MAIL ORDER BRIDE SERIES
NO. 10
1865
USA
AL & JOANNA LACY

# LET THERE BE LIGHT

OTHER BOOKS BY AL LACY

**Angel of Mercy series:**
*A Promise for Breanna* (Book One)
*Faithful Heart* (Book Two)
*Captive Set Free* (Book Three)
*A Dream Fulfilled* (Book Four)
*Suffer the Little Children* (Book Five)
*Whither Thou Goest* (Book Six)
*Final Justice* (Book Seven)
*Not by Might* (Book Eight)
*Things Not Seen* (Book Nine)
*Far Above Rubies* (Book Ten)

**Journeys of the Stranger series:**
*Legacy* (Book One)
*Silent Abduction* (Book Two)
*Blizzard* (Book Three)
*Tears of the Sun* (Book Four)
*Circle of Fire* (Book Five)
*Quiet Thunder* (Book Six)
*Snow Ghost* (Book Seven)

**Battles of Destiny (Civil War series):**
*Beloved Enemy* (Battle of First Bull Run)
*A Heart Divided* (Battle of Mobile Bay)
*A Promise Unbroken* (Battle of Rich Mountain)
*Shadowed Memories* (Battle of Shiloh)
*Joy from Ashes* (Battle of Fredericksburg)
*Season of Valor* (Battle of Gettysburg)
*Wings of the Wind* (Battle of Antietam)
*Turn of Glory* (Battle of Chancellorsville)

**Hannah of Fort Bridger series (coauthored with JoAnna Lacy):**
*Under the Distant Sky* (Book One)
*Consider the Lilies* (Book Two)
*No Place for Fear* (Book Three)
*Pillow of Stone* (Book Four)
*The Perfect Gift* (Book Five)
*Touch of Compassion* (Book Six)
*Beyond the Valley* (Book Seven)
*Damascus Journey* (Book Eight)

**Mail Order Bride series (coauthored with JoAnna Lacy):**
*Secrets of the Heart* (Book One)
*A Time to Love* (Book Two)
*Tender Flame* (Book Three)
*Blessed Are the Merciful* (Book Four)
*Ransom of Love* (Book Five)
*Until the Daybreak* (Book Six)
*Sincerely Yours* (Book Seven)
*A Measure of Grace* (Book Eight)
*So Little Time* (Book Nine)

# Let There Be Light

## MAIL ORDER BRIDE 10

## AL & JOANNA LACY

Multnomah® Publishers *Sisters, Oregon*

LET THERE BE LIGHT

© 2002 by ALJO PRODUCTIONS, INC.
published by Multnomah Publishers, Inc.

International Standard Book Number: 1-59052-042-4

Cover design by Kirk DouPonce UDG/DesignWorks
Cover illustration by Vittorio Dangelico

Printed in the United States of America

*Multnomah* is a trademark of Multnomah Publishers, Inc., and is registered in the U.S. Patent and Trademark Office.
The colophon is a trademark of Multnomah Publishers, Inc.

FOR INFORMATION:
MULTNOMAH PUBLISHERS, INC., POST OFFICE BOX 1720, SISTERS, OREGON 97759

Library of Congress Cataloging-in-Publication Data
Lacy, Al.
    Let there be light : Al and Joanna Lacy.
        p. cm. -- (Mail order bride)
    ISBN 1-59052-042-4
    1. Prisoners of war--Family relationships--Fiction. 2. Mail order brides--Fiction. 3. Women pioneers--Fiction. 4. Arizona--Fiction. 5. Revenge--Fiction. I. Lacy, Joanna. II. Title
    PS3562.A256 L49 2002
    813'.54--dc21                                                2002009316

02 03 04 05 06 07 08 09 — 10 9 8 7 6 5 4 3 2 1 0

This book is affectionately dedicated to our faithful fans in Salem, Virginia:

*Lawrence and Rebecca Snapp and their daughter, Charlotte. God bless you!*

NUMBERS 6:26

# Prologue

THE ENCYCLOPEDIA BRITANNICA reports that the mail order business, also called direct mail marketing, "is a method of merchandising in which the seller's offer is made through mass mailing of a circular or catalog, or advertisement placed in a newspaper or magazine, in which the buyer places his order by mail."

Britannica goes on to say that "mail order operations have been known in the United States in one form or another since colonial days but not until the latter half of the nineteenth century did they assume a significant role in domestic trade."

Thus the mail order market was known when the big gold rush took place in this country in the 1840s and 1850s. At that time, prospectors, merchants, and adventurers raced from the east to the newly discovered goldfields in the west. One of the most famous was the California gold rush in 1848–49, when discovery of gold at Sutter's Mill, near Sacramento, brought more than forty thousand men to California. Though few struck it rich, their presence stimulated economic growth, the lure of which brought even more men to the west.

The married men sent for their wives and children, wanting to stay and make their home there. Most of the gold rush men were single and also desired to stay in the west, but there were about two hundred men for every woman. Being familiar with the mail order concept, they began advertising in eastern newspapers for women to come west and marry them. Thus was born the "mail order bride."

Women by the hundreds began answering the ads. Often when men and their prospective brides corresponded, they agreed to send no photographs; they would accept each other by the spirit of the letters rather than on a physical basis. Others, of course, did exchange photographs.

The mail order bride movement accelerated after the Civil War ended in April 1865, when men went west by the thousands to make their fortunes on the frontier. Many of the marriages turned out well, while others were disappointing and ended in desertion by one or the other of the mates, or by divorce.

In the Mail Order Bride fiction series, we tell stories intended to grip the heart of the reader, bring some smiles, and maybe wring out a few tears. As always, we weave in the gospel of Jesus Christ and run threads of Bible truth that apply to our lives today.

*And God said, Let there be light:*
*and there was light.*
GENESIS 1:3

—⁓—     —⁓—     —⁓—

*For God, who commanded the light to shine out of darkness,*
*hath shined in our hearts,*
*to give the light of the knowledge of the glory of God*
*in the face of Jesus Christ.*
2 CORINTHIANS 4:6

# *Introduction*

IN MALACHI 4:2, God tells us that the day is coming when the Sun of righteousness shall arise with healing in His wings. The Sun of righteousness is also the Son of God.

There is only one sun in our solar system, and there is only one Mediator between God and men. As at sunrise each day, the sun dispels the darkness of night; so Jesus Christ, the Sun of righteousness, dispels the spiritual darkness in the human heart when that heart is opened to Him.

When the Scripture speaks of the "light of the glorious gospel of Christ" (2 Corinthians 4:4), the very light of the gospel is the Sun of righteousness, Jesus Christ!

Jesus said in John 12:46, "I am come a light into the world, that whosoever believeth on me should not abide in darkness." As the earth cannot abide in darkness where the sun is shining, neither can a human heart abide in darkness where the Sun of righteousness shines.

"For God, who commanded the light to shine out of darkness, hath shined in our hearts, to give the light of the knowledge of the glory of God in the face of Jesus Christ" (2 Corinthians 4:6).

There is an ancient allegory written for children based upon the premise of this verse, but serviceable to adults.

Once upon a time to a cave, deep underground, came a voice calling: "Mr. Cave! Mr. Cave! Come up to the earth's surface and see my light!"

The cave called back, "Who are you?"

"My name is Mr. Sun. Come up and see my light."

The cave retorted, "I don't know what you mean. There isn't anything but darkness."

"Oh, but there is! Come up and see!"

Finally, Mr. Cave ventured forth and was surprised to see brilliant light everywhere. Looking up to the sun, he said, "Come with me and see my darkness."

"What is darkness?" asked Mr. Sun.

"Come and see."

So Mr. Sun accepted the invitation. In his blazing brightness, he entered the cave, looked around, and asked, "Where is your darkness?"

Where the Sun of righteousness is, there is no darkness! We praise the Lord that He has used our novels to shine the gospel light into the hearts of many of our unsaved readers, and they have come to know the Lord Jesus Christ as their personal Saviour.

May this final book in the Mail Order Bride series be a blessing to our Christian readers, and may it also be used of God to open sin-darkened hearts and say, "Let there be light."

# 1

IT WAS TUESDAY AFTERNOON, May 5, 1863. Beneath a clear, sunny Missouri sky, the train rolled southwestward toward Kansas City. The early spring day was unusually warm and in the coach just ahead of the caboose, lovely twenty-two-year-old Lorna Lee turned to elderly Madeline Rudeen. "It's a bit stuffy in here, don't you think?"

Madeline's wrinkles deepened around her mouth as she smiled and fanned her face with her hand. "It certainly is. Would you mind lifting the window a little?"

Lorna smiled. "I was going to ask if you'd mind if I did that very thing."

Lorna and Madeline had boarded the train in Chicago and had barely talked enough to become acquainted. Madeline had fallen asleep shortly after the train had slipped into its gentle sway and the wheels settled into their rhythmic clicking beneath the coach. She had only awakened for brief moments until some twenty minutes ago.

When Lorna raised the window, a fresh breeze swept in accompanied by a louder sound of clicking wheels.

"Ah, that's better," said Madeline.

"Yes." Lorna paused, then said, "We haven't been able to talk very much since we left Chicago. Where are you bound, Mrs. Rudeen?"

"Topeka, Kansas. That's the train's next stop after Kansas City. Topeka is my home. I've been visiting my oldest son and his family in Riverdale, just south of Chicago."

At that moment, the train moved onto a trestle over a wide, sunlit river. As Lorna looked down at the rolling water, Madeline said, "That's the Missouri River, dear. In case you didn't know."

"I knew it was in the Kansas City area, but that's about all. I've never been here before."

The front door of the coach opened, and the conductor entered. Moving along the aisle, he called out, "Kansas City…fifteen minutes! Kansas City…fifteen minutes!"

Madeline looked at Lorna. "So where are you going, dear?"

"Mogollon, Arizona."

"Oh, really? Just where is Mogollon?"

"It's in eastern Arizona. Do you know where Holbrook is?"

"Oh yes. It's just a few miles west of the Petrified Forest. I read about it in a magazine not long ago."

"All right. Mogollon is thirty miles west of Holbrook."

Madeline frowned. "There are no railroads in Arizona yet, are there?"

"No. The train I'll take out of Kansas City will get me to Santa Fe, New Mexico. I'll have to take a stagecoach from Santa Fe down to Albuquerque. I'll board another stagecoach there, which will take me all the way to Mogollon."

Madeline nodded. "So you've got a long trip ahead of you."

"Yes."

At that instant, the train started to slow down. Passengers began leaving their seats to take hand luggage out of the overhead racks.

"Do you need to get past me to take down your bag, dear?" asked Madeline.

"No, that's all right. I'll get it when the train stops." Lorna felt a cool gust of air sweep through the opening in the window. She pressed her face to the glass. "I see some dark clouds gathering to the north. We just might be in for a thunderstorm."

"That'll cool the air for sure."

No sooner had Madeline made her comment than a jagged bolt of lightning stabbed through the dark clouds. A few seconds later, a low, rumbling thunder could be heard.

"I think you're right, dear," said Madeline, craning her neck to peek out the window. "One thing is for sure. God is in control of the weather, and a little rain would be refreshing right now."

"You're right about that. I just hope it holds off until I change trains."

The terminal came into view and the train slowed. The whistle on the big engine let out a blast, and within a few minutes, the train chugged to a halt in the depot.

Lorna stood up, moved past Madeline, and retrieved her small bag from the overhead rack. Passengers were making their way toward both doors. Lorna looked down at Madeline with a smile. "It was nice to have met you, Mrs. Rudeen. I hope you have a safe journey the rest of the way to Topeka."

"Thank you, dear. And you have a safe journey all the way to Mogollon."

"I'm trusting the Lord to see to that," Lorna said softly, smiling again. "Good-bye." With that, she slipped into the line of passengers and stepped off the train into the cool, refreshing air. She could hear distant thunder as she made her way amid the crowd and passed through one of the doors that led inside the terminal.

It took her only seconds to locate the large chalkboard in the center of the depot. Threading her way through the crowd, she made her way to the chalkboard. Her heart sank when she found the schedule of the Santa Fe–bound train on the board with a chalk message next to it, saying that it had been delayed indefinitely.

Lorna sighed. Her nerves were already a bit on edge with the prospect of what lay ahead in Mogollon. She was anxious to get there, have the initial meeting, and see how things would develop.

Squelching the anxiety, she wheeled and headed for the ticket counter. There were three agents taking care of people who stood in line. Behind them, at a large desk, was a young man in a wheelchair, operating a telegraph key. Lorna chose the shortest line. *Lord, I really need to get to Mogollon as soon as possible.*

Some ten minutes had passed when the man in front of Lorna turned and walked away. As she set her bag down and stepped up to the counter, the silver-haired agent said, "May I help you, young lady?"

"I hope so, sir," she said a bit timidly, placing her ticket in front of him. "As you can see, I'm booked on the train to Santa Fe. What can you tell me other than it's delayed indefinitely?"

The agent looked at the ticket, lifted his billed cap and dropped it back in place. He met her gaze. "Well, Miss Lee—it is *Miss* Lee, isn't it?"

"Yes, sir."

"There's been a battle between Union and Confederate forces near Dodge City, Kansas. The battle is over, but the Confederates tore up a section of the tracks, and there's been no word as yet from the railroad officials as to when they expect the damage to be repaired. Since we've gone through this kind of thing before, my own guess is that it will be done within twenty-four hours." He placed the ticket in her hand. "If you will check with me periodically, I'll let you know when we get word. I see you're going by stagecoach to Albuquerque, then on to Mogollon."

"Yes."

"Once we know about the train's schedule, we'll wire the Wells Fargo office in Santa Fe and set up new stage reservations for you."

"Thank you," said Lorna, then sighed wearily, placed the ticket in her purse, and looked at the large front windows of the terminal. A sign across the street caught her eye, and at the same moment, her stomach growled from hunger. She looked back at the agent. "Sir, do you think it would be all right if I stepped across the street and had a bite to eat at the diner?"

The man grinned in an attempt to calm her fears. "Sure. You'll have plenty of time to do that. Check with me when you come back. Have yourself a nice meal."

"Thank you, sir." Lorna picked up her bag. "I won't be gone long."

When Lorna stepped out of the terminal, she found the wind gusting, and noted that the clouds were now about to cover the sun. She waited for the traffic to clear, bent her head against the wind, and set her gaze on the diner. A break came seconds later, and as she made her way across the street, she thought, *A cup of tea and a bowl of hot potato soup sound tasty.*

There was no one in line at the ticket counter when Lorna returned to the terminal. The same agent she had talked to before was at the counter and saw her coming.

A smile broke across his face as she drew up, wiping rain from her face. "Well, young lady, did you have a nice meal?"

"Sure did."

"Raining out there, I see."

"Mm-hmm. The small drops are turning into big fat ones. Looks like we're going to get a good shower. Any news about my train?"

"Nothing yet, I'm sorry to say." He tossed a thumb over his shoulder. "Lenny, there, is waiting faithfully at the telegraph key for word."

Lorna looked past the agent at the young man in the wheelchair, who heard what the agent said. "Are you booked on the Santa Fe train, ma'am?"

"Yes."

"Well, stay close by. I'll let Charlie know when we get word."

The silver-haired man grinned. "I'm Charlie."

Lorna nodded. "I had that figured out."

A man in a suit came out of a back room, handed Lenny a sheet of paper, and told him to get it on the wire immediately.

Lenny glanced at the paper and nodded. He began working the telegraph key, and the man returned to the office. Lorna watched while Lenny clicked out the Morse code and let her eyes run over the wheelchair.

Charlie noticed her glance. "Lenny was in the War, Miss Lee. Union side, of course. Got both of his legs blown off by a cannon-ball."

Lorna bit her lips as her mind went to Mogollon. "Oh. I'm sorry. He seems like a nice young man."

"That he is, ma'am."

"War is such a terrible thing. Not only fills graves, but leaves many a soldier with wounds they will carry for the rest of their lives."

"Yes, ma'am. Terrible thing."

A customer was approaching the counter. Lorna smiled at Charlie. "I'll be sitting over here in the section close by, sir. I'll check with you periodically, but if word comes in, please let me know, even if I should fall asleep."

"Sure will. And if nothing's come by the time I go off duty at six o'clock, I'll tell the agent on night shift about you. We work twelve-hour shifts, here, so I'll see you in the morning, even if you get word this evening. At best, your train won't be in till sometime tomorrow."

Lorna thanked him, pivoted, and walked to the nearest section of seats, where a few other people were sitting. She found the hardwood benches less comfortable than the seats in the railroad coaches, but weary, she soon fell asleep.

Lorna slept until nearly ten o'clock. She sat up straight, rubbed the back of her neck, and looked toward the ticket counter. There was one agent on duty, as well as another man at the telegraph desk. The people around her were all asleep. She rose to her feet, stretched her arms, and made her way to the counter.

The agent gave her a smile. "May I help you, Miss Lee?"

Her eyebrows arched. "You know my name?"

"Yes. Charlie pointed you out when I came on duty. I'm supposed to let you know if word comes in about your Santa Fe train. So far, we've heard nothing. Probably won't until morning."

Lorna thanked him and went back to her seat. Once again positioning herself as comfortably as possible, she closed her eyes, and soon fell asleep. She awakened a few times during the night and looked toward the ticket counter. Each time, there was no sign of the agent, nor the man who had been at the telegraph desk. She figured they were sitting where she could not see them.

She awakened again when sunlight was just beginning to stream through the terminal's east windows and saw Charlie behind the counter. She could hear the telegraph key clicking. She jumped up and rushed to the counter. "Good morning, sir. Any word, yet?"

"It's coming in right now, Miss Lee," said Charlie, turning to look back at Lenny.

Lorna glanced at Lenny, who smiled at her and raised a finger to indicate that the message would be completed shortly. Seconds later, the clicking stopped. Lenny finished writing the message, then handed the paper to Charlie.

The agent read it quickly and looked at Lorna. "The train is on its way, Miss Lee. They say it will arrive at ten o'clock this morning. It is scheduled to leave here at eleven."

"Oh, that's good!"

"If you will let me have your ticket again, I'll have Lenny wire the Wells Fargo office in Santa Fe and make new reservations for you."

As Lorna handed him her ticket, Charlie said, "You go ahead and sit down. I'll let you know when we get the message back from Wells Fargo."

Lorna returned to her seat. She could hear Lenny tapping out the Morse code on the telegraph key. People were now coming into the terminal, and the other two agents appeared behind the ticket counter.

Lorna heard the telegraph key clicking, and when some thirty minutes had passed, she saw Charlie motioning to her. She hurried to the counter, and he laid the ticket in front of her. "You're all fixed up now, Miss Lee. You'll be in Santa Fe at ten o'clock tomorrow morning, and you have a reservation on the eleven-thirty stage to Albuquerque and the three o'clock stage from Albuquerque. You will spend the night in Gallup and arrive in Mogollon at four o'clock on Friday afternoon."

Lorna thanked him, went across the street to eat breakfast at the diner, then headed for the spot in the depot where she would board her train.

The train came in as promised, and Lorna climbed aboard at the conductor's first call. When the train pulled out of Kansas City, she was sitting by herself on a coach seat. She watched the landscape for a while, then took her Bible out of the handbag that lay next to her and began reading. A half hour later, she laid her head back, closed her eyes, and spent time with the Lord in prayer.

On Thursday morning, Lorna pressed her face to the window and watched as the train chugged into the depot at Santa Fe. The elderly woman sitting next to her had boarded at Dalhart, Texas, and had family meeting her.

They stepped off the train, bid each other good-bye as the woman's relatives rushed up, and Lorna made her way to the baggage coach where she told a baggage handler she needed her small trunk taken to wherever the Wells Fargo people would pick it up. The baggage handler told her there would be a Wells Fargo wagon right out front. He would bring her trunk, and the wagon driver would take her to the Fargo office, which was three blocks away.

Some twenty minutes later, Lorna was at the Wells Fargo office where she soon boarded the eleven-thirty stage bound south for Albuquerque.

Just before three o'clock that afternoon, Lorna boarded the westbound stage in Albuquerque with two men in their forties and a young woman about her age. Her heart pounded with excitement as she realized how close she was getting to Mogollon. She would be there at four o'clock tomorrow afternoon on this very stagecoach.

Outside, the stage driver and shotgunner were checking the harness, making ready to pull out.

The young woman and Lorna were seated together, facing the two men. They introduced themselves as George Stallworth and Lester Franklin, explaining that they were government Indian agents. They worked with the Navajo and Hopi tribes in Gallup.

Lorna smiled. "My name is Lorna Lee, and I'm on my way to Mogollon."

The young woman said softly, "My name is Rhonda Clark, and I'm going to Holbrook."

Lorna studied Rhonda, telling herself that Rhonda was quite pretty, but she was a troubled person.

The driver stepped up to the window on Lorna's side and ran his gaze over the faces of his passengers. "Everybody ready to go?"

The Indian agents and Lorna nodded. Rhonda looked at him, but did not respond. The driver called for his shotgunner to climb aboard, then climbed up himself. The Wells Fargo agent stood at the door of the office, bid the men up in the box good-bye, and the stage pulled away. Within a few minutes, they were out of Albuquerque, headed due west, and the horses were put to a steady trot. The stage rocked and swayed on the uneven ground as the sun continued its downward slant toward the western horizon.

Stallworth and Franklin talked Indian business together, sharing papers that each carried in his briefcase.

Lorna noted that Rhonda kept her face turned toward her window, discouraging any conversation between them. Seated on the north side of the coach, Lorna stared out her own window at the rugged San Mateo Mountains, lost in thoughts and daydreams about her future in Mogollon.

At one point, as the stagecoach crossed a bridge over a small stream, Lorna heard Rhonda sniffle. Her sensitive heart was touched when she turned to see silent tears threatening to spill from Rhonda's closed eyes. The men were deeply involved in their conversation. Lorna was careful not to call their attention to herself or Rhonda as she took a lace hankie from her dress sleeve and extended it to her. "Here, honey."

A tear started down Rhonda's cheek as she looked at Lorna. "Thank you, but I have one." Even as she spoke, she opened her purse and took out her own hankie.

While Rhonda dabbed at her cheek, then her shadowed blue eyes, Lorna said, "Are you going to Holbrook to live or are you just going for a visit?"

Rhonda sniffed. Her voice was strained. "To live. What about you?"

A smile spread over Lorna's lovely features. "Permanent. I'm going there to marry a very handsome man."

"Oh. I see. And what's his name?"

"Jack Sparks. He is an ex-Union soldier. He had been a captain. He now manages the town's hardware store."

"How was he able to get out of the army with the Civil War going so strong?"

"Medical discharge. Jack was fighting under Brigadier General Nathaniel Lyon in the Battle of Wilson's Creek near Springfield, Missouri, on August 10, 1861. During the battle, a Confederate cannonball exploded near him. A piece of shrapnel hit his left eye. It destroyed the eyeball. Jack now wears a patch over his eye."

"Oh. I'm sorry."

Lorna pulled a photograph out of her purse and handed it to her. "That's Jack, standing outside the hardware store. Doesn't he have a winsome smile?"

Rhonda nodded. "Yes. Too bad such a handsome man has to wear an eye patch for the rest of his life."

"Yes, but the patch isn't going to make any difference to me. Soon after Jack's discharge from the army, he went to Mogollon, where his uncle lives. His uncle owns the hardware store. When he learned of Jack's being wounded and discharged from the army, he offered him the job."

"That's nice," said Rhonda, handing the picture back to her. "How long have you known Jack?"

"I've never met him. We've only corresponded through the mail."

A look of pure horror suddenly captured Rhonda's features. "Oh no! Don't tell me you're going to be his mail order bride!"

Lorna gave her a strange look. "That's exactly what I'm going to do."

Rhonda set her jaw and clenched her teeth. "Don't do it, Lorna. It will only end up in heartache."

Lorna frowned. "Were you a mail order bride?"

"Yes."

"Want to tell me about it?"

The obvious resentment that was inside Rhonda Clark came out as she told Lorna she was born in Columbus, Ohio. Her life was a lonely one, and a year ago, because of her loneliness, she answered a mail order bride ad in the *Columbus Star*. The ad had been placed by a Lieutenant Philip Clark, who was stationed at Fort Craig, New Mexico, which was about a hundred miles south of Albuquerque.

She came to New Mexico, believing that everything was going to be wonderful. She would be married to a handsome young army officer and find adventure in the west. As soon as she married Philip, she knew she had made a mistake. He treated her like dirt and acted like she was his maid instead of his wife. After ten months of this kind of treatment, she went to a judge in nearby Socorro and obtained a divorce.

Touched deeply by Rhonda's sorrow, Lorna said, "I'm sorry,

honey. So you're going to Holbrook to live, you said."

"Yes. I'm going to live with a cousin and her husband." Her features twisted. "Lorna, don't do it. Don't marry this man you've never met. Get off in Gallup and wait for the next stage to Albuquerque. Where's home?"

"South Bend, Indiana."

"Well, head back to South Bend as fast as you can. Don't marry a man you've never met. This mail order bride system is a failure. An utter failure. Save yourself some horrible heartache, Lorna. Go back home and marry some guy you've known for a long time."

Lorna was disturbed by the woman's words but countered, "Rhonda, it's not going to be that way with Jack and me. Both of us have prayed earnestly about this, and we feel certain that the Lord has chosen us for each other."

Rhonda's mouth turned down. She rolled her eyes. "Praying isn't going to help either one of you. If there is a God, He doesn't care what happens to any of His creatures. You're a fool if you go ahead and marry this stranger."

"Oh, but prayer most certainly has already helped us to know that we will be happy together, Rhonda. This is because Jack and I know Jesus Christ as our personal Saviour, and—"

"Don't give me any of that Jesus stuff!" clipped Rhonda. "I don't want to hear it."

By this time, the men were looking at them, having heard Rhonda's outburst. They looked at each other, adjusted themselves on the seat, but said nothing.

When Lorna looked back at Rhonda, she had her arms folded over her chest and was looking out the window. The stubborn look on her face told Lorna she was not about to listen to anything she had to say.

The stage arrived in Gallup on time. The Indian agents told the young women good-bye and hurried away. Crew and passengers would stay in a small lodge for the night. They were given supper by the Wells Fargo agent and his wife.

That night as Lorna lay in the feather bed, she told the Lord that even though she was nervous about going to Mogollon as Jack's prospective mail order bride, she had peace in her heart because He had given it to her. She knew He was leading her, and that Jack's letters had strongly indicated that He had also led him to answer her inquiry to his ad in the *South Bend Journal,* asking her to come to Arizona with the future of becoming his wife.

"Lord," she said, "please don't let what Rhonda told me today put any doubts in my heart about Jack. I'm asking You to guide both of us once we have met and I stay in the boardinghouse while we get acquainted. Both Jack and I only want Your will for us, Lord, and You know the peace You have given me about coming out west to become Mrs. Jack Sparks. We are so sure that You have chosen us for each other."

The next morning, after breakfast with the Wells Fargo agent and his wife, the stage driver and shotgunner, Rhonda and Lorna, and a well-dressed couple in their early forties boarded. The young women sat on the seat where they had been the day before.

When the stage was once again moving across the rolling land, the man smiled and said, "Ladies, I am Pastor David Denison of Mogollon, and this is my wife, Clara."

"Oh!" said Lorna, her eyes lighting up. "I know who you are. Jack Sparks has told me about you in his letters."

"And you're Lorna Lee," said Clara. "Jack has told us so much about you. We've been eager to meet you."

"We sure have," said the pastor. "I didn't realize you would be on the same stage with us."

"Well, I wouldn't have been, but my train was delayed getting to Kansas City, so I'm running later than expected. The Fargo agent in Santa Fe told me Jack would be notified of my new arrival time."

"I'll tell you this much," said Denison, "Jack is one excited young man. He has shown your picture to everybody in the church, and I imagine by now he's shown it to everybody in town."

Lorna smiled. "I'm excited too, Pastor Denison. As you well know, we both have absolute assurance that the Lord has chosen us for each other."

"I have counseled him from day one about the mail order bride ad, and he has shown me every letter that came in response. Clara and I have no doubt you are God's choice for Jack."

"I'm so glad. Have you and Mrs. Denison been in Gallup very long?"

"Just a week. I was preaching a revival meeting for a pastor friend of mine."

Lorna nodded. "Jack has told me what a great preacher his pastor is."

Denison's features tinted. "Well, Jack may be a little prejudiced since I'm the one who had the privilege of leading him to the Lord."

Rhonda kept her eyes out the window as Lorna and the Denisons talked about Jack and their plans to marry. Lorna asked about Jack's first approach to the pastor about putting a mail order bride ad in eastern newspapers.

"Well, Jack came to me back in February. He said he felt it was time he was getting married, but there were no Christian young women in Mogollon who were not already engaged." He chuckled. "Clara and I have twin daughters, Mary and Martha, who at that time, were sixteen. They're seventeen, now. But because Clara and I had declared that our daughters could not marry until they were at least eighteen, Jack knew they were too young to consider."

Clara smiled at Lorna. "Jack asked my husband what he thought of the mail order bride system."

Rhonda flicked a glance at Clara, then looked back out the window.

"I told him of other Christian couples I know whom the Lord had brought together by the mail order bride system," said the pastor, "and I told him the Lord could do it for him too. I cautioned Jack to make sure he made it plain in his ad that he is a born-again man looking for a born-again bride, and to ask for her testimony of salvation when she responded to the ad."

"Well, he did," said Lorna.

Denison grinned, nodding. "He received several letters of response, Lorna. And he let Clara and me read them. Most of them were good letters, but Jack just didn't have peace about responding to them...until your letter came. Clara and I both felt there was something special about you. Your testimony was as clear as could be, and the three of us prayed together about it. Jack had such peace that he immediately had that picture taken in front of the hardware store and sent it with the letter."

"And it was some letter," said Lorna. "Jack didn't want to keep any secrets from me. He sent the picture because he wanted me to see the patch over his eye. He gave me pertinent information about himself and his family, and told me about getting the wound in the battle at Wilson's Creek. He wanted me to get the full impact of his disfigurement right off and not to have to face a shock when I came to meet him. He even asked that I seriously consider his handicap before we proceeded any further."

"That's Jack," said Clara.

"Well, I did consider it. Very seriously. My heart knew before my head did that this was the special man the Lord had reserved for me. I wrote back and told him so, and that after much prayer, I felt I should come to Mogollon as his prospective mail order bride. His next letter was so sweet. He included the money for my travel expense and said to come as soon as possible. I wasted no time preparing for this trip west, and I can hardly wait to meet him."

At that moment, Rhonda turned and looked at Lorna. "I sure hope it works out for you."

"Thank you," said Lorna. "Rhonda was a mail order bride," she said to the Denisons, "but it didn't work out."

"Oh, I'm so sorry," said Clara.

"Did you bathe it in prayer beforehand?" queried the pastor.

Rhonda shook her head stiffly. "I don't believe in prayer, and I don't want to talk about God." With that, she turned to look out the window once again.

Lorna shrugged as she looked at the Denisons and mouthed, *I tried to talk to her about the Lord, but she refuses to listen.*

The Denisons nodded sadly.

When the stage rolled into Holbrook, Lorna and the Denisons bid Rhonda good-bye, and she walked away with her cousin and her husband.

Watching them go, Lorna said, "I wanted so desperately to reach her for the Lord, but she just wouldn't listen."

"That's always a heartbreaker," said the pastor.

Moments later, the stagecoach rolled out of Holbrook.

Clara leaned close to Lorna and took hold of her hand. "Tell you what, honey—if it works out between you and Jack as we believe it will, I want to make your wedding dress for you. I've made them for several brides in our church. Will you let me do it?"

Lorna's face was beaming. "I sure will!"

AS THE CIVIL WAR CONTINUED, the battles became fiercer and the bloodshed grew worse. Wives, mothers, sweethearts, and entire families of both the North and the South lived in constant dread that their men in uniform would never come home again.

On Thursday morning, September 22, 1864, young Jenny Linden was behind the counter at Henderson's General Store in Harrisburg, Pennsylvania, waiting on a customer when she heard the door open and looked past the woman to see the delivery man from the *Harrisburg Journal* come in. He was carrying a stack of papers.

Jenny handed the woman her change, and as she walked away, Jenny watched Wiley Owens place the stack of newspapers on the empty stand next to the counter. "Morning, Jenny," said Wiley.

"Is there bad news in the paper, Wiley?"

Wiley licked his lips nervously. "Jenny, I know how you feel about Nate Conrad, and…ah…well, on the front page of the paper, there's an article about a bloody battle that took place near Winchester, Virginia, on Tuesday. Over a hundred men were killed on each side. About twice as many were wounded. And… ah…well—"

"What is it, Wiley?"

Owens cleared his throat nervously. "Well, Jenny, some of Pennsylvania's troops under the command of General William T.

Sherman were involved in the battle, including Nate's Seventh Pennsylvania Artillery."

Jenny's features lost color. Her lips were moving, but she couldn't seem to get the words out.

Wiley stepped closer to her. "Jenny, just because there were many casualties in the battle doesn't mean that Nate was one of them. I knew when you looked at the front page of the paper, you'd see that Nate's unit was in the battle and that it would upset you."

A shaky hand went to Jenny's mouth and tears filmed her eyes.

"Jenny, you mustn't let it get to you. You've got to hold on to the hope that Nate is all right, and one day when this awful war is over, he will come home to live out his natural life."

At that moment, Zack and Emma Henderson—the proprietors—came out of the office at the rear of the store, having heard Wiley's words.

Emma put an arm around Jenny and said, "Wiley's advice is sound, honey. You've got to keep a positive attitude about Nate's safety in the War, as well as your father's."

Zack glanced at the stack of newspapers on the stand, then looked at Owens. "Wiley, was anything said in the article about the Third Pennsylvania Cavalry Division being involved in Tuesday's battle?"

"No, sir. The Third Cavalry Division wasn't mentioned."

Jenny drew a shuddering breath. "I'm glad for that. At least Papa wasn't in that battle. I…I just wish I knew if Nate was all right."

Emma's arm was still around Jenny. She kissed her cheek. "Honey, I have a good feeling way down deep about Nate. I just know he's all right."

Jenny managed a smile. "You're such a dear, Emma. Whenever I need encouragement, you always have a way of giving it to me."

"You just keep it up, Emma," said Wiley. "Well, I've got more papers to deliver. See all of you later."

Emma patted Jenny's cheek. "It's going to be all right for both your papa and Nate, honey. How about your mother? Has she met her new doctor?"

"Not yet, but Dr. Griffin is to pay her a visit about five o'clock this evening so he can go over her problem and get acquainted with her."

For a moment, Jenny and the Hendersons discussed the fact that the Linden family physician, Dr. Wayne Maddox, had felt the need to sell his practice and go into the service as an army doctor. Maddox had sold his practice to Dr. Adam Griffin just this past week.

Customers were coming into the store as Emma said, "I'm glad to know that your mother will get the new doctor's attention right away."

It was toward the end of the day, and while the last shadows cast by the setting sun were fingering their way into the general store, Zack and Emma were waiting on customers at the counter while Jenny was working at the fabric display table nearby. She had been busy for over an hour, arranging new bolts of brightly colored fabrics on the table from the latest shipment that had arrived in early afternoon.

After having leaned over the table for some time, Jenny straightened and stretched the kinks out of her back. Letting her eyes roam carefully over the display, she rearranged one of the bolts, then ran her hands gently over the soft, colorful cloth. *I sure would love to have a new dress made out of this wonderfully soft, deep blue wool,* she thought. *Right now, money in the Linden household is too scarce to even be thinking this way. Maybe when this horrible war is over and Papa is back home and working again, Mama and I can make some new dresses.*

Taking a step back, Jenny looked over her handiwork one last time.

Satisfied, she returned to the back side of the counter, and while Zack and Emma continued taking care of customers, she began refilling the candy jars that were bunched at both ends of the counter.

Dusk was rapidly encroaching into the small parlor where forty-year-old Myrna Linden sat in her rocking chair near the window that overlooked the street. In her hands, she held a photograph of her husband in his uniform. Pressing the photograph close to her heart, she stared forlornly into space while tears streamed down her cheeks.

Her mind was tortured as she thought of William facing death every day while the horrible Civil War went on. Myrna had no idea where her husband's unit was fighting, for General Sherman's troops were spread over several Confederate states.

Myrna wiped tears from her face and looked at the photograph. Her lips quivered. "Oh, William, I love you so much. I want the War to be over so you can come home. Almost every night, I hear Jenny crying herself to sleep in her room, wanting her papa to come home safely."

Myrna jumped when the knock came at the door. "Oh!" she whispered as she laid her husband's picture on the nearby table and rose from the rocking chair. "I knew Dr. Griffin was coming."

She glanced at the clock on the wall and noted that it was almost five-thirty. Moving a bit unsteadily, Myrna left the parlor and moved through the hall to the vestibule. When she opened the door, a man stood there, holding a black medical bag in one hand and a briefcase in the other.

"Hello, Mrs. Linden," he said warmly. "Sorry I'm a bit late."

Myrna matched his smile. "That's all right, Dr. Griffin. I understand how house calls are. You can't always get away when you plan to. Please, come in."

As she led the doctor into the parlor, Myrna became aware that the parlor was dim. "Please sit over there in that overstuffed chair, Doctor. I'll light these lamps, then we can talk."

She lifted the glass chimney of the first lamp with a shaky hand and picked up a match. She made an attempt to strike the match, but couldn't get it to flare.

"Here," said the doctor, placing his medical bag and the briefcase next to the chair, "let me do it for you."

Myrna watched the young doctor light both lamps.

"There, that's better, isn't it, Mrs. Linden?"

"Yes, it is. Thank you." She glanced around the cozy room, now aglow with soft light. "Please sit down." She slid her rocker so she could face him in the glow of the nearest lamp.

The doctor sat down in the overstuffed chair. He picked up the briefcase, opened it, and took out a folder. "I have your file right here. I've read it over so I could know what I needed to about you when we had this meeting. I'm sure it was difficult for you to lose Dr. Maddox."

"Yes. I was really upset when he told me he was selling his practice so he could become an army doctor, but I felt much better when my daughter, Jenny, did some investigating and learned that you were a fine physician and were coming to Harrisburg with a good and successful practice behind you in Baltimore."

Griffin grinned. "Well, I'm glad you feel okay about me."

He opened the folder and took out the papers. "I would like to go over your records with you to make sure I understand all about your illness."

"Of course."

He glanced at the papers. "Dr. Maddox says that you suffer with a condition he diagnosed as manic depression."

"Yes." Myrna's eyes were fixed on his face.

The doctor met her gaze. "It says here that your husband, Captain William Linden, is in the Third Pennsylvania Cavalry Division under the command of General William T. Sherman."

"That's right."

"Tell me about your depression. When did it come on?"

"Well, this time, it was shortly after William went to war—just over three years ago."

Griffin's eyebrows arched. "This time? Oh, I recall that you did experience a similar depression several years ago."

"Yes. Twelve years to be exact. June of 1852. When I gave birth to a baby boy. He died two days later, and I went into the depression. The record will show, Dr. Griffin, that within a year after the baby's death, I was nearly back to normal."

The doctor was flipping pages. "And didn't I read in here that you did suffer brief times of depression over the years when you came under stress of one kind or another?"

"Yes. But none of it was as bad as when I lost the baby, or when the Civil War broke out and William told me he felt it was his duty to fight for the Union and he was going to sign up. Right after he left the house to go downtown and sign up, I went completely to pieces. I went into a deep one that time, Doctor. When William came home after signing up and found me in that condition, he said he was going to back out. He couldn't go off and leave me like that."

Griffin looked up from the papers. "So why did he go?"

"It was my doing. Other men were enlisting all over the North and leaving their families because they felt it was their duty to do so. William felt strongly that he should go too. I admired this in him and told him he should go; that Dr. Maddox and Jenny would take care of me. He did as I said, but when he was gone, and I knew he was facing enemy guns, I became much worse."

Griffin nodded. "I'm glad to know these details, Mrs. Linden. Since the records indicate that Dr. Maddox has had you on paraldehyde, and it definitely helps you to a degree, I'll keep you on it."

"I appreciate that, Doctor."

Griffin nodded and looked back at the papers. "Dr. Maddox's records show that you have been slowly but steadily losing weight."

"Yes. I simply have no appetite, Doctor. And the more I think about William being out there on those battlefields with bullets and cannonballs flying every direction, the less desire I have to eat."

"I understand, but it concerns me. I know a loss of appetite is quite often a by-product of depression. But I can't let you keep on losing weight. I'm going to do some in-depth study on it and see if I can help you regain your appetite."

Myrna gave him a wan smile. "If I could have my husband home and no longer a target for Confederate guns, Doctor, I'd get my appetite back in a hurry."

Griffin smiled in return. "That, m'lady, is out of my hands."

"Of course, but I do want you to know, Dr. Griffin, that I appreciate your concern for me."

"Well, you're my patient now, and that puts you on my concern list. How's your paraldehyde supply?"

"I have about half a bottle left."

"All right. I brought one with me, just in case you were running low. Half a bottle is low in my estimation, when you need it like you do." As he spoke, Griffin opened his medical bag and produced a fresh bottle, setting it on the small table next to his chair. "And by the way, this bottle is a gift from your new doctor as a token of appreciation that you have given up your husband and the income he once produced, so he might be out there doing his part to bring this war to an end."

Tears welled up in Myrna's eyes. She took a linen handkerchief from a dress pocket and dabbed at her eyes. "That's very kind of you, Doctor. Thank you."

"It's the least I can do," he said, pulling a stethoscope from the black bag. "Now I want to check your vital signs. You just relax, and I'll have it done shortly."

Rising from the chair, he put the earpieces in his ears and listened to her heart. He commented that the heart sounded a bit weak, but at least was steady. A regular diet of solid food would help. Next he listened to her lungs, asking her to take deep breaths, hold them, then let the air out through her nose.

Griffin noticed that while he was doing his examination, Myrna kept folding and unfolding the handkerchief as her hands rested in her lap.

Satisfied with the sound of her lungs, he took out a thermometer and checked her temperature, which turned out to be normal. Then taking out his pocket watch, he compared her pulse with the ticks of the second hand. "Pulse is normal. I'm glad for that."

As he was replacing the watch into his vest pocket, he looked into Myrna's pale face. His well-trained and experienced eye missed nothing. Though her vital signs were all well within normal range, he was very aware of the empty look in her lovely blue eyes. There was a fragile quality about Myrna Linden, and her thin hands continued to nervously fold and unfold the linen handkerchief.

While putting the thermometer and stethoscope back into his medical bag, the doctor said, "Tell me about your daughter. I didn't check her records. How old is Jenny?"

"She's eighteen. She finished high school last May, graduating with excellent grades."

"Good. What does she do now?"

"She works as a clerk at Henderson's General Store on Main Street in downtown Harrisburg."

"How is she coping with her father being in the War and constantly in danger?"

"Well, she doesn't have any symptoms like mine, Doctor, if that's what you mean. Of course, Jenny is equally as concerned about her father facing death almost every day. Jenny and her father have a very special relationship. I've seen many fathers and daughters who were close, but these two are especially close. William adores that sweet girl, and she adores him as well. If you would see them together, you would know what I'm talking about."

"I'm glad for that, Mrs. Linden. When he comes home, they will have a very special reunion too."

Myrna managed a smile and nodded. She took a quick breath and said in an almost inaudible voice, "War is so foolish. All it does is tear up people's lives. Seldom does anything good come from it. As I told you, William would have stayed home with me if I hadn't insisted he follow his sense of duty and do like thousands of other Union men and perform his part in the War."

"Well, all of us wish this terrible thing had never happened, and now that it has, we can only hope that it won't last much longer."

Myrna's eyes filled with tears again. "I'm trying desperately to keep myself and this household together here, but I'm woefully aware that with each passing day, the chances of William coming home safely grow slimmer. Every time we read about the battles in the newspapers, it seems they become more intense, and a greater percentage of men are killed. And if not killed, then maimed and disfigured. In the face of this, my depression becomes an almost unbearable burden with which to cope, Doctor."

"I understand, Mrs. Linden. And the War is daily taking its toll on the families with loved ones on the battlefields, as well as the men in uniform. I have a son in the army."

"You do?"

"Yes. And it is terribly hard for my wife and me, knowing Brad is facing enemy guns almost every day."

"Oh, bless your hearts. Then you know by experience what Jenny and I are going through."

"Yes, ma'am. Leona—my wife—cries herself to sleep every night."

Myrna moved her head back and forth slowly. "This horrid war has been going on for over three years now, Dr. Griffin. Maybe one of these days it will be over."

Griffin sighed as he tightened the buckle on his medical bag and stood up. "I sure hope so. Well, it's after six o'clock. I'd better be getting home. Leona will have supper on."

Myrna rose from the rocker. "I will walk you to the door, Doctor. I wish Jenny could have come home while you were here. I want her to meet you. They don't close the store till six, and then they have to do a little cleaning up before they can leave."

"I'm sure I'll get to meet her soon," said Griffin. "She sounds like a very nice girl."

They were moving toward the parlor door. "Oh, that she is. Would you like to see a picture of her?"

"Of course," said the doctor as they stopped and Myrna stepped to the mantel.

Picking up a framed photograph of her daughter, Myrna moved to Griffin and handed it to him. "This is Jenny's graduation picture."

The doctor looked at the lovely blonde in the photograph and smiled at Myrna. "She's beautiful, Mrs. Linden. And I think I can guess the color of her eyes. Blue, right?"

"Yes. As blue as the sky, Doctor."

Griffin detected a spark of light in Myrna's eyes as she spoke of her daughter. He grinned. "Just like her mother's."

She smiled as the doctor placed Jenny's picture back in her hand. "Well, maybe a shade bluer. I wish I had her blond hair, instead of this mouse brown color.

"Don't be too hard on yourself, Mrs. Linden. Your hair is the same color as Leona's, and I love it." He glanced at Jenny's picture. "I have an idea that lovely girl has a lot of young men interested in her."

"She does indeed, but all of them are away in the War, and she just stays home and takes care of me when she's not working at the store."

"She really does sound like a nice girl."

Another smile tugged at the corners of Myrna's mouth. "There's none better, Doctor." She looked at the picture in her hand. "I'll walk you to the d—" Her eyes fell on the photograph that lay on the table by her rocker, which she had been looking at when the doctor knocked on the door. "I have a picture of William in his uniform over here. Would you like to see it?"

"Certainly."

Myrna hurried as best she could, set the framed picture back on the mantel, and picked up the one on the small table. Hurrying back, she handed it to him. "This is my William."

Griffin set eyes on the photograph and nodded. "He is a fine-looking man, Mrs. Linden. He has the look of an army officer in his eyes."

She raised her eyebrows and looked at the picture. "Hmm. I never thought of that. I guess he does. But even so, I want him home and out of the army."

"That day will come," said Griffin. "Well, I'd better get going, or Leona will fry my hide if I'm late for supper!"

When the doctor was gone, Myrna carried William's picture with her and sat down once again on the rocking chair. Slanting the picture toward the lamplight, she sighed. "Oh, William, I miss you so much."

And tears began to flow.

# 3

IN DOWNTOWN HARRISBURG, Zack Henderson was moving about, dousing the coal oil lamps in the general store while his wife and Jenny Linden were behind the counter, arranging pencils and paper pads for business the next day.

"Well, that about does it," Emma said with a sigh.

Purse in hand, Jenny moved around the end of the counter and picked up one of the newspapers off the stand. "Guess so. I sure don't want to forget Mama's paper."

Emma headed toward the front door, which now had the closed sign facing the street on its window. Pulling it open, she looked back at Jenny, who was coming her way while double-folding the newspaper and placing it under her arm. "Does your mother really read every page in the paper every evening?"

"Every *word*," Jenny said, chuckling as the two women stepped outside. "She really loves to read her paper. If I would forget to bring it to her, she wouldn't know what to do after supper until bedtime."

Zack put out the last lamp, which left the store in darkness except for the shadows cast by the light that streamed through the windows from the street lamps outside. As he stepped out and locked the door, Jenny ran her gaze both ways. The lamplighters had already done their job on Main Street.

Emma hugged Jenny. "You and your mother have a nice

evening. We'll see you in the morning."

"Sure will," said Jenny. "Good night to both of you."

The Hendersons bid Jenny good night and headed up the street. Jenny carried her purse and the newspaper and made her way the opposite direction. Already, Main Street was almost deserted. When Jenny reached the first intersection, she turned the corner and headed toward the residential area where the Linden house was located. The street lamps were few and far between on the residential streets, but Jenny was used to walking home in the dark.

When she reached the next block, which was overshadowed by lofty trees and bathed in the dim light coming from the street lamps on the corners, she headed across the street. Almost every house in the block ahead of her had lights twinkling in their windows. She had barely reached the other side when from behind her, she heard rapid footsteps.

She turned just in time to see the shadowed figures of two boys, close on her heels, running toward her. One of them snatched the purse from her hand, and both boys laughed as they kept on running.

"Hey!" she shouted. "Come back here!"

They were still laughing as they paused to look back at her, then ran on.

Jenny spied a length of tree limb lying next to the walk. She picked it up and hurled it at the legs of the boys. The one who had the purse in hand was a step or two behind his friend, and when the flying limb struck his ankles, his feet tangled in it. He went down with a yelp while his friend kept on running. Before he could get up, Jenny bent over and yanked the purse out of his hand.

She had rolled the newspaper up tight, and wielding it like a club, cracked him across the face. "Who do you think you are, kid?" she hissed. "You had no business taking my purse!"

The boy threw his arms up to protect his face and burst into tears.

Jenny gave him one more slap with the paper, looked down at him with burning eyes, and snapped, "You'd better be glad I'm only half mad! Now, get out of here!"

Myrna Linden was sitting in the rocking chair, looking at her husband's photograph by the light of the nearby lamp when she heard footsteps on the porch stairs. She looked up through the window to see Jenny crossing the porch.

Myrna glanced back at the uniformed man in the picture. "Well, darling, here's our beautiful daughter, home from work."

Seconds later Jenny entered the parlor. She had folded the newspaper back to its usual form. Myrna noticed that Jenny's face was pale and her eyes showed worry.

"Hello, Mama," Jenny said softly as she approached the rocking chair. "How are you doing?"

Myrna managed a smile as her daughter drew near. "I'm doing all right, honey."

Jenny leaned over and kissed her cheek. "Good. I love you."

"I love you too. What's wrong? Did something happen at the store to upset you?"

Jenny figured the episode she had with the boy who had snatched her purse wasn't worth mentioning. "No, Mama, nothing happened at the store. But the *Journal* has some bad news."

Myrna frowned, looked at the folded paper in Jenny's hand, then met her gaze. "Something about the War?"

"Yes."

Myrna reached for the newspaper.

"There was a fierce battle near Winchester, Virginia, two days ago. A large number of men on both sides were wounded, and many were killed. The battle involved some of Pennsylvania's troops under the command of General Sherman."

It was Myrna's turn to have a pale face. "W-was your father's unit involved?"

"No, Mama."

Myrna sighed. "Oh, I'm so glad."

Jenny's features pinched. Her voice choked as she said, "But Nate's Seventh Pennsylvania Artillery was in the battle."

"I see. Well, I hope Nate is all right."

"I hope so too. It upset me pretty bad when Wiley Owens came in with the papers and told me about the battle and that some of

Pennsylvania's troops were in it. Wiley and the Hendersons tried to encourage me about it. They told me I should keep a positive attitude about Nate's safety in the War."

"Just like we have to do about your papa. But it's…it's so hard."

Jenny clenched her teeth. "Why can't the government do something about this? It's so frustrating to read in the newspapers of these battles involving men we love, but to have to wait for what seems like an eternity to get any information."

"That it is, honey. It is almost more than I can bear. I wish there was a way we could know, but there isn't."

Jenny let out a sigh and sat down on the sofa. "I'll go start supper in a few minutes, Mama. I just need to sit down and catch my breath."

"Of course, honey," said Myrna, unfolding the newspaper to expose the front page. "I wish Nate had some family in Harrisburg to come home to when the War is over. But at least he has friends."

"He has me, Mama. I'm more than a friend."

Myrna flicked a glance at her but did not comment.

Jenny sat quietly with her hands folded in her lap, her thoughts on Nate and the yearning inside her to know if he was all right.

Myrna hastily read the front page article about the battle. Her features twisted and tears filmed her eyes. "Oh, Jenny, this is terrible. What a useless waste of human life, let alone all the blood that was shed by the wounded men."

Jenny's eyes flashed fire. "That's for sure, Mama. And it's the fault of those Confederate leaders. They started the War. The Rebels fired the first shot. If they hadn't rebelled against the United States government in the first place there wouldn't have been any Civil War, and those thousands of men already killed in the past three and a half years would still be alive. Papa would be home where he belongs, running his lumber company, and Nate would be home working his job at the Harrisburg Water Department. I'd like to have that Jefferson Davis in my gun sights!"

Myrna studied her daughter's fiery eyes and stonelike face. Since Jenny was quite young, she had displayed a flinty temper and a bent for vengeance against anyone who, in her mind, had done someone wrong. "Now, Jenny, you shouldn't talk that way. Just calm down.

The people of the South are human too. Their rebellion against the government came when they were told that they would have to put a stop to slavery.

"The people of the South felt strongly that the federal government had no right to tell the states what they could or couldn't do. In their minds, the federal government was interfering with the rights of the individual states to govern their own commerce. I'm loyal to the Union, honey, but I can understand how the Southerners feel. You need to try to see the South's side of the issues of states' rights and slavery."

"Mama, as far as I'm concerned, the plantation owners in the South wouldn't need slaves if they would let go of some of their wealth and use it for wages to pay their help, rather than make them live as chattel. If they had been reasonable about this in the first place, there wouldn't be any Civil War going on. All of those men who have been killed on the battlefields would still be alive."

Myrna wiped tears. "Honey, I don't want any men being killed—Northerners or Southerners. But since the two armies are indeed fighting each other, I'm glad, at least, that your papa's unit wasn't in this battle near Winchester."

"I'm glad Papa's unit wasn't there, Mama, but—but—" Suddenly Jenny burst into sobs.

Myrna laid the newspaper aside, rose from the rocking chair, and moved unsteadily to the sofa. She sat down beside her daughter and wrapped her in her arms. Jenny laid her head on her mother's breast. "Oh, Mama, I love Nate so much. I don't know what I would do if he got killed. And…and he might have been killed in that battle on Tuesday!"

"Now, honey, what did Wiley Owens and the Hendersons tell you about keeping a positive attitude about Nate's safety in the War?"

Jenny sniffed. "But, Mama, it's so hard. So very hard."

"Yes. I know. But if you can keep a positive attitude, it will be a lot easier on you. I know I'm not the one to speak with authority on this, since I've been so depressed with your papa gone, but Wiley and the Hendersons are right. Honey, I have a feeling that Lieutenant Nate Conrad is all right, even though he was in that awful battle. Think of it this way—many more men made it through the battle than were killed."

Jenny wiped tears from her face and kissed her mother's cheek. "That is the way to look at it. Thank you. I'll go start supper."

As Jenny rose from the sofa, Myrna looked up at her. "I'll come help you."

"I'll let you set the table, Mama, but until I'm ready for that, you just sit back over here in your rocking chair and read some more of the paper."

With that, Jenny offered her hand. Myrna took it, and Jenny helped her to her feet. As she was guiding her mother toward the rocking chair, she said, "Oh! I just remembered! Your new doctor was to be here at five o'clock. I'm sorry. My mind was so heavy about Nate that it slipped my mind. He did make it, didn't he?"

Myrna settled onto the rocker. "Yes, he did. And I like Dr. Adam Griffin very much."

"Well, good! I assume he did a thorough examination."

"Oh yes. He checked my heart and lungs, and took my pulse and my temperature. He brought my file with him and went over the records."

"And he is in agreement with the treatment Dr. Maddox was giving you?"

"Absolutely."

"That's good. No changes, then."

"Right. He left me a new bottle of paraldehyde, so I have a sufficient supply. He did say that he is very concerned about my weight loss. He said a lack of appetite usually goes with manic depression, and he is going to do a study on depression and see if he can find a way to bring back my appetite."

"He sounds like a good doctor. I'm anxious to meet him. I'm glad you like him and that he is going to take good care of you. This daughter of yours would also like to see her mother get some flesh back on her bones."

Myrna smiled up at her.

Jenny picked up the newspaper and placed it on her mother's lap. "You read. I'll let you know when I'm ready for the table to be set."

As she headed for the kitchen, Jenny was trying to think of something to prepare for supper that might tempt her mother to eat more than her usual few bites. *Ham steak!* she thought. *Yes! I almost forgot that I bought the ham steaks at the meat market yesterday.*

She knew her mother loved ham steak and red-eye gravy. She also loved Jenny's big thick buttermilk biscuits.

Entering the kitchen, Jenny built a fire in the cookstove. While the stove was getting hot, she went to the pantry and selected two good-sized potatoes, as well as the makings for the biscuits. By the time she had the potatoes peeled, the stove was hot, and soon the kitchen was filled with the tempting aroma of ham sizzling in the skillet, buttermilk biscuits baking in the oven, and hot coffee steaming from the pot on the stove.

With everything cooking as she desired, Jenny went to the parlor. "Okay, Mama. You can come and set the table now."

The two walked to the kitchen together, and as Myrna began setting the table, Jenny checked on the food that was cooking and then busied herself at the counter of the cupboard, slicing raw carrots and celery.

While setting the table, Myrna paused with the silverware in her hands. "Jenny, I'm worried about you."

Jenny looked over her shoulder. "Worried about me?"

"Yes."

"Concerning what?"

"Nate."

Jenny turned all the way around. "What do you mean?"

"Honey, it really worries me that you have so much love for Nate, and yet you have no assurance that he is in love with you. I can see a broken heart coming."

Jenny closed her eyes. "Mama, I assure you that Nate is not going to break my heart. He loves me." She opened her eyes. "He does. He really loves me."

"And you base this on what? May I remind you that a few days after Nate went off to the War, I asked you if he had committed himself to you. Remember?"

"Yes, and I—"

"Your exact words were 'not really.' And then you said, 'But,

Mama, I know in my heart that Nate loves me and one day will make me his bride.' Remember?"

"Yes, Mama. I remember. But even though Nate didn't come right out and say he loved me and wanted to marry me, I know it is so because of his actions. You know the old adage: Actions speak louder than words. My heart tells me that Nate loves me, and when he comes home from the War, he will ask me to marry him."

Myrna began placing the silverware setting at Jenny's plate. "Honey, I think you were misreading his actions. You and Nate had known each other for almost ten years when he went off to the War. You started dating him for a full year before that. You wouldn't date anyone else during that time, but he dated other girls. And though he dated you many times, he never once stated anything positive about being in love with you, or that the two of you had a future together. I seriously doubt that Nate has any plans to marry you. For sure, this is not the normal way for a young man to act toward the girl he loves and wants to marry. When it's normal, he will come right out and say so."

Without comment, Jenny turned around and went back to work on the carrots and celery.

Myrna placed silverware at her own plate, then moved up behind Jenny and slipped an arm around her. "Honey, I just don't want you to get hurt. Don't let your heart tell you things are wonderful when they're not."

Jenny laid down the paring knife and looked deep into her mother's eyes. "Mama, you simply do not know Nate like I do. I am positive he is in love with me. And I am positive he has marriage in mind. Whenever the War is over, he will come home and propose. I'm sure of it." Her brow creased. "That is—that is, if he—he is still alive."

As Jenny began sniffling, Myrna gripped both her upper arms. "Now, now, honey. With all these other things you're positive about, don't let down on your positive attitude about Nate's safety in the War."

Jenny nodded, biting her lips.

"I'll help you take the food from the stove," said Myrna. "I see we've got ham steaks in the skillet."

Jenny served their plates and carried them to the table, which was covered with a white cloth embroidered with yellow daisies. Returning to the stove, she poured two steaming cups of coffee and placed one beside each plate.

When the two sat down at the table, Jenny was still having a difficult time with worry. She looked at the food and felt like a lump was in her throat and a hot ball of lead had settled in her stomach. She wondered if she could swallow a bite. However, she knew that in order to entice her mother into eating, she would have to find a way. Ham steak, red-eye gravy, and buttermilk biscuits were among Myrna Linden's favorites, but if her daughter didn't eat, she might not eat, either.

Jenny dug in and her mother followed suit, bragging on her daughter's cooking skills. While they ate, they discussed the War, commenting on what it would take to end it. They agreed that President Abraham Lincoln was working hard with his military leaders in an effort to bring the bloody War to an end.

Jenny was actually unaware of what was going into her mouth. Soon she realized that her plate was empty, and a quick glance across the table revealed that her mother had eaten a good portion of her own food.

Smiling, Jenny reached across the table and patted her mother's thin, blue-veined hand. "I see my choice for supper was a good one, Mama. You ate more than you have at one meal in a long time."

Myrna smiled in return, her eyes showing a bit of a sparkle. "Yes, dear. I really am trying. I want to do everything I can to cooperate with Dr. Griffin. Maybe he'll soon have some answers for me with this appetite thing."

Jenny was about to make a favorable comment when suddenly, as if a shade had been pulled down over her mother's face, the smile disappeared from her lips and her eyes took on that dreaded vacant look that had haunted Jenny since her father had gone off to the War.

Myrna's lips began to tremble and her voice was hollow. "If only I could hear from your father. If only he would come home." Desperation joined the hollow sound. "I...I think I'm going to die if my William doesn't come home soon."

Jenny rose from her chair, moved around the table, and put an arm around her mother's shoulders. Leaning down close, she spoke softly into her ear. "Now, Mama, what about your positive attitude? You've got to take care of yourself so you will be here when Papa comes home. As hard as President Lincoln is working to bring the War to an end, it will come soon."

The vacant look was still in Myrna's eyes. "Do…do you really think so?"

"Yes. We must hang on to that hope. Now you sit there and concentrate on the day Papa will come home to us while I clean up the table and do the dishes."

Jenny was concerned while she did her cleanup work, for each time she looked at her mother, the blank stare was still there. It was as if Myrna Linden was in a world all her own.

When she was finished, Jenny was pleased to see her mother focusing more normally. She took her hand and said, "Come, sweet Mama. Let's go into the parlor."

Myrna moved unsteadily down the hall with her daughter gripping her tightly. Jenny noticed that she was shivering a bit. When they entered the parlor, Jenny slid the rocking chair close to the small fireplace, then settled her mother in it. "Night's chill is in the air, Mama. Let me cover you, then I'll light a fire."

Jenny stepped out of the parlor long enough to take a large afghan out of the hall closet. She spread the afghan over her mother's shoulders, then hurried to light the fire. When it was burning, she leaned over and hugged her. "There now, Mama. You'll feel the heat shortly. When it gets going, you'll be all nice and warm."

The vacant eyes were beginning to focus even better. A tiny smile appeared. "Thank you, Jenny. You are such a good girl. What would I ever do without you?"

Jenny leaned close and looked into her mother's eyes. "That's one thing you never have to worry about, Mama. No matter what, I will be here for you until Papa returns from this dreadful war."

Another tiny smile appeared. "That means more to me than I can ever tell you."

"You're my mother. And I want you to know that even when Papa is home, and I am married to Nate, I will always be close by so I can look after you."

Myrna cleared her throat gently and said, "I'd like to read the rest of my newspaper, now."

Jenny moved quickly, picked up the paper, and placed it in her mother's hands. "You enjoy every word, Mama. I'm going to sit right here on the sofa and read that new novel I started last night."

Myrna watched her daughter go to the bookshelf on the other side of the room. As Jenny picked up the book and headed toward the sofa, Myrna asked, "What's the name of the novel?"

Jenny lifted the book so her mother could see the cover. "It's called *Toward the Sunset*. See?"

Myrna focused on the cover, which showed a blazing sunset, and nodded. "What's it about?"

"It tells the story of a wagon train going out west—the hardships of the trail, including sickness, bad weather, and savage Indians. Their final destination is Los Angeles. So far, it's really good."

"Well, I hope you enjoy it to the last page."

"Someday I'd like to go out west and see it for myself, just like the people in this novel. The Kansas plains, the Colorado Rockies, the Arizona desert, Los Angeles, and the Pacific Ocean."

With her nerves now calm, Myrna began reading her newspaper. Jenny was immediately involved in her novel.

Mother and daughter had been reading for over two hours when Jenny glanced at Myrna while turning a page, and saw her head bobbing and her eyes drooping. Closing the book, she left the sofa and laid a hand on her mother's shoulder. "All right, sweet Mama, time for bed."

Jenny guided her mother down the hall to her bedroom, helped her put on her nightgown, tucked her into bed, and doused the lamp on the bedside table. Myrna was asleep instantly. Jenny leaned over, kissed her forehead, then left the room.

She went back to the parlor, doused the lamps there, and went to her room.

When she was in her nightgown and ready to put out her own lamp, Jenny glanced at the magazine that lay on the nightstand. It was the latest edition of *Harper's Magazine*, which she had purchased at Henderson's store a few days earlier. Picking up the magazine, she ran her eyes over the photograph on the cover, which showed a group of weary, bedraggled Union soldiers in a wooded area, looking into the camera.

Jenny had already read through the magazine, but it held her interest because it had an article about battlefields in the South, along with several photographs of battlefields in Virginia, Tennessee, Georgia, and Arkansas. Inside the magazine, the editor explained that the photograph on the cover was taken in Virginia.

She looked at the cover for a long moment, then looked inside once more to view the photographs of the other battlefields. Each one had Union soldiers in a small group, looking at the camera. In some, there were cannons close by. Others showed small tents in the background, indicating that the soldiers were camped on the very ground where they had fought the Confederates.

Jenny's eyes teared as she focused on a picture of two Union officers who were on a battlefield in Tennessee, standing over the bodies of four of their men who had been killed that day. One of the officers slightly resembled her father. "Oh, Papa," she said, "I want you to come home before some Rebel bullet takes you from us. Mama needs you. I need you. Please come home, Papa."

Jenny closed the magazine, doused the lantern, and crawled into bed. As the darkness surrounded her, she wiped tears on the sheet. "Oh, Papa, I love you so much. And I miss you so much. Please come home."

Her mind then went to Nate Conrad. "Oh, Nate, even though you have never put it in so many words that you love me, I know you do. Please come home so one day we can meet at the altar to become husband and wife."

Soon, Jenny fell asleep with tears still on her cheeks.

JENNY LINDEN FOUND HERSELF walking alone through a dense forest. It was late afternoon. The mossy smells invading her nostrils told her she was in the Deep South, and the air was so still it clung to her like a shroud. The sky was overcast with clouds that seemed to be made of smoke. With all the trees that surrounded her, there was not a bird to be seen...or heard.

She was coming to a clearing. Suddenly she saw a myriad of uniformed men lying dead on an open field, along with several dead horses. Her hand went to her mouth, and she swallowed hard as she stepped out of the trees and let her eyes roam over the sea of torsos that were sprawled in three directions. Some were lying on top of others, their heads and limbs twisted.

Jenny halted. She smelled burned gunpowder and blood. A foreboding atmosphere hung over the battlefield, like the calm before a tornado. Somehow she felt that she should keep walking among the dead. Forcing her feet to carry her forward, she moved slowly, weaving among the corpses that were clad in both gray and blue.

Barely breathing, Jenny looked down at the lifeless form of a Confederate officer. He lay faceup, his vacant eyes staring toward the sky. His revolver was in his hand, held in a death grip.

A few feet ahead of her lay a Union officer. A quick glance at the emblems on his shoulders told her he was a captain. Her eyes went to his face. Suddenly she drew a quick, sharp breath. A shiver touched her spine. "Papa!" Captain William Linden lay dead, with two slugs in his chest.

As she stood over her dead father, the sight she beheld set her limbs trembling with horror. It was as if a fist were tightening and twisting in her chest. She dropped to her knees, touched the cold face, and began to cry in great wracking sobs. "Papa-a-a-a! No! Papa, don't be dead! Papa, please don't be d—"

Abruptly, Jenny was aware of two Confederate soldiers standing over her. One was tall and slender, the other, short and stumpy. They both started laughing.

The tall one grinned at her evilly. "What's the matter, girlie? You don't like to see a dead Yankee?"

Jenny heard a triumphant ghostly Rebel yell coming from somewhere across the field. Suddenly a powerful unquenchable rage claimed her. She jumped to her feet and screamed, "This is my father! You filthy Rebels killed my father!"

The stumpy man in gray threw his head back, laughed, and held his ample stomach. "Too bad, girlie! Your father's dead. We killed him, and we're glad!"

Jenny wheeled, dashed to the body of the Confederate officer, bent over, and wrested the revolver from his tight grip. Swinging back the hammer, she lined it on the stumpy soldier. Her eyes glittered dangerously. "You killed my father. So you're glad, eh? Well, let's see how glad you are about this!"

The revolver bucked in her hand as it roared, and the Rebel went down with the bullet in his heart. The thin one sprang toward her, eyes wild. Jenny snapped the hammer back, took aim, and squeezed the trigger. The slug dead-centered the Rebel's forehead, and he went down in a heap.

Jenny's blood was boiling. "You killed my father! How does it feel, dirty Rebel? Huh? How does it feel? Nobody kills my father and gets away with it!" With that, she fired two more bullets into his head.

Jenny moved to the other Rebel corpse. "You killed my father. How do you like it, fatso?" She put the last two bullets in his head, then threw the gun down and ran toward her father's body. "Papa! Papa-a-a-a!"

Suddenly, Jenny was awake, sitting up in her bed. "Papa-a-a-a! Papa-a-a-a!" She threw her hands to her face and sobbed, "Oh, Papa, don't be dead! Please don't be dead!"

The bedroom door opened, and by the soft moonlight that was coming through the windows, Jenny saw her sleepy-eyed mother framed in the doorway. "Honey, are you all right?"

Jenny drew a shaky breath. "Yes, Mama. I…I was having a nightmare. I'm all right. Sorry I woke you up."

"That's okay, honey. I've had my share of nightmares for the past three years, as you well know. Do you think you can go back to sleep?"

"Uh-huh. It may take a few minutes, but I'm sure I can."

"Well, sleep peacefully this time, honey," said Myrna as she stepped into the hall and closed the door.

Jenny's face was soaked with sweat. She wiped it with the sheet, lay down, and turned on her side. Within ten minutes, she was fast asleep.


The rising sun wove its golden fingers through the windows into Jenny's room, and when it touched her eyelids, she rolled over and opened her eyes. "It can't be morning already," she mumbled.

Her weary brain protested at the thought of a new day starting so soon. She had gone through another nightmare shortly after getting back to sleep. She rubbed her puffy eyes while trying to rid her memory of the horror imbedded there.

She took a deep breath, let it out slowly, and sat up. After a few seconds, she swung her legs over the edge of the bed and tried to stretch the kinks out of her back. She glanced out the window at the pink and gold sunrise, and thought about her father and Nate. She wondered where in the South they might be, and if they were able to see the sun rising on another day.

Jenny rose from the bed to get ready. It took her a little longer than usual, for she stopped often to contemplate her nightmares and ponder on what they might mean. A strong feeling of dread hovered over her as she walked down the hall toward her mother's room to awaken her.

When Jenny turned the knob and pushed the door open, she was surprised to find her mother up and dressed. Myrna was at the dresser mirror, putting the finishing touches on her hair with a brush. She looked at Jenny in the reflection, noting her tired eyes. "Did you have another nightmare?"

Jenny nodded. "Yes."

"I thought so. I heard you cry out, but it was only for a moment, so I decided not to disturb you. I figured you would go back to sleep quicker if I left you alone."

"How's your appetite, Mama? You think you can put down a good breakfast?"

Myrna laid the hairbrush on the dresser and turned around. "I'm really not feeling any hunger to speak of, honey. How about you?"

"I'm not very hungry, either. How about leftover biscuits dabbed with butter and jam and some hot black tea?"

Myrna walked toward her daughter. "That would be just fine."

Soon they were seated at the kitchen table with steaming cups of tea next to plates that held two biscuits each. As they drank the tea, it seemed to revive them some.

Myrna looked across the table at Jenny. "Want to tell me about the nightmares?"

Jenny shrugged. "If you want to hear it."

"I do."

"All right. The first one took place on a battlefield somewhere in the Deep South. I could even smell the moss."

"Really?"

"Mm-hmm. I was walking through a thick forest toward an open field when I saw all these bodies of men and horses strewn everywhere."

Jenny went on to describe the nightmare in detail, and when she finished by telling how she had shot the two Confederate soldiers dead who were laughing because they had killed her papa, then put slugs in their heads just for the sake of vengeance, Myrna shook her head. "Honey, it's a good thing you're not a man. If you were, you would take vengeance on every Confederate soldier possible, making him wish he had never donned a gray uniform."

A strange light filled Jenny's eyes. "I most certainly would,

Mama, right down to General Bobby Lee. Then I would go after President Jeffie Davis, himself. And before I killed him, I would make sure I told him what a low-down cuss he is."

Myrna touched the tips of her fingers to her temples. "Jenny, I hope no one ever crosses you. That person would certainly wish he—or she—hadn't, when you got through with them."

Jenny laughed. "You're right, Mama. When somebody purposely does someone else wrong, they deserve to suffer for it."

Myrna took a small bite of biscuit, chewed it briefly, then swallowed it. She took a sip of tea. "Tell me about your other nightmare."

"Well, I found myself in an army camp where Nate was, and a Rebel spy had come into the camp, dressed in Union blue. Somehow I knew the man was a spy, and that he was there to kill Lieutenant Nate Conrad. I saw the spy enter Nate's tent and ran that direction, shouting a warning to Nate. There was a scuffle inside the tent, and by the time I stepped in there, the spy was dead with a knife in his chest.

"Nate was standing over him, breathing hard, and his eyes were wide as he looked at me and thanked me for calling out the warning. He asked how I knew the man was a spy. I told him I didn't know. I just knew it. I...I looked down at the dead man, realizing that he would have taken Nate from me if I hadn't called out the warning. I was angry, Mama. Really angry. I needed to vent my vengeance on him. Even though he was dead, I grabbed Nate's revolver from his holster and put all six bullets in the dead man's face."

Myrna's pale features twisted with revulsion. "Jenny, I wish you didn't have such a vengeful spirit. What you did in both of those nightmares scares me."

Jenny laughed again. "Mama, Mama. Those were only dreams."

"I know, but—"

"But I will tell you this, Mama," Jenny said in a serious tone, "if anyone ever harmed you or Papa or the man I love, they would taste of my vengeance, for sure."

Myrna did not comment. She picked up what was left of the biscuit and put it in her mouth. While she was chewing it, Jenny said,

"How about another biscuit, Mama?"

Myrna shook her head. "Not now, dear. Maybe I'll have it for a midmorning snack."

"Well, all right, but Mama, I do wish you would try to eat more. You seem to be losing weight almost every day."

Myrna nodded. "I'll try, honey. Maybe Dr. Griffin will come up with a solution to give me back my appetite."

"I sure hope so. It grieves me to see you wasting away like this."

Myrna reached across the table and patted her daughter's hand. "Don't you be worrying about me. One of these days this horrible war will be over and your papa will come home. I'll be fine, then."

Jenny squeezed her hand. "You just hold on to that dream, won't you?"

Myrna put a hand to her mouth and her eyes filled with tears. "I'll try."

Jenny rose from the table. "Mama, I'm going to make a stew before I leave for work. Will you keep wood on the fire in the stove so it can simmer all day?"

Myrna nodded.

"All right. Now, let's get you into the parlor."

After settling her mother in the rocking chair in the parlor and wrapping a light shawl around her shoulders, Jenny returned to the kitchen. She prepared carrots, potatoes, onions, and chunks of beef for the stew, and put them into a heavy pot. She added wood to the fire and placed the pot at the back of the stove to simmer.

Moments later, Jenny entered the parlor, kissed her mother's sunken cheeks, and stepped outside into a glorious, sunny fall day. Even her spirits were lifted a little as her tired eyes took in the array of color amid the trees that lined the street. When she reached the sidewalk, she turned and waved at her mother, then hurried off to work.


There were a few customers waiting in front of the store when Jenny arrived. Pressing a smile on her lips, she said, "Good morning, folks. I'll see if I can speed things up in there so we can get you in a little early."

"That would be nice, Jenny," said a young mother, who was holding a toddler in one arm while gripping the handle of a baby carriage with an infant inside.

Jenny stepped inside and found Zack and Emma busy behind the counter, making ready for the day's business. She greeted them.

"How's your mother today?" asked Emma as Jenny moved behind the counter.

"A little better, Emma. She still has her good moments and her bad ones. But I think she's having a few more good ones since Dr. Griffin was there to see her yesterday. He was a real encouragement to her."

"I'm glad for that. She needs all the encouragement she can get."

Jenny had her cash drawer ready quickly. "I told those folks outside that I'd see if we could open a few minutes early for them. I'm ready if you are."

Zack grinned and headed around the end of the counter. "Okay, Miss Fix-it, we'll just do that."

As the hours passed and customers came into the store, most of them, as usual, talked about the War. Some spoke of particular battles that had been fought of late and voiced their sorrow for the Union soldiers who had been killed. Others spoke their sorrow for the Union soldiers who had lost limbs, for those who had lost their eyesight, and for those who had been captured and were languishing in dirty, disease-infested Confederate prison camps.

In early afternoon, Jenny and Emma were working the counter. Both had lines of a half-dozen customers as they tallied up the bills and sacked goods. In both lines, people were discussing different aspects of the War and its casualties while they waited.

In front of Jenny, the woman she was waiting on was in conversation with the man just behind her. They were talking about the Union soldiers who were being killed on Southern battlefields and dumped in shallow graves without embalmment or coffins, where their bodies would rot while being devoured by worms.

Suddenly Jenny dropped the pencil she was holding, put her hands to her mouth, and began to weep. While the man and the woman, along with the rest of those in line stared at her, Emma stepped to Jenny and laid a hand on her arm. "What's wrong, honey?"

Jenny bit her lips and looked at Emma through her tears. "All of this war talk, Emma. I just need a few minutes to get a hold of myself."

"Go on back to the office. Zack is over there in the hardware section. I'll get him to take over for you here."

Jenny nodded. "I'll be back as soon as I can."

While the customers looked on, Jenny hurried from behind the counter and made a run for the office at the rear of the store. Entering the office, she closed the door behind her, sat down at the desk, and laid her head in her hands. While she wept, her mind went wild. Her thoughts rushed to her father. She got a mental picture of his body lying in a shallow grave somewhere in the South. Seconds later, the picture in her mind changed, and she saw him in the midst of battle. He was crouched behind his dead horse, firing his revolver at approaching Confederate soldiers, when suddenly a cannonball hit and exploded.

When the smoke cleared, Jenny could see her father lying on the ground, alive, with an arm missing and blood flowing. She gasped and muffled a sob.

Suddenly the mental image changed again. This time, she saw her father confined in a Rebel prison camp, dying of some horrible disease with no one there to take care of him or comfort him.

"Oh, Papa! Oh, Papa! I can't stand these horrible thoughts. Please come home before any of these things happen to you!"

After sobbing for a few more minutes, Jenny gained control of herself. She went to the washroom and bathed her face in cold water. When she had dried her face, she touched up her hair and returned to the counter.


That evening at closing time, Jenny bid the Hendersons good night and headed for home. While she walked, she thought of the mental images that had assaulted her mind concerning her father earlier in the day. Suddenly, she was getting images of Nate, seeing him in the same kind of predicaments. Shaking her head to rid herself of the pictures, Jenny felt the strong desire to wipe out every Southern man who put on a gray uniform.

The Linden house came into view. She thought of her mother's words spoken at breakfast that morning: *Jenny, I wish you didn't have such a vengeful spirit.*

She smiled to herself and said aloud, "Mama, if people do bad things, they deserve what comes to them."

At supper, Jenny was concerned that her mother ate very little of the beef stew, but she knew it would do no good to try to force her to eat more.

As usual, mother and daughter spent the evening in the parlor with Myrna reading that day's edition of the *Harrisburg Journal.* Jenny read three more chapters of her novel.

At bedtime, Jenny tucked her mother in, and as she walked down the hall toward her own room, her mind was fixed on Nate Conrad. She missed him terribly, and there was only one way to ease the pain of it.

Upon entering her room, she sat down at her small desk and took out paper and pen. She closed her eyes, trying to think what she should say. After a minute or so, she dipped the pen in the inkwell and began her letter.

Friday, September 23, 1864
My darling Nate,

Yes, this is the nineteenth letter I have written to you since you went off to fight in the War. And, since there is no mail service to wherever you are, this letter will go into the desk drawer with the other eighteen for you to read when you come home. As I have told you in the other letters, I write these periodically because somehow it makes me feel close to you.

I want to say once more, my darling, that I love you with all my heart, and I miss you so terribly. I see so many women here in town who miss their husbands, sons, and sweethearts. But none of them miss their men as much as I miss you. I know you miss me too, and we can talk about our lonely hours during the War when we are living in our own home here in Harrisburg as husband and wife.

Until then, my precious Nate, don't ever forget that you are the only one for me. If at night, you will look up at the stars and remember that I am looking at those same stars, you will feel closer to me.

All my love,

Your Jenny

Jenny wiped tears while she blotted the ink, then read the letter over. "Someday, when we're married, darling," she said softly, "we can let our love grow deeper as you read these letters while we're cuddled together on our sofa in our own house."

Before folding the letter, Jenny planted a kiss on the spot where she had started with "My darling Nate." She then opened a drawer and took out the small stack of letters which were tied with a pink ribbon. She slid the letter on top, placed the stack back in the drawer, and closed it.

Jenny picked the lantern up from atop the desk, left her room, and moved down the hall to her mother's room. Opening the door quietly, she peeked in. By the light of the lantern, she saw that her mother was fast asleep. A smile curved her lips as she whispered, "I love you, Mama."

She closed the door quietly and returned to her own room. Moments later, in her nightgown, Jenny doused the lantern's flame and slipped down between the sheets. Once again, her mind went to her father. A lump rose in her throat. "Papa, I love you and I miss you so much."

Memories of her childhood flooded Jenny's mind. She talked to her father about one incident after another that happened when they were together in days gone by.

After reminiscing for several minutes, she said, "Papa, every one of those precious moments only serve to make me love you even more. Thank you for all the wonderful memories you gave me. We can talk about them when you come home."

Soon Jenny cried herself to sleep.

The next morning, Jenny arrived at Henderson's General Store, and at opening time, with Zack and Emma at her side, she busied herself waiting on customers.

As usual, the prominent subject among the customers was the Civil War and its casualties. While doing her job, Jenny tried to block the War talk from her mind, but there came a moment early in the afternoon when she was having flashes of mental pictures concerning her father and Nate—just like the ones that had tortured her the day before. Suddenly, as she finished sacking goods for a customer, she broke down and began to cry.

Emma excused herself to the customer she was serving. "Honey, what's wrong?"

Jenny met Emma's gaze. "It's all this War talk. I can't stand constantly hearing about it. You know…with Papa and Nate—"

"I understand, honey."

Zack leaned close. "Emma, business is slowing down now. I can handle it. Take Jenny back to the office and talk to her."

Emma took Jenny by the hand and quickly led her back to the office.

When they stepped inside, Emma closed the door and folded Jenny in her arms. "Sweetie, I know your heart is heavy. You not only have your mother's depression to deal with, but you have had to live with the fact that you may never see your father and Nate again."

Jenny sobbed for several minutes, clinging to Emma. When she gained control of her emotions, Emma released her, allowing her to dry her tears. Jenny kissed Emma's cheek. "Thank you for being such a true, caring friend to me."

Emma kissed Jenny's cheek in return. "And thank you for being such a sweet girl. Yes, and for being such a good friend too."

"I'm ready to go back to work now."

"All right. Let's go."


It was late in the afternoon when Zack reminded Emma that he had an appointment with the president of the Bank of Harrisburg concerning the loan for the new house they wanted to build. Knowing it would take a while, he asked Emma to close up for him, adding that he would be home by suppertime.

Soon it was six o'clock and time to close the store. Jenny locked the door and hung the closed sign in the window. She turned to Emma, who was taking the money out of the cash drawers and placing it in a metal box. "I'll go tidy up the office a bit before I go."

Emma smiled. "Thanks, honey. I'll be back to put this money in the safe in a couple minutes."

As Jenny was heading toward the rear of the store, she heard a tap on the front door, and Emma calling out that the store was closed. Shaking her head at the way people acted sometimes, Jenny entered the office and began her cleaning job.

Out front the customer looked through the window on the door and said loud enough for Emma to hear, "Please, ma'am. Let me in."

Emma noted that he was a young man with a full beard. Rounding the end of the counter, she approached the door, unlocked it, and opened it a few inches. "What do you need?"

"I'm just passing through town, ma'am, and I need a few food items. I won't take much of your time."

Emma smiled. "All right. Come in."

"Thank you," said the young man.

Emma closed the door and locked it. As she started to turn around, she said, "If you'll tell me what you need, I'll help you find—" The words stuck in her throat when she saw the small revolver in his hand, which was pointed directly at her face. "Wh-what do you want?"

"I want the money from the cash drawer. You were just taking it out, weren't you?"

Emma's mouth had gone dry. "Well, yes, but—"

"Just go back there behind the counter and give it to me."

Emma's face was gray as she started toward the counter with the robber on her heels.

At the rear of the store, Jenny heard the male voice. She started out of the office and halted quickly when she saw the bearded man holding the gun on Emma as she was moving behind the counter. Quickly assessing the situation, Jenny stepped back into the office so the robber wouldn't see her. He obviously thought Emma was in the store alone, giving him the perfect opportunity to relieve her of the money in the cash drawers.

Jenny's heart was pounding wildly, but she had a plan in mind instantly. Crouching low, she moved out of the office quickly and silently moved down the aisles of shelves to the hardware section. Several ax handles leaned against the wall. She grasped one, and keeping low, headed in a line that would bring her up behind the robber.

Behind the counter, Emma's fear had her shaking. She dropped some of the money on the floor.

The robber snapped, "Hurry, lady! Pick it up!"

Emma froze, clinging to the edge of the counter.

The robber slapped her face. "I said pick it up!"

Emma gasped, let out a whimper, and stumbled back against the wall.

Hastening along her chosen path in a crouch, Jenny heard the slap, the whimper, and Emma's stumbling feet.

Her temper flared.

She felt her blood heat up.

Just as she came to the end of a row of shelves where she could see the robber from behind, he was leaning over the counter and stuffing money in his pockets. She moved with the swiftness of a cougar, swung the ax handle, and cracked him savagely on the head. He went down like a poleaxed steer and hit the floor, unconscious.

Emma blinked at the sight before her and shakily moved back up to her place at the counter. She looked down at Jenny who was foraging through the man's pockets, pulling out the stolen money.

Jenny paused, looked up at Emma, and said, "Get the police!"

In a bit of a daze, Emma hurried to the door, unlocked it, and swung it open. A man was passing by on the sidewalk. "Harry!" cried Emma. "Get the police! A man just tried to rob us!"

Harry Weems was a regular customer of the store. He stepped up close enough to see the bearded man lying unconscious on the floor, with Jenny emptying his pockets. "Right away!" He turned and ran down the street.

Emma closed the door and leaned against it, trying to clear her head. A moment later, she turned around and saw Jenny behind the counter, placing the money in the cash box. Keeping a wary eye on the man on the floor, Emma hurried back behind the counter. "H-Harry Weems is going for the police."

"Good," said Jenny, closing the lid on the metal box.

Emma clung to Jenny's hand. "Th-thank you for coming to my rescue, honey."

Jenny's features reddened. She looked back at the robber. "He would dare to slap you! I'd like to bash—"

The robber was stirring. He moaned, shook his head to clear it, and sat up. Jenny grasped the ax handle, which was leaning against the wall behind her, and with eyes blazing, hurried around the end of the counter.

Emma looked on in amazement as Jenny stood over the bearded man and hissed, "You scum!" With that, she swung the ax handle and cracked his head again. The impact of the blow flattened him on the floor. He was out cold.

Jenny's anger was a molten flame in her brain. She lifted the ax handle over her head. "You would dare slap my friend and rob her!"

The ax handle came down on his head again, then Jenny hurried behind the counter and gathered Emma in her arms.

AT MEMORIAL HOSPITAL in Frederick, Maryland, on Saturday morning, September 24, hospital superintendent Dr. Homer Walton stood at the front of the small assembly room and watched as his staff of physicians, nurses, and medical assistants was gathering before him. He glanced at the clock on the wall. It was 6:47.

Two minutes later, all the staff members were present, and seated.

Walton ran his eyes over their faces. "Ladies and gentlemen, I needed to have this meeting with you just before the seven o'clock shift change, so I could make all of you aware of what is about to happen. I assume that most of you heard about the battle that took place near Winchester, Virginia, this past Tuesday."

Heads were nodding.

Walton continued. "I received a wire late last night from Union army headquarters in Washington, D.C., stating that a train is on its way to Frederick, carrying ninety-three wounded Union soldiers from that battle. It will be arriving about noon today. Since we are already almost to capacity in the military ward, this number of patients arriving is going to put a tremendous load on us. We'll have to put some of our present patients on cots so the new ones can have the beds.

"From the information I received in the wire, I know there will be several amputations to perform, and a good number of the men will need surgery for bullet and shrapnel removal. Others are not wounded so severely. I know this is going to add exceedingly to your workload, but you have each demonstrated before that you are willing to labor long and hard to care for the men who have bravely fought on the battlefields for the Union cause."

Heads were nodding again.

Walton smiled. "You're a great bunch. If I had my way, every one of you would be given a medal of honor from Congress. All right. You're dismissed."

As the meeting broke up and the day staff went to work, every preparation possible was made so they would be ready when the train brought in the ninety-three wounded men.


The train arrived in Frederick just before noon. Several army wagons were at the depot to take the wounded Union soldiers to Memorial Hospital.

Medical carts and stretchers were employed to bring the patients into the hospital from the wagons. Some of the wounded men were taken directly to the military ward, while the greater number was hurried to the surgical unit. There, the staff physicians did quick examinations to determine the order in which the amputations and surgeries should be done. Nurses and their assistants in the military ward went to work to patch up the men who were less seriously wounded.

By three o'clock in the afternoon, men who had had surgery and amputations were being brought into the crowded ward and placed in beds made available by other patients being placed on cots.

One young officer was lifted from a medical cart and placed on a bed, while a nurse and her assistant stood by. The officer was still unconscious from the morphine which had been administered before his surgery. One of the attendants handed the nurse the wounded officer's chart, then he and his partner hurried away with the cart to pick up another patient.

"Loretta, you go ahead and make him comfortable. I'll look over his chart," Millie Ross said.

"All right, Millie," said Loretta. She adjusted the pillow under the patient's head, then moved around the bed, tucking sheets and covers close around his body. When she was finished, she studied the pale face of the unconscious soldier for a moment, then turned to Millie. "The surgery was on his lower back?"

Millie looked up. "Yes. The surgeons had to take a piece of shrapnel out. It says here that it was quite large, but no serious damage was done to the spine."

Loretta nodded. "That's good. At least he will walk again. How many severed spines have we seen from what cannonballs have done to our soldiers?"

"A lot of them. And bayonets too."

"Yes. And how horrible it is to have to stand by when they are told that they will never walk again."

Millie looked at the unconscious young officer with compassion. "He's going to be here a good while for recuperation, but at least he won't have to live the rest of his life paralyzed."

Another medical cart was seen coming through the door.

Millie raised her hand to get the attendants' attention, and pointed to a vacant bed further down the line. They nodded, acknowledging that they understood. Millie hung the chart at the foot of the young officer's bed. "Okay, Loretta. We'll let this one rest. I'll come back and check on him after we take care of this next patient."

Some thirty minutes later, Millie hung the chart of the big husky Union sergeant on the foot of the bed. The sergeant was already beginning to come out of his unconsciousness. "Loretta," said Millie, "you stay with him. I'll go check on our young officer over here."

Loretta was dabbing a wet cloth on the sergeant's forehead. She nodded. Millie turned and moved along the line of beds, looking at each patient as she passed them. One of them called out, "Hello, Millie! Why don't you come and hold my hand? It really hurts."

She smiled, waved him off, and moved up to the bed of the young officer, who now had his bleary eyes open and was looking around.

Millie bent over him. "Lieutenant, can you see me?"

He ran his tongue over his lips and tried to focus on her face.

Millie could tell he was still quite disoriented from the morphine. "Are you thirsty, Lieutenant?"

He licked his lips again and nodded.

She picked up the cup that was on the small table beside his bed and poured it half full from the water pitcher. She placed one hand behind his head and carefully lifted it as she put the cup to his lips. "Just sip it slowly."

When he had sipped all the water he wanted for the moment, Millie set the cup on the table. "You can have more when you're ready."

He tried to smile while still attempting to focus on her face. He could barely make out her features, but what he could see told him that she was very pleasant to look at. Her voice was so soft and sweet. He wondered if he was dreaming.

She picked up a cloth, dipped it in water, wrung it out a little, and placed it on his forehead. He told himself he wasn't dreaming. The coolness he felt was real. "Wh-where am I?"

Millie leaned down close. "You're in Memorial Hospital, Frederick, Maryland."

"Oh. Now I remember. The train…"

"Yes. The train brought you here. Your chart says you are Lieutenant Nathan Conrad of the Seventh Pennsylvania Artillery Division, and that the surgeon had to take a large piece of shrapnel out of your lower back."

Nate Conrad ran his tongue over his lips again. "Yes. Nurse?"

"Yes, Lieutenant?"

He worked his jaw for a few seconds. "How—bad?"

"Do you mean, will you walk again?"

He closed his eyes. "Y-yes."

"There was no serious damage to your spine. You will walk again."

His eyes opened and a smile curved his lips. "Oh. Wonderful. I won't be a cripple."

"No. You—"

Suddenly, Lieutenant Nate Conrad's eyes closed and his body relaxed. Millie smiled. He was under the influence of the morphine again. She removed the cloth from his forehead, laid it on the table, and smiled down at him. "You rest now, Lieutenant. I'll check on you later."

She started to walk away, then paused for a moment, and fixed her eyes on the sleeping face. *There is something special about this one,* she thought. Then giving herself a mental shake, she left his bedside to attend the mountain of duties still awaiting her attention.

During the next hour and a half Millie stayed busy with other patients, but twice sent Loretta to check on Lieutenant Nathan Conrad. The first time Loretta returned, she reported that the lieutenant was still asleep. The second time, she drew up beside Millie, who was taking a wounded soldier's temperature, and said softly, "He's coming out of it, Millie."

The redhead turned and looked across the ward and focused on Nate Conrad's bed. He was rolling his head back and forth slowly, and rubbing his eyes.

Looking at her assistant, Millie said, "You finish up here, Loretta. I'd better go see about him."

When Millie drew up beside Nate's bed, he was mumbling something that didn't make sense and still rubbing his eyes. Millie took hold of his hands to stop the rubbing and looked down into his eyes. They were glassy and unfocused.

Millie had started her nursing career just after the Civil War began in the spring of 1861. She had become quite used to the muttering of wounded soldiers who were awakening from under the influence of anesthetics. They seldom made any sense.

After a few minutes, the patient went quiet again and slipped back into his deep sleep.

An hour later, she went to the lieutenant's bed and found him awake, but still a bit disoriented. She had to tell him once again where he was and assure him that he would walk again. His pain was severe, so after feeding him what broth she could get down him, she administered a strong dose of laudanum.

Millie rested the lieutenant's head back on the pillow, placed the cup on the table, and tucked the covers up under his chin.

He looked at her with dull eyes, then tried to adjust his position in the bed. Sudden pain shot through his back. He grimaced and said something once more that didn't make sense.

She smiled and spoke softly. "No more talking now, Lieutenant. Lie still and let the laudanum do its job. The laudanum will help you to rest. By the time you wake up in the morning, I'll be here for another shift."

His eyes drifted closed before the last words left the lovely nurse's mouth.

When Millie's twelve-hour shift was about over, she made it a point to stop at Lieutenant Nathan Conrad's bed once more. He was sleeping soundly.

That evening in Harrisburg, Pennsylvania, Jenny Linden entered the parlor, made her way to the rocking chair, and kissed her mother's cheek. She placed the day's edition of the *Harrisburg Journal* in her hands. "You can read while I go start supper, Mama."

Myrna looked up at her daughter with fearful eyes. "Is there anything in the paper about more battles?"

"Not this time. There's one small article on the first page about a couple of skirmishes, but none that involved Papa's unit or Nate's."

Myrna sighed. "That's good news."

Jenny let a frown crease her brow. "I have to tell you something, Mama."

"What?"

"We had a man try to rob the store today."

"Oh? *Try*, you say. But he was unsuccessful."

"He was unsuccessful."

"No one was hurt, I hope."

"No."

"Tell me about it."

Jenny gave her mother a detailed account of the attempted robbery, including how she had knocked the robber out with the ax handle. She finished by saying, "Mama, the policemen who came to the store and took the robber to jail told me that Chief Wymore will be coming to the house to talk to me sometime this evening."

"Do you know why?"

"Not really. I guess he just wants to hear the story directly from me. You go ahead and read your paper. I'll let you know when you can come and set the table."

Supper was over, the kitchen was cleaned up, the dishes were done, and mother and daughter were busy with their reading in the parlor when there was a knock at the door.

Jenny closed her novel, laid it on the table beside the sofa, and rose to her feet. "That will be Chief Leonard Wymore."

She dashed into the hall and hurried to the door. When she opened it, she saw a middle-aged man with a well-trimmed mustache that matched his salt-and-pepper hair. The badge on his chest reflected the light from the lantern that burned in the vestibule. He removed his hat. "Miss Jenny Linden?"

"Yes, Chief Wymore. I've been expecting you. Please come in."

The chief stepped inside. Jenny closed the door, took his hat, hung it on a peg by the closet, and led him into the parlor. She introduced him to her mother, explained that her father was a Union captain in the War, then they sat down on the sofa.

Wymore smiled at Jenny. "Miss Linden, I want to tell you that I very much appreciate the courageous thing you did to foil the robbery. The Hendersons appreciate it too, I assure you."

Jenny smiled in return. "They have already expressed it, sir. This robber...was he already wanted by the law?"

"I'll say he was. His name is Rufus Hickam. He was in Sing Sing Prison in Ossining, New York, for armed robbery. He broke out four weeks ago and has been on the run. When he gets out of the hospital, he will be returned to the prison with an addition to his original fifteen-year sentence."

Jenny's eyebrows arched. "Hospital?"

"Didn't the officers tell you they were taking him to the hospital?"

"No. He was still unconscious when they carried him out of the store to the police wagon. His head was bleeding some, but one of the officers had tied the robber's handkerchief around his head. I figured they were taking him to the jail."

"Well, Hickam is in the hospital, handcuffed to his bed with an officer sitting just outside his room. I stopped by the hospital on my way over here to look in on him. The doctor who stitched up the gash in Hickam's head said he had been struck in the head three times. Did you have a hard time rendering him unconscious?"

Jenny shook her head. "No. I knocked him out with the first blow. He had stuffed the money in his pockets. I had to empty them out. By the time Emma and I were putting the money in the metal cash box that goes in the safe, that no-good was coming to. So I hit him a second time and knocked him out again."

"So why did you hit him the third time?"

Jenny's features tinted. Her eyes were like pinpoints as she said levelly, "Did Emma tell you what that low-down skunk did to her?"

"You mean the slap in the face?"

"Yes." Her features darkened and her eyes flashed. "I was so mad at that dirty beast for slapping Emma, I cracked him over the head one more time, just for good measure!"

"Oh, I see."

"Chief Wymore," spoke up Myrna, "my Jenny has a bit of a flinty temper."

Wymore nodded. A grin curved his lips. "Well, Mrs. Linden, sometimes a little bit of temper can be a good thing." He turned to Jenny. "I commend you, Miss Linden, for having the courage to take on Rufus Hickam and thwart the robbery, but—"

"But what, Chief?" Jenny's eyes still had a fiery quality. "That criminal had no business striking Emma. He had that third blow coming."

"I know you had to have been strung out emotionally, Miss Linden, but you could have cracked Hickam's skull with that third blow and killed him. If you had, you'd be facing manslaughter charges. I'm glad Hickam is still alive, and that the doctors say he will live. I really would've hated to arrest you if he had died. You need to keep a check on that temper. It could get you in real trouble."

Jenny's lips were pulled into a thin line. "I'm glad I didn't kill him, Chief, but on the other hand, he shouldn't have robbed Emma, nor should he have slapped her. In my anger, I was only getting even for what he did to her."

Wymore shrugged, rose to his feet, and stood over Myrna. "It was nice to have met you, Mrs. Linden. And I hope this war is over soon so your husband can come home."

Myrna's eyes filled with tears. "Thank you, Chief Wymore. It was nice to have met you, too."

Jenny walked the chief to the door, and as he stepped out onto the porch, he turned and smiled. "I'll say this for you, little lady: if I was in trouble, I sure wouldn't mind having you there to help me. Hickam won't be able to hide the fact that he was foiled by a woman. It's going to be in the newspapers. They'll know about it at the prison before he gets back there. He's going to have a tough time living it down."

Jenny shrugged. "Ask me if I care."

The chief rubbed the back of his neck. "Good-bye, Miss Linden."

"Good-bye, Chief Wymore. Thanks for coming by."

When Jenny entered the parlor and sat down on the sofa once more, Myrna said, "The chief is right, honey. You need to keep a check on that temper. You really shouldn't have hit that robber in the head when he was already down and out."

Jenny squared her jaw. "If he didn't want his skull cracked, he should have stayed out of Henderson's store."


On Sunday morning at Memorial Hospital in Frederick, Maryland, Millie Ross spent a few minutes with Dr. Gary Medford—who had done Lieutenant Nathan Conrad's surgery—then moved into the ward to begin her day's work and headed straight for Conrad's bed. As she drew up, she saw that he was awake.

He looked up at her, his eyes much clearer than they had been the day before. He managed a tiny smile. "Hello."

"Hello yourself, Lieutenant. You're looking a little better."

"I feel a little better, ma'am."

"Do you remember me?"

"Oh yes. You're my main nurse on the day shift. You were so kind to me, and I really appreciate it."

"Is your back hurting?"

"I have some pain, but it's much better than yesterday. One of the night nurses gave me some more laudanum three or four hours ago."

"You were so groggy from the morphine yesterday. I wasn't sure if you would remember any part of it."

Nate frowned. "I probably can't remember a whole lot of it, but I do remember you and your kind bedside manner. However, there is one important thing I can't seem to recall."

"And that is?"

"Your name."

Millie smiled. "I can tell you why you can't recall it."

"Yes?"

"I never told you it."

"Oh. Well, a man should know his nurse's name."

"It's Mildred Ross, Lieutenant."

At that instant, Loretta appeared. "Well, Millie, I see our patient is awake and clear-eyed."

"Yes," said Millie, glancing at her then back at Nate. "Lieutenant Conrad surprises me. He remembers more from yesterday than I figured he would. And he's feeling a little better."

Loretta looked at the patient. "That's good, Lieutenant. I'm glad there is improvement. Are you hungry?"

Nate nodded slowly. "I am."

Loretta turned to Millie. "I'll go get him some porridge and some coffee."

"All right. In the meantime, I'll check his bandages."

Loretta hurried away.

Millie picked up his chart from where it hung at the end of the bed and glanced at it. "I see it was at 4:15 that you were given the laudanum. As soon as you've had your breakfast, Lieutenant, I'll give you another dose. I'll also check your temperature and your pulse at that time. Now, can you roll on your side so I can look at the bandages?"

"I think so."

Millie helped him roll onto his side, found the bandages intact and that there was no excessive bleeding. She helped him roll onto his back once again and tucked the sheet and covers around him. "Everything is looking good."

*Not as good-looking as you*, he thought, then said aloud, "I'm glad for that. I remember how relieved I was when you told me yesterday that my spine wasn't seriously damaged and that I would walk again."

Millie smiled. "You amaze me, Lieutenant. I'm surprised that you recall so much. You really had a big dose of morphine for your surgery. Sometimes it totally fogs the mind for several hours."

"Maybe it was because I had such a nice nurse."

Millie's face tinted. "You are so kind."

There was a brief silence, then Nate said, "Miss Ross, is Frederick your home?"

"Yes. My parents are both deceased. I live in an apartment with two other nurses about my age."

"So we're both orphans. My parents are dead too."

"I see. Lieutenant, I know from your chart that you are in the Seventh Pennsylvania Artillery Division. So I assume your home is in Pennsylvania."

"Yes, ma'am."

"Where in Pennsylvania?"

"Harrisburg."

"That's in eastern Pennsylvania, isn't it?"

"Yes. Little over a hundred miles due west of Philadelphia."

She nodded, then reached to the end of the bed and picked up the chart. Looking at it, she said, "Lieutenant, I noted when I read this yesterday that Dr. Medford, who did your surgery, wrote here that you had both external and internal damage by the shrapnel, even though your spine was not damaged severely."

"That doesn't surprise me."

"Well, with this in mind, I talked to Dr. Medford when I first arrived for work this morning and discussed it with him. He says that you will probably be five or six months in recuperation here at the hospital. It will depend on how well you heal whether you can return to active duty or not. As I'm sure you know, the army will muster you out if Dr. Medford deems you questionable for further combat."

Nate let a slight grin capture his mouth. "Miss Ross, if you can be my main nurse for the recuperating time, I won't mind at all if it takes even six or seven months to get healed up."

Millie smiled.

"Ah…"

"Yes, Lieutenant?"

"It *is* Miss Ross, isn't it?"

She smiled again as she saw Loretta coming with a breakfast tray in her hands. "Yes, it is. Time for breakfast."

In the days that followed, Millie Ross gave the wounded lieutenant the best of care and all the attention he wanted. In the process, they became better acquainted.

One day, after Millie had changed the bandage on Nate's back—with Loretta's help—Millie tucked the covers around him and said, "Lieutenant, your wound is healing well."

Loretta was walking away, and Nate patted Millie's hand affectionately. "Thank you, Miss Ross, for the excellent care you are giving me. If I had parents to write home to, I'd sure brag about you."

"You are so kind." She warmed him with a smile. "Lieutenant Conrad, I would like for you to drop the 'Miss Ross,' and just call me Millie."

The smile had its effect on Nate, as well as the request to call her by her nickname. He gave her a lopsided grin. "All right, Millie. It's a deal. That is, if you will drop the 'Lieutenant Conrad' and just call me Nate."

Millie giggled. "All right, Nate, it's a deal!"

He studied her eyes for a moment. "Millie?"

"Mm-hmm?"

"Ah…ah…are you engaged or involved seriously with anyone?"

She locked her gaze with his. "I have a few men I date periodically, but no engagement, and nothing serious."

The smile that spread over his face was more than she had seen up to that point. "I'm glad to hear that."

Millie giggled again. "Well, that must mean that *you* aren't engaged or serious about someone."

"Right. Like you with the men, I have some lady friends up in Harrisburg I've dated periodically, but there's nobody special."

Millie tried to hide the relief she felt, but Nate picked up on it. Secretly, he felt a glow inside. He knew he was falling in love with Millie Ross, and there was reason to believe she was falling in love with him.

6

IN HARRISBURG, PENNSYLVANIA, on Friday morning, October 14, Jenny Linden was alone at the counter at Henderson's General Store.

The lowering gray sky that Jenny had awakened to that morning was finally beginning to drop its heavy burden of icy rain. Through the large windows, she could see it pelting the dusty street and stripping the few remaining leaves from the skeletal trees in view. People were moving along the sidewalks, bending their heads against the wind-driven ice crystals.

Jenny had a fire going in the store's potbellied stove and a pot of coffee brewing, which she would indulge in later.

A few customers had come and gone, and at the moment, there was one woman at the counter, whom Jenny was waiting on. Jenny saw Wiley Owens come in, carrying the day's edition of the *Harrisburg Journal.* He brushed the icy rain from his face. "Hello, Jenny."

Looking past her customer, Jenny smiled at Wiley and greeted him as he moved up to the empty stand at the end of the counter. He began removing the papers from a canvas bag which protected them from the rain.

Jenny's customer picked up her paper sack, thanked her, and turned to leave.

"Thank you, Mrs. Burton," said Jenny. "Come again."

"Oh, I will," she said, and hurried out the door.

Jenny turned to Wiley, who was stacking the papers on the stand. "I think this rain is going to turn to snow before long."

He gave her a quick smile. "Probably will."

"Wiley, is there more in today's paper about the War?"

"'Fraid so. The front page is full of news about a bloody battle that took place near Rome, Georgia, two days ago."

Jenny was about to ask Wiley if he knew what military units fought in the battle, but two customers came through the door, greeting her, and Wiley hurried out, giving her a wave.

Three more customers came in a moment later. While Jenny was waiting for the five customers to pick up their items and bring them to the counter, she glanced at the newspapers on the stand. She was eager to read about the battle, but told herself she would have to wait for a lull in business before she would be able to get to it.

More customers came in, brushing the ice crystals from their coats and hats while Jenny was taking care of the others. Soon there was a line of nearly a dozen people in front of the counter. Jenny was hastily tabulating bills and stuffing paper sacks in an effort to keep any of them from having to wait too long.

When a couple stepped away, her next customer was Max Akers, a bookkeeper at one of the local department stores. As he laid his items on the counter, Max smiled. "Nice to see you, Jenny. As you know, my wife usually does the grocery shopping, but she's down with a cold, so here I am."

"I'm sorry to hear that Susan is ill, Max. I hope she'll get over the cold soon."

"I'm sure she will. Jenny, I haven't seen you since the robbery took place here. I want to commend you for what you did to help the police catch that escaped convict." He leaned closer and grinned. "I'm glad you gave that Rufus Hickam an extra whack on the head, even when he was already out cold."

Jenny smiled as she finished tabulating the small bill. "How do you know about that? The newspaper account didn't report the extra whack."

Max chuckled. "Oh, word gets around." He leaned even closer. "Maybe you should have saved the taxpayers some money and given him another good whack. I mean…a *really* good one."

Jenny put the items in a paper sack and took Max's money. As he thanked her and walked away, his words about a third whack went through her mind. *See there, Chief Wymore, not everybody agrees with your soft-touch philosophy.*

More customers came and went. Some bought the newspapers, along with other items they had come in to purchase. Finally, about eleven o'clock, the wintry rain was coming down hard, driven by stronger winds, causing the people of Harrisburg to seek sanctuary in their homes, and business in the general store trickled to a halt.

Giving a huge sigh of relief, Jenny straightened the pencils and work pads on the counter, then went to the big potbellied stove in the center of the store and tossed more logs on the fire. Using a poker, she stirred the flames. The fire flared up quickly, putting off a rosy glow and instantly warming up the area around it. The coffeepot was steaming.

Jenny poured herself a mug of the brew and carried it to the counter. She then went to the newspaper stand, picked up a paper, and returned to her spot behind the counter. The wind outside was now howling fiercely. She glanced out the windows while spreading the paper out before her, and saw that the icy rain was still pelting them hard. She could barely see anything on the street.

A shiver ran through her body. She turned, lifted her shawl from a hook on the wall, and draped it over her shoulders. She took a sip of the coffee, set the cup down, and put her attention on the front page of the paper.

She saw that on Wednesday, October 12, there was a battle on Coosaville Road, just outside the city of Rome, Georgia. The Union troops involved in the battle were under the command of General William T. Sherman, and the Confederate troops were under the command of General John Bell Hood.

Jenny noted the statistics. Reportedly, 114 Union soldiers were killed, 229 wounded, and 176 were missing or captured. On the Confederate side, 87 were killed, 137 wounded, and 43 were missing or captured.

As her eyes moved down the page, they suddenly bulged and her heart leaped in her chest when she read that the Third Pennsylvania

Cavalry Division had been involved in the battle. "Oh, Papa!" she said. "You've got to be all right! You just have to!"

At that moment, the door opened, and Zack and Emma Henderson came in, followed by two male customers, who were in conversation with Zack.

So entangled in her own thoughts and concern over what she had just read, Jenny was completely unaware of the people coming in until a draft from the open door ruffled the pages of the newspaper. When she lifted up her fear-filled eyes, Emma was first to notice. She removed her coat, shook the ice crystals from it, and hurried around behind the counter to the girl. Hanging the coat on a wall hook, she said, "Jenny, what's wrong?"

Zack's conversation with the two male customers suddenly cut off as he heard Emma's words and noted Jenny's puckered brow and sheet-white face. "Excuse me, gentlemen."

Jenny pointed a trembling finger at the front page of the newspaper. "Papa's Cavalry Division was in a battle near Rome, Georgia, on Wednesday. Lots of Union soldiers were killed."

Emma folded Jenny in her arms. "Now, honey, your papa is probably all right. Remember, you must do your best to keep an optimistic frame of mind about him, and cling to the hope that one day he will come home alive and well."

Jenny took a deep breath and steadied herself. "You're right, Emma."

Zack reached over the counter and patted Jenny's shoulder. "You're a brave girl, honey. Everything is going to turn out all right. You just keep believing it."

Jenny took another deep breath. "I'm doing my best, Zack. And you two are so encouraging. Thank you."

That evening, when Jenny left the store with the day's edition of the *Harrisburg Journal* in her hand, the wind had died down and a light snow was falling. She dreaded having to tell her mother about the bloody Coosaville Road battle and that her father was involved in it.

Jenny wished she could keep it from her mother, but she knew if she didn't bring the newspaper home, Myrna Linden would know something was wrong. Jenny would be forced to tell her the truth anyhow. In her mother's weakened condition, the news that the Third Pennsylvania Cavalry Division was involved in the fierce battle could be devastating. Her mother would think the worst and it would play havoc with her emotional problems. She was already in a low state of mind with the War still going on; not knowing when or if she might ever see her husband again could be the last straw.

As Jenny neared the Linden house, she could make out a horse and buggy parked in front. When she was turning into the yard, Dr. Adam Griffin was coming out the door. Light from the lanterns in the parlor put a glow on the porch. She hurried up on the porch as he was about to descend the steps. "Dr. Griffin, is something wrong with Mama?"

"Oh no," he said, giving her a smile. "You remember, I told her I was going to do some study on manic depression to see if there is anything new in medical science to help give her some appetite."

"Yes."

"Well, I did, and since it was time for a house call anyway, I wanted to let her know what I had found out."

"And?"

"There are two French doctors in Paris who at present are testing barbituric acid. Do you know what that is?"

"No, sir."

"Well, it's a new discovery. It has a tranquilizing effect on a person's mind and nervous system. And these doctors say they believe it will increase the appetite for people like your mother. As I said, they are in the testing stage now, but it offers hope for your mother, and I wanted to tell her about it. More time is needed, but at least it is encouraging to know the doctors are optimistic."

Jenny smiled. "That's for sure. Thank you for this good news, Doctor."

Griffin turned to leave. "I'll keep you and your mother posted as I hear more, Jenny."

"Thanks, again."

As the doctor moved off the porch and headed for his buggy, Jenny turned to see her mother looking at her from the rocking chair by the parlor window. Jenny thought of the news she was about to spring on her, and a grave look settled on her face.

Myrna had a fire going in the parlor stove, and the lamps in the room gave off a mellow glow, dispelling the gloom of nightfall. When her daughter came in, Myrna saw Jenny's troubled expression. "Honey, did Dr. Griffin tell you something he didn't tell me?"

Jenny moved toward the rocking chair. "No, Mama. It was the same good news about the work of the French doctors that he told you. I'm really encouraged about it."

"Well, honey, you don't look encouraged."

Jenny bent over and kissed her mother's forehead. "This is something else, Mama."

Myrna's eyes went to the newspaper in Jenny's hand. "Something in the paper?"

Jenny sighed and put the paper in her hand. "Yes. I wish you didn't have to know, but it's there on the front page."

Myrna opened the paper and began to read. Jenny laid a hand on her shoulder.

It took a minute for Myrna to come to the place in the article where the army units involved in the battle on both sides were listed. Her eyes widened when they focused on William's division. "Oh no!" she cried, and broke into tears. "Oh no! Jenny, your papa was probably killed!"

Jenny bent down and took hold of both her hands. In a soft tone, and using the same tactics that Emma Henderson had used on her earlier that day, she tried to calm her down and to convince her that she should keep on optimistic outlook on the situation. At first it looked like Jenny's efforts would fail, but with the help of an extra dose of paraldehyde, Myrna eventually calmed down and weakly agreed with her daughter that she must keep a positive outlook on William's situation.

Myrna dabbed at her tears with a hankie while Jenny kept a hand on her shoulder. "Honey, I just couldn't live if something happened to your papa. He…he must come home to me whenever the War is over——which I hope is soon——so we can have our life together."

Jenny sighed. "I want Papa to come home too. And I feel the same way about Nate. I just couldn't live without him. I'm so very much anticipating the day he comes home to me. And when he does, we'll take up where we left off. Shortly thereafter, there will be wedding bells."

Myrna closed her eyes.

Jenny stayed, her hand gripping her mother's shoulder firmly, while talking in low tones about keeping up their optimism. There was a hollow note in Jenny's voice, which told her mother that some of the optimism she spoke of was really not there. She kept her thoughts about it to herself.

When the paraldehyde had calmed Myrna down some, Jenny said, "Mama, I'm going to cook supper now. Does anything sound especially appetizing to you?"

Myrna was ready to tell her daughter that she wasn't at all hungry, but turning to look up at her, she read the deeply troubled look that remained in Jenny's eyes. Not wanting to add to her daughter's anxiety, she pulled a smile from deep in her heart. "I think a poached egg and some toast would taste good on this chilly night, honey. And maybe some peppermint tea."

Her response had the desired effect, and the troubled look on Jenny's face softened into a pleasant smile. "I'll have it ready in just a few minutes, Mama. Do you want to stay here and read more in your paper, or would you like to come into the kitchen and keep me company?"

"I'll just do that, dear," Myrna replied, and arm in arm, the two inwardly grieving women left the parlor, each bent on comforting the other.

On the same day, at Memorial Hospital in Frederick, Maryland, more Union casualties from battles and skirmishes all over Virginia were being brought in. There was room for them now, because some soldiers wounded months earlier had been released and a number of those brought in from the Winchester battle had died.

Dr. Homer Walton, as usual, was supervising the entrance of the new patients into the hospital. When he had seen to it that those in need of surgery had been taken to the surgical section and the others were getting the attention they needed as they were placed in the military ward, he was passing along the long line of beds heading for his office. As he drew near Lieutenant Nathan Conrad's bed, he saw Conrad's surgeon, Dr. Gary Medford.

Dr. Medford was just finishing an examination of the wound, and Nate was rolling over on to his back.

Dr. Walton smiled down at Nate, then looked at the surgeon. "So how's our patient doing, Dr. Medford?"

"The wound is healing slowly, Doctor," replied Medford, helping Nate adjust his covers. "It will be a couple of months before Lieutenant Conrad will be able to leave the bed to periodically sit in a wheelchair. Then of course, it will be a month or so beyond that before he can be on his feet, walking with crutches. If he does as I expect, he'll graduate from the crutches in a short time to a cane, and one day, will be able to lay aside the cane."

Nate managed a smile. "That sounds like a long time, Dr. Medford, but it's a whole lot better than if you had told me I would never walk again."

Suddenly a female voice came from the row of beds. "Dr. Walton! Dr. Medford!"

Nate recognized the voice. It was Millie Ross. He swung his gaze that direction as both doctors walked toward her. Millie was standing at the bed of Corporal Eddie Truitt, who had been under Nate's command in the battle at Winchester. He knew that Eddie had been seriously wounded with a bullet very close to his heart and had suffered many complications since being at the hospital, but Millie had told him that the doctors thought he would make it.

Nate's eyes were riveted on the scene. Both doctors were leaning over Eddie, working furiously as Millie helped them. Soon it became obvious to Nate and everyone else in the ward that Corporal Eddie Truitt was dying. Nate closed his eyes. "Oh no! Not Eddie!"

When he opened his eyes and looked in that direction again, Millie was sadly pulling a sheet up over Eddie's face. Dr. Walton called for a cart, and the body was taken away.

Nate clenched his teeth. Sick at heart for his Union comrades who had already lost their lives as a result of the Winchester battle, but grieving especially over Eddie, Nate began to weep. His head was down as his body shook from the sobs.

Suddenly he felt a tender hand on his shoulder. He looked up through his tears into the face of Millie Ross.

Millie's features were pinched and compassion was in her eyes. "Nate, are you all right?"

"Not really," he said. "Seeing my close friend, Eddie, die really got to me. Eddie was a good soldier, Millie, and this makes the seventh soldier who has died here in the ward from my unit since we were brought here after the Winchester battle. There were nine others who never made it through surgery. It—it's just so hard to lose them."

Millie bent down close to his face, kept her hand on his shoulder, and talked to him in soft tones, trying to comfort him. Her nearness to him and the compassion she was showing served to ease his grief, and after a few minutes, Nate's weeping ceased.

On the verge of tears herself, Millie stroked his cheek. "I wish I could take the pain for you, Nate. I knew you and Eddie were good friends. I've never lost a close friend to death, but I can imagine how it hurts—especially because Eddie was under your command when he was shot. Just remember, I'm right here for you. If—"

"Miss Ross," came the voice of Letha Phillips, the head nurse on the day shift, "I need to talk to you as soon as you are finished taking care of Lieutenant Conrad."

With that, the woman headed toward the nurse's station.

Nate noticed a frown crease Millie's brow as she watched Letha Phillips walk away in a rather stiff-legged manner. "Millie, is something wrong?"

She looked back at Nate. "I think so. I've never had her talk to me in that tone of voice."

"What could you have done to deserve that kind of treatment?"

Millie shrugged. "I don't know, but I'm going to find out. I'll see you later." With that, Millie headed toward the nurse's station.

Letha Phillips was talking to another nurse when Millie drew up. Letha glanced at her with a sharp look in her eye, then finished what she was saying to the other nurse.

As Letha turned to face her, Millie asked, "What did you want to talk to me about, Mrs. Phillips?"

"Let's go in here, so we can talk in private." Letha led her into a small room nearby, opened the door, and gestured for her to enter. Millie stepped in, and Letha closed the door.

There was guarded curiosity in Millie's eyes as she waited for Letha to speak.

Letha put a stern gaze on her. "Millie, I happened to notice the attention you were giving Lieutenant Conrad, and what I saw did not look good."

Millie batted her eyelids in surprise at Letha's tone. "What do you mean?"

Letha drew a deep breath. "Millie, you shouldn't have bent so low over his face. It almost looked like you were going to kiss him. And you shouldn't have been stroking his cheek like that, either. This was just too much familiarity for a nurse to be showing a male patient."

"Oh. I…I'm sorry, Mrs. Phillips. I didn't mean to do something wrong. Nate——Lieutenant Conrad was grieving over Corporal Eddie Truitt, who just died there in the ward. The corporal had been under Lieutenant Conrad's command in the Winchester battle. They had been close friends. I was just trying to comfort him."

Letha grinned crookedly. "Tell me, Millie, doesn't Lieutenant Conrad mean just a bit more to you than your other patients?"

A slight blush colored Millie's features. "Well…ah…you could say that. I liked the lieutenant very much when I first met him, and I like him even more now."

Letha's eyes softened. "I can understand that. You are a single young lady, and he is a single young man. From what I have observed, he likes you very much too. But the two of you must not allow this to show while he is a patient here in the hospital."

Millie nodded. "I understand, Mrs. Phillips. I just got carried away this morning when Nate was so torn up over his friend's death. I'll be more careful from now on."

"Please do. Ah…"

"Yes, ma'am?"

"Have you two declared special feelings for each other?"

"No. Not really. But I will tell you that I do have special feelings for him, and I know he has them for me. And when we do actually declare these feelings to each other, I'll make sure that we keep it to ourselves so I don't appear unethical in my profession as a nurse."

Finally, there was a hint of a smile on Letha's lips. "Thank you, dear. This is what I was concerned about. You may go back to him now."

When Millie returned to Nate, she explained to him what the head nurse talked to her about. "Nate, I owe you an apology."

"For what?"

"Well, for…for appearing so familiar by my actions."

Nate looked up into her eyes. "May I ask you something?"

"Of course."

He cleared his throat nervously. "Well…*do* you feel something special toward me?"

A smile graced her lips. "Yes. I feel something very special toward you."

Nate started to take hold of her hand, but stopped short. "Millie, I feel something very special toward you too. You don't need to apologize to me for your actions this morning when you were trying to comfort me. I loved them. You are such a sweet, kind, and compassionate person. I wanted so much to respond by kissing the hand that was caressing my cheek. But I see Mrs. Phillips's point. We'll need to be careful not to show our affection while I am a patient here in the hospital."

Millie nodded.

Nate grinned up at her. "We can talk a little later about how it will be after I'm dismissed from the hospital."

Millie smiled. "We will just do that. A little later."

7

ON THAT SAME FRIDAY, OCTOBER 14, Confederate Captain Henry Wirz—commandant of the Andersonville Prison Camp some forty-five miles southwest of Macon, Georgia—gathered the major portion of his guards in front of his small log cabin near the camp's only gate. They stood in four rows.

"Men," said the captain, running his eyes over their faces, "I just received a wire from General John Bell Hood in Rome, Georgia. He informed me of a battle that took place two days ago just outside that city. General Hood's wire went on to say that he and his regiment took ninety-one Union soldiers as prisoners during the battle. Those ninety-one prisoners are being brought by train to Macon, then they will be transported from Macon to us by wagons. They will arrive here at the camp sometime tomorrow afternoon."

Some of the guards' faces twisted as they looked at each other; there was a buzzing of voices.

Wirz had lost the use of his left arm in the Battle of Seven Pines in 1862. While it hung like a dead limb from his shoulder, he raised his right arm and waved his hand. "Men, listen to me! I don't like having to crowd this prison even worse, but there is no choice in the matter. We'll have to make room for the ninety-one new prisoners."

Sergeant Dan Tyler, who was known by all to be the epitome of optimism, raised his hand from his position in the first row. "Captain, may I say something?"

Wirz nodded. "Yes, Sergeant."

Tyler let a smile spread from ear to ear. "Look at it this way, sir…that's ninety-one fewer Yankees that our troops out there on the battlefields will have to fight."

The other men laughed, and Wirz joined them.

When the laughter subsided, Wirz set appreciative eyes on Tyler. "Sergeant, I wish I could learn to look on the lighter side of things like you do."

Dan Tyler, who had black hair and dark-brown eyes, smiled again. "Captain, I used to look on the dark side of things all the time, and then the change came into my life."

Wirz knew what was coming next, but saw no way to stop it. He waited for Tyler to proceed.

"That change came as I have told you, sir, when I heard the gospel and invited the Lord Jesus Christ into my heart as my Saviour. He dispelled my darkness and filled my heart, soul, and mind with His marvelous light. Sure, life has its hard times, especially for those of us who are fighting this war, but with Jesus in my heart, everything is brighter."

Some of the other guards were speaking their agreement with the sergeant when Captain Wirz said, "Gentlemen, I must get back into my office."

Lieutenant Harry Fisher, who headed up the prison camp guards, said, "Captain, any special orders about where we should place these new prisoners when they get here?"

"Just put them wherever you can. Let those prisoners who have comrades from the same units stay together. As we have already seen, it makes for a more pleasant camp with pals sharing the same areas. We don't coddle anybody, but it helps the atmosphere around here if the prisoners have a measure of contentment."

"Yes, sir."

Wirz turned and entered his cabin.

Tyler turned and gave a wide grin to those guards who had spoken their agreement with his testimony. Among them were his closest friends, Corporals Clay Holden and Joel Stevens.

Lieutenant Fisher looked around at the men. "We'd better get busy and decide where we're going to put the new prisoners, men. I have a little assignment for Sergeant Tyler. As soon as I explain it to him, I'll take the rest of you with me and we'll make preparations."

The men began talking in small groups. Tyler stepped up to Fisher, waiting for his assignment. "Just a minute, Sergeant." Fisher motioned to the latest guard to join the camp, who had arrived late the night before on an army wagon from Macon.

The new guard smiled and made a quick move to the lieutenant. "Yes, sir?"

"Have you met Sergeant Tyler yet?"

"No, sir, but I'll tell you this—I like him already."

"Well, good." Fisher grinned. "I'm going to have him give you a little tour of the camp, so you'll know about the place. He will fill you in on some important things and answer any questions you might have." He introduced the man to Tyler. "Sergeant, this is Corporal Willie Botham."

Tyler offered his hand, and Botham gripped it in a friendly shake. "What is your first name, Sergeant?"

"Dan."

"Short for Daniel? Like in the Bible?"

"That's it."

"I want both of you men to report back to me when the tour is over," said Fisher.

Tyler nodded. "Will do, sir. Let's go, Corporal."

As Fisher left to approach the men who were waiting, Tyler ran his hand in a wide circle. "As you can see, Corporal, the entire camp is surrounded by that twelve-foot-high stockade fence."

"Yes," said Botham, noting the guard towers that stood just outside the stockade on all four sides, positioned some two hundred feet apart. Three guards stood in each tower, rifles in their hands.

"And this gate over here is the camp's only entrance. There are no other gates."

Botham nodded.

"Well, let's take a walk so I can show you the whole place."

As the corporal moved up beside him, Tyler headed parallel with the stockade fence at a distance of about forty feet. "The camp covers a total of twenty-seven acres inside the fence, Corporal. We also lay claim to the prison graveyard outside the stockade on the north."

"Well, I'm glad it's on the outside."

Tyler grinned. "Where are you from?"

"Knoxville, Tennessee, Sergeant. Actually from a farm some ten miles east of Knoxville. That's where I was born."

Tyler's eyes brightened. "I'm from Tennessee, too."

"Oh, really? What part?"

"I was born and raised on a cattle ranch some thirteen miles west of Chattanooga."

Botham's face beamed as he extended his hand. "Well, put 'er there, Sergeant! It's always good to meet another person from Tennessee."

Tyler shook his hand for the second time. "That's for sure! The greenest and most beautiful state in the Confederacy, and twice as beautiful as any other state in the country, or any of the territories."

"I agree 100 percent. And I have to brag that Davy Crockett was born just a few miles from where I was, near Greenville. What a hero! As I'm sure you know, he died bravely helping to defend the Alamo in San Antonio, Texas."

"Of course."

"My dad met him once."

"Oh, really?"

"Mm-hmm. In 1833, when Davy was elected the second time as a U.S. representative of Tennessee. He used to talk about it a lot. Of course, I wasn't born till 1843, seven years after Davy was killed at the Alamo. He was really one of dad's heroes."

"Well, he's a hero to all of us Tennesseans."

"I want to tell you why I told Lieutenant Fisher that I liked you already, even though we hadn't met."

"How come?"

"It was your testimony. I love Jesus too. I took Him into my heart as my Saviour when I was twelve years old."

"Wonderful!" Tyler extended his hand. "Put 'er there, Corporal!" And they shook hands for the third time.

As they continued to walk slowly, Botham said, "Since you were raised on a cattle ranch, you had to have had horses."

"Oh yeah. Did we ever."

"I love horses. On our farm, ours were draft horses, but I sure loved to work with them."

"For sure. In fact, it was because of my love for horses that I was in a cavalry unit up till six months ago. At that time, I was assigned here at the prison camp because there was a shortage of guards."

"Oh. That must have been hard for you."

"It was. Have you met Corporal Clay Holden and Corporal Joel Stevens?"

"No."

"Well, you will. Great guys and good Christians too. We were in the same cavalry unit together. They were given their assignment to Andersonville at the same time I was and came here with me."

"I see."

Tyler and Botham were ascending a slight rise. The sergeant stopped, and pointing around the compound, said, "You can see the entire camp from here."

Botham ran a panorama of the full twenty-seven acres. The Union prisoners milled about, looking sad and dejected. Letting his line of sight flit from one group to another, he said, "Sergeant, my heart goes out to them. These men we call our enemies have the same hopes and dreams that we do. They just picture them becoming a reality in a different part of this country."

Tyler sighed. "Yes. They have families and friends up north, even as we have here in the South. This war was none of their doing, just like it was none of our doing. Like us, they are human and part of God's creation. I'm sure many of them are Christians, and it grieves me that we brothers in Christ have to fight each other on the battlefields and be at odds even here in this prison."

Botham nodded, a mournful look clouding his face. "Our Christian brothers out there in those dusty blue uniforms may have ideals a little different than ours because they are Northerners and we are Southerners, but basically, we're cut from the same cloth."

"Yes. That's true. I'm just praying that this senseless war will soon be over. Blue or gray, we need to get this thing over with so all of us can be free to spin our own daydreams and plan a better future."

Botham turned his sad eyes on Tyler. "I know there have been wars and rumors of wars since man's early days on this earth, but I don't pretend to understand it."

"Well, it started when Cain declared war on his brother, Abel, and murdered him. 1 John 3:12 tells us that Cain was of that wicked one—the devil. So we know that behind all the wars that mankind has waged is Satan. Jesus said he was a murderer from the beginning."

Botham nodded. "That has to be it, Sergeant. I hadn't thought of it in that light before."

"We know that God is in control, Willie. He has a plan, and in that plan, He allows war, just like He allowed Cain to murder Abel. He has a purpose for everything He does and allows, and we must trust in the Lord with all our hearts, and lean not unto our own understanding. One thing for sure: we know that all things work together for good to them who love God. On this earth we may never know the reason that God allowed this Civil War, but while we're here, we know that all things are working together for the good of God's children. Right now, I can't see beyond this disease-infested prison camp, but the Lord is already in my future, just waiting for me to get there."

Willie grinned. "You're a real encouragement, Sergeant. The only thing for you and me is to walk with the Lord, serve Him with everything that is in us, and leave our lives in His powerful hands."

Dan Tyler laid his hand on Willie's shoulder. "That's it, brother."

Willie once again ran his eyes over the scene before them. "I know this place has the reputation for being the worst prison camp in the South, but there isn't a prison camp—Union or Confederate—that is fit for human beings."

"True," said Tyler.

"From what I know, Sergeant, this one is so bad because it is so overcrowded, and we're extremely short on food, clothing, blankets, shelter, and medical supplies."

"That's part of it. Another is that the overcrowding has produced much pollution. That little stream down there that bisects the compound is the prison's chief source of water. It also serves as the garbage dump for the cookhouse, and it is a breeding spot for mosquitoes, flies, lice, and fleas."

Willie shook his head. "At least I had a nice clean tent to sleep in last night. But look out there. Those shelters the prisoners have are just rude, tattered canvas tents."

Tyler swung a finger to a spot a little to their left. "Not even that much over there. Those shelters are made of worn-out blankets and ragged old clothing stretched on sticks." He swung his finger a little further. "Look over there. They have no tents or shabby cloth shelters at all. They have simply dug holes in the ground and covered them with threadbare blankets."

Willie shook his head again. "What's it going to be like when winter comes? I know it gets quite cold in this part of Georgia in December, January, and February, and even snows at times. I would think many of the prisoners would die of exposure to the weather with so little shelter."

"No doubt," Tyler said sadly. "As you probably know, this camp was opened last February. Some of the prisoners did die during those first few weeks because of exposure to the cold weather."

"I was told that there have been many deaths even since then because of disease."

"Mm-hmm. Most of the prisoners who were brought here were already weakened from months or years of confinement in other Confederate prison camps. Some thirteen thousand men died here from February through September. That was over fifty a day. And now it's only getting worse. Just a week ago, on one day, we had a hundred and twenty-seven men die from disease or malnutrition—or both. That's one death every eleven minutes. I'll show you the graveyard in a few minutes."

Willie wiped a palm over his face. "How many prisoners do we have here right now?"

"Over thirty-three thousand. When the camp first opened, it had seven thousand five hundred inmates. By May there were fifteen thousand, and by July, there were twenty-nine thousand. And now, in spite of all that have died, as I said, there are over thirty-three thousand crammed into these twenty-seven acres." He chuckled dryly. "And now, we have to make room for ninety-one more."

"Whew! If this war goes on much longer, the Confederacy will have to come up with another prison camp."

"For sure. But maybe the Lord will see to it that this war doesn't last much longer. Well, let's move on."

As they descended the low rise, Tyler pointed toward the stockade fence that surrounded the compound. Have you noticed our escape deterrent?"

Willie nodded. "You mean the guard towers?"

"Well, they're there to enforce the deterrent if any prisoners decide to try to escape. See that single rail on posts?"

Willie ran is gaze along the inside of the stockade, noting the single rail no more than four feet high, on posts. "Yes."

"As you can see, the wooden rail is some fifteen feet from the stockade fence. That ominous cordon is called the 'dead line.' Of course, that frail structure is no physical barrier, but the prisoners have all been forewarned of the consequences of venturing beyond it. They know that Captain Wirz has instructed the guards in the towers to shoot any man who dares move past the dead line."

"I see. Have any prisoners tried to escape?"

"They have. Since February, more than fifty prisoners have been shot and killed who moved past the dead line in an attempt to scale the stockade wall and escape."

Suddenly the air was filled with loud shouts. Tyler and Botham turned to see Lieutenant Harry Fisher and a half dozen other guards forcing ill-tempered prisoners to move their crude shelters to one side or the other in order to make room for the new prisoners who would be coming in.

Abruptly, one of the prisoners jumped a guard in an attempt to grasp his revolver. The guard wrestled with him, and at the same time, another guard cracked the prisoner on the head with the barrel of his gun, dropping him on the ground unconscious. Other prisoners stood by, poised, as if they were going to make a move while looking on with hate-filled eyes.

Fisher's gun was already drawn. He swung the muzzle on them and snapped back the hammer. "Forget it! The first man that makes a false move will be shot. Now settle down and get those shelters moved like I told you!"

A wild-eyed prisoner leaped at Fisher, screaming at him. Fisher's revolver roared, and the man went down.

Dan Tyler shook his head. "Some of them never learn."

While the other prisoners looked on, their faces stony, two guards picked up the dead man and carried him toward the gate. Two others picked up the unconscious man and carried him toward his crude shelter.

"I hope you can see that we mean business," Fisher said. "If you rebel, you will taste of the same. Now let's get those shelters moved like I said."

Dan turned to Willie. "Well, let's go out to the graveyard."

They walked together to the camp's gate and moved past three guards while a fourth opened the gate for them. They passed through the gate, and Dan led Willie north through a small patch of cottonwood trees. They soon came to a short slope, and just ahead of them was a large plot of ground with several shallow mass graves. Willie noted that four bodies were being placed in the grave by guards, along with the man who had just been shot by Lieutenant Fisher.

They drew up several yards short of the new mass grave, which was simply a ditch hollowed out by guards with shovels. It was approximately ninety feet in length and most of it was covered with dirt, where bodies had already been placed recently.

Willie looked around at the other graves and sighed. "Yes, Sergeant, I sure hope this war will end soon."

Dan Tyler's face was grim. "Can't come too soon as far as I'm concerned. Well, let's head back. The tour ends here."

As they headed back toward the enclosed camp, Willie said, "If the War ended today, I'd be one happy man, Sergeant. I have a beautiful Christian girl waiting for me back in Knoxville. I'd love to go home and make her my blushing bride."

Dan looked at him and grinned. "What's her name?"

"Betty Sue Wilkins. And is she gorgeous! She's blond and has big blue eyes. And of course, I'd like to go home to be with my parents and my three brothers and two sisters, too."

"I hope it happens real soon, Willie. And I hope it works out well for you and Betty Sue."

"How about you, Sergeant?" asked Willie. "Do you have a girl waiting for you back home?"

Dan shook his head. "No one special. The Lord just hasn't brought that special girl into my life yet. My parents are both dead, and I don't have any brothers and sisters. So there's not much to go home to."

"Oh. I'm sorry. But you must have friends back home who would love to see you."

"Oh yes, but I have different plans. My pals Clay Holden and Joel Stevens and I have talked seriously about the three of us going out west somewhere when the War is over. We'd like to begin life anew on the frontier—possibly on a cattle ranch."

"Hey, that sounds great, Sergeant! I've heard a lot about the west. Wide open spaces. Mountains whose peaks are so high, no trees will grow up there. Deer aplenty, along with moose, elk, and antelope. I'd like to at least see it someday, myself."

Dan chuckled. "Well, maybe someday after you've married Betty Sue, the two of you could make a trip to whatever part of the west my pals and I settle in and come see me. I'd love to meet that gorgeous blonde!"

"Tell you what, Sergeant, that sounds good to me. Maybe we can just do that. And…ah…by that time, you will have found that girl the Lord has picked out for you, married her, and settled down on some big cattle ranch out there."

Dan sighed. "Yeah. That sounds wonderful. And I have to tell you, Corporal Willie Botham, the girl of my dreams is also blond and has big blue eyes."

"Well, you can't have Betty Sue! She's mine."

Dan laughed. "Oh, I wouldn't want to take another man's blond, blue-eyed dream girl. The Lord has one all picked out for me somewhere. And when it's His time, He will bring her into my life."

Willie grinned at him. "A man can't go wrong looking at it that way, Sergeant. And like I said, when you've already found her and married her and settled down on that big cattle ranch, maybe Betty Sue and I can come and visit you."

## 8

AT SIX O'CLOCK ON SATURDAY EVENING, October 15, at Memorial Hospital in Frederick, Maryland, Corporal Nate Conrad opened his eyes at the sound of someone beside his bed, and found himself looking into the face of Millie Ross.

Millie smiled down at him. "Come on, sleepyhead. Wake up. It's suppertime."

Nate rubbed his eyes. "Guess I was napping a bit."

She giggled. "Napping? When I passed by here five minutes ago, you were sleeping like a log."

"Okay, okay. It gets boring lying here in this bed. Sleeping helps relieve the boredom. At least when I'm sleeping—" He looked at the bed to his right. The patient was busy being fed by one of the nurses, and they were occupied in conversation. He glanced to the bed at his left, and it was still unoccupied, as it had been since the patient who occupied it had been dismissed from the hospital that morning.

Millie raised her eyebrows. "At least when you're sleeping *what?*"

Nate grinned. "At least when I'm sleeping, I can dream about a certain pretty redheaded nurse, and I can even hold hands with her. Something I'm not allowed to do when I'm awake."

Millie shook her head with a smile, turned, and drew the wheeled cart up to her side.

Nate sniffed. "Smells good. What's for supper?"

"Well, since you and I are Yankees, this may be hard to get off my tongue…but it's *southern* fried chicken."

He whispered, "Don't tell anybody, but I love southern fried chicken! In fact, I've never even heard of *northern* fried chicken, have you?"

"Can't say that I have. I also have mashed potatoes with chicken gravy, cornbread, and green beans for you."

"Well, let's get to it!"

Since Nate was now able to sit up in the bed for short periods, Millie helped him to a sitting position, tied a napkin around his neck, and placed a tray on his lap. The food was transferred from the cart to the tray, and as the patient began eating, Millie said, "Has anyone told you the War news today?"

Nate swallowed the chicken he was chewing. "No. Bad?"

"Well, not as bad as it has been lately. No major battles. Just some skirmishes. You know we're always about two days late getting the news."

He took another bite of chicken. "Mm-hmm."

"Let me tell you about the Maryland vote before I tell you about the skirmishes."

Chewing, Nate smiled and nodded.

"Were you aware that the people of Maryland were voting Thursday to adopt a new state constitution?"

"No."

"Well, they did, and the new constitution included abolition of slavery."

Nate's eyebrows arched. "Oh, really? I knew that even though Maryland has a lot of Southern sympathizers, it is definitely a Union state. But I didn't know the slavery issue hadn't already been settled here."

"Well, it has, now."

"Do Maryland's civic leaders expect a problem over it from the Southern sympathizers?"

"Apparently Governor Peabody doesn't think so. There was quite an article in the newspapers about it. He was interviewed by several newspaper reporters at the same time on Thursday evening when the votes had been counted. He says the Southern sympathizers in Maryland don't want trouble over it. There is enough trouble with the War going on."

"Good. What about the skirmishes?"

"There was one at Cedar Creek, Virginia, on Thursday. A unit of ours collided with a unit of Rebels about the same size. A total of fourteen men were killed. Also on Thursday, General Jubal Early's troops took on Union troops at Fisher's Hill, which is only a few miles from Cedar Creek. Eleven were killed, the newspapers said. Our troops were led by Major Leonard Saunders, who was wounded in the fight. In fact, Major Saunders was brought here, along with five other men from his unit. They arrived about an hour ago. Major Saunders is undergoing surgery right now. He will be put in this bed next to you."

Nate glanced at the empty bed. "Oh? Well, I've heard a lot about Major Saunders, but I've never met him. Is his wound serious?"

"Not too serious. He took a bullet in the thigh of his left leg."

"Oh. Well, I'm glad it's not life threatening."

As Nate was finishing his meal, Millie said, "My shift is almost up. You rest well tonight, won't you?"

He swallowed his last morsel of cornbread. "I will if I can manage to dream some more about that redheaded nurse."

Millie gave him a sidelong glance while removing the dishes and eating utensils from the tray. "Corporal Nathan Conrad, you are a case."

At that moment, Nate noticed Millie's roommates, nurses Paula Thompson and Nancy Field, draw up. They had their coats on, and Paula was carrying Millie's coat.

"Millie, are you ready to go?"

"Will be as soon as I deliver this cart back to the kitchen."

The nurse who was attending the patient next to Nate said, "I'll take it for you, Millie. I have to take my own cart back to the kitchen. You go on home."

Millie thanked her, parking the cart where the nurse could easily take it with her. Looking down at Nate, she said, "Now, you rest well, Corporal."

He grinned at her with a twinkle in his eye. "I will, Miss Ross."

Millie shook her head, smiling. "Good night, Corporal."

"How about wishing me sweet dreams?"

She blushed. "All right. Sweet dreams."

Paula and Nancy bid the corporal good night, and Millie walked between them as they headed for the door. When they reached the end of the line of beds, Millie looked back. Nate smiled and waved to her.

When the three nurses stepped out into the nippy fall air and moved down the street toward their apartment building, Paula said, "Millie, honey, I've noticed something lately."

"What's that?"

"It seems to me that you spend more time than is necessary with Corporal Nate Conrad."

"I've noticed that too," said Nancy. "What about that, Millie?"

Millie chuckled dryly. "You two are imagining things."

Paula giggled. "I don't think so. There's a certain light in your eyes when you look at him."

Millie was not ready to admit to her friends that she was definitely falling in love with Nate. She would withhold that information until Nate had declared himself in the matter. "You two are seeing things. If you're noticing a light in my eyes it's because I love being a nurse and taking care of my patients. You both need to put a check on your imaginations."

Paula and Nancy laughed heartily, but said no more on the subject.


Nate Conrad was lying on his bed with his eyes closed when he heard activity at the unoccupied bed next to him. He opened his eyes and saw two of the night nurses preparing the bed by turning the covers down. A pair of male attendants drew up with one of them pushing a cart.

Nate watched as the attendants carefully lifted the heavyset man off the cart and placed him on the bed.

As the attendants wheeled the cart away, the nurses did what they could to make the major comfortable. He was still under the influence of the anesthetic. They checked his vital signs, then one of them noticed that Nate was still awake. "Corporal," she said, keeping her voice low, "this man is Major Leonard Saunders. If he should awaken you at anytime during the night and you see that he is in pain, will you give us a holler?"

"Sure will, ma'am. I'm a great admirer of Major Saunders. I can hardly wait to meet him."

When Millie Ross awakened the next morning with beams of the sun shining into the room, she saw Paula and Nancy getting out of their beds.

"Good morning, Millie," said Nancy, while putting on her robe. "Sleep well?"

"Sure did," she said, throwing back the covers and sitting up.

Paula giggled, swinging her gaze on Nancy. "Well, now we know, don't we?"

"We sure do. And we don't need to put a check on our imaginations, because we didn't imagine it."

Millie threw her legs over the edge of the bed. "You didn't imagine what?"

Paula giggled again. "Well, you were talking quite loudly in your sleep last night. Woke both of us up."

"And we now know that you are head-over-heels in love with the handsome Corporal Nate Conrad," said Nancy. "You were calling him 'Nate darling' in your dream and pouring out such sweet words, telling him how very much you love him."

"You also told him that you think Harrisburg would be a nice place to live."

Millie blushed as a smile spread and threw her hands up. "What can I say? You heard it from my own mouth. I'm in love with the guy."

"And he's in love with you, too, isn't he?" said Paula.

"Well-l-l, he hasn't come out with the exact words 'I love you,' but I know he loves me. He is the perfect gentleman and is working up to it slowly."

Millie's roommates smiled at each other, then Nancy asked, "How much longer will Nate be in the hospital?"

"There's no way to know exactly at this point, but the doctors are saying he will be here at least five more months, maybe six."

Paula laid a hand on Millie's shoulder. "Honey, I'm glad for what's happening between you and Nate. It's just too bad the two of you can't have some privacy so you could talk to each other freely and be able to show some affection."

"Yes," said Nancy. "I understand why there have to be rules concerning nurses becoming romantically involved with the male patients, but when two people are genuinely in love with each other, they should be able to express it and show it."

Millie nodded. "I'd sure like to be able to do that, and from the look I see in Nate's eyes and some of the things he says, I'm sure he would too."

Paula squeezed Millie's shoulder. "Maybe when Nate is able to occupy a wheelchair, you can wheel him somewhere that you can at least have enough privacy to express yourselves without other hospital personnel or other patients being able to listen to what you say."

A smile curved Millie's lips. "Maybe this will be possible. I sure hope so."

"Of course, honey," said Nancy, "if this develops between you and Nate, the day will come when you will have to leave here and go to Harrisburg with him. And, of course, there will be wedding bells."

Millie's eyes brightened. "Oh, won't that be the day?"

It was almost seven o'clock when Millie, Paula, and Nancy arrived at the hospital to start their shift. Millie's first duty was to check on each patient who had been assigned to her. Her desire was to go to Nate first, but not wanting to give the head nurse or anyone else in authority a reason to reprimand her, she took them in order.

Some thirty minutes later, she came to Nate, who was her fifth patient in a list of twelve.

Nate's face beamed as he looked up and smiled at her. "My, oh my, you sure look lovely this morning, Miss Ross. I like the way you have your hair styled. I mean, I like each style you use, but you look exceptionally beautiful today."

The heavyset man in the next bed grinned. "Now, Corporal Conrad, you are not supposed to flirt with the nurses."

Nate chuckled nervously. "I wasn't flirting, Major. I was just stating a fact. Miss Millie Ross, I would like to introduce you to Major Leonard Saunders."

"Good morning, ma'am," said the major. "I'm happy to meet you."

Millie smiled. "And I'm happy to meet you, sir. Are you feeling all right this morning? I know you had surgery yesterday afternoon."

"I'm doing fine, thank you. My nurse, Miss Walker, is taking good care of me."

"Excellent," she said, then turned her back to Saunders and looked down at Nate. There was love in her eyes. Nate's heart skipped a beat. "Well, Corporal, I need to get to the usual—checking your vital signs and all that."

Nate wanted to tell her that she'd better check his heart first, since it was skipping one beat after another, but he refrained.

While Millie was checking his vital signs, Nelda Walker drew up to the major's bed to check his bandage. She spoke to Millie, then put her attention on the major.

Nate kept an eye on the major and his nurse, and when they were engaged in conversation, he drew Millie's attention by pointing to his lips and silently mouthed, *I love you, Millie!*

It was Millie's turn to have her heart skip a beat. Her eyes lit up. Making sure no one was looking, she silently mouthed in return, *I love you too!*

At that instant, she was checking his pulse. The beat picked up and she smiled down at him.

Nate ran his eyes to the major and the nurse and to the sleeping patient on his other side. Knowing that he had a private moment, he took hold of Millie's hand, squeezed the forefinger and the middle finger together, and planted a kiss on them. The lovely redhead casually looked around, and when she was sure no one was looking, she pressed the kiss on her fingers to her lips. Nate's face was beaming as he silently mouthed again, *I love you!*

Before dawn that morning, just outside Rome, Georgia, the ninety-one Union prisoners who were to be taken to Andersonville Prison

Camp were being escorted at gunpoint to a train with three boxcars behind the engine and coal car. Some of the Confederate soldiers were carrying lanterns.

In the engine cab, engineer Walt Benson and fireman Link Hazzard were looking out the window. Hazzard had the fire going in the boiler, and the steam was almost up to power.

The fireman shook his head. "I can see their faces well enough by the light of the lanterns to discern that those Yankees are scared spitless."

"Wouldn't you be if you were going to Andersonville? They know about the death rate there."

"I guess everybody from the Atlantic to the Pacific and from Canada to Mexico have heard about Andersonville, Walt. I've been hearing about it since March, and I was in Kentucky at the time. I never dreamed when the army brought me to this part of Georgia last week that I'd actually be hauling prisoners to Macon so they could put them in wagons and take them to that disease-ridden prison."

Benson sighed. "Well, I guess it's something you and I can both tell our grandchildren about someday."

A Confederate captain was coming their way. As he drew up, he said, "Okay, Walt. We're locking them in the boxcars right now. You can pull out in five minutes."

"All right, sir. Steam's up. We're ready."

Five minutes later, Walt Benson gave the throttle a shove, and the big engine lurched forward. The couplings between the cars rattled with a deep thunderous sound and the train was rolling south.

Soon they were amid fields and forests as the engine belched black smoke toward the star bedecked sky. The powerful headlight shone on the gleaming twin tracks ahead, which seemed to become one as they disappeared a hundred yards in the distance in the predawn darkness.

In each of the three boxcars, a single lantern hung overhead, giving off a glow of pale yellow light and casting the shadows of the heartsick prisoners on the hard wooden floor where they sat.

In the third boxcar, Captain William Linden—who was the leader of A Company in the second battalion of the Third

Pennsylvania Cavalry Division—was sitting on the floor in a corner at the rear with his back braced against the boxcar wall.

Linden let his eyes roam over the other thirty men in the boxcar. Most of them were silent as they huddled in small groups, their heads hanging low. A few were talking in subdued voices that could barely be heard by anyone outside their group over the rumble of the steel wheels beneath the car.

The captain was feeling the same dread of Andersonville as were the rest of the men. His stomach flipped over at the thought of it. He wondered how many of the ninety-one men on the train would live to see their homes and families again. Squaring his jaw, he determined that he would be one of them.

This line of thought sent his mind to his wife and daughter at home in Harrisburg. He wished he could at least get word to Myrna and Jenny that he was still alive, but there was no possible way to do it. "Jenny," he whispered, "I know you are taking care of your mother. Please, honey, do all you can to keep her from sinking deeper into her depression. I know you're both wondering if I'm alive, and if so, if I am in one piece. No way to let you know. But someday this dreadful war will be over, and in spite of the disease and filth of Andersonville, I'll come home to you."

At that moment, Linden saw three of the men under his command making their way toward him from the other end of the car. Focusing on them in the dim light, he saw that their faces were grim.

No, not grim.

*Angry.*

Lieutenant Edgar Toomey, Sergeant Keith Lewis, and Corporal Todd Zediker hunkered down in front of Linden, their glaring eyes burning his face.

Toomey, whose buckteeth always protruded past his lips, sneered at Linden. Keeping his voice low so the men in the car could not hear him, he hissed, "It's your fault, Linden! All your fault!"

The captain met his hot gaze with steady eyes. "You can say that all you want, Toomey, but you're wrong."

"Well, you're the commander of A Company, ain't you? Huh?"

"That I am."

"Okay. In that battle at Coosaville Road, sixteen of our men were killed—including my little brother, Lester! Twenty-one were wounded, and are now in the hands of those Confederate doctors, who'll let 'em die as sure as the sun comes up in the east! And the rest of us are on this train, goin' to Andersonville so we can die of disease or starvation, or both! And it's all your fault!"

Linden felt scorched by the flaming eyes of all three men. His own anger surfaced, making a dark tide shade his face. A glitter leaped into his eyes. "I'm telling you again: it is not my fault!"

"You're a liar, Linden!" Lewis was breathing hard. "I heard Edgar warn you just before we entered into the battle with those stinkin' Rebels, that if we didn't withdraw and ride quickly to the safety of that nearby forest to the west, we were all gonna get killed or captured along with those other Union troops who were already fightin' those Rebels who outnumbered us all."

"I heard Edgar's warnin' to you, too," growled Zediker. "We had that one opportunity at that precise moment of time. It was head for the protection of that forest unnoticed by the enemy and not battle such a large number, or end up like this. Oh, but no, you wouldn't listen. Now, look what's happened! Now, what's left of our company is on our way to that horrible Andersonville Prison. And it *is* all your fault!"

Linden bristled. "Don't you guys have any sense at all? I told you this when you spoke your warning, Edgar, and I'm telling you again. If I had led A Company away from a battle that was already in progress, and we had taken refuge in the forest to save our own skins when our comrades were already greatly outnumbered, it would have been a cowardly act, and the rest of us would have been charged with desertion in the face of battle. Those of us who lived through it to the end of the War would face the shame of our cowardice for the rest of our lives."

"Call it what you want, Captain, but my brother's dead, as are fifteen other men in our unit," Toomey snarled. "As I said, those wounded ones the Rebels picked up off the battlefield won't get proper care from the Rebel doctors. They'll all die! And the rest of us are gonna die in that rotten disease-infested Rebel prison camp at Andersonville."

"Right!" snapped Lewis. "If you'd listened to Edgar, his brother would still be alive, as well as the other fifteen men, and we wouldn't be ridin' in this dirty boxcar toward that filthy prison camp!"

"Yeah," said Zediker. "You and your big sense of honor. Look what it got us!"

Linden looked at them with dull hostility. "May I remind you that you are speaking to a superior officer, and that I am also your assigned leader? If we do get out of this, I'll have to report you to the army officials in Washington."

All three regarded him with hate-filled eyes, but did not reply.

Linden fixed his eyes like hot pinpoints on Toomey. "Let me also remind you, Lieutenant, that you and I are both from Harrisburg and will be living in the same town together when this war is over. You are sowing seeds that will be a crop of trouble later."

"Hah!" said Toomey, showing his buckteeth in fury. "Neither one of us are gonna live to ever see Harrisburg again!" Then he said to his pals, "Let's go back to the front of the car. It stinks worse back here."

Linden watched as they stood up and walked away, without looking back.

When the trio reached the other end of the car, where they had been sitting before, they tightened into a knot and sat down.

Toomey spoke in a low voice so only his two friends could hear. "I'm tellin' you this much—even if I do live till the end of the War and get to go home, Linden's gonna die! I'll see to that!"

*9*

MAIL ORDER BRIDE SERIES
NO. 10
1865
USA
AL & JOANNA LACY

MYRNA LINDEN WAS IN A FRIGHTENING nightmare, observing swarms of infantrymen and cavalrymen clashing amid cannons and rifles on some Southern battlefield. Foot soldiers were dropping by the dozens, as were cavalrymen and their horses. Cannonballs were exploding, sending fragments of metal and flaming bodies twisting through the air.

Suddenly she caught sight of William on his horse, leading his company in the battle. Seconds later, cannonballs struck all around William. The smoke and fire enveloped him and his horse, and when the smoke drifted away, she saw both of them lying on the ground, dead.

She screamed, "William! William! Please don't be dead! Please don't—"

"Mama! Mama!" Jenny's voice came to her ears, penetrating her nightmare.

Myrna opened her eyes to see her daughter standing over her. She reached for her. "He's dead, Jenny! Your papa's dead!" And suddenly she was shrieking, rolling her head back and forth.

Jenny shook her. "Mama! Mama! It's all right. I'm right here with you."

Myrna closed her eyes and shrieked till her throat seized shut, then gasped for breath. When Jenny called to her again, she opened her eyes, still trying to catch her breath.

Jenny stroked her forehead. "Mama, you were having another one of your bad dreams. It's all right. Everything is fine."

Myrna stared at her with wide, frightened eyes. Her face shrunk around her cheekbones, giving her a grimace of perpetual sorrow. Desperation was in her tight voice. "Jenny…Jenny…he's dead. Your papa's dead. I saw him die in an explosion of cannonballs. He's dead! He's dead!"

Jenny sat down on the bed and wrapped her arms around her mother's neck. "No, Mama. It was only a bad dream. Papa is still alive. He'll be coming home to us soon."

Myrna's body began to shudder. Jenny pulled back and looked into her tear-misted eyes. Her skin was flushed and her eyes had taken on the hollow look Jenny had seen so many times before.

"Mama, settle down now," she said softly. "You just had another one of your bad dreams. It's morning. You rest while I go fix you some breakfast."

Myrna nodded and closed her eyes.

Jenny stood up and wiped a palm over her own tired face. Her mother had been having one bad dream after another for the past three nights, and Jenny had slept no more than a couple of hours each of those nights.

Her eyes were red-rimmed. She looked almost as ravaged as the tormented woman who lay under the blankets.

Jenny's brow furrowed as she looked down at the face that once was so lovely. *She's getting steadily worse. It was bad enough when my baby brother died, but this torment over Papa is devastating. I'm watching her sinking deeper into her depression every day. She's dying a little at a time right before my eyes.*

Tears filled Jenny's eyes and were spilling down her cheeks. She started to turn away, but stopped when she heard her mother say weakly, "Jenny…"

She bent over her. "Yes, Mama?"

Myrna lifted a trembling hand toward her. Jenny took hold of it. "Honey, I…I'm sorry to be such a problem."

Jenny squeezed the hand. "Mama, you're not a problem. I love you. I just wish I could make everything all right for you."

The sun was filling the room with its bright glow. Myrna looked up at her daughter admiringly, thinking how trim and statuesque she was. Her sky blue eyes were so full of expression. The blond locks were so radiant that to Myrna they seemed a halo. "Thank you for being so good to me, honey."

Jenny managed a smile and caressed her mother's pale cheek. "You don't have to thank me for that, sweet Mama. You just relax. You'll have breakfast in bed like the last two mornings. Only today I won't have to leave you and go to work. It's my day off. I will have to be gone for a little while, though. I'm going to go fetch Dr. Griffin for you. He isn't due for four more days, but I want him to know about these bad dreams that have so upset you these past three nights. I'll ask him to come see you today."

Myrna nodded.

Jenny bent down and kissed her mother's forehead. "I'll wash my face and brush my hair, then I'll fix your breakfast."

Myrna nodded again, and Jenny hurried through the door. She went first to the kitchen where she built a fire in the cookstove. Leaving it to pop and crackle, she went to her own room, where she poured water into the wash basin and washed her face. When she was drying it, she looked in the mirror and said to her reflection, "Jenny, it's a good thing Nate's not here to look at you. You look like death warmed over."

She brushed her hair, then combed it into a tight bun at the nape of her neck, using two long hairpins to hold it in place. Going to the closet, she donned a warm brown dress trimmed with a wide cream-colored bertha collar. She pinched her cheeks to bring some rose into them, then powdered her face lightly.

Noting again the weary look in her eyes, she threw palms upward and said, "That's as good as it's going to get today."

In the kitchen, Jenny put another log on the fire, then dipped water from the bucket, filled the teakettle, and set it on the stove. She also filled a small pot, and while both were heating, she scooped a small measure of oatmeal from the tin and poured it into the pot.

She sat down at the table, and while she waited for the water to boil in both pot and teakettle, Jenny's thoughts ran to Nate. She wondered where he was in the South and what he might be facing that day. Shaking her head to rid her mind of his danger, she began daydreaming about the day Nate would come home to her. She pictured that first moment, imagining how wonderful it would be. She was forming a mental image of their wedding when the teakettle began to whistle, spewing hot water from its spout that sizzled in small drops on the stove. As she rose from the table and stepped to the stove, a dark thought pressed itself into her mind: *Nate isn't coming home. And neither is Papa. They're both dead and buried beneath the sod somewhere in Southern soil.*

"No!" she said aloud. "No! They both must come home!"

Her heart was still heavy and doubtful as she hurriedly finished preparing her mother's breakfast. She made the tray as attractive and tempting as possible, and carried it up the hall toward her mother's room. Along with the teapot, cups, and bowl of oatmeal, was the bottle of paraldehyde.

When she entered the room, she was astonished to see her mother sitting up, with her back resting against a couple of pillows. This thrilled her, but her elation was short-lived when she moved up to the bed and saw the tragic emptiness in her mother's eyes.

Jenny placed the tray on the bedside table. "Okay, Mama. Here's some hot tea and some oatmeal."

Myrna frowned when she saw only one cereal bowl. "Aren't you going to eat, dear?"

"I'm just not hungry right now, Mama. I brought two cups, though, so I could have some tea with you."

Jenny poured the tea into a cup, let her mother sip it for a moment, then set it down and picked up the bowl of hot oatmeal and placed a spoon in it. "Here you go, Mama. See if you can eat it all, okay? Then I'll give you your paraldehyde."

Taking the bowl, Myrna lifted the spoon and began eating. Jenny poured tea into the other cup, and sipped it slowly. When Myrna had eaten half the oatmeal, she said, "Honey, that's all I can do."

Jenny sighed, took the bowl, and put it on the tray. She gave her mother a heavy dose of paraldehyde, then handed her the cup of tea to finish.

Myrna took a couple more sips of tea, then handed the cup to Jenny.

"Thank you, honey." With that, she laid her head back on the pillows and closed her eyes.

Gazing down at her mother's pallid features brought tears of frustration to Jenny's eyes. "I'm so sorry that your life has turned out like this, Mama. So very sorry."

Myrna opened her dreary eyes and set them on Jenny, but did not respond.

"Mama, you need to lie down again. Let me help you."

When she had her mother lying comfortably, Jenny said, "See if you can nap a little, Mama. I'm going after Dr. Griffin. I'll be back shortly."

Jenny leaned down and planted a kiss on Myrna's forehead, then picked up the tray and carried it back to the kitchen. Making quick work of the cleanup job, she put on her coat and returned to her mother's room to check on her. When she stopped at the door and saw that her mother was sleeping, she turned and hurried out the front door of the house.

It was a magnificent autumn day. The air was brisk under a brilliant blue sky. The trees still had a few golden red leaves, and as she walked down the street, the beauty of it all overwhelmed her. As she drew within a block of the doctor's office, she said, "Please, Dr. Griffin, please help my mama."

When Jenny returned to the house and stepped up on the front porch, she saw her mother at the parlor window, sitting in her rocking chair. She was weeping and wringing her hands, saying something Jenny could not distinguish.

Jenny hurried inside and rushed toward the parlor. Even before she reached the parlor door, she could hear her mother babbling. "He's dead! My poor William is dead! He will never come home to me!"

Jenny dashed to her and took hold of her hands. "Mama, listen to me! Papa isn't dead. He's alive and will come home to you when the War is over."

"No, Jenny! Your papa is dead! He's never coming home!"

"Dr. Griffin will be coming soon, Mama. He had some patients with appointments, but as soon as he finishes with them, he'll be here. He will be able to help you."

Myrna sniffed. "Jenny, if your papa doesn't come home, nobody can help me! I'll just collapse and die."

"Mama, I'm going to give you some more paraldehyde. You've got to settle down. I'll be right b—"

Jenny's words were interrupted by a knock on the front door.

Myrna's eyes widened. "Honey, did you lock the door? That may be your papa! Maybe he's home! If the door was unlocked, he would come in. Hurry, honey! Go let your papa in!"

Jenny felt her stomach twist. "Mama, the War isn't over. It can't be Papa. It's probably Dr. Griffin."

Myrna frowned, her eyes losing focus. "Dr. Griffin?"

"Could be. I had to walk back. He has a horse and buggy."

Myrna blinked and shook her head, as if there were cobwebs trying to clog her brain. Her eyes were wild. "Jenny! Your papa's dead, isn't he? He isn't coming back…ever!"

There was another knock on the door.

"No, Mama. He's not dead. Settle down. I've got to go to the door."

Myrna threw her head back, and what burst from her lips was a shrill, frightened scream that echoed through the house.

Jenny ran into the hall and dashed to the door. When she opened it, she was glad to see the face of Dr. Adam Griffin.

"Jenny, is that your mother screaming?"

"Yes. Please hurry. Like I told you this morning, she thinks Papa is dead."

Myrna was still screaming. The doctor bolted ahead of Jenny, who followed close on his heels. When they entered the parlor, Myrna was sitting on the floor in front of the sofa, her head bobbing loosely on her neck. Her mouth hung open and her blank, staring eyes were at a demented angle. She stopped screaming when she saw the doctor come in. "He's dead, Doctor. William is dead. He isn't coming home. I can't stand it. I can't stand it!"

Griffin leaned down. "Mrs. Linden, let's get you up here on the sofa."

She looked at him blankly as he set his medical bag down, took hold of her arms, lifted her to her feet, and eased her down on the sofa. He knelt in front of her and took hold of both trembling hands. "Mrs. Linden, there is no reason to believe that your husband is dead."

"Yes, there is. I saw cannonballs explode and kill him! I saw it, Doctor! I saw it!"

While Jenny looked on, biting her lips, Griffin worked with Myrna for several minutes, trying to convince her that what she saw was only a dream. She kept shaking her head, insisting that William was dead and would never be coming home.

When Griffin saw that talking to her would do no good, he picked her up in his arms and said to Jenny, "When did she last have a dose of paraldehyde?"

"This morning, just before I came to your office. I gave her an extra large dose. I was about to give her some more when you knocked on the door."

"All right. Would you bring my bag? I have some in there. I'll give her some."

When they entered Myrna's room, the doctor laid her on the bed. She continued to stare at him while mumbling something indistinguishable in a dazed tone of voice. Dr. Griffin asked Jenny for some water and a cup. She watched him mix sedative powders and saw her mother get a heavy dose of paraldehyde, along with the strong sedative.

A few minutes later, Myrna was fast asleep.

Dr. Griffin set compassionate eyes on the worried daughter and said, "Jenny, I'll leave the rest of this paraldehyde and these sedative powders with you. Give both of them to her in the dosage I just did three times a day. I'll write them down for you. Make the last one just before her bedtime."

After writing the dosage down on a slip of paper, he gave it to Jenny. "I'll be back about this time tomorrow to check on her. If you need me before then, send a neighbor to let me know."

Jenny nodded, her face void of color. "All right, Doctor. Thank you."

When Dr. Griffin was gone, Jenny sat down on the overstuffed chair near her mother's bed. She looked at her sleeping mother for a long moment, then tears surfaced. She bent her head down and put her hands over her face. "Oh, Papa, we need you here so very much. I'm afraid Mama's going to do just as she said…collapse and die. All the medicine in the world isn't going to help her if she gives up on living. She needs you, Papa. And so do I."

Jenny sniffled and wiped tears with the palms of her hands. As she was doing so, her thoughts went to Nate Conrad. An ache rose in her heart. She stood up, made sure her mother was still sleeping, left the room, and made her way down the hall to her own room.

She was still sniffling some when she sat down at her small desk. With shaking hands, she took out paper and pen, thumbed tears from her eyes, and concentrated on what she wanted to say to the man she loved.

Memories of her times with Nate flooded her mind. They served only to more intensify the ache in her heart. It took a moment to calm herself, then Jenny dipped the pen in the inkwell and began to write.

Friday, October 14, 1864
My darling Nate,
Well, sweetheart, here it is. Letter number 20. I need desperately to feel closer to you. Since the news came that your artillery unit was in the Winchester, Virginia, battle, I have had to reach deep inside to keep up hope that you are alive and well. And I have to admit that sometimes I am hanging on by a thread.

I'm so frightened, darling. All my hopes and dreams are wrapped up in you and the love we share for each other. If anything happened to you, and you didn't come home to me when the War is over, I would just collapse and die. I love you with all of my heart, and life without you would be hopelessly empty.

I miss you so very much. Like I said in my last letter, I know you miss me too. And I am trying to hang on to the dream in my heart that we can talk about our lonely hours when we are married and living in our own home here in Harrisburg, when all this horrible loneliness and uncertainty is over.

Until then, my love, don't forget that you are the only one for me.

All my love,

Your Jenny

By the time she had signed the letter, Jenny was weeping. She pressed it close to her face as if it were Nate. "Oh, darling, I love you so very much. I hope somehow, wherever you are, you can feel the presence of my love and my thoughts."

When she stopped weeping and dried her face with a handkerchief from a desk drawer, Jenny saw that her tears had smeared the letter so that most of it was unreadable. She used a blotter to dry the paper, then folded and planted a kiss on it. She then opened the drawer that held the small bundle of letters and placed it on top of the others.

Jenny rose from the chair and sighed. "Well, it's time I cleaned this house up good, as I always do on my day off."

Though her body felt the strain of so little sleep the past three nights, she swept every room except her mother's, and used a feather duster after sweeping. In the kitchen, she mopped the floor, then polished the table and gave the counter a good scouring. While doing these familiar chores, it a brought a calmness to her and a small contented smile curved her lips.

She went back to her room and changed the linens on her bed, making a mental note to do the same for her mother when she awakened. She would then do the washing.

With everything done as much as possible at that point, Jenny returned to her mother's room. As she moved up quietly beside the bed, Myrna Linden was still in a deep sleep.

Jenny stroked her mother's hair softly. *The sedative is really working. She needs the rest, for sure.*

Her stomach rumbled, reminding her that she had only had a cup of tea since supper last night. She noted by the clock on her mother's dresser that it was almost noon.

As she walked back toward the kitchen, Jenny admired the clean house, and was pleased with her hard work of the morning. Letting herself daydream for a moment, she pictured what her own home would be like when she and Nate married.

There was a pang in her heart as the impression forced itself into her thoughts: *That is, if he lives through the War to come home to me.*

Entering the kitchen, Jenny stoked up the fire in the stove, put a pot of coffee on, then sliced a piece of cold roast beef. She cut a wedge of pungent cheese and after slathering two slices of bread with creamy butter, made a sandwich. When the coffee was hot, she sat down and enjoyed the sandwich and coffee, along with a soft molasses cookie.

As Jenny was cleaning up after eating, a deep feeling of lassitude invaded her already weary body. She went to her mother's room, and when she found her still sleeping peacefully, she sat in the over-stuffed chair nearby. Her eyes grew heavy immediately, and in less than a minute, her chin fell to her chest and her own eyes closed in sleep.

More than three hours had passed when Jenny was drawn from her slumber by the sound of her mother's covers rustling. She raised her head, rubbed her eyes, and found her mother looking at her. She sat up straight and let a tiny smile curve her lips. "How are you feeling, Mama?"

Myrna smiled back. "I'm better, honey. You were sleeping when I woke up a few minutes ago. I had to change positions. I'm sorry if I disturbed you."

Jenny rose from the chair and took hold of her mother's hand. "It's all right, Mama. I'm just glad you're feeling better. Your eyes are much clearer than they were this morning."

"Jenny…I—"

"What, Mama?"

"I was just thinking…"

"Yes?"

"Is…is there some way you could find out from army headquarters in Washington, D.C., if your papa survived that battle near Rome, Georgia? Certainly they would know."

Jenny shook her head. "No, Mama. I didn't tell you, but I investigated this very thing a few days ago. I went to the army recruiting office downtown. They told me that the army knows with reasonable accuracy how many men are killed, wounded, and missing in battles, but they do not register the dead and missing for public information. The army simply doesn't have the personnel to handle such a formidable task."

Myrna's countenance fell. "Oh."

Jenny raised the hand she held to her lips and kissed it. "Mama, we'll just have to wait till the War is over. Papa will come home to us."

"How can you be sure?"

"Well, I can't, but we have to keep our hopes up. It's the same thing I have to do about Nate. We can't give up, Mama."

Myrna's eyes filled with tears. Jenny leaned down and hugged her, and Myrna clung to her for several minutes.

When Myrna let go, she wiped her tears with the sheet. "What would I do without my precious daughter?"

Jenny smiled. "You'll never have to worry about that. I'll always be close to you, even after Nate and I get married."

Myrna bit her lips again and patted Jenny's hand. Her eyes grew heavy, and within a few minutes, she settled into a light sleep.

Jenny sat back down in the overstuffed chair. She told herself she would have to continue to encourage her mother by putting on an optimistic attitude, though the optimism was only on the surface. Inside, she feared that she would never see her father or Nate again.

That night, after administering the paraldehyde and the sedative to her mother per Dr. Griffin's specifications, Jenny crawled wearily into her bed. Her thoughts were on her father and Nate as she fell asleep.

Moments later, in her dream, she was standing in the Harrisburg railroad station, watching the army train roll in. The crowd of people all around her was in a jovial mood, talking about how the Civil War had ended weeks before and they were eagerly waiting for their beloved soldiers to arrive.

When the train rolled to a halt with a loud hiss from the bowels of the engine, Jenny's anxious blue eyes darted from coach to coach as uniformed men began to get off. Wives, mothers, and sweethearts were rushing to the men.

Suddenly, she saw her father appear on the rear platform of one of the cars, looking around. She ran to him. "Papa! Papa! Papa!"

A smile broke over his face when he spotted her, and he hurried down the steps. "Jenny, honey," he said, "you're prettier than ever!"

She clung to him with all her might. At the same moment, she looked over his shoulder and to her delight, she saw Nate getting off the train. Their eyes met, and Nate dashed to her. She let go of her father, and was folded into Nate's arms while Captain William Linden looked on with a smile.

After a few minutes of exchanging words of love, Jenny and Nate drew back to look into each other's eyes.

Nate drew a deep breath and smiled from ear to ear. "Sweetheart, I love you so much."

"And I love you so much, darling," she said.

Nate looked at Captain Linden. "Sir, I want to ask you something very important."

William smiled. "Of course, Lieutenant. What is it?"

"May I have your daughter's hand in marriage?"

Jenny's heart was banging her ribs as she waited for her father's reply.

William's smile was still there. "Of course, young man. I know that both of you love each other, and I'm happy to give my permission."

Suddenly Jenny was sitting up in her bed, breathing heavily. Moonlight was streaming through the window, giving the room a silver glow. *Only a dream,* she thought. *I can only hope that both Papa and Nate live to make that moment come true.*

# 10

It was late in the afternoon on Saturday, October 15, when the army wagons from Macon pulled through the gate of Andersonville Prison Camp with the new group of ninety-one Union prisoners.

At gunpoint, several guards ordered the prisoners to get out of the wagons and assembled them in front of Captain Henry Wirz's log cabin, just inside the gate. They were told to stand at attention, which they did, though most of them did it reluctantly.

Inside the cabin, Lieutenant Harry Fisher stood at one of the small windows while the prison commandant sat at his desk. Fisher turned and said, "They're ready, sir."

Wirz nodded, rose from his desk chair, and headed toward the door. Fisher preceded him and opened the door. The captain put on a stern face and stepped past Fisher, who closed the door and followed, halting at the captain's side, a half step to the rear.

Wirz introduced himself, then laid down the rules to the new prisoners in a harsh voice, warning that if the rules were broken, the guilty parties would suffer the consequences, which were always severe. Wirz pointed out the dead line around the inside of the stockade fence. He cautioned them about prisoners moving inside the flimsy cordon, then told them the number who had been shot to death who had ignored the rule.

An invisible cloud of gloom hung heavily over the men in blue uniforms.

Wirz let his line of sight roam over the group, noting that there was one captain and three lieutenants. "We're heavy on inmates, so we're short on canvas and blankets. We'll provide what we can, and you boys will have to make do." He pointed with his head toward the man behind him. "This is Lieutenant Harry Fisher, chief of the prison guards. I warn you, he is not the man to rile. Obey any and all orders he gives you immediately, without question or comment. Lieutenant Fisher, I want you to take a sufficient number of your men and lead these new prisoners to the area they will occupy."

Fisher took a step that brought him close to the commandant's side. "Yes, sir."

Wirz lifted a finger, signaling that he wanted to say something else. Eyes roaming the enemy faces, he said, "Since winter is not far away, if you Yankees want to dig holes in the ground in your assigned spot to help give some shelter from the cold nights, you will be given shovels. You will do the digging while these armed guards look on." The commandant's face hardened. "If any of you should try to use the shovels as weapons against the guards, you will be shot down like rabid dogs! We have plenty of space in our graveyard outside the stockade. There is sufficient room for your dead body. Keep that in mind at all times."

The prisoners stood silently, exchanging troubled glances.

Wirz returned to his cabin, and Fisher chose ten guards to accompany the new men to their assigned area they would call home.

While Fisher and the guards were escorting the new men past areas occupied by Union prisoners who looked on in silence, Lieutenant Edgar Toomey slipped up beside Captain William Linden and whispered, "You got us into this mess, Linden. If you'd listened to me, we wouldn't be in this pig sty of a prison camp."

"I would rather be in this prison camp than to be free and know I was a cowardly deserter."

Toomey's face darkened. "Are you callin' me a cowardly deserter?"

"That's exactly what you are!"

Toomey released a gust of hot breath and moved back with his friends, Lewis and Zediker. Keeping his voice low, he told them what Linden had just said. As they looked at Toomey with frowns on their brows, he hissed, "He's gonna die! One way or another, I'm gonna kill 'im!"

When they reached the area the new prisoners would occupy, Lieutenant Harry Fisher stood before them. He pointed out the small piles of tattered cloth and canvas, along with some broken tree limbs that could be used to support them as shelters.

"Now listen to me. You are to stay in this area, which as you can see, is bordered by a line of small stones around the perimeter. All the areas in the compound are marked off the same way. You are not to move among the other prisoners. That is a hard and fast regulation. Believe me, you don't want to face the consequence of disobeying this edict. When it's time for meals or bathing in the stream that runs through here, you will be led by guards. The privies are quite visible from here. You will visit them one at a time and walk the path that leads directly to them. Never step off the path. Guards will be watching you at all times. Break the rules, and you will be sorry."

At that moment, two guards approached the area. One was carrying a roll of canvas, and the other bore two sturdy pieces of tree limbs, uniform in length, along with four short ones to be used as stakes. "What is your name, Captain?" asked Fisher.

"William Linden," came the soft reply.

"Well, Captain Linden, I have ordered a tent for you. We supply them for those prisoners with the rank of captain or above."

Linden shook his head. "Thank you, Lieutenant Fisher, but I can't do that. My shelter should be no better than those of my men."

"Hey, Captain!" spoke up a lieutenant. "It's all right. We men of A Company want you to take it, right, fellas?"

There was a chorus of voices expressing agreement. Abstaining were Toomey, Lewis, and Zediker.

When Linden shook his head, declining, the same voices pressed him to accept Fisher's offer. Finally, Linden nodded, ran his gaze over their faces, and said, "All right, since you insist. And thank you."

Toomey, Lewis, and Zediker looked at each other with sour expressions on their faces.

The guard who held the canvas placed it in Linden's hands, and the other guard gave him the lengths of tree limbs and the stakes.

When the guards left, the men went to work to make themselves shelters with what little materials had been provided.

Edgar Toomey picked up his share of cloth, canvas, and broken tree limbs, and glared at Captain Linden, who was stretching out the canvas to set up his one-man tent. While Toomey was putting the materials together to make his crude shelter, he glanced at the nearest area to the east, which was some thirty yards away. He saw a husky Union sergeant who was adjusting a pole on a complete one-man canvas tent. His eyes bulged. He told himself the tent couldn't belong to a mere sergeant. It had to belong to an officer. But when the sergeant slipped inside and closed the flap, he knew the tent was his.

Looking around, Toomey couldn't see any guards nearby. He headed across his own assigned area in the direction of the adjacent one.

"Hey, Edgar!" came Corporal Todd Zediker's voice.

Toomey paused and looked over his shoulder at him.

"Where you goin'?"

"Just takin' a little walk. See you later." With that, he crossed the line of small stones and hurried toward his destination.

Keith Lewis drew up beside Zediker, watching Toomey go. "What's he doin'?"

Zediker shrugged. "I haven't the least idea."

Suddenly, Captain William Linden was beside them. "He's fixing to get himself in trouble, that's what he's doing."

Both of them looked at Linden coldly.

He met their frigid eyes. "You two are going to suffer if you continue to follow him. He's on a beeline for the whipping post."

Without a word, they turned their backs on him and walked away.

Linden glanced across the open area as Toomey was stepping over the stone line at the other area, shook his head, and went back to setting up his tent.

Some of the men in the other area looked at Toomey askance as he moved past them and approached the tent belonging to the sergeant. Standing over it, he called, "Hey, Sergeant! Come out here! I'm Lieutenant Toomey of A Company, Third Pennsylvania Cavalry."

The flap snapped back, and the burly sergeant crawled out, rising to his feet. He had a neck like a tree trunk, shoulders and arms to match, and a square, rugged face. He eyed Toomey quizzically. "Aren't you trespassing, Lieutenant?"

Toomey ignored the question. "I want this tent."

The sergeant's features stiffened. "Well, you can't have it."

"I outrank you, and I'm taking the tent. How did you get it, anyway? You're just a sergeant."

"Well, you're just a lieutenant. Only captains, majors, colonels, and generals get tents. It just so happens that I did Lieutenant Harry Fisher a good turn a few weeks ago, and he gave me the tent. If you want a tent, you'll have to get it elsewhere. And may I remind you that you are outside your own bounds?"

Toomey's eyes blazed. "Who are you to talk to me like that?" His right fist stabbed a lightning-fast punch to the sergeant's jaw, knocking him down.

The sergeant bounded to his feet, shook his shoulders, and sent a blow to Toomey's jaw, flattening him. He lay there stunned, shaking his head and blinking.

Suddenly three guards were on the scene. One of them was Sergeant Dan Tyler, who bent over, grasped Toomey's hand, and hoisted him to his feet. "Lieutenant, what are you doing out of your area?"

Toomey scrubbed a palm over his eyes while still shaking his head. He stared hard at Tyler and surprised him by hooking a terrific right to his temple.

Before Toomey could move another muscle, the other two guards seized him, wrestled him to the ground, and pinned him there. While Dan Tyler was getting up, one of the guards who held Toomey said, "You're gonna be sorry you hit Sergeant Tyler! Lieutenant Fisher saw it, and is on his way. You'll taste of the whip now."

Tyler stood over them, rubbing his jaw. Fisher quickly drew up. He glared down at the man who was held in the iron grip of the two guards. "What's your name, Lieutenant?"

Toomey swallowed hard. "Edgar Toomey."

"Well, Edgar Toomey, you are going to be punished severely for striking Sergeant Tyler. Pick him up, men. He's going to the whipping post."

Toomey's face turned gray.

The other prisoners in the area looked on, as well as those in nearby areas. The guards in the towers were watching, and one close to the gate was hurrying down the stairs. When he reached the ground, he dashed toward the commandant's cabin.

Dan Tyler took a step closer to Fisher. "Lieutenant…"

"Yes?"

"How about letting it go this time? Toomey is understandably under a heavy strain, having just arrived here at the prison camp. Since it was me he punched, I'm asking you to spare him the whipping. He needs discipline for leaving his area, but not the severity of the whip."

Toomey set astonished eyes on Tyler, wondering why this Rebel sergeant would want to show him mercy—especially after he had just punched him and knocked him down.

Fisher was pondering Tyler's words when Captain Henry Wirz appeared, panting. "What's going on, here?"

Dan Tyler explained to Wirz that Toomey had punched him, and gave the same reason to him as he had to Fisher for leniency in the first offense.

At that instant, the Union sergeant stepped up. "Captain Wirz, this all started when Toomey came into this area and demanded that I give him my tent because he outranks me. When I told him he couldn't have it and reminded him that he was out of his area, he punched me. I punched him back, and before he could get up, Sergeant Tyler and these other two guards showed up."

Wirz set his eyes on Toomey. "You broke the rule on leaving your area. For this, you will be made to stand at attention for the rest of the day, and all night. You will be denied supper and breakfast. And because you would dare to strike one of the guards, you will be given twenty lashes at the whipping post in addition to these other punishments."

Tyler cleared his throat gently. "Sir, I—"

"Request denied, Sergeant. I appreciate your commiseration for this man, but he needs to learn his lesson. Take him to the whipping post. I'll be right behind you to give instructions to Sergeant Landrum."

Tyler gripped Toomey's arm. "Let's go. The whipping post is over there by the barn and corral."

Reluctantly, Toomey walked alongside Tyler as they moved across the compound. Toomey noticed the men in his area looking on. Captain William Linden was shaking his head.

Tyler and Toomey were several steps ahead of Wirz, Fisher, and the other guards. Toomey glared at Tyler. "How come you tried to keep me from bein' whipped? We're enemies. And besides that, I punched you."

"I'll tell you why. I'm a Christian, Lieutenant. And as a born-again child of God, I wanted to show you compassion. I know being captured and locked up has to be very rough on a man."

Fire leaped into Toomey's eyes and wrath reddened his face. In a mocking, singsong manner, he said, *"You wanted to show me compassion.* Bah! I hate you born-again types who think you're so high and mighty. You're just a bunch of hypocrites who want to make yourselves look good with your facade of compassion."

"You're wrong," Dan said. "It is just that we born-again types have experienced the compassion of the Lord Jesus Christ in forgiving our sins and saving our souls. We want to show the same kind of compassion and forgiveness to those who have wronged us."

Toomey spit on the ground and swore. "You hypocrite! If I could get you alone, I'd beat you to a pulp! Then the real Dan Tyler would surface, wouldn't he?"

"Cool down, Toomey. You're only going to make things harder on yourself."

Suddenly Toomey leaped a step ahead of Tyler, pivoted, and swung a fist at his face. Tyler dodged the blow and sent a thrust to his jaw, knocking him down.

Captain Wirz and Lieutenant Fisher rushed up, as well as the guards.

"Pick him up!" commanded Wirz.

Two of the guards lifted a dazed Toomey to his feet, holding him securely. Wirz's features were beet red as he faced Toomey. "Just for swinging at Sergeant Tyler, you're going to get an additional ten lashes at the whipping post. Maybe that'll settle you down!"

While Toomey was trying to shake the cobwebs from the walls of his brain, he was dragged to the whipping post. His brain was clearing when he focused on a massive man with sergeant's stripes on his shirt. There was a bullwhip in his hand. The tail of the whip lay in a coil on the ground. Toomey's jaw slacked.

Wirz stepped in front of him. "Lieutenant Toomey, meet Sergeant Whip Landrum. His real name is Bartholomew, but I think you can guess why we call him Whip."

Toomey's face was now deathly pale.

One of the guards removed Toomey's shirt, then he was tied to the whipping post with a leather thong. His entire body quivered.

A half dozen horses in the corral looked on curiously.

"Okay, Whip," said the commandant. "Give him thirty lashes."


When the whipping had been administered, Edgar Toomey's back was laced with bright red welts. Some were seeping blood. His wrists were released from the leather thong, and a guard held him up while another one put his shirt on him.

Captain Wirz stood before Toomey again. "Sergeant Tyler is going to escort you back to your area. I hope you will learn your lesson by the time it's all over, Lieutenant Edgar Toomey." Then he said to Fisher, "Assign two guards to watch this man all night in his area. They are to make sure he stands at attention the entire time. He will get no supper tonight and no breakfast in the morning."

Toomey gave Wirz a dull look, but remained silent.

Dan Tyler took hold of Toomey's arm. "Let's go, Lieutenant."

As Dan was escorting the man back to his assigned area, Toomey looked at him with hate-filled eyes.

Dan sighed. "You had better get over this rebellious spirit, Lieutenant, or there will be more discipline."

Toomey's lips were tight against his teeth.

When they reached the area, all the men were looking on. Captain William Linden stepped up to meet them. "Edgar, when are you going to learn that you can't buck the whole world?"

Toomey's face was like a metal mask. In spite of it, the pain he was experiencing showed in his eyes. "I got nothin' to say to you, Linden."

Keith Lewis and Todd Zediker were waiting. Toomey moved past Linden and drew up to his friends. Tyler was still at his side.

Lewis asked, "Are you hurtin' much, Edgar?"

"Naw. The whip didn't hurt at all. I'm fine."

Lewis and Zediker exchanged glances and shook their heads.

Dan saw the two guards coming who would be with Toomey until morning.

He looked at Toomey. "We both know the whip did hurt you, Lieutenant. I hope the pain eases soon."

Toomey's eyes were like bits of slate. "Haven't you got someplace to go, you pious hypocrite?"

Dan held his gaze for a few seconds. "Your guards are here." With that, he turned and walked away.

Zediker's brow furrowed. "Your two guards?"

"Yeah. For mixin' it up with Tyler I got whipped, and for leavin' my assigned area, I gotta stand at attention from now till mornin'. They're here to see that I do it. No supper. No breakfast."

"You should know better than to resist a guard," said Lewis, "and you shouldn't have gone over there to that other area."

While the guards were drawing close, Toomey set cold eyes on Dan Tyler. "Someday when this war is over, I'm gonna find that Dan Tyler and beat him to a pulp."

Zediker eyed him with amazement. "The guards told us that Tyler tried to persuade Wirz not to have you whipped, even though you punched him. I don't understand your hatred for the man."

"Tyler is one of those religious fanatics that calls himself a born-again Christian. I can see right through him. His supposed effort to keep me from bein' whipped was only to make himself look good. He's nothin' but a two-faced hypocrite."

The guards drew up. "Toomey, we're going to put you over here at the edge of the area. You will stand at full attention until we tell you to do otherwise. If you give us any trouble, you'll pay a little visit to Whip Landrum again. Got it?"

Toomey gave them a bland look. "Yeah. I got it."

As the weeks passed, Edgar Toomey continued to be a problem, especially to Dan Tyler. Because of the rules laid down by Captain Wirz, Tyler was forced to see that Toomey was disciplined in various ways for his rebellion.

On Saturday, November 5, Dan was at the infirmary getting a damaged ear stitched up when Captain Wirz came in. Dan was sitting on the examining table while the prison physician worked on the ear. Wirz said, "Your pals Clay Holden and Joel Stevens came to my cabin and told me that Toomey jumped you and tried to tear your ear off, Sergeant. Is that so?"

"Yes, sir."

"Well, he's crossed the line, now. This is enough. He has been whipped four times and put under all kinds of discipline, but nothing seems to work. This is the fourth time he has attacked you. I'll order a firing squad for dawn tomorrow."

Dan's features pinched. "Please, sir. I'm the only one Toomey has attacked physically. Don't kill him. I know we have no way of putting him in solitary confinement, or I would say we should do that. But please don't kill him."

Wirz sighed. "That goes against your Christian principles, does it?"

"Yes, sir. To kill the enemy in battle is one thing, but to put him before a firing squad is another. He has not committed a capital crime."

Wirz thought on it. "Well, I could have him put in wrist and ankle chains. Would you object to that?"

"No. He definitely needs to be constrained."

"All right, Sergeant. I'll have him put in chains. Is his ear going to be all right, Doctor?"

"He'll be fine, Captain."

On Tuesday, November 22, when Toomey had just been whipped again for trying to attack Sergeant Dan Tyler in spite of his chains, he was lying facedown on the ground next to the hole he had dug for himself. Lewis and Zediker were at their spots close by. Tyler crossed the area and drew up to him. Pain showed in Toomey's face as he twisted his head and looked up. "What do you want?"

"When are you going to learn, Toomey? Do you like pain?"

Toomey only glared at him.

Tyler looked at Lewis and Zediker. "You two better talk some sense into your friend's head."

When Tyler was gone, Lewis said, "Edgar, your hatred for Tyler is gonna end up gettin' you killed if you're not careful."

"That's right," put in Zediker. "He ain't done nothin' to make you hate him like you do."

"He's done enough," Toomey said flatly. "There's only one person on this earth I hate more than him, and that's William Linden. One day, Linden is gonna die at my hand."

Lewis looked at him. "Well, you can do it after the War is over, if you don't get beat to death with Landrum's whip before that. In the meantime, why don't you wise up? You've got scars on your back and you're chained like a wild beast. Didn't Tyler tell you a week ago that if you started acting right, he would see to it that those chains came off?"

"Yeah."

"Then use your head, man. Straighten up and save yourself some misery."

Toomey thought on it for a long moment. "Okay, guys, you're right. I won't attack Tyler anymore. It'd be good to have these chains off. I'll track him down after the War and give him his well-deserved beatin'. As for Linden, I'll find the right time to take care of him."


On Friday, December 23, at Memorial Hospital, Lieutenant Nate Conrad was sitting in a chair beside his bed, gazing out a nearby window at the snow-covered landscape. It had snowed every day for the past week, and even now snow was falling from a pewter-gray sky in big fat flakes.

Nate was healing slower than he had hoped, but at least he could now leave his bed for a few hours a day to sit in the chair with the help of one of the male attendants.

In spite of the slow healing process, Nate was a happy man. He and Millie were falling deeper in love every day. Though they were not allowed time alone in some private place, they had been able to talk in whispers to each other at times and express their love.

Despite the wool blanket covering his legs, Nate shivered when a gust of wind slammed against the window, driving the snow against it and obscuring his view. He gripped the arms of the chair as he painfully lifted his feet up and down, doing the exercises prescribed by Dr. Gary Medford. It was two days before Christmas, and Nate considered his ability to move his legs the best Christmas gift of 1864.

He could see it snowing outside. His thoughts went to Millie, who was busy with her other patients. Though their plans were only tentative at that point, he knew the day would come when he would make Millie his bride. A vision of her beautiful face came before him, bringing a smile to his lips.

*I want to be able to give her a whole man, not one tied to a chair,* he thought. *I must walk again, but first I have to graduate to a wheelchair. And that can only come when I can operate these legs well enough to get in and out of it, as Dr. Medford said.*

Clenching his teeth against the pain that stabbed his back, he concentrated on moving his legs up and down again. This time he did it for five minutes. He rested again for a few minutes, then began the exercises again. He kept it up for another five minutes.

Millie had been watching him from the far side of the ward. Tears made a path down her cheeks as she witnessed his valiant attempts to do his exercises.

"You can do it, my love," she whispered, gripping one hand with the other. "And one day we will meet at a church altar and we can repeat our vows before a preacher."

ON NEW YEAR'S DAY 1865, Lieutenant Nate Conrad was sitting in the chair next to his bed, doing his leg exercises. It was midmorning, and he was thinking of Millie Ross, who at the moment was in a meeting with head nurse Letha Phillips and some of the other nurses.

In the beds on either side of him were Captain Brent Stoffell and Sergeant Bob Kirgan. Both men had been there since mid-December.

Kirgan smiled at him. "I'll say one thing for you, Lieutenant. You're persistent. I can tell you still feel pain in your back when you exercise those legs, but you keep it up anyway."

"Mm-hmm," grunted Nate, keeping the legs in motion. "I want to graduate from this chair to one with wheels on it. Dr. Medford won't let me do it until I convince him I'm ready. I can't graduate from a wheelchair to crutches unless I first get in the wheelchair."

"Any idea how soon you might get your wheelchair?" asked Captain Stoffell.

"Dr. Medford told me last week I was close. As you know, he examined me yesterday, but I couldn't get a committal from him. I sure hope it's soon."

Kirgan looked down the long row of beds. "Hey! Lookee there, Lieutenant! Dr. Medford's coming this way, and he's pushing an empty wheelchair."

Nate turned to look. "He sure is! But…maybe it's for someone else."

Stoffell chuckled. "We'll soon find out."

Nate's pulse quickened as Dr. Gary Medford drew near and he wheeled the chair to a stop at his bed.

A broad smile lit up Medford's face as he set his eyes on Nate. "Well, Lieutenant, guess what? Your time has come. I talked to Dr. Walton after examining you yesterday, and we're in agreement that you are now ready for this wheelchair. Your back is healed sufficiently that it can take the pressure of wheeling the chair. A great deal of this is because you have done your leg exercises so consistently. You can now move around the ward and get to know the other soldiers who are confined to their beds."

Nate's face immediately showed the joy he felt.

"Dr. Walton told me that he is going to sign the official papers that will get you a medical discharge from the army. He and I agree there is no way you could return to active duty."

"This is good news, Doctor. Of course, if I could, I would go back to the War, but my back is telling me I couldn't do it."

The doctor smiled again and ran his gaze to the men on both sides. "I've got some more good news."

"What is it, Doctor?" asked Stoffell.

"Word just came by wire to Dr. Walton from a doctor friend of his at one of Washington's big hospitals. The experts in Washington are saying there are some strong indications that the South is losing the War. These experts, which include President Abraham Lincoln, are predicting that the Confederacy will surrender within six months, seven at the longest."

"Wonderful!" said Nate. "If anybody has his hands on the pulse of the War, it's the president."

Brent Stoffell sighed. "I sure hope he's right. As soon as I get out of here, I want to go home to my wife and children."

"I don't have a wife and children," spoke up Bob Kirgan, "but I've got a sweetheart who's waiting at home for me. Plus my parents."

At that moment, excited voices were heard at the beds nearest the front door of the ward as nurses began telling the patients the same news.

Nate looked that way. "Can I get in my wheelchair, now, Doctor? I've been looking forward to this for so long."

"Sure. Let me help you."

Before the doctor could take hold of Nate, he was on his feet, steadying himself with the arm of the chair. "I've been getting myself out of bed and into this chair for quite some time, now, Doctor. I have to hang on to one, then the other, so if you'll steady the wheelchair for me, I'll get myself in it."

Dr. Medford gripped the wheelchair. "All right. I'm watching. Just be careful."

Using the arm of the chair to steady himself, Nate took hold of the wheelchair and eased into it. "Ah! This feels good!"

The doctor bent down in front of him. "Lift your feet so I can let down these footrests."

Nate lifted his feet. The doctor let the footrests down. "I'm going to stay with you for a few minutes while you wheel yourself around. Go ahead."

Nate gripped the hand rims and put himself in motion. Besides Stoffell and Kirgan, other men in the area were watching and began to cheer. He rolled himself one direction for a few seconds, then turned around and went the other direction. When he came back to his bed, Dr. Medford said, "You're doing great, Lieutenant. Don't overdo it. Especially this first day. You'll need to work your way into it."

Nate nodded. "I see what you mean. My arms are feeling it already. I've been laid up too long."

"Keep that in mind. Let me tell you this. My plan is to have you up on crutches by the first week of February."

Nate's eyes brightened. "Now you're talking!"

"I knew that would perk you up. If you continue to do as well as you have in the last few weeks, you just might be able to go home by April."

"That's music to my ears, Doctor. Believe me, I'll keep working at it."

At that moment, Letha Phillips appeared, her gaze fixed on Nate. "Well, well, what have we here? Lieutenant, I'm so glad you finally have graduated to a wheelchair."

"Me too, ma'am. Thank you."

"Miss Ross will certainly be glad to see this." The look in her eyes told Nate she knew that he and Millie had a special closeness.

Nate nodded. "Yes, ma'am. I'm sure she will."

Letha gave him a grin and walked away.

"I'll leave you, now," said Medford. "You can wheel yourself around a little more, but don't go at it too long—more than a half hour."

"I'll go easy, Doctor. Promise."

Medford patted his shoulder. "All right. And when you need to get back in bed, you have somebody help you. I don't trust the brake on this wheelchair. That's an order, understand?"

Nate saluted. "Yes, sir, General Doctor Medford, sir!"

Stoffell and Kirgan laughed. The doctor chuckled.

For the next half hour, Nate visited men who were confined to their beds. They talked about home, family, and the message of hope that had come that day, encouraging them that the War would soon be over.

Nate was wheeling away from a soldier's bed, intending to return to his own bed when he saw a smiling Millie Ross coming toward him. He wheeled her direction.

"Oh, this is wonderful! I'm so glad to see you in this wheelchair!" said Millie.

"It feels great, I'm telling you. And guess what?"

"What?"

"Dr. Medford said his plan is to have me up on crutches by the first week of February."

"Oh, darling, I—" Suddenly, Millie put a hand to her mouth, looking around to see if anyone had heard her. If they had, no one showed it. She bent low over him. "That's really encouraging. I'll do anything I can to help see that it happens."

"I'm sure you've heard about President Lincoln's prediction that the Confederates will surrender in six or seven months."

"Yes! Oh, I hope he's right."

"Me too. Everyone in the North and the South needs to get back to a normal life."

"So how long have you been wheeling around in the chair, Lieutenant?"

He grinned. "I like 'darling' better."

Millie blushed.

"I've been wheeling around about half an hour. Dr. Medford told me not to overdo it. I was just heading back to my bed."

"Good. Dr. Medford is right. Using your arms to put the wheels in motion is bound to put a strain on your back."

"I can tell that. But…ah…there wouldn't be as much strain if someone were to push me back to my bed."

Millie smiled. "Just *someone?*"

Nate lowered his voice. "Well, just someone who has red hair, is strikingly beautiful, her initials are M. R., and she's a nurse in this hospital."

"Lieutenant Conrad, that kind of talk will get you a ride for sure."

Nate grinned. "Do you think you might be able to get permission from Mrs. Phillips to let you wheel me out into the hall, since I've been confined in this ward so long?"

"Well-l-l…"

He whispered, "If you could do that, we might find a place where we could talk more privately than right here, or at my bed where other patients, as well as nurses and their assistants, are so close by."

A smile graced her lips. "I'll wheel you back to your bed. You can stay in the wheelchair while I go ask Mrs. Phillips."

"Those are welcome words. Let's go."

Millie wheeled Nate to his bed, parked the wheelchair beside it, and hurried toward the nurse's station.

Brent Stoffell said, "Nate, I'm so glad you finally got your wheelchair."

"Me too," came Bob Kirgan's voice.

"Thanks, guys. It's a real encouragement. It means I'm just that much closer to being dismissed from the hospital. I can hardly wait to go home."

Stoffell chuckled. "When you're dismissed and you head for home, are you going to take Miss Ross with you?"

Nate chuckled back and put a surprised look on his face. "Hey, Brent, that's a good idea! I hadn't thought of that!"

Both men laughed.

"Yeah, sure," said Stoffell. "Who do you think you're kidding?"

"I don't know what you're talking about."

"You're not fooling us, Lieutenant Nathan Conrad," said Kirgan. "It's written all over both of you. You two are in love, aren't you?"

Nate grinned. "Okay, so you guys figured it out. But we can't show it openly, since I'm a patient and she's employed by the hospital."

"I can understand that," said Stoffell. "But when you do leave here, you *are* taking her with you, aren't you?"

"I sure want to, but since we've had no privacy at all, I haven't even been able to ask her to marry me. This isn't something you try to whisper when other people are as close as you guys. However, at this moment, she's seeking permission from Mrs. Phillips to wheel me out into the hall. If permission is granted and we can find a reasonably private spot, I'm popping the question today."

Both men smiled and were about to comment when Millie returned. "Letha granted me permission to take you for a ride in the hall as long as I have you back in that bed to rest inside half an hour."

"Well, what are we waiting for?"

As Millie wheeled him away, the two soldiers grinned at each other.

When they passed through the door into the hall, Nate looked around. "Oh, so that's what it looks like out here. I'd forgotten."

Millie chuckled.

As they moved slowly along the hall, Nate pointed to a spot up ahead where there was a large bay window. "How about if we pull over at the window?"

"Sure."

Millie rolled the wheelchair up close to the window. "How's that?"

"Perfect." He glanced outside at the snow-blanketed hospital grounds. "It's nice to get a different view than I've had in the ward."

People were moving up and down the hall in a constant stream.

Nate looked up at the redhead. "Since time is short, and we can finally talk without someone listening, I...I want to ask you a question."

She smiled and leaned against the windowsill. "What is the question?"

Nate started to take hold of her hand, but checked himself, remembering there were people passing by.

"I wish we could hold hands too. Go ahead with your question."

Nate's heart was fluttering. It came out quickly. "Millie, when I get out of the hospital, will you marry me?"

Tears filmed her eyes. "Nate, darling, I've been living for this moment, and I've already said yes in my heart. Now, I'll say it with my lips. Yes, I will marry you."

Joy had Nate's face beaming. "Oh, Millie, my sweet, I love you so much."

"And I love you so much." Love light was glowing from her misty eyes.

"I sure would like to seal it with a kiss, sweetheart, but this will have to do for now." As he spoke, Nate took hold of her hands, making it look like she was helping him adjust his position in the wheelchair. Quickly, he planted a kiss on each hand.

Millie brushed a tear from her cheek and put both hands to her lips as if to lift the kisses from them. "Darling, if President Lincoln and the other Washington experts are correct, the War will be over in June or July. I wish it would end today, but if…if it ended early in June, we could have a June wedding."

"How about an April wedding?"

"Hmm?"

"When Dr. Medford brought me my wheelchair, he told me that Dr. Walton is going to sign the papers that will give me a medical discharge from the army, and he also told me that he thinks I'll be able to go home by April."

"He did? Oh, that's wonderful! Well, if that's the case, of course it will be an April wedding. I assume you want to get married in Harrisburg."

"Well, actually, I was thinking that we'd get married right here in Frederick as soon as I'm released from the hospital. The wedding will be a small one, of course, but at least Paula and Nancy could be there."

"I'd like that."

"All right, it's settled. I'll take you home as my blushing bride."

Millie moved to him, leaned over, and took hold of his hands. "Here, let me help you adjust yourself again."

Nate grinned as she kissed both of his hands. He pressed the places where she had kissed them to his lips. "Okay, it's sealed with kisses now."

Tears of joy brimmed in the eyes of both of them. For the moment, Nate and Millie were content to just look at each other, reading the love that dwelt there.

After a moment, Nate said, "I wanted to be at least up on crutches before I asked you to marry me, so you'd see that you wouldn't be marrying a man who couldn't walk at all; but I just couldn't wait any longer."

A fresh wave of love warmed Millie's heart. "I've watched you work tirelessly, exercising your legs as Dr. Medford had urged you to do, but I had already made up my mind that if you asked me to marry you, I was going to do so regardless of how long it would take you to walk again. And even if I knew you would never walk again, I would still marry you."

"Oh, I wish I could hug you."

"I wish you could too. But our day will come, darling."

"It can't come too soon for me. I can hardly wait to show you off to my friends in Harrisburg."

"Darling, speaking of Harrisburg…"

"Yes?"

"I assume there's a hospital."

"Oh yes. It's a large one too."

"Do you think I might be able to get a job there? Since you might not be able to go to work for a while, my income would take care of us."

"I have no doubt they would hire you immediately. They are always short of nurses."

"All right. We'll get married as soon as you're released from the hospital. We'll go to Harrisburg and build our lives together in your hometown."

Nate closed his eyes. "I'm the most fortunate man in all the world."

"I'll do my best to keep you thinking that."

He looked up at her tenderly. "I don't think it, sweetheart, I *know* it. Please...please help me adjust myself in this wheelchair again."

When their hands met, Nate kissed both of Millie's hands again.

Suddenly, it struck Nate that he could hear no footsteps and no voices in the hall. He looked both directions. "Millie, for the moment, we're alone."

"Yes, I see that." Quickly, she bent down and they stole their first kiss.


At Harrisburg a cold, hard winter had set in. During the warmer months, Jenny Linden had taken her mother for walks on Fridays and Sundays, her two days off from work. But now—in January—Myrna remained inside every day, with a fire crackling in the parlor's fireplace and in the kitchen stove. She occupied herself with what housework she could do, and watching people and vehicles pass by on the snow-laden street from the parlor window.

Dr. Adam Griffin was coming by the house once a week to check on her and to keep her supplied with paraldehyde and sedative powders, which to a degree, were helping to keep her stable. Jenny had her hands full, however, trying to keep her mother's spirits up concerning her father. Myrna was having frequent nightmares, where she observed Captain William Linden being killed in one violent way or another. Only by administering large doses was Jenny able to keep her mother from sinking deeper into her depression.

Jenny and Myrna talked daily about President Lincoln's words—as reported continually in the newspapers—which were designed to give the people of the North hope that the Civil War would be over soon. Lincoln's optimism helped Jenny to cling to the hope that both her father and Nate would be coming home in a few months.

Late one cold, snowy Sunday afternoon, the two were sitting side by side near the parlor window, watching buggies and carriages pass by on the street. People could be seen through the falling snow, walking along the sidewalk with their heads bent against the cold wind.

The scene was gray, marked only by the spider-web tracery of trees—firs, their needles dark green beneath the clumps of snow on every bough; and bare oaks and maples, their limbs spindly.

At one point, Jenny went to the kitchen to put an apple pie in the oven. From time to time, she made a trip to the kitchen to check on the pie.

Soon evening came on, pulling the gray of the heavily clouded day through the yards, past the frozen lawns, and from the snow-muffled houses with their tightly-closed windows. Jenny left her chair and lit the three lanterns in the parlor, filling the room with a soft yellow glow. She returned to her chair, sat down, and sighed.

Myrna turned and smiled. "I wish your papa was here to enjoy the evening with us."

"Oh yes, Mama. And Nate too."

Jenny had written her twenty-fourth letter to Nate Conrad the night before and had placed it in the drawer with all the others for him to read when he finally came home. But having written the letter, she was feeling the warmth of the love she was sure Nate had in his heart for her.

Turning to her mother, Jenny said, "Mama, do you realize if President Lincoln is right—and I hope he is—that by the time all of this snow is melted away, it won't be long till Papa and Nate come home."

Myrna turned her tired eyes on her daughter. "Why do I keep having bad dreams about your papa being killed in the War if he is coming home to us?"

Jenny reached over and patted her arm. "Please, Mama. I keep telling you those are only bad dreams. Nothing more. They go with your depression, but there is no reason to believe they are anything more than horrible nightmares that will be gone as soon as Papa walks through that door. You've got to hold on to that."

Myrna's brow furrowed. "I'm trying, honey, but it's so hard."

"Just remember the love he has for you. This will help you, Mama. It sure helps me as I think of Nate. He and I have such a deep love for each other. We're going to be so happy when he comes home and we get married."

"Honey, I need to ask you something."

"What, Mama?"

"If...if it really should turn out that your papa doesn't come home from the War, but Nate does—what are you going to do with me?"

"Mama, what do you mean?"

"I mean, if you marry Nate, you'll be making your own home. I...I can't stay here alone."

Jenny rose from her chair, bent over, and kissed her mother's forehead. "If it should be that Papa doesn't come home from the War, sweet Mama, Nate and I will take you into our home. I would never abandon you."

Tears swelled up in Myrna's eyes. "Thank you, honey. Thank you."

Jenny kissed her forehead again. "I've been thinking, Mama, it might be a nice change to have our supper in here by the fireplace. Would you like that?"

Suddenly, Myrna gasped, her eyes fixed outside. Her hands flew up to her mouth. "Jenny! Look! It's your papa! He's come home!"

Jenny focused her eyes on the obscure figure of a man moving in the haze of falling, swirling snow. Her heart banged her ribs. "Mama, I can't make out who it is. It's too dark to see his face."

Myrna clapped her hands. "It's William, that's who it is! My bad dreams were just bad dreams. Oh, Jenny, your papa has come home!"

The man was almost to the porch. Jenny whirled, picked up one of the lanterns, ran across the room, and darted into the hall. She hurried to the front door and pulled it open just as the sound of footsteps were heard scrunching snow on the porch. The glow of the lantern exposed the man's face.

"Oh! Dr. Griffin!"

Dr. Adam Griffin wiped snowflakes from his face and smiled. "Hello, Jenny. I was just making a house call at the Montgomery house three doors down, and I thought since I was so close, I'd walk over here and see how your mother is doing."

"Please come in."

When Griffin stepped through the doorway, Jenny closed the door and faced him. "Mama's been about the same, Doctor. She—she spotted you coming into the yard, and with the blowing snow and darkness gathering, she thought it was Papa coming home."

"I see. Guess I should have driven the buggy down here."

"No, no. It's all right. Let's go into the parlor so she can see that it's you."

When Griffin followed Jenny into the parlor, Myrna was on her feet, staring at them, her countenance showing the tension she was feeling. Abruptly, the muscles of her face relaxed. "Oh. Dr. Griffin. I thought you were William."

He moved up close to her. "Yes, Jenny told me. I'm sorry it's only your doctor, but as I explained to Jenny, I was down here at the Montgomerys' making a house call. Since I was so close, I thought I'd stop in and see how you are doing."

"Well, you did give me a start, but other than that, I'm doing all right. If only William was here, I'd be doing excellently."

"I understand. If President Lincoln is right, the War will be over in a few months, and William will indeed be coming home."

Griffin then excused himself and left.

Jenny slid Myrna's rocking chair close to the fireplace and tossed a couple of fresh logs on the fire. "Mama, I was asking you about our eating in here for a change. Would you like to eat here by the fire?"

Myrna made her way to the rocking chair and sat down. "That would be nice, honey."

"All right. You sit there and soak up the heat, and I'll get supper ready."

In the kitchen, Jenny pulled the apple pie from the oven and set it on the counter of the cupboard to cool. She added more wood to the fire in the stove, then put tea leaves into the teapot. She already had water heating in the teakettle, which was shooting steam from its spout.

She poured the hot water into the teapot and left it to steep, then made split pea soup with slices of ham, and put it on the stove. Next, she sliced cornbread and buttered it.

She sat down at the kitchen table and waited for the soup to get hot. While waiting, Jenny let her thoughts go to the day she and Nate would marry. *Just think,* she mused, *I'll be Mrs. Nate Conrad. Sounds wonderful!*

When the food was ready, she rubbed a hand over her tired eyes and pushed herself up from the table. The pungent aroma of the split pea soup permeated the kitchen, and Jenny's stomach growled from hunger.

She filled two bowls with the steaming soup and placed them on a tray, adding a small plate of cornbread. When she had put the teapot and two cups on the tray, she carefully carried it to the parlor.

Myrna smiled widely when her daughter entered the room. "That smells delicious, dear. Thank you for working so hard to tempt my appetite."

Jenny placed the tray on the small table that stood by the rocking chair. "You are so welcome, Mama. It is always rewarding to see you eat what I put before you. After all, we don't want Papa to come home and find you a shadow of your former self, do we?"

When Jenny had made sure everything was right for her mother, she brought a straight-backed wooden chair from across the room and sat down, facing her over the small table.

The fire burned brightly in the fireplace and the lanterns gave a rosy glow to the faces of mother and daughter as they enjoyed their repast. They talked quietly about William and Nate coming home in June or July, and periodically gazed out at the falling snow lazily making its way toward the ground past the lace-curtained window.

# 12

MAIL ORDER BRIDE SERIES
NO. 10
1865
USA
AL & JOANNA LACY

IT HAD SNOWED MOST OF THE NIGHT. Mounds were piled against the house and covered the yard when Jenny Linden opened the front door of the house to leave for work.

The sky had cleared just before dawn and the brilliant sun shone down from a clear blue sky. As she closed the door and moved down the porch steps, making deep imprints in the snow, Jenny's breath hung in the still, cold air. Glittering snowflakes, like thousands of diamonds, seemed to dance on the billowy snow.

Jenny squinted against the glare as she carefully picked her way through the eight-inch depth toward the sidewalk. When she reached it, she turned, painted a smile on her face, and waved a gloved hand at her mother who sat in her rocking chair at the parlor window.

Myrna gave a tiny, weak wave back, then dropped her hand into her lap and stared at her daughter.

Jenny's heart felt like a chunk of lead. She paused for a moment, gazing at the forlorn figure in the rocking chair. *She's got that longing look in her eyes again. She'll sit there all day, watching for Papa to come walking into the yard.*

Jenny became suddenly aware of the freezing temperature and the iciness creeping into her feet. She pulled her coat collar up, lowered her chin into it, and moved briskly down the street toward downtown Harrisburg. Her mind was clouded with worry over her mother, but she was still very much aware of the beauty of the bright winter morning.

When Jenny reached the general store, she opened the door and stepped inside. A blast of welcome warm air accosted her. Zack had a roaring fire going in the potbellied stove, and it had warded off the deep chill that had been in the store from the long, cold night. She smiled as she saw that Emma had the coffeepot on top of the stove. The mixed aromas of hot coffee and burning wood permeated the air.

Stomping the snow from her high-top shoes, Jenny moved up to the stove, took off her gloves, stuffed them in her coat pocket, and rubbed her hands together while holding them over the stove. At that moment, she heard footsteps coming from the direction of the office at the rear of the store.

Emma's eyes lit up as she appeared, carrying three coffee mugs. "Good morning, Jenny."

"Good morning, Emma. That coffee sure smells good."

"Well, let's just get some of it in your tummy." As she spoke, Emma set two of the mugs down on a small table near the stove and poured the other one full of coffee. She handed the mug to Jenny. "Here, honey. Sip on this. It'll warm you up on the inside while the stove thaws you on the outside. I'll be right back. Zack wants some coffee too."

"Oh yes! Thank you, Emma. This will have me thawed out in a minute." Jenny sipped gratefully as she watched Emma fill a mug for her husband and hurry away. She set the cup down, took off her coat and scarf, and carried them to the pegs on the wall behind the counter. She straightened the heavy sweater that she had worn under her coat and welcomed the warmth it gave her.

Emma was back shortly, and when she returned, Jenny was at the stove again, sipping her coffee. "This sure hits the spot."

"I'm having some right now, myself." Emma filled her own mug, then the two women discussed President Lincoln's latest comments about the soon end of the War. They drained their mugs just in time to open the store. Jenny went to the window, flipped the closed sign to the other side, and in less than two minutes, customers were filing in.

At midmorning Jenny was at the counter alone, waiting on a customer, when she saw the door open and two young women come in. Laura Denton and Shirley Atwood were in her high school graduating class. She liked both of them, but was a bit cautious of them because they were born-again Christians and talked a lot about Jesus Christ, the Bible, and their church.

Jenny looked past her customer and smiled. "Hello, Laura. Hello, Shirley. Nice to see you."

Smiling back, both young women greeted her warmly, unbuttoned their coats, and headed toward the long rows of shelves to find the items they had come to purchase.

Jenny finished with her customer and another came to the counter, carrying groceries in a hand basket. She had just finished with that person when Laura and Shirley approached the counter with their goods.

"Some snow we got, huh?" said Jenny.

"Enough," said Shirley with a giggle.

Jenny totaled the bills separately, and when they had paid her, she began bagging the items. While she was doing so, she and the girls talked about the War and President Lincoln's messages with the prediction that the Confederacy would surrender within a few months.

Jenny filled the final paper bag, and with a trace of sadness in her eyes, she slid it toward Laura. "I'm glad your fathers weren't allowed in the army when the War broke out. It's really difficult having my father in the War, with no way of communication. Mama is having serious depression problems with him gone, not knowing whether he is dead or alive. It's pretty rough on me too. I'm so worried that Papa may never come home, and that Mama is going to completely lose her mind if he doesn't."

Laura reached across the counter and squeezed Jenny's hand. "My heart goes out to you with this load on your shoulders, Jenny. I'm sure your mother's depression problem is having an awful effect on you, let alone the load you carry about your father being in danger on some battlefield in the South."

Jenny's lower lip quivered. "It's pretty hard."

"We're so sorry, Jenny," said Shirley, leaning close and patting her other hand. "I wish this didn't have to be."

Laura squeezed Jenny's hand again. "Honey, if you and your mother had Jesus in your hearts and lives, He would give you peace and comfort that no one else can."

Shirley nodded. "That peace and comfort would not only be yours concerning your father's state in the War, but concerning your own eternal destiny. We love you and your mother, but it's heaven or hell, Jenny, depending on what you do with Jesus Christ. He is the only one who can cleanse your sins, forgive them, and give you a place in heaven. If you will open your heart to Him, you'll be in heaven forever. But if you don't, it's eternity in hell."

"Both of you have talked to me about this several times at school, and as I told you each time, this being born again and washed in the blood doesn't make sense to me," Jenny said, frowning. "I just can't see it."

"The reason you can't see it is because Satan has you blinded. The Bible says so. Shirley and I have given you the gospel over and over. If you would just let the gospel light shine into your spiritual darkness, you would see it and be saved. Both of us had to do this, as has every person who has become a child of God by the new birth. Every human being comes into the world blinded spiritually by the devil. If you would believe the gospel and open your heart to Jesus, you would have God's guarantee of heaven when you die, and while going through life here on earth, you would have God's peace that passes all understanding."

Jenny noted that other customers were standing in line for service.

She looked past Laura and Shirley, then smiled weakly. "Thanks for shopping here, ladies. It was nice to see you."

Laura and Shirley exchanged glances, picked up their packages, and stepped aside. "We'll be praying for you, honey," Laura said.

"We sure will," Shirley assured her.

Jenny afforded them another faint smile, then started adding up the bill for the next customer.


On Tuesday morning, February 5, at Andersonville Prison Camp, Sergeant Dan Tyler was at the gate in conversation with the two guards in the tower when they saw an army unit coming toward them from the north. The Confederate flag they were carrying was flapping in the breeze.

"Who do you suppose that is?" said Corporal Alan Fleming, focusing on the ten men on horseback.

"Looks like the kind of unit that makes up an escort for an important military leader," said Corporal Jerry Weston.

Dan Tyler nodded. "We'll soon find out. I'll wait. If it's somebody who wants to see the captain, I'll escort them to his cabin."

Moments later, the riders drew up to the gate. Alan Fleming said from the side of his mouth, "From the insignias on the shoulders of the man on the gray roan, he's a general."

"You're the number-one gate man at the moment," said Tyler. "Find out who he is and what he wants."

Fleming stepped to the railing and raised his voice so he could be heard. "Yes, sir, General? What can we do for you?"

The silver-haired man with the droopy mustache replied, "I'm General Stewart Morrison from Fort Benning up by Columbus. I'm on my way down to the army post at Palmyra near Albany. Since we had to pass close by here on the way, I thought I'd stop and spend a few minutes with my old friend, Captain Henry Wirz. Is he here?"

"He is, sir."

Dan stepped up beside Fleming and looked down at Morrison. "General, I'm Sergeant Dan Tyler. I'll escort you to the captain's quarters."

"Much obliged, Sergeant."

Moments later, the men in the escort unit were being taken to the mess hall while Dan Tyler led General Morrison up to the captain's cabin and knocked on the door.

"Enter!" came Wirz's voice.

Dan opened the door. "Captain, I have General Stewart Morrison. He would like to see you."

Wirz sprang from the chair behind his desk. "Stew! I...I mean—"

"It's all right, Captain," said Dan. "He told me you were old friends. I won't tell anybody you called him Stew."

Both officers laughed.

Wirz and Morrison shook hands, then Morrison said, "Henry, I can only stay a few minutes. I'm on my way down to the army post at Palmyra. Just thought I'd stop for a few minutes."

"Could you stay for lunch?"

"Sorry, no. Sergeant Tyler was kind enough to let my men grab some coffee while I'm visiting you. But when I say a few minutes, I mean no more than thirty of them."

Wirz nodded. "All right. Then we'll make do with a half hour's chat. I've got some coffee on the stove. Want some?"

"Sure."

Wirz set his gaze on Tyler, who was about to back out the door. "Sergeant, when General Morrison leaves, I need you to have Lieutenant Edgar Toomey brought to me. I've got to have a talk with him."

"I understand, sir. I'll watch for General Morrison to leave, then I'll have Corporals Holden and Stevens bring him to you." With that, Dan stepped out and closed the door.

Wirz gestured to an overstuffed chair near the potbellied stove. "Have a seat, Stew."

Wirz poured coffee for both of them and sat down, facing his friend.

They chatted about the early days in the Civil War when they served in the same regiment together, then Wirz asked, "So what's your trip to Palmyra about?"

"The condition of the Confederacy."

Wirz's eyebrows arched. "You mean in light of what Lincoln is telling everybody up North?"

"Yes. The morale of our troops is falling quickly because they can see what Lincoln sees. I received a dispatch from General Robert E. Lee, asking me to meet with General P. G. Beauregard at Palmyra. We have to find a way to encourage the troops."

Wirz sighed. "And how are you going to do that, Stew? Lie?"

Morrison shook his head, stared at the floor a moment, then raised his eyes to Wirz. "That's about it. Ever since the Confederate currency was devalued in October of '63, things have gotten worse financially. You've seen it. I know the problem you're having here with prisoners starving to death because you don't have enough food to feed them. And I've noticed that some of your guards are looking pretty thin too."

"It's been bad. I won't try to kid you. Our food allotment from the government is pretty small. First and foremost, the guards have to have food. So with the prisoners getting less to eat, more and more of them are coming down with scurvy because of the lack of proper nourishment. The only thing that's helping the food problem right now is that so many of the prisoners are dying from pneumonia brought on by exposure to the winter weather. We don't have shelter for most of the men, and they're dying like flies. Infections are killing them fast too. With the unsanitary conditions brought on because we have no soap for the prisoners to use when they bathe or wash their clothes, nor do we have disinfectants to kill the germs in their areas, they're dying right now at the rate of over seventy a day. Other than pneumonia, scurvy is killing most of them."

Morrison sighed. "The reputation of this place is known far and wide."

"Yeah, I know. It isn't because we want it this way, but when they give me over thirty thousand prisoners to feed and try to keep alive, but don't provide enough food and medicine, it gets disastrous."

"I know that, Henry. The Confederacy is just about broke. We're running out of gunpowder and bullets, as well as cannonballs. Soon we'll have to fight those Yankees with knives, bayonets, clubs, and fists."

Wirz was squeezing his hands together until the knuckles were white. "Stew, we're done for, aren't we?"

Morrison drew a shaky breath and let it out slowly through his nose. "General Beauregard and I can't let on to our men that it's this bad, as can none of the other Confederate military leaders, but yes…we're done for. Lincoln knows this. That's why he can be so encouraging to the people up North and to the Union Army. It's just a matter of time. As you know, Lincoln is predicting the Confederate forces will collapse by June or July, but he's being generous. I'd say we might have till the first part of April at best."

Wirz's features were pale. "Well, I guess all we can do at this point is to keep doing our jobs as best we can."

Morrison stood up. "That's about it. Well, Henry, I've got to get going. It's been nice seeing you."

Wirz walked the general to the gate where the other men of the unit were waiting for him. They mounted and rode out. By the time Wirz reached his cabin, Corporals Clay Holden and Joel Stevens were on the porch with a sullen Edgar Toomey between them.

Toomey regarded Wirz with a dull look as he drew up, opened the door, and said, "Inside."

Wirz sat down at his desk, and Toomey was made to sit on the wooden chair in front of it while the corporals stood flanking him.

The captain's eyes were hard as he looked at Toomey across the desk. "I'm sick and tired of your attitude toward Sergeant Dan Tyler, Toomey. This is going to change, or you're going to face discipline that'll make you wish you were never born."

Toomey's jaw jutted. "I haven't laid a hand on him since that day back in November when I tried to choke him with my wrist chains."

"I know, but I'm getting daily reports from the other guards that you are pouring out verbal abuse to him continually. Now I want it stopped."

"Tyler hasn't tattled on me?"

"No. It's the other guards who have told me. And when I allowed your chains to be removed a month ago, it was the other guards who told you that I did it at Sergeant Tyler's request. He didn't tell you himself, did he?"

Toomey cleared his throat. "Well, no. He didn't."

Wirz frowned. "Don't you have an ounce of appreciation in you? I'd think you would want to thank him."

Toomey's eyes were wintry. "He just did it to make himself look good to you and the other guards. You know, like he was a saint or somethin'. I don't like him."

"Well, you'd better give it a try."

"Certainly there can't be a rule at this pig sty you call a prison camp, forcin' the prisoners to like all these Rebel guards."

Wirz looked at him silently.

"Well, is there such a rule, Captain Wirz?" demanded Toomey. "If so, I'd like to see it in writin'."

"Of course there is no such written rule, and I can't force you to like Sergeant Tyler, but you can keep it to yourself and quit being insolent to him. This isn't a request, Lieutenant Toomey. It's a command. Break it once more, and you'll wish you were never born."

Toomey didn't like the look in Wirz's eyes. "All right, Captain, I'll keep my hatred for Tyler to mys—"

"*Sergeant* Tyler," corrected Wirz with a rasp in his voice.

Toomey cleared his throat. "I'll keep my hatred for *Sergeant* Tyler to myself."

"You'd better mean it. No more warnings."

Toomey nodded. "I got it."

Wirz looked up at the men who flanked the prisoner. "Get him out of here."

Holden and Stevens ushered Toomey out the door and while they were walking toward Toomey's area, Stevens said, "You'd better heed what Captain Wirz said, mister. I've seen the captain get angry at insolent prisoners before. You don't want to find out the hard way just how mean he can get."

Toomey did not reply.

"Did you ever find out that Captain Wirz had once ordered you to be shot by a firing squad?" said Holden.

Toomey looked up at him, eyes wide. "No."

"Well, he did. And it was Sergeant Tyler who talked him out of it."

"You don't say?"

"I *do* say."

"Hmpf. Well, whattya know?"

"So you see, he saved your life."

Toomey chuckled dryly. "Yeah. For his own glory. It just made him look good to Captain Wirz."

Clay Holden laid hold on Toomey's arm with a tight grip and pulled him to a stop. Joel Stevens took hold of Toomey's other arm.

"Tell me, Toomey—why do you hate Sergeant Tyler?" asked Holden.

"I've got my reasons."

"Let's hear them."

"All right. First of all, I despise these hypocritical born-again Christians who think they're better than everybody else."

"Well, I'm one of those born-again Christians and so is Corporal Stevens. We don't think we're better than anybody else. We're simply sinners saved by the grace of God. And we know for a fact that this is also Sergeant Tyler's way of thinking. We are his closest friends, and we know him well."

Toomey sneered and shook his head. "Well, there's plenty more reasons to hate him."

"Like what?"

"The countless times he's had me disciplined for no reason at all."

Holden looked at him incredulously. "You're either a liar, or you've lost your mind."

"We happen to know that every time Sergeant Tyler had you disciplined, it was because you were guilty of breaking Captain Wirz's rules," said Stevens.

Holden nodded. "Sergeant Tyler was only doing his duty to see that you were disciplined for it. He would be wrong not to."

Toomey bit his tongue. Having just learned that Wirz had actually ordered his execution by a firing squad had put the fear into him. If he spouted off at Holden and Stevens, it would get to Wirz's ears. He would say no more.

The corporals delivered Toomey to his area and walked away.

In Toomey's heart, wrath toward Tyler was growing. Tyler could have overlooked his breaking of the rules, but he didn't. He saw to it that he was disciplined. The pious hypocrite.

Keith Lewis and Todd Zediker went to Toomey and asked him what Wirz wanted to see him about. He told them, then said it had only served to make him hate Tyler the more. Someday when the War was over, he would find Tyler and get even with him.

"Well, a lot of things will get settled when this war is over," said Zediker.

Toomey glanced toward Captain William Linden's tent, where the captain was talking to two of his men. "Maybe I'll get to settle it with Linden even before the War is over. I wouldn't be facin' Tyler's schemes to get me punished, or Wirz's threats, or the rest of these Rebel beasts in this pig sty if Linden had listened to me that day outside of Rome. My little brother wouldn't be dead, either."

"That's for sure," agreed Lewis. "Every bit of it is Linden's fault. Him and his so-called allegiance to the Union and his so-called honor as a leader of soldiers."

Toomey was breathing hard as he kept his eyes on Linden.

"Yeah. Not only would Lester still be alive, so would the rest of them that were killed that day. And when I see the men of Company A dyin' with pneumonia and all those other sicknesses, it makes me hate Linden even more. The man is gonna die. Sooner or later, I'll find a way to kill 'im. And I hope it's sooner."

Lewis nodded. "Yeah. Me too."

"Can't come too soon for me," Zediker said.


Time moved on. On Friday night, March 24, Edgar Toomey was awakened by a moaning sound. He sat up in the rectangular hole that was his bed, and realized it was Keith Lewis, who was in the hole on his right. Laying aside the thin, tattered blanket that covered him, he sat up. Lewis moaned again.

On Toomey's other side, Todd Zediker began to stir.

Toomey climbed out of the hole, crawled to Lewis, and said in a low tone, "Keith, what's wrong?"

Lewis was grinding his teeth. He moaned again. "I…I'm hurtin' bad, Edgar."

"Where?"

"Lower midsection all the way to my knees. Really bad. I…I think it's…scurvy."

Toomey knew the symptoms. So many men had died of scurvy. "Lie still. I'll go get some guards so they can take you to the infirmary."

As Toomey was rising to his feet, he heard Zediker say, "Edgar, what's the matter?"

"It's Keith. He's sick. I think it's the scurvy."

"Oh no."

"Come over here and stay with him while I go for some guards."

"Sure. Go on."

Toomey zigzagged among the crude shelters in the direction of the closest guard tower, where lanterns burned, giving off light in a wide circle. When he reached the line of small stones that bordered his particular area along the path that led to the privies, he moved a few steps along the path, waiting for one of the guards to spot him.

It happened quickly. A guard called, "Who goes there?"

"Lieutenant Edgar Toomey!"

"All right, Toomey. Hurry and get your business done at one of the privies."

"It's not that! We've got a sick man over here. Corporal Keith Lewis. I think he's got the scurvy!"

"Go on back. I'll see that two guards are there shortly."

The guards were there within a few minutes. They picked Lewis up, assuring Toomey and Zediker they would awaken the prison physician immediately, and carried the sick man toward the infirmary.

When the guards returned a half hour later, Toomey and Zediker were still awake. They were informed that Corporal Keith Lewis did indeed have scurvy.

When the guards were gone, Toomey said hotly, "It's Linden's fault, Todd. We wouldn't be in this rotten place if he'd listened to me."

As with all of the prisoners who had lingering sicknesses, Keith Lewis was kept in the infirmary, which was made up of several shanties. Three days later, Todd Zediker came down with it.

Both men only grew worse, and Lewis died on Thursday, April 6. When Edgar Toomey stood at the edge of his area and watched Keith Lewis's body being carried out the gate for burial in the prison camp's graveyard, his blood was hot. He renewed his vow to kill Captain William Linden.

Todd Zediker died two days later.

There was a brutal expression on Toomey's face as he turned and went back to his crude shelter after watching the body being carried out. He looked at the empty rectangular holes on both sides of him with a smoky flare in his eyes. His arms hung straight, his hands heavy-knuckled. His jaw made a determined cut against the sunlight that bathed his face. "You'll pay, Linden. You'll pay."

13

MAIL ORDER BRIDE SERIES
NO. 10
1865
USA
AL & JOANNA LACY

ON SUNDAY NIGHT APRIL 9, Edgar Toomey lay awake in the rectangular hole in the ground. His blood was to the boiling point, and he could hardly breathe for the loathing that coursed through his body.

William Linden must die tonight.

There was silence across the compound, except for the night breezes soughing through the trees, which were sprouting their leaves. A half moon hung in a star-spangled sky above, partially covered at times by drifting clouds.

Just before midnight, Toomey slipped out of his blanket and crawled up to ground level, staying on his belly. The compound was dimly lighted by the lanterns that hung high on the guard towers, leaving dark shadows between the circles of light. Toomey pulled the pocket watch from his trousers, angled it toward the lantern light of the nearest tower, and nodded. *I was right. It'll be midnight in three minutes.*

He slipped the watch back into his pocket and crawled some twenty yards in the shadows to a patch of trees where many limbs had fallen on the ground from the winter's high winds. Staying on his belly, he searched among the broken limbs until he found a section of limb some twelve inches in length that was sturdy and had a sharp point.

He looked back toward the towers. The guards were moving slowly along the edges of the platforms, rifles in hand. On the ground were other guards who were doing patrol duty near the dead line.

Crawling slowly and glancing periodically toward the towers and the guards, Toomey moved in the shadows to the small tent occupied by Captain William Linden. He could hear the soft, even breathing inside. Glancing once more toward the towers and the guards, he gripped the sharp length of tree limb and crawled past the flap into the tent.

Moments later, Edgar Toomey's heartbeat was expanding like thunder through his whole body as he crawled into the hole that was his bed.

He lay there a few minutes, breathing heavily. A grin of triumph was on his face.

When his breathing returned to normal, he crawled back out of the hole and stood to his feet. Pulling the watch from his pocket, he slanted it toward the lantern light and noted that it was 12:20. He looked toward the nearest tower and saw the guards moving slowly around the perimeter of the high platform, their eyes searching the shadowed compound.

He pocketed the watch, and with steady steps, he threaded his way amid the sleeping men of what was left of A Company to the path that led to the nearest privies. Stepping onto the path, he moved slowly, knowing that any second the guards would spot him.

A call came quickly. "Lieutenant Toomey, do you need to go to the privies?"

Toomey stopped and looked toward the guard. "Yes."

"Take care of your business quickly and get back to bed."

"Sure will."

Toomey picked up his pace and hurried toward the privies. A few minutes later, he came out, waved at the guards, and moved with haste to his hole in the ground.

The next morning, when the men of A Company were ordered by the guards to join the Union soldiers of five other areas and walk to the mess hall for their thirty-minute breakfast shift, they soon entered the hall and sat down at the tables under the watchful eyes of the guards.

Lieutenant Harry Fisher stood before them and observed as guards began calling the roll, with sheets of paper in hand, overlooking the names that were scratched out. Each man answered with a "Yo!"

Edgar Toomey's heart was banging his ribs. When the guard assigned to A Company read off the name of Captain William Linden and there was no reply, Toomey cupped a hand over his mouth and grinned.

Lieutenant Harry Fisher picked up on Captain William Linden's absence immediately.

While the prisoners were looking around as if they could not believe Linden would bypass breakfast, Fisher glanced at Corporal Joel Stevens. "Corporal, will you go to Captain Linden's tent and check on him, please?"

"Yes, sir. With all the sickness that's in the camp, Lieutenant, I'd say Captain Linden is probably coming down with something." With that, Stevens left the mess hall and headed across the compound toward the area marked off for A Company.

When he entered the area, he hurried up to Linden's tent. The flap was still down. "Captain Linden, are you in there?"

Dead silence.

"Captain Linden?"

Not a sound.

Stevens leaned down, pulled back the flap, and stuck his head inside. What he saw made him catch his breath and sent a tingle up his spine. He moved in and knelt beside Linden's form. A sharp length of tree limb was buried deep in his chest. He pressed fingers to the side of Linden's neck, intending to see if there was a pulse. The coldness of his skin and the lack of a pulse told him the man indeed was dead.

Back in the mess hall, Edgar Toomey was eating his small ration of grits and cornbread, acting as if all was normal. He kept a watchful eye on the door and smiled to himself when he saw Corporal Joel Stevens enter and rush up to Lieutenant Fisher. Since the prisoners were not allowed to talk during meals, all was quiet in the mess hall except for the tinkling sound of eating utensils. Everyone heard Stevens tell Fisher he found Captain William Linden dead in his tent; he had been stabbed through the heart with a sharp stick.

"Let's go tell Captain Wirz," Fisher told Stevens. The two went out the door.

As they neared the cabin, Wirz was just coming out the door with Sergeant Dan Tyler. They saw the two men hurrying toward them and waited.

Wirz frowned. "Something wrong?"

"Yes, sir," said Fisher. "When the roll was called for A Company at breakfast, Captain Linden was not there. I sent Corporal Stevens to see about him. He found him dead in his tent."

Wirz's eyebrows arched. "Hmm. He hasn't been on the sick list as far as I know."

"It wasn't sickness, sir," said Stevens. "Somebody killed him. He's got a length of tree branch buried in his chest."

Wirz looked at Tyler. "Let's go take a look." Then he said to Fisher and Stevens, "You two come with us."

Breakfast was almost over. Edgar Toomey was gloating within. William Linden had finally paid for the deaths of Lester Toomey, Keith Lewis, Todd Zediker, and a host of other men of A Company. He was draining the last of the weak coffee from his cup when he saw the door open and Captain Henry Wirz come in with Lieutenant Harry Fisher, Sergeant Dan Tyler, and Corporal Joel Stevens on his heels.

Wirz stepped to a central spot so all could see and hear him. "Men, give me your attention."

Most of the prisoners in the mess hall were already looking at him.

"I have an announcement. Captain William Linden was murdered in his sleep last night."

Underneath the tabletop, Edgar Toomey was silently clapping his hands.

The other Union soldiers were showing their shock at the news.

Wirz went on. "Listen to me, men. You are our enemies, and we are your enemies. But even though Captain Linden was an enemy soldier, there will be an investigation. Murder is wrong, no matter who the victim is. Captain Linden was a human being and had the right to live as we all do. He never broke any of the rules that bring capital punishment in the camp. This is a dastardly deed, and I will do my best to find the guilty party and bring him to justice."

Edgar Toomey felt warmth flowing through his body. Vengeance was his, and soon he would also have his vengeance on Dan Tyler. He had concocted a plan and would do his best to make it work.

The prisoners filed out of the mess hall to give room for the next shift to have their breakfast. Their faces showed the grief they felt that another Union soldier was dead. When they returned to their respective areas, there were whispers that some low-down Rebel guard had done the dastardly deed.

Linden's body was carried outside the stockade to the prison graveyard two hours later and buried along with eleven other prisoners who had died of various diseases in the infirmary during the night.

Shortly after the burial, Corporal Willie Botham and a new guard named Corporal Ted Hobson were moving along the path that led past the A Company area when they saw a Union officer wave to get their attention.

"Who's that?" asked Hobson.

"Lieutenant Edgar Toomey. He's a real troublemaker."

"Oh yeah. A couple of the guards were talking about him yesterday. From what I could pick up, he's Sergeant Dan Tyler's number one antagonist in this place."

"You've got that right."

Toomey drew up. He swept a glance over the face of the new guard, then settled on Botham. "Corporal Botham, I need to see Captain Wirz. It's very important that I talk to him in his office."

"What's it about?"

"I'd rather tell the captain."

"The first thing he's going to ask me when I tell him you've requested a meeting with him is what it's about. If I tell him you refused to give me that information, he'll turn you down. Besides, you can't see him alone anyway. There have to be two guards present anytime the captain talks to a prisoner personally in his office."

Toomey nodded. "All right. It's about Captain Linden's murder. I know who did it."

"Oh? Who?"

"Let me at least divulge that when I meet with the captain. Since you're the messenger, you'll probably be one of the guards who'll be in on the meeting, won't you?"

"I would say so."

"Then you'll hear it at that time. Please go tell him. It's urgent, believe me."

"All right."

Toomey kept his eyes on both guards as they hurried toward the captain's cabin. He watched them go inside, and they emerged only seconds later. Toomey grinned to himself. *I knew that would get the ol' boy's attention in a hurry.*

Minutes later, Captain Henry Wirz was seated at his desk with Toomey standing before him, flanked by Botham and Hobson.

Wirz did his best to mask the aversion he felt toward Toomey as he looked up at him. "So I'm told you know who murdered Captain Linden."

"I sure do."

"Let's hear it."

"Sergeant Dan Tyler."

Wirz let a smirk curve his mouth. "Lieutenant Toomey, when are you going to let this hatred you have for Sergeant Tyler die?"

Toomey stiffened. "This has nothin' to do with that. I know what I saw."

Wirz sighed and shook his head. "Tell me what you saw."

"It was twenty minutes after midnight when I woke up and had to use the privy. While I was walkin' the path to the privies, by the lantern light from the closest guard tower I saw Tyler—uh, Sergeant

Tyler go into Captain Linden's tent with a narrow piece of wood in his hand. He didn't know I saw him."

"And just how did you know the precise time?"

"Well, when I climbed out of that hole I sleep in, I took out my pocket watch just to see what time it was." He dug into his pocket and pulled out the watch. "Here. This is it. It works. Check it out."

Wirz glanced at the hands of the watch and noted that they were indicating the correct time at the moment. He knew Toomey too well, and the accusation against Dan Tyler infuriated him. Hard emotion lurked behind his eyes—eyes which glittered with a potent awareness of deception. "You're a liar, Toomey! Sergeant Tyler is a fine man and an excellent soldier. He would not murder anyone."

Toomey shrugged. "I know what I saw. I just felt I should tell you about it. You *did* say in the mess hall this mornin' that it was a dastardly deed and you'd do your best to find the guilty party and bring him to justice."

Wirz glared at him.

"Well, that is what you said, wasn't it, Captain?"

"Yes."

Toomey shrugged again. "I did my duty. I came here and told you what I saw. If you want to verify that I visited the privy at twelve-twenty last night, you can ask the guards who were in that area. They saw me. I'm tellin' you the truth, Captain. I clearly saw Sergeant Tyler enter Captain Linden's tent with the stick in his hand."

Wirz's eyes flashed with indignation. "I'm going to make you tell this to Sergeant Tyler, face to face!"

"Bring him here. I'll be glad to do that."

Wirz held Toomey's steady gaze as he rose from the desk chair. "I'll just do that."

Wirz went to the door, opened it, caught sight of a guard walking by, and called to him, telling him to find Sergeant Dan Tyler and tell him to come to his office immediately. He then returned to his desk and sat down, staring at Toomey.

Toomey sniffed and rubbed his nose. "Don't look at me like that, Captain. I'm tellin' you the truth."

"Uh-huh. All you've done since you came here was to show hatred and contempt for Sergeant Tyler. I still say you're lying. And

I'm telling you right now, this kind of accusation against Sergeant Tyler can result in greater punishment than you've imagined. You sure you don't want to change your story before he gets here?"

"Absolutely not. I'm tellin' you the truth. You should be commendin' me for reportin' what I saw, not threatenin' me. Tyler—Sergeant Tyler went into Captain Linden's tent carryin' the stick that Corporal Joel Stevens found buried in his chest. He should be punished for his crime."

The sounds of booted feet were heard on the cabin porch. Willie Botham turned and opened the door. "Come in, Sergeant."

Dan Tyler stepped in, glanced at Hobson and Botham, fixed his eyes on Edgar Toomey for a second, then drew up beside Botham. "You wanted to see me, Captain?"

Wirz nodded. "Yes. Lieutenant Toomey has come to me with an accusation against you, and I told him he was going to have to accuse you to your face."

Tyler turned to Toomey. "I'm listening."

Toomey's jaw firmed. "I saw you go into Captain Linden's tent while he was asleep last night, carryin' a stick. The one you plunged into his heart."

Dan held Toomey's gaze for a few seconds, then turned to Wirz. "He's lying through his teeth, Captain. As you well know, he hates me. He's probably the one who put the stick in Captain Linden's heart so he could accuse me of it."

Toomey bugged his eyes. "That's preposterous! Why would I kill a fellow Union soldier, especially the leader of my company?"

"You must've had something against Captain Linden and after murdering him in his tent, you made sure the guards saw you a little later so you could lie and frame the man in this camp that you hate the most."

Toomey stared at him uncompromisingly. "You've got a vivid imagination, Sergeant."

"Just what time last night did you see me go into Captain Linden's tent with that stick in my hand?"

"Twenty minutes after midnight."

Tyler turned to the captain. "Sir, after shift change at eleven o'clock last night, Clay Holden and Joel Stevens were with me in my tent till exactly one-fifteen. We were having Bible study and prayer together. They'll verify it."

This was a jolt to Toomey, but he kept up his facade as Wirz said, "Corporal Botham, will you go find those two men and bring them here, please?"

Botham headed for the door. "Yes, sir."

"And Corporal…"

Botham turned around. "Yes, sir?"

"Don't tell Holden and Stevens what Sergeant Tyler said about them being in his tent last night. In fact, don't tell them anything that's been discussed here, including Lieutenant Toomey's accusation."

"Yes, sir." Botham was out the door quickly.

Wirz looked up at Toomey. "You want to change your story before Corporals Holden and Stevens get here?"

Toomey's eyes were steady, cold, and without expression. "Why should I? Like I told you, Captain, I'm tellin' you the truth. My captain was murdered last night. I saw the killer go into his tent, carryin' the weapon that took his life."

Wirz moved his head slowly back and forth. "I've met some expert liars in my time, Toomey, but you take the cake."

Toomey pulled his lips back over his buck teeth and folded his arms.

"No doubt due to a lifetime of practice," said Tyler. "It takes a lot of practice to be this cold and calculating about accusing a man of murder when you know he's innocent."

Toomey's eyes settled on Tyler. They were so black and elliptic; they made him think of a bull rattlesnake. He imagined the white lines running from the eyes over scaly skin to the corners of his mouth and almost heard him hiss and shake his rattles.

Voices were heard outside, drawing near, followed by boots scraping on the wooden floor of the porch. The door opened and Corporal Willie Botham stepped in with Clay Holden and Joel Stevens on his heels. "They were close by."

Wirz nodded. "Good."

Dan Tyler's friends looked at Edgar Toomey, then Holden turned to Wirz. "What's this about, Captain?"

Wirz ran his gaze between them. "What time did you two men go to bed last night?"

Deep lines etched themselves across Holden's brow. "Well, about one-thirty, sir. Why?"

Wirz focused on Stevens. "That right?"

"Yes, sir."

"What were you doing prior to that?"

"We were in Sergeant Tyler's tent, studying the Bible and praying, sir. What's wrong?"

Wirz ignored the question. "Tell me exactly what time the two of you went to Sergeant Tyler's tent and exactly what time you left it."

Holden and Stevens exchanged glances, then Holden said, "Captain, all three of us went to the sergeant's tent immediately after shift change at eleven o'clock, and Joel and I were there until exactly one-fifteen. Joel had looked at his watch when we finished our prayer time and commented that we'd better get to bed."

"And you never left the tent at any time between the time you entered it and when you left at one-fifteen."

"No, sir. Neither did Sergeant Tyler. What is this all about?"

"Lieutenant Toomey came to me and said that he saw Sergeant Tyler enter Captain William Linden's tent at exactly twelve-twenty last night. And that he had a stick in his hand—the stick that you found buried in his chest, Corporal Stevens."

Surprise showed on the faces of both men.

"Well, that's a lie, sir," said Stevens. "At twelve-twenty, we were in the sergeant's tent, like we told you, and he was with us."

Toomey laughed. "Sure, I expect your pals to lie for you, Sergeant Tyler. You had this all set up to make yourself look innocent. You murdered my good friend and superior officer, Captain William Linden, and you oughtta hang for it!"

Captain Wirz opened his mouth to say something, but before he could get a word out, he was interrupted by a loud shout just outside the gate, accompanied by rapid, pounding hooves: "The War is over! The War is over!"

Wirz looked at Botham and Hobson as he rose from his chair. "Watch him."

Corporals Holden and Stevens followed Sergeant Tyler and the commandant as they bolted out the door. The rider was now coming through the open gate, which was held by one of the guards, and when he saw Wirz, he slipped out of the saddle and dashed up to him. Guards were running up from all over the compound.

Botham and Hobson brought Toomey out on the porch of the cabin.

"Captain Wirz," said the rider breathlessly, "we've met, but I don't know if you remember me. I'm Lieutenant Kyle Kimbrough from the army post at Macon. A wire came to us early this morning from Confederate headquarters in Richmond. It said that yesterday at Appomattox Courthouse, Virginia, General Robert E. Lee surrendered to General Ulysses S. Grant. We lost, but at least the War is over!"

The Confederate guards and their commandant stood with pale faces.

Captain Wirz ran his gaze over the gathering group. "Men, this is sad news in that we've been defeated, but it's really no surprise. We've known deep in our hearts that with the economic problems in the Confederacy, it was inevitable. At least, in time, now, we can all go home to our families. There will be no more bloodshed, and in a matter of a few weeks, I'm sure, both Union and Confederate prison camps will be emptied."

Word was spreading all over the camp, and by this time, prisoners were running like stampeding cattle toward the gathering at the gate, followed by guards who were trying to get them to stop. Guards in the towers were shouldering their rifles.

Wirz signaled them to hold their fire and allowed the Union horde to gather before him. They were whooping for joy.

The guards were circling the gleeful prisoners, holding their guns at ready position.

Wirz let them have their moment of celebration, then raised his hands for them to get quiet. When they did, he lifted his voice so all could hear. "You've had your time of celebration, men. Now I want all of you to go back to your areas. All rules are still in effect and will be until you are shipped north, which no doubt will be in a few weeks. You are still our prisoners until then and I expect you to conduct yourselves as such. Anyone who gets out of line will be dealt with as if the War was still on."

The prisoners hugged each other and obediently made their way back to their assigned areas. Lieutenant Edgar Toomey was allowed to go with them.

Moments later, in the presence of just Clay Holden and Joel Stevens, Dan Tyler turned to the commandant. "Captain Wirz, what are you going to do about Captain Linden's murder?"

Wirz scrubbed a palm over his face. "Sergeant, I know you didn't do it, and though I suspect—as you do—that Toomey did it, there is no way I can prove it. There is nothing I can do."

BIRDS TWITTERED AS THEY FLITTED among the tree branches in Harrisburg on Monday morning, April 10. Jenny Linden looked up at them. "I wish I were as happy and carefree as you little birdies are. Maybe someday…"

When she neared Henderson's General Store, a few customers were clustered around the door, as usual, waiting for the store to open. They greeted Jenny as she drew up. She managed a smile. "Are the Hendersons in there, yet?"

"Yes," replied a middle-aged woman. "They're at the counter getting things ready."

Jenny stepped to the door and put her hand on the knob. "I'll see if I can hurry it along and we can open a few minutes early."

As she opened the door, an elderly man in the group chuckled. "You're a real sweetheart, Jenny."

She moved in, smiled at him, and closed the door. *I'm actually Nate's sweetheart, Mr. Creighton. And I love him so.*

Zack and Emma looked at her from behind the counter. Both said, "Good morning, Jenny," in unison.

She headed toward them. "Good morning to you too. How are my favorite bosses this morning?"

Emma smiled. "Fine."

"Fair to middling," said Zack.

"Just fair to middling, Zack?" said Jenny, moving behind the counter.

Emma shook her head. "He didn't get much sleep last night, honey."

"Back pain again?"

"Yes," said Zack. "I ran out of my salicylic acid powders. I'll go over to the pharmacy in a little while and get some more."

Suddenly they heard people shouting out in the street.

Zack frowned. "What's going on out there?"

The shouting grew louder and the customers outside the store were lifting their voices in elation, joining them.

Zack moved around the end of the counter. "Let's see what this is all about."

Emma and Jenny were right behind him.

When Zack pulled open the door, people were hugging each other on the sidewalks while laughing gaily. Some were weeping.

Emma and Jenny moved out the door. Zack looked at Frank Creighton, who was wiping tears from his wrinkled cheeks with a bandanna. "Frank, what's all the excitement about?"

"The War is over, Zack! The War is over! Here's Hank Keller. Tell them, Hank!"

Hank Keller was a middle-aged man who worked at one of Harrisburg's department stores and was a regular customer at the general store. His eyes danced in a bright face. "Zack, on my way to work, I pass the newspaper office every day. A few minutes ago, some of the *Journal* employees were coming out the door, shouting. A wire had just come from army headquarters in Washington. Yesterday at Appomattox Courthouse, Virginia, Bobby Lee surrendered to General Grant. The War's over and we won!"

"Oh, that's wonderful!" said Zack, then turned and gathered Emma and Jenny in his arms. "It's over, sweet ladies! The War's over!"

Tears bubbled in Jenny's eyes as she bounced on the balls of her feet. "I can't believe it! Am I dreaming?"

Emma playfully pinched Jenny's arm. "Did you feel that?"

Jenny wiped tears. "Yes, I did."

"Then you're not dreaming, honey! The War's over, and your papa will be coming home!"

"Yes, oh yes! And Nate too!"

More people were appearing on the street, shouting their elation. Zack squeezed his wife and Jenny. "Well, ladies, it's time to open up the store. I wish we carried firecrackers in stock. If we did, we'd make a pile of money today!"

The joyful noise grew steadily louder in downtown Harrisburg as rejoicing customers entered the general store to make their purchases. The War's end was the only subject in the aisles and at the counter.

It was almost nine o'clock when the Hendersons and Jenny heard the voice of Wiley Owens as he came in, carrying the day's edition of the *Harrisburg Journal*. "Hey, everybody! Wanna see some marvelous headlines?"

Wiley immediately had the attention of everyone in the store. He stepped to the empty stand by the counter, laid the bundle of newspapers on it, and picked up one paper. He flashed the front page and waved it about so all could see. "Look at this!"

The large, bold headlines read:

## WAR IS OVER!
## LEE SURRENDERS!
## UNION VICTORIOUS!

The customers raised their voices in happy shouts while many waved their hands over their heads.

Jenny stood in a state of pleasant shock. She had waited for what seemed an eternity for this news and had a difficult time taking it all in. Her mind seemed to be going in a dozen directions at once. *Can it really be true? Is the horrible War finally over?*

She would try Emma's way again. Making sure no one was watching her, she pinched the flesh of her left arm with her right hand. A smile spread over her face. *Yes! It's really true! I'm not dreaming. Papa and Nate will soon come home!*

Wiley Owens returned to the street where he had left his cart, and pushed it on up the street, waving one of the newspapers and shouting.

When business slacked, Zack left the store to pick up some more salicylic acid powders at the nearby pharmacy. He was back in fifteen minutes, and after mixing himself a dose and downing it, he returned to his place at the counter.

When Jenny saw that business had slowed even more, she turned to Emma. "Would it be all right if I run home and tell Mama the War's over?"

Before Emma could reply, Zack said, "You go on, Jenny. I want you and your mother to have some celebration together. Can you be back by ten-thirty? Business will no doubt pick up by then."

"Of course. I'll be back by then."

With her feet propelled by the excitement, Jenny ran all the way home, pausing only to greet people she knew who wanted to comment joyfully on the War's end.

When she reached her block and ran toward her house, she was surprised to see her mother on the front porch, standing amid a small group of neighbors. Tears of joy were streaming down Myrna's cheeks. When she spotted her daughter running across the yard, she cried, "Jenny! Oh, Jenny!"

Jenny bounded up the steps and folded her mother in her arms. "Mama, Papa's coming home! He's coming home!"

"Yes, honey! Papa's coming home! It's been years since we've had anything to celebrate. Now at last, your papa will be coming home to us!"

The neighbors rejoiced, knowing how hard it had been on Myrna with her depression problem and the load that Jenny had borne in caring for Myrna. When their emotions had settled, Jenny thanked the neighbors for coming to share the good news of the War's end with her mother. The neighbors were joyful that Captain William Linden would be coming home.

As Jenny took Myrna inside and they headed for the parlor, Myrna set her teary eyes on her daughter. "Honey, how did you get off work?"

"Business slowed as it usually does between nine-thirty and ten, Mama, so I asked Emma if I could come home and tell you the good news. Zack asked if I would be back by ten-thirty, so I've got to head back. I had no idea that the neighbors would come and tell you about the War being over."

"I was surprised they thought to do it, but I'm sure glad they did."

Myrna settled in her rocking chair. Jenny leaned over and hugged her. "See you at lunchtime, Mama. You just sit here and daydream about Papa coming home."

"I'm going to do just that."

Jenny rushed out the door and darted down the porch steps. She paused long enough to smile at the lady in the parlor window with tears of joy streaming down her cheeks, then waved and hurried away.

Myrna did exactly as her daughter had said. Rocking the chair, she closed her eyes and let her imagination take her to the day not far away when her husband would come home.

At lunchtime, Jenny entered the house to find her mother looking better than she had in a long time. They enjoyed lunch together, talking about happy days to come. When Jenny left to return to the store, Myrna was once again sitting in the rocking chair.

Jenny kissed her cheek. "Just spend the afternoon daydreaming, sweet Mama. Papa will be home soon."

When Jenny went out the door, her heart felt lighter than it had in four years.


That evening at supper, Myrna and Jenny were euphoric as they talked about the War coming to an end, even sooner than President Abraham Lincoln had guessed.

Myrna looked across the table at her daughter with a light in her eyes that Jenny had not seen in four years. "Honey, it's like I'm dreaming."

"I know, Mama. I feel the same way. But it's real, believe me. The War's over, and Papa's coming home to us."

"How long do you think it will take for your papa to be discharged?"

"It's hard to say. But I'd guess it would take at least a couple of weeks. And then, depending on where he is, it will take some time for the army to get him here on a train. So we may be looking at something like three weeks before he's here in our arms."

Myrna dropped her fork and put a hand to her mouth. "Oh, Jenny, I've tried to imagine what it will be like when I first see him. It's been so long."

"It has, but I have a feeling it'll be like he's never been gone. You and Papa can just pick up where you left off."

Myrna wiped a tear from her cheek. "I'm so happy."

"Me too, Mama. And I have an idea."

"What's that?"

"When it comes close to the time for Papa to arrive, I'd like to decorate the house. You know: lots of pretty flowers, and I'll make little signs that welcome him home. We'll put them all over the house."

"Oh yes! That's a marvelous idea!"

Jenny went quiet for a moment while she cleaned up her plate. Myrna saw a dreamy look come into Jenny's eyes. "What are you thinking, honey?"

Jenny took a sip of tea, set the cup down, and smiled. "I was thinking about the first moment I see Nate. Oh, Mama, I'm so excited."

"Jenny, I haven't said anything about this for a long time, but please be careful with your heart. I don't want it broken."

"Mama, I—"

"You have no guarantee that Nate will be coming home to you as if you were his fiancée, or even as if you were his special girl."

Jenny giggled. "I'll show you, Mama. You just wait and see! Nate is in love with me, and if I'm not able to be at the railroad station when his train comes in, he'll be knocking on that front door minutes after he gets off the train!"

Myrna smiled, but the smile didn't reach her eyes. "I hope so, honey. I hope I'm wrong, but please keep a guard on your heart until he actually declares that he is in love with you and wants to marry you."

Jenny giggled again. "Like I said, Mama. That's exactly how he feels. You just wait and see."

The next morning, Jenny bent down and kissed her mother's forehead. "You go on daydreaming, sweet Mama. I'll see you at lunchtime."

"All right, honey. Try to keep your mind on your work."

"It'll be a struggle, but I'll manage." She glanced out the parlor window. "What a glorious spring day! Just look out there, Mama! I haven't seen the sun shine so brightly since that horrible war began. Maybe soon our lives can be normal again, and we can have a happy future to look forward to."

Myrna looked up and smiled. This time the smile reached her eyes. "Yes, sweetheart, now you can concentrate on your own future and you won't have to worry about me. Your papa will be here, and our own lives can resume where we left off the day he boarded the army train and pulled out of Harrisburg."

Jenny went out the door and was walking down Main Street, enjoying the happiness the townspeople were showing over the War's end. Strangers and people she knew stopped her on the street to share their elation. Some of the women hugged her, saying how glad they were that her father was coming home.

Happy tears flowed down Jenny's cheeks as she shared their joy and anticipated the moment her father would arrive home. In the back of her mind, she also anticipated the marvelous day when Nate would arrive home and take her in his arms. She told herself Nate would probably propose shortly thereafter—or maybe he would even ask her to marry him when they first came face to face! A tingle slithered down her backbone.

When Jenny arrived at the general store, she found Zack and Emma on the sidewalk having their own time of rejoicing over the War's end with the customers who were there ahead of opening time.

Jenny joined in with them, then followed the Hendersons inside so they could prepare to open the store. Soon the door was opened and it was business as usual, along with jovial talk about the upcoming arrival of the men of Harrisburg who survived the War.

Jenny and the Hendersons were behind the counter waiting on customers when they saw Wiley Owens come in, carrying his stack of newspapers. He lifted up one copy of the day's edition. "Hey, everybody! The front page of the *Journal* has a message from President Lincoln! Let me tell you about it."

Wiley quickly had everybody's attention. The customers who were in line at the counter stayed in place, but the rest of them gathered around Wiley, anticipating what they would hear from the president. He held the paper open so everyone could see the front page. "President Lincoln has sent word to all the newspapers in the Northern states, stating that the men of the Union army who are mustering out will begin arriving in their hometowns by rail in about two weeks. There will be announcements posted in the railroad stations giving the arrival times of the trains."

A loud cheer went up, and Emma put an arm around Jenny, smiling at her.

Wiley went on. "The president also says that those Union soldiers who were confined in the Confederate prison camps will be arriving in their hometowns by rail anywhere from three to four weeks later than the other soldiers. Announcements will be posted in the railroad stations concerning their arrival times too."

Jenny's heart was pounding in her chest. She looked at Emma. "Will you let me have time off to be at the railroad station for each train to arrive, so I'll be sure to be there when Papa arrives?"

"Of course, honey. You'll have no way of knowing which train your father will be on, so you can plan to be there for each one until he arrives."

"You sure can, Jenny," Zack said.

Jenny thought about her dream—the one in which both her father and Nate arrived on the same train. Her heart pounded even harder. She hoped her mother would feel like going to the station with her.

Wiley Owens left the store, and the customers who had collected around him went back to their shopping. Jenny and the Hendersons were once again tallying bills and bagging goods.

When it was almost noon, Jenny hurried out the door and headed down the street. She was eager to tell her mother what President Lincoln had said. It was now definite that her father would be home within a couple of weeks.

As she moved along Main Street, greeting people and being greeted in return, she came to a sudden stop. Her jaw dropped in astonishment at the sight before her. Jenny's feet seemed glued to the sidewalk. *My mind is playing tricks on me.*

She closed her eyes, thinking the delusory vision would be gone when she opened them again. But when she opened them, Nate Conrad was still standing there on the sidewalk in front of Baldwin's Clothing Store, no more than thirty yards from her. He was talking to two of his young friends—Stan Galley and Bruce Laird, both of whom had physical infirmities which kept them from entering the army.

Jenny's heart was fluttering. She willed her leaden feet to move. She never took her shocked eyes off of Nate as she headed toward him. She was puzzled as to how Nate got home so soon and wondered why he hadn't already come into the general store to see her.

As she drew closer, she saw that Nate was leaning on crutches. Her eyes widened. She put a hand to her mouth. *Oh no! He was wounded in battle!*

Jenny's rapid movement toward him caught Nate's peripheral vision. He turned his head as she drew near and adjusted himself on the crutches. "Hello, Jenny!"

Stan and Bruce both greeted her warmly.

"Hello, Stan. Hello, Bruce." She looked at the crutches, then into Nate's eyes. "Wh-what happened to you?"

"Cannonball exploded close to me during a battle near Winchester, Virginia, back in September. Big piece of shrapnel hit me in the lower back."

"I…I read in the newspaper about your unit being in that battle. D-did it damage your spine?"

"No, and I'm plenty thankful for that. I've been recuperating at Memorial Hospital in Frederick, Maryland."

Jenny moved up close and slid her arms around his neck. "Darling, how long have you been home?"

The heads of both Stan and Bruce turned at her use of the word *darling.* They were stunned at the embrace she was putting on Nate.

Nate's face lost color as he drew back in her grasp. "I've been back in Harrisburg since last Friday."

Jenny let go of him and stepped back. There was hurt in her voice as she said, "You've been home five days, and you haven't come to see me? Why?"

Nate glanced at his friends, who were looking puzzled. He took a shaky breath. "Jenny, I—" His eyes flicked past Jenny.

Jenny turned and saw a lovely redhead coming out of Baldwin's Clothing Store, carrying a small package. She was looking directly at Nate, smiling. As she drew up, she glanced at Jenny, then back at Nate. "Sweetheart, who is this young lady?"

Jenny stiffened at the other woman's use of *sweetheart* and glared at her with hot eyes.

Nate cleared his throat uneasily. "Honey, this is Jenny Linden, a longtime friend of mine. Jenny, this is my wife, Millie."

Jenny felt the breath leave her lungs as though someone had punched her in the stomach. "Your *wife?*" she huffed. "What do you mean, your wife? You were promised to me! We were going to get married when you came home from the War!"

Millie took a sharp breath and swerved her eyes on Nate, who said, "Now look, Jenny, there was never any such promise. Where did you ever get that idea?"

Jenny's chest tightened with emotion and her throat seemed to swell.

"Why, those times when we were together the last few months before you went away to the War. You—you—"

"I never said anything about us getting married at *any* time—before or after the War!"

Jenny's anger had her breathing hard. Her thoughts seemed to be composed of cobwebs. "But—but—"

"Nate never even mentioned you, Jenny," Millie said. "It sounds like you misconstrued his friendship to be more than it was."

Suddenly the anger within her took control. Jenny bared her teeth and knocked the package out of Millie's hands.

Millie gasped, her eyes flashing.

Jenny's right hand shot out and slapped Millie across the face. "You shut up! You don't know that you're talking about!" Then she wheeled on Nate and started beating on his chest with both fists. "You're a cheating, two-timing low-down cur dog!"

People on the street were gawking at the scene, eyes wide, mouths hanging open.

Stan and Bruce grabbed Jenny and pulled her off of Nate just as he stumbled backward and fell to the ground. Millie bent down to help him up while Stan and Bruce held Jenny tightly in their arms.

She struggled to free herself. "Let go of me! Do you hear me? I said let go of me!"

But Nate's friends kept her restrained.

Nate was on his feet, balancing on the crutches. He stared at Jenny Linden as if he could not believe what he was seeing.

She screamed at the young men to release her, but still they held on.

Millie picked up her package and gave Jenny a hard look. "Come on, Nate, let's go home."

Jenny was still screaming, but Stan Galley and Bruce Laird hung on as Nate hobbled away on his crutches with Millie at his side.

The furious blonde was spraying saliva as she put her gaze on the couple. "Hey, woman! You're a man-stealer! Nate, you're a dirty, traitorous snake-in-the grass!"

Nate and Millie reached the corner, made a quick turn, and headed down the side street.

After several steps were taken, Millie pulled Nate to a stop. Her eyes searched his stunned face. "Honey, are you all right?"

He nodded. "Yes. I'm just so shocked at this incident with Jenny. I can hardly believe it. But I'm not concerned about me." There was apprehension in his voice as he ran shaky fingers over the red welts on Millie's cheek. "Are you all right, sweetheart?"

Tears pooled in Millie's eyes, but a tiny smile rimmed her lips. "I'm fine, darling. But I will say that I've never been through anything like that before."

"I'm sorry. Really…I'm at a total loss as to what that was all about. I dated Jenny, yes, even as I dated a number of girls, but I never gave her any reason to believe that I was in love with her or wanted to marry her. You were right when you told her she had misconstrued my friendship to be more than it was. Please believe me. I have never had any serious feelings for Jenny, and I *never* gave her any reason to think I had intentions of marrying her."

Millie gave him a broad smile. "Of course I believe you, darling. Let's just go home and forget this horrible incident. I'm sure you're getting tired, and you need to lie down and rest."

A contented smile crossed Nate's face. "Always a nurse, aren't you?"

"I will always be, at least where you're concerned. Come on. My husband and patient needs his rest."

In front of Baldwin's Clothing Store, as soon as Nate and Millie disappeared around the corner, Jenny Linden hissed at Stan and Bruce, "Let go of me! I mean it! Right now!"

People on the street were still staring.

Bruce looked at Stan. "Shall we let her go?"

"Only if she's cooled down and promises to leave the Conrads alone."

"I'm not going to bother them," Jenny said coldly. "They aren't worth it."

Stan nodded. "All right."

Both men let go at the same time.

Jenny scowled, gave them both a piercing look, then wheeled and stomped down the street.

# 15

MYRNA LINDEN WAS HAVING EVEN A BETTER DAY than she had experienced the day before. She had even accomplished some chores around the house. Knowing that William would be coming home soon had given her the reason she needed to strive to get well. Bright sunshine filled the house with welcome light, and with her chores done, she opened a couple of side windows in the parlor.

Going to the large window at the front of the parlor, she looked out and was amazed to see tulips blooming in an array of colors along the path in the front yard that led to the street. "My, my," she breathed, "they seem to have blossomed overnight. It's been such a long and dismal winter, but now the War is over and spring is in the air!"

Myrna settled into the rocking chair with a sigh. "Oh, William, I haven't been this happy since the day Jenny was born. You're coming home to me, darling. You're coming home to me!"

Lost in her own state of anger as she walked hurriedly along Main Street, Jenny Linden was unaware of the people who spoke to her. She acknowledged no one. When they were ignored, the people stared after her, murmuring among themselves, wondering what was wrong.

One woman commented to her husband, "I hope she hasn't received bad news concerning her father."

The husband watched Jenny march stiffly down the street. "Something's wrong, that's for sure."


Myrna was rocking the chair gently in her reverie when movement on the sidewalk caught her attention. She focused on the figure turning into the yard and smiled. "There's my Jenny—"

She caught her breath.

The look on her daughter's face made Myrna's heart sink. "Oh no," she mumbled as she rose from the chair and headed for the parlor door. "Something is wrong, dreadfully wrong. William? Has Jenny somehow learned that her father isn't coming home?" Myrna stepped into the hall just as Jenny came through the front door.

Jenny saw the shadow of apprehension in her mother's eyes just before Myrna said with a quiver in her voice, "Jenny, is something wrong? Did you hear bad news about your papa?"

Jenny had to clear her throat before she could speak. "No, Mama, there is no bad news about Papa."

"Well, you're upset about something. What is it?"

As they entered the parlor, Jenny said, "The most horrible thing in all my life just happened to me on my way home."

Myrna's brows pinched together as they stopped in the middle of the room, facing each other. "Come. Let's sit down so you can tell me about it."

"I don't want to sit down, Mama. You go ahead."

Myrna's frown deepened as she eased into the rocking chair, looking up at her obviously frustrated daughter. "Tell me, honey."

Jenny's breath was sawing in and out of her lungs. She bared her teeth and clenched her fists. "I was on Main Street, approaching the corner where Baldwin's Clothing store is. Suddenly I saw Nate standing there, talking to Stan Galley and Bruce Laird."

Myrna gasped. "Nate?"

"Yes."

"How come he's home ahead of the rest of the army?"

"I'll tell you about that later. I rushed up to him and threw my arms around his neck. I knew something was wrong right then, Mama. He didn't respond as if he was glad to see me at all. Then I turned around, and here stood this redheaded hussy that he introduced as his wife."

Myrna's hand went to her mouth. She stared at Jenny for a brief moment, then spread her fingers. "His wife?"

"Yes. He was unfaithful to me, Mama. He went off to the War and found himself a wench to marry!"

Myrna bit her lower lip. "Didn't I tell you not to set your heart on Nate?"

The cords in her throat tautened like steel cables. Jenny's face suddenly became a crimson blur. "Why do you have to rub that in? Why?"

Myrna's eyelids fluttered, and she looked as if Jenny had slapped her face.

"Don't look at me like that!" Jenny hissed. "It's bad enough what Nate did to me. I sure don't need my own mother rubbing salt in my wounds!"

Myrna seemed to cave in.

Ignoring her, Jenny paced the floor in a temper fit, shaking her fists as she stormed all over the parlor, calling Nate Conrad and his new wife more choice names.

At one point, when pivoting at the corner of the wall near the front window, Jenny saw her mother slumped in the rocking chair. Her head was tilted forward. She was shaking severely. Her eyes were staring vacantly toward the floor, and she was mumbling incoherently. Tears were making furrows down her mottled cheeks, dripping off her chin.

Jenny's heart lurched in her breast. She dashed to her, sank to her knees, and took Myrna's hands in her own. "Oh, Mama, I'm so sorry for upsetting you. What have I done?" Her own tears began to flow. "Mama, I'm sorry. Please forgive me. Please say you forgive me!"

Myrna's lips were so pale that they stood out disconcertingly, like scars, against her blotched complexion. There was no response. Myrna continued to shake and mumble inarticulately while staring into nothingness. There was not so much as a flicker in her eyes.

"Oh no. I've got to get help." She let go of her mother's hands and laid them in her lap. "Mama, I'll be right back."

She dashed out the parlor door, swung open the front door, bounded down the steps, and ran as fast as she could across the yard toward the Bowden house next door. John Bowden was retired and home most of the time. He and Dorothy would help her.

The Bowdens, who were in their midsixties, were sitting on their front porch. John was reading the day's edition of the *Harrisburg Journal* and Dorothy was knitting.

As Jenny crossed into the Bowden yard, holding her skirt above her ankles while she ran, Dorothy saw her coming. "John. Something's wrong at the Linden house."

John looked up and lowered his paper. When he saw the frightened look on Jenny's face, he rose to his feet and moved toward the porch steps. "Jenny, what's wrong?"

Jenny drew up. "It's Mama! I need to get her to the hospital. Would you take us?"

"Of course. I'll go hitch up the buggy."

Dorothy was now at John's side. "Jenny, I'm going along. I'll go over to the house with you."

Moments later, the Bowden buggy was racing through the streets of Harrisburg in the direction of the hospital. Jenny and Dorothy were in the rear seat with Myrna between them. Myrna was still shaking, mumbling, and staring vacantly into space. When answering the Bowdens' inquiry as to what happened, Jenny did not give them the real reason. She simply told them that her mother went into her present state suddenly, without provocation.

When they arrived at the hospital, John carried Myrna, as he had done at the house. The receptionist at the front desk knew Jenny and her mother, and was aware of Myrna's depression. She called for a pair of orderlies, who came quickly with a stretcher. The receptionist told Jenny that Dr. Adam Griffin just happened to be at the hospital, visiting patients. She would find him and send him to the examining room. While the orderlies were carefully placing Myrna on the stretcher, Jenny thanked the Bowdens for bringing them to the hospital and asked if they would go by the general store and tell the Hendersons what had happened.

"Of course," said John. "I'll leave Dorothy here with you."

"Thank you, but it won't be necessary. Dr. Griffin will no doubt give Mama a strong sedative. Once she's asleep, I'll head on back to the store. Please tell Zack and Emma I'll be there as soon as I can."

John nodded. "All right."

"Honey," said Dorothy, "is there anything else we can do for you?"

Jenny managed a smile. "Not right now, but I'll sure call on you again if I need you. Thanks for being such a help to me."

The Bowdens went away, and Jenny followed the stretcher into the examining room. Dr. Griffin arrived when the orderlies were placing Myrna flat on her back on an examining table. He saw immediately the state Myrna was in, and asked Jenny to take a seat across the room. He began his examination by checking her vital signs, then started talking to her in low tones. Jenny watched as the doctor talked to her mother, and was pleased when she saw her begin to respond.

Dr. Griffin worked with Myrna for several minutes, talking to her, and asking questions. When he was satisfied that his patient was at least partially coherent, he set eyes on Jenny and motioned for her.

As Jenny joined the doctor at the examining table, Myrna looked up at her and raised a hand toward her. Jenny took her hand, then looked at the doctor. "She's better already, Dr. Griffin. Her eyes are focused, and I saw her talking to you."

Myrna nodded. "Jus' a li'l bit, honey."

"She's in a very deep state of depression, Jenny," said Griffin. "I just gave her a strong sedative. But before I did, I asked her what brought this on. She said she couldn't tell me. What was it?"

Jenny bit her lip. She really didn't want the doctor to know, but since her mother was listening and her mind was clear enough to know what she was saying, she would have to tell the truth. She cleared her throat nervously. "Dr. Griffin, it isn't that Mama couldn't tell you, it's that she *wouldn't*. She doesn't want to make me look bad."

Griffin frowned. "Go on."

Jenny sighed. "Well, I've been in love with a young man since before he went off to the War four years ago. I thought he was in love with me, but I was wrong. Today I ran into him on Main Street. He had come home with a medical discharge last Friday. He had his new wife with him."

"Oh. I see."

"Doctor, by the time I got home, I was half out of my mind with anger and grief. I stormed around in front of Mama, and when she reminded me that she had warned me not to set my heart on the man, I blew up at her. That's what sent her into this deep state of depression."

Griffin shook his head. "Jenny, your mother is very fragile. I've told you that. You must be very, very careful not to do or say anything that can upset her."

"I know. Even though I was so angry, I should have thought of Mama and not of myself. It won't happen again. I'm sorry. Thank you for your kindness to Mama."

The doctor nodded. "I'll need to keep her here in the hospital a few days so she can be tended to properly."

"I understand, and that's the way I want it."

Griffin looked down at Myrna, whose eyes were closed. She was breathing steadily. "The sedative has already taken effect, Jenny. I'll leave orders for her to be kept right here on this table for a couple of hours before they put her in a room. There will be a nurse with her at all times. She'll probably sleep till tomorrow morning."

Jenny thanked Dr. Griffin again for the good care he gave her mother, saying she would come back that evening after work and check on her.

Upon returning to the store, Jenny told Zack and Emma that her mother was deep into depression when she got home, so she had the Bowdens take them to the hospital in their buggy. She explained that Dr. Griffin was going to keep her mother there a few days for observation. She apologized for being late. The Hendersons told her they understood, and both said they hoped Myrna would get better quickly.

That evening when Jenny arrived at the hospital, she was given her mother's room number by the receptionist, and when she entered the room, a staff physician was checking Myrna's vital signs. The doctor told Jenny that her mother was still sleeping heavily under sedation and wouldn't awaken until sometime in the morning. She wouldn't be clear-minded until evening. He explained that the nurse who had been assigned to her mother for the evening shift was out of the room for the moment, but was keeping a close watch on her.

As Jenny left the hospital and headed home, her mind went once again to Nate Conrad, and her anger toward him grew hotter. By the time she entered the house, she was so angry that she could do nothing but pace the floor of the parlor and rail at Nate as if he could hear her. She was also irate at Millie for daring to steal Nate from her.

In her anger, Jenny found herself picking up a flower vase, ready to smash it on the floor. She caught herself just before throwing it down and took a deep breath. "If I smash anything, it'll be something that belongs to that two-timing skunk and that man-stealing hussy!"

The next day after work, Jenny Linden went to the hospital to check on her mother. When she stopped at the receptionist's desk, the woman said, "Hello, Miss Linden. I happen to know that your mother is awake and is talking quite clearly. Her assigned nurse is with her."

Jenny thanked her and headed for room twenty-four. When she drew up to the room, the door was open. Her mother was sitting up with pillows at her back, and the nurse was standing beside the bed, talking to her.

As Jenny stepped into the room, the nurse turned and looked at her.

Jenny stopped in her tracks, her eyes wide.

It was Millie Conrad.

Myrna was just focusing on her daughter when Jenny's face flushed with fury. "Get out of here, you brazen man-stealer! I don't want you in the same room with my mother!"

A staff doctor was passing by, but hearing Jenny's outburst, he stepped into the room. "What's going on here?"

Jenny turned her fiery eyes on the doctor. "I want this woman out of my mother's room, and I want her to stay out!"

"Why? What has Mrs. Conrad done?"

"Don't make me tell you, Doctor! Just get her out of here! Right now!"

Puzzlement captured the young physician's features. "Mrs. Conrad, please leave the room and send Della Martin in here."

Millie gave Jenny a hot glare, wheeled and hurried from the room.

Myrna's lips quivered as she looked up at her daughter. "Honey, I didn't know she was Nate's wife."

"It's all right, Mama. It's no fault of yours."

The doctor rubbed his chin. "I would really like to know what Mrs. Conrad did."

"She stole the man I was to marry, that's what she did."

"Oh. Recently?"

"Yes. Recently. I didn't know she was a nurse, and I didn't know she worked here. But I don't want her caring for my mother."

Head nurse Della Martin came into the room. "Dr. Faulkner, Millie said you wanted to see me."

The doctor quickly explained to Mrs. Martin what Jenny had just told him. When she understood the situation, she promised Jenny that Mrs. Conrad would not tend her mother anymore. Jenny thanked her.

Dr. Faulkner left, but by this time, Myrna was starting to slip into her disconsolate state once more. The nurse worked with her, trying to calm her, and after some twenty minutes, was successful. She told Jenny she would assign another nurse to her mother, but it would take a half hour or so. Jenny told her she would stay till then.

When Della Martin was gone, Jenny took her mother's hand. "Mama, really, I had no idea Nate's new wife was a nurse, nor that she worked in this hospital. Finding her right here in your room was just more than I could stand. I'm sorry I upset you again."

"I understand, honey. I'm glad to see you."

When the new nurse arrived, Jenny kissed her mother, saying she would see her tomorrow evening, and left the room.

As she walked down the hall, the wrath she felt toward Nate and Millie was burning like a volcano inside her. She stopped at the receptionist's desk and asked when the next shift of nurses would be coming in. She was told that the shift changed at eleven o'clock.

Jenny thanked the receptionist and took a seat in the lobby where a chair was in the shadows. She waited until she saw Millie pass through the lobby just after eleven o'clock, then followed her outside. Nate was there in a buggy with its lanterns lit, waiting for her.

There were a few buggies for hire just outside the hospital door. Jenny waited till the Conrad buggy was in motion, then hurried to the nearest buggy for hire, climbed in, and told the driver to follow the buggy that just picked up that nurse. As the driver pulled away from the hospital, Jenny said, "That nurse and her husband are friends of mine. They recently eloped and got married. I don't want them to know I'm following them, so stay back a ways. I just need to know where they live so I can pay them a surprise visit sometime soon."

The driver followed at a safe distance, and soon they saw Nate and Millie pull into the yard of a small white frame house. As the buggy moved on past the Conrad house, Jenny smiled and told the driver she appreciated his help. She then had him take her up to a house a block from her home, as if she lived there. She paid the driver, went toward the bogus house as if she would enter it, then when he pulled away and turned the corner, she hurried to her own house.

The next morning Jenny went to work as usual. At noon, she skipped lunch to take a walk and get a good look at the Conrad house. Just as she was drawing near, she saw the Conrads come out of the house and head for their buggy. Though Nate was on crutches, he balanced himself on them and helped Millie into the buggy.

When she was seated, she leaned toward Nate, and they kissed. Jenny's blood heated up.

When they drove away, Jenny chuckled. "This couldn't have worked out better." Quickly she made her way to the alley and hurried into the Conrads' backyard.

As she stepped up on the back porch, she looked around for something with which to break the window in the door if it was locked. She turned the knob and was pleased to find it unlocked.

A few minutes before three o'clock that afternoon, Nate left Millie at the hospital and headed the buggy back home. Dark clouds were gathering in the sky and thunder was rumbling in the distance.

When he arrived home, he parked the buggy next to the small barn in the backyard, removed the horse's harness, led him into the small corral, and pitched him some hay.

When Nate moved through the back door and stepped into the kitchen, what he saw took his breath. The cupboard doors were open, and every plate, cup, saucer, and bowl lay on the floor in shattered pieces. The table was overturned, as were the chairs. The glass chimneys of the lamps also lay shattered on the floor.

"Oh no!" Hobbling on the crutches, he hurried toward the front of the house. There were shattered flower vases on the floor in the hall and the flowers lay on the floor, crushed by the feet of the intruder.

In every room, paintings had been taken from the walls and broken, and figurines lay on the floor, smashed. The mirrors were cracked, and in the bedroom, the blankets were on the floor and the sheets and pillowcases were torn to shreds.

His voice quivered as he said, "Why would anyone do a horrible thing like this? Who—"

He immediately thought of Jenny Linden, remembering the scene on the street in front of Baldwin's Clothing Store and recalling the things Millie had told him about Jenny's conduct when she found her in her mother's room at the hospital.

"It had to have been Jenny." He hobbled back through the house, surveying the damage once again. "This is terrible. Millie has worked so hard to make this place cozy and comfortable. She doesn't deserve this. And neither do I."

He balanced himself on the crutches and turned one of the chairs upright. Easing wearily onto the chair, Nate let his eyes wander over the room and the scattered pieces of glass and china on the floor. Letting his mind go back to the days prior to the War, he tried to recall what he possibly could have said or intimated to cause Jenny to arrive at the conclusion that he was in love with her and wanted to marry her. *We were friends. We dated several times, but there was nothing serious between us.*

Nate considered going to the police and telling them he was sure Jenny Linden had done this, but there would be no way to prove it. Instead he would go to the general store and ask to talk to her privately. Maybe another try would convince Jenny that she had no right to think he was coming home from the War with plans to marry her.

After doing what he could to clean up the mess in each room, Nate went to the barn, harnessed the gelding, hitched him to the buggy, and drove away, sick at heart. He dreaded the moment when he would pick Millie up at the hospital that night and have to tell her of the devastation in the house.


At the store, Jenny gave no indication to the Hendersons that anything was amiss. She carried on with her work as usual.

Emma was working beside her at the counter, but along with Zack she knew from the customer grapevine about the altercation the day before between Jenny and the Conrads in front of Baldwin's Clothing Store. They had learned it while Jenny was gone at noontime.

Emma knew more trouble was brewing when she looked up and saw Nate enter the store. His face was as cloudy as the spring storm that was gathering outside.

Jenny first heard the crutches thumping on the floor, then raised her eyes and looked past the customer in front of her. The look on Nate's face told her he had found the wreckage she had left in his house. Apparently he was there to accuse her. *Well, he can't prove a thing.*

Jenny's customer walked away. Nate said calmly, "Jenny, could you spare a moment to talk to me privately?"

Before Jenny could reply, Emma spoke up. "Go ahead, Jenny. I'll handle the counter. If it gets stacked up, I'll holler for Zack."

"Let's go out to the alley. We can talk there," Jenny said.

When they were outside the store and in the privacy of the alley, Nate said in a low voice, "I know it was you who entered our house and made havoc because of your anger toward me."

Jenny frowned and looked shocked. "I don't know what you're talking about."

"Yes, you do. Don't lie to me. I saw you in action in front of Baldwin's, and Millie told me what you did at the hospital. Now, Jenny, there was no call to do what you did in our house. I've come here to ask you to explain to me what I ever said or did to make you think I was in love with you and wanted to marry you."

Jenny's temper flared inside her. She slammed the heels of both hands against his chest with all her might. The unexpected impact knocked him off balance. He stumbled backward and fell on his back.

Jenny stood over him, her features livid. "I never want to see you again, Nate Conrad! If you ever come around me again, I'll have you arrested for harassment!"

With that, Jenny went back into the store and slammed the door.

Slowly and with great difficulty, Nate brought his body to a sitting position. He ground his teeth, so insufferable was the pain in his lower back. His entire frame was trembling.

He looked up and down the alley to see if there was anyone to help him. His eyes encountered only a vacant view. "I…I can't sit here like this. It's going to start raining any minute."

Even the smallest movement shot pain through his back, but with determination to get up, he grasped both crutches, and inch by inch, got his feet under him. With herculean effort, he pushed himself upright and got the crutches under his arms.

Sweat beaded on his brow and his body continued to tremble. The alley began to spin before his eyes. A black vortex was trying to swallow him when suddenly he felt strong arms seize him, and he leaned heavily into the welcome support. His foggy head began to clear, and quickly, the vortex was gone. He focused on his rescuer, who was a tall, burly, blunt-featured man with dark curly hair.

"You all right, mister?" came the man's deep voice.

Nate drew a shuddering breath. "I am now, thanks to you."

"What happened?"

"I…uh…was just walking down the alley, here…and I lost my balance. Got shot up in the War, and I'm still trying to learn to walk on these pesky crutches. My buggy is parked out on Main Street. Would you mind helping me get out there?"

"Be glad to. My wagon's right back there at the end of the alley. How about I go get it? I'll put you in the wagon and drive you out to your buggy."

"Great. Thanks."

"You just lean up against the wall and hang on," said Nate's new friend. "I'll be right back."

With that, the big man was gone.

Nate leaned against the wall and shook his head. *Jenny really hates me. I've got to be careful and protect Millie from her.*

The clatter of a wagon was heard as tiny raindrops began to fall. He looked to the end of the alley and saw the man driving toward him. He hopped out. "It's starting to rain, mister. How about I tie your horse and buggy on the back of the wagon and take you all the way home? I've got a tarp we can put over our heads."

"Sounds good to me."

"It may be tough getting you up on the seat. Just rest your weight on me and let me do the work."

With a little time and a great deal of effort, Nate was placed on the seat. His friend hopped up beside him and drove out to the street. Nate pointed out his horse and buggy, and soon they were headed for the Conrad house with the gelding's reins tied to the back of the wagon.

The ride was short, but with every bounce, a groan escaped Nate's tight lips. The rain was still soft and light. When they pulled up in front of the house, Nate thought that the little white frame home never looked so good.

When the horse and buggy had been put away, the big man helped Nate from the wagon and assisted him up onto the back porch.

Gasping between words, Nate said, "How…can…I…ever… thank…you?"

"No need, friend. Just glad I came along when I did. Anything more I can do for you?"

Nate shook his head. "No, thank…you. I can…get myself in the house. But I need to know your name."

"Sure. James Fair. And you are?"

"Nate Conrad."

"Have you got a missus to tend to you?"

"Yes. In fact, my wife is a nurse. I'll be fine. Thank you, Mr. Fair. Maybe we'll meet again sometime."

"You betcha, pal. Well, I better get going. I think we're about to get a real downpour." With that, he climbed into the wagon and drove away.

Nate moved with great care as he entered the kitchen. He went to the washroom and opened the medicine cabinet. He was glad Jenny hadn't touched it. He took out his bottle of laudanum, went to the cupboard, and mixed it with a cool cup of water.

He swallowed the mixture, then limped on his crutches to the bedroom and laid his pain-wracked body on the bare mattress.

Before sleep claimed him, he was vaguely aware of the rain beating violently on the roof of the house and against the windows. *Made it just in time.*

ON SATURDAY MORNING, APRIL 15, the news spread all over Harrisburg that President Abraham Lincoln had been shot the night before at Ford's Theatre in Washington, D.C., by the famous stage actor, John Wilkes Booth. The president was reported to be in critical condition, and the law was on the trail of Booth. The people of Harrisburg were terribly upset.

As Jenny Linden headed home after work that evening, she dreaded telling her mother that President Lincoln had been shot, but Myrna had a right to know and would find out eventually, anyway. It was best to go ahead and tell her.

Myrna took it hard, but clung to the hope that the doctors who were attending the president would be able to save his life.

The next day, John and Dorothy Bowden arrived home from church and knocked on the Linden door. They told Jenny that word had come last night from Washington to the owners of the *Harrisburg Journal* that President Lincoln had died Saturday morning.

Myrna wept for some time upon hearing the awful news, but when Jenny reminded her that Papa would be coming home, she held tight to that anticipated event, which eased her grief over the death of President Lincoln.

On Tuesday, April 19, the *Harrisburg Journal* carried the story of

Vice President Andrew Johnson being sworn in as president at the Capitol Building in Washington on Monday. The *Journal* also reported that federal authorities now knew that John Wilkes Booth had fled south into Maryland and were hot on his trail.

On Thursday, April 27, newspapers across the northern states reported that the assassin's trail had led the authorities into Virginia, and John Wilkes Booth had been shot and killed by Union soldiers the night before in a barn near Bowling Green, Virginia, where he had been hiding.

On Saturday, April 29, Jenny was busy at the counter in the general store when she saw John Bowden come in. John waited until Jenny's customer walked away, then stepped up and smiled. "I was driving past the railroad station, so I stopped and went in to see if there was any word about when the trains carrying the military men of Harrisburg and the surrounding area might be arriving."

Jenny's eyes lit up. "Yes?"

"There are posters announcing that during the first two weeks of May, a number of trains will be coming. They explain that it will depend on where the men were in the South when the War ended, as to when they will arrive. The arrival dates of the trains will be posted in the station two days in advance."

"Oh, John, thank you for doing that. I was going to go to the depot on my way home after work and see if there was any information."

"I figured you would, so I thought I'd save you the trip. Anyway, honey, your papa's going to be home sometime in the next couple of weeks."

Tears shone in Jenny's eyes. "Yes! And what a wonderful day it will be when he does!"

When she went home for lunch and told her mother John's news, Myrna brightened up quickly. Even though Myrna had taken the president's death hard, this news put a brightness on her face, and she was still talking about William's soon return as Jenny left the house to go back to work.

That evening after supper, Myrna did what she could to help her daughter decorate the house with the cloth flowers Jenny had fashioned. The flowers were adorned with bright-colored ribbons that added to the beauty of the flowers and made each room look festive.

Myrna followed Jenny into each room and watched her pin up the signs she had made, welcoming Captain William Linden home.

When all the decorations and signs were in place, Myrna wrapped her arms around Jenny. "Oh, honey, finally your papa is coming home! Finally, we can get our lives back to normal, and we'll be so happy!"

Jenny pushed the pain and disappointment over Nate aside and hugged her mother tightly. "Yes, Mama. We're going to be so happy. Papa is coming home!"

On Monday, May 1, Jenny made her own trip to the railroad station before going home after work and found a sign that said the first military train would arrive at approximately 2:00 P.M. on Wednesday, May 3. The next one would come in at about the same time on Friday, May 5. Further notices would be posted shortly.

With this report, Myrna showed even greater improvement. The next day, Jenny informed the Hendersons of what the sign in the depot said, and they told her she could have time off each day the trains came in, so she could be there to meet her father. She thanked them both with a hug, and they spoke their joy that Captain William Linden would soon be home.

On that same day, Dr. Adam Griffin made his regular house call on Myrna and left a note for Jenny, saying he was pleased with the progress her mother had made since she first learned that the War was over three weeks ago, and that he was sure once Captain Linden was actually home, Myrna would improve even quicker. One day in the not-too-distant future, she would be completely out of her state of depression.

Jenny was elated when she read the note and celebrated by taking her mother for a walk in the nearby park, where they watched the sun go down together while talking of William's soon return.

The next day at 2:00 P.M. Jenny was at the railroad station, along with hundreds of other excited people. There were two coaches behind the engine and coal car, and eagerly, she ran her gaze between the coaches, watching the front and rear platforms for her father to appear.

When the last man had gotten off to be surrounded by loved ones and friends, Jenny headed home to let her mother know that Papa hadn't been on that train. This did not discourage them. There were more trains to come. Their loved one would be on one of them.

On Friday May 5, Jenny once again stood on the platform along with hundreds of excited people, but when the two coaches had emptied out, there was no Captain William Linden. Jenny felt a tinge of envy as she watched the men in uniform being welcomed enthusiastically with hugs, kisses, and handshakes. But she reminded herself that more trains would be coming. She would have her turn to dash up to a returning soldier and hug him and kiss his cheek.

Signs in the depot announced that there would be more information about coming trains within a few days. Jenny returned on Saturday, but no further notice had yet been posted. The same thing was true on Sunday. However, on Monday, May 8, she found notices posted that two more military trains would be coming to Harrisburg: one on Wednesday, May 10, and the last one on Friday, May 12.

Jenny and her mother were optimistic that William would be on one of those two trains. When Captain William Linden did not get off the train on Wednesday, Jenny and Myrna knew without a doubt that he would be on the Friday train.

When Jenny arrived at the depot on Friday, she threaded her way through the crowds toward the platform where the military train was scheduled to stop and unload its passengers. While making her way in that direction, Jenny found several people crowded around a fresh sign in the center of the terminal. She joined the group.

The sign was announcing that on Tuesday, May 16, a government train would be coming in from Richmond, Virginia, with fifty-three soldiers from Harrisburg and the surrounding area who had been incarcerated in several different Confederate prison camps at the time the Civil War came to an end on April 9. The train was to arrive at 3:00 P.M. The sign made it clear that this would be the only train that would bring Union men who had been in prison camps.

Jenny moved on, feeling the excitement build inside her. *Papa will be on the train today.*

Once again she joined a happy crowd of people who were eagerly waiting for the train to arrive.

At just after two o'clock, the military train came chugging into the depot and ground to a halt. The crowd pressed close, wanting to get a look at the faces of the men as they stepped out on to the platforms at the front and rear of both coaches.

Jenny's heart throbbed with anticipation as she pushed through the press to a frontal position. Her eyes flitted back and forth between the coach platforms as men began coming out the doors and moving down the steps. Jenny had to keep shifting positions to allow people to get past her to the men as they got off the train.

In less than ten minutes, the last man stepped down and was immediately in the arms of his family members.

Jenny found herself standing alone, still running her eyes from platform to platform.

Her heart sank.


Myrna was sitting in her rocking chair at the parlor window, eagerly waiting for a glimpse of Jenny and her father to come into the yard. Her hand went to her mouth when she saw her daughter moving along the sidewalk alone, her head a bit low and a sad look on her face.

She rose to her feet and headed for the parlor door. Could it be that her nightmares were true? Was William shot down in battle?

Myrna opened the front door of the house just as Jenny reached the top of the porch steps. "Jenny…your papa wasn't on this train, either?"

Jenny shook her head and folded her mother in her arms. "No, Mama. He wasn't."

Myrna started to mumble.

Jenny eased her hold on her mother, moving back so she could look her in the eyes. "But Mama, there's one more train coming. Don't give up."

The focus came back into Myrna's eyes. "I thought this was the last train."

"Well, it is the last train to bring the men home who were on battlefields, but there was a big sign in the railroad station announcing that a government train will be coming in on May 16 from Richmond, Virginia. It will be carrying fifty-three men from Harrisburg and the surrounding area who were in different Confederate prison camps. It has to be that Papa was in one of those prison camps."

Relief showed in Myrna's eyes. "Oh yes. That's it. Your papa was in one of the prison camps. I hope he wasn't in that horrible Andersonville Prison Camp."

Jenny bit her lower lip. "Me too, Mama. If he was, he's probably as skinny as a rail. But don't you give up. Papa will be home next Tuesday. Now I've got to get back to work, because Zack and Emma are waiting to hear if Papa was on today's train."

"Of course. Will you go tell the Bowdens on your way to work, honey? They're waiting to hear too."

Jenny kissed her mother's cheek. "Will do. You go sit down and rest. I'll see you this evening."


Just before three o'clock in the afternoon on May 16, Jenny entered the Harrisburg station, doing her best to buoy her spirits. Her father *had* to be on this train.

As before, excited people gathered on the platform next to the tracks where the train was to stop. This crowd, however, was much smaller than the previous ones.

Jenny thought of the decorations that were still on display in the Linden house and all the welcome-home signs. A chill slithered down her spine. *What if*— No! She would not let herself think about what it would be like if her father never came home. He *had* to be on this train.

The sound of the engine's whistle preceded the clanging of the bell. All eyes were on the train as it rolled to a halt.

Jenny Linden's heart was in her throat as she positioned herself so she could see both platforms of the single coach. Men began to come out the doors. Some were frail and sick-looking. Others, in better health, helped them down to be welcomed into the arms of loved ones and friends.

Jenny began counting as the haggard men left the coach.

People moved around her to welcome their loved ones home from the prison camps.

At the rear of the coach, Jenny spotted three faces of Harrisburg men that she knew. All three men were very thin. One of them was Corporal Jed Wilkes. Another was Corporal Truman Sibley. The third was Lieutenant Edgar Toomey, whom she had met on two or three occasions at social functions before the War. When she saw his parents and siblings gather around him, she recalled that Toomey had never married.

While still counting the men as they got off, Jenny's ears perked up when she heard Toomey tell his family members that his younger brother, Lester, had been killed in the battle near Rome, Georgia. There were sudden tears and open sobs at the news. Jenny recalled quickly that the newspaper reported that her father's unit had been in that battle.

When the emotions settled some, Toomey told his relatives that he and the other men of A Company who had survived the battle had been captured and put in the Andersonville Prison Camp.

Jenny recalled that her father's unit of the Third Pennsylvania Cavalry Division was A Company. This meant that Toomey was definitely in her father's unit.

Jenny continued to watch for her father, feeling sure that since Edgar Toomey and the other men of her father's unit had been in Andersonville, he must have been there too.

As the men continued to file out of the coach at both ends, Jenny's heart was growing heavy. Forty-four men had come out so far and her father was not among them. He *had* to be one of the other nine.

They kept coming. More wives, children, mothers, fathers, siblings, and other relatives and friends were feeling the relief of seeing their loved ones coming off the train.

Jenny was still counting...fifty-one...fifty-two...*fifty-three.*

Her father was not among them.

A pained expression crossed Jenny's face. *I must have counted wrong. Papa has to be on this train! There will be no other!*

Her hungry eyes continued to watch both doors, but they remained painfully empty. *Maybe Papa's too ill to get off by himself. Yes, that's it!*

Jenny bounded up the steps of the front platform of the coach and moved inside. Her eyes quickly scanned the inside of the coach.

There were only empty seats.

Her heart felt like it dropped all the way to her toes. Her mouth was suddenly bone-dry. "He isn't here," she gasped. A fresh wave of panic washed over her. "Papa isn't coming home. What am I going to do?"

Feeling numb all over, she left the coach and moved down the platform steps. She saw Jed Wilkes and Truman Sibley walking away with their relatives and friends, but Edgar Toomey was still standing close by, telling those gathered around him about the atrocities of Andersonville Prison.

Summoning strength from deep within, Jenny rushed up to the group and set her eyes on Edgar Toomey. "Please excuse me, Lieutenant Toomey. Do you remember me?"

Toomey stopped what he was saying and looked at her. "Why, yes. You're Jenny Linden, Captain William Linden's daughter." He forced a pleasant look on his face. "What can I do for you, Miss Jenny?"

"I heard you say that you were in A Company...my father's unit."

"Yes."

"Papa hasn't come home yet, Lieutenant. Can you tell me about him? Was he in Andersonville Prison with you?"

Toomey excused himself to the group of relatives and friends, saying he would be right back. He took Jenny by the hand and led her aside so no one else could hear their conversation. "Miss Jenny, your father was indeed in Andersonville with what was left of A Company after the battle near Rome, Georgia. I...I don't how to tell you this, except to say it straight out. Your father is dead."

Jenny stared in open-mouthed shock. Her heart kicked inside her chest. "D-dead?"

"Yes. Your father was murdered by a guard in the prison. His name is Sergeant Dan Tyler."

She suddenly broke into tears, and Toomey feigned compassion on her, taking her into his arms. "I'm sorry, Miss Jenny. I hate to be the one to break this to you."

When she finally gained control of her emotions, Toomey released her and told her how Sergeant Dan Tyler had mistreated her father repeatedly.

Jenny drew a shuddering breath. "Oh-h-h-h. Why did he murder Papa?"

"Well, because of this mistreatment by Tyler, bad blood developed between them. Tyler couldn't stand it because your father stood up to him. Finally, Tyler sneaked into your father's tent one night and stabbed him to death."

These words served only to put Jenny back in sobs. Toomey held her in his arms again, but inside, he was rejoicing once again that the captain was dead. After a few minutes, Jenny's sobbing faded. Attempting to gain control of her emotions, she wiped tears, breathing raggedly.

"Miss Jenny," said Toomey, "if you need confirmation of what I just told you, Corporals Truman Sibley and Jed Wilkes, who got off the train with me, can substantiate it."

Jenny shook her head. "Your—your word is good enough for me. I don't need to ask them."

"Are you sure? I'd be glad to run after them. They're probably out in the parking lot."

"No, no. It's all right." She drew another shuddering breath. "Was this Sergeant Dan Tyler punished by the Confederate authorities for murdering my father?"

"Absolutely not, Miss Jenny. No Confederate authority is going to punish one of their own for ridding the world of a Yankee soldier. Especially a Yankee officer. Tyler got off scot-free."

Jenny struggled to maintain her composure. "Do you know where this cold-blooded murdering Rebel lives?"

"No. I never did hear where Tyler was from."

Jenny nodded. "Well, thank you for telling me about Papa. I'm sorry to have butted in on you."

"Don't be sorry, little lady. I'm sorry I had to be the one to tell you about your brave father."

As Jenny walked away, her insides were churning with mixed emotions: grief at the death of her father and wrath toward the man who had murdered him. She wished she could keep the bad news from her mother, but told herself it would be impossible. Mama had to know. However, if she could get by with it, she would spare her mother the horrible details.

She considered taking her mother to the hospital so she would have the proper medical care when she was told of her father's death, but Myrna Linden would know something was seriously wrong if she was told they were going to the hospital. Even if Jenny could get Dr. Griffin to come to the house before she told her mother the bad news, she would know something was wrong and think the worst, anyway. There was no other way to do it, but to be honest and tell her the truth.

When Jenny arrived home and mounted the steps of the front porch, she looked through the parlor window and saw that her mother was asleep in her rocking chair. Dreading what the news was going to do to her mother, Jenny steeled herself and walked through the door.

Myrna stirred when Jenny entered the parlor, rubbed her eyes, and focused on her daughter's drawn features. Her mouth went dry. "Oh no. He wasn't on this train, either?"

Jenny moved up to her and took her hand. "Papa's dead, Mama. I don't know any other way to break it to you."

Myrna burst into tears. Jenny told her about Lieutenant Edgar Toomey being on today's train. Toomey had said that Papa had died while in the Andersonville Prison Camp.

By this time, Myrna was staring blankly into space and mumbling incoherently. Jenny dashed to the Bowdens' house, explained how she just learned that her father had died at Andersonville Prison Camp, and what the news did to her mother. She asked if they would take them to the hospital.

Upon entering the hospital with Myrna Linden, Jenny found Della Martin at the receptionist's desk and quickly explained what had happened. Myrna was immediately taken into an examining room, and a messenger was sent from the hospital to go to Dr. Adam Griffin's office and tell him the state Myrna was in.

The Bowdens stayed in the waiting room with Jenny.

Almost a half hour had passed before Dr. Griffin rushed into the examining room. Another fifteen minutes had passed when the doctor came into the waiting room. Jenny and the Bowdens rose to their feet as they observed the serious look on Dr. Griffin's face.

"Jenny, I hate to tell you this, but your mother is in bad shape." He repeated what Della Martin had told him in the examining room about Captain William Linden's death in the prison camp, wanting to be sure he knew the facts. Jenny told him he had them right.

The doctor sighed. "Jenny, she is going to need constant care. We've got to keep her here in the hospital."

Jenny nodded. "Of course, Doctor. I want her to have the best of care."

"I want you to go on home. This blow has hit you hard too. You won't be alone, will you?"

"We'll stay with her, Doctor," said John Bowden.

"Good. Go now, Jenny. Come back in the morning."

As the Bowden buggy moved through the streets of Harrisburg, Jenny told her neighbors that she really needed to have some time alone. She would be all right. They told her they understood, but that if she needed them, all she had to do was step outside her door and call for them. She asked if they would go to the general store, notify the Hendersons of what happened, and tell them she would have to have time off from work to spend at the hospital. The Bowdens assured her they would take care of it.

When Jenny arrived home and entered the house, her heart felt like it was made of cold lead. Suddenly the decorations and the signs she had made for her father seemed to mock her. In a rage, she ripped the signs off the walls and threw the flowers in a trash can on the back porch. All the while, she screamed repeatedly that she was going to hunt down Sergeant Dan Tyler and kill him.


Day after day, Jenny fed on the anger that was coursing through her toward the man who had murdered her father. Myrna was steadily growing worse, drawing deeper into her depression and away from her daughter.

Jenny's mind went continually to the man who had taken her father from her, and she resolved that wherever Dan Tyler was, she would find him. He was going to pay for this with his own life. She was so full of hatred toward Tyler that she had no appetite. She fed on the deep need of revenge that consumed her. Tyler would be sorry one day.

As the days passed, Jenny stayed by her mother's side as if her presence was paramount to Myrna's healing. Pale and wan, she often whispered to her unresponsive mother, begging her to come back to her.

Della Martin was finally able to get Jenny to start eating again, but the portions she put down were very small. Della also did her best to convince Jenny that she needed to rest her mind and body. Jenny only shrugged and continued her vigilance, all the while making plans of vengeance on Dan Tyler.

On the sixth day since Myrna had been hospitalized, Jenny was standing over her bed. Her mother had been incommunicable the entire time, even though she was awake from time to time. Myrna did no more than mumble and stare blankly into space. At the moment, Myrna was sleeping.

Jenny looked down at her with sad but loving eyes.

Suddenly Myrna jerked, shook her head, opened her eyes for a few seconds, made a guttural sound, closed her eyes, and went limp. Jenny dashed into the hall to find a nurse. The first one she saw was Millie Conrad. Ignoring her, she ran up to a nurse who had treated her mother and was just coming out of a nearby room. "Please! My mother is getting worse. Hurry!"

When the two of them entered the room, the nurse saw that Myrna's face was purple, and quickly checked her pulse and looked for a sign that she was breathing. After a few seconds, she turned to Jenny. "I'm sorry, Miss Linden. She's gone."

Jenny collapsed on a chair and began sobbing uncontrollably. The nurse hurried to the door, and calling to another nurse, told her to bring one of the staff doctors immediately.

The doctor arrived quickly. While the nurse was trying to console Jenny, she asked the doctor to examine the dead patient to see if he could tell the cause of death.

After examining Myrna's body for several minutes, the doctor stepped to Jenny. "Miss Linden, your mother died of a stroke. As you know, I have attended her many times since she has been here. One of the predisposing conditions that brings on a stroke is hypertension, which your mother has been suffering all along. Hypertension often thickens the arteries, which is called arteriosclerosis. It did so in your mother's case. The thickening of her arteries finally took its toll. I'm sorry."

"You're very kind, Doctor," said Jenny. Her throat was tear-clogged, but her mind went to Dan Tyler. *He's the one who's going to be sorry.*

# 17

THREE DAYS LATER, JENNY LINDEN STOOD beside her mother's coffin at the cemetery. Zack and Emma Henderson had closed the store so they could attend the simple graveside service, conducted by the Bowdens' minister. Jack and Dorothy also stood with Jenny, as did Dr. Adam Griffin.

The undertaker and an assistant stood back several feet, waiting to put the coffin in the ground when Jenny and her friends were gone.

The radiant sunshine that brightened the cemetery was a mockery to Jenny because of the darkness that seemed to surround her. While the minister was speaking words that meant little to her, Jenny stared forlornly at the deep rectangular hole that waited to receive her mother's body.

There was very little money to spend on the funeral. The coffin was a plain pine box. Myrna's body was wrapped up to her neck in a beautiful quilt she had made shortly after William had gone off to the War. It had often adorned her bed. Now it would be used to cover her lifeless form in the darkness of the grave.

The minister finished his brief message and nodded at Jenny. Jenny stepped to the open coffin, carrying a small bouquet of flowers she had gathered from her own yard. The Hendersons, the Bowdens, and Dr. Griffin moved up behind her.

Jenny bent down and kissed her mother's cold cheek. Choking on the tears that clogged her throat, she managed to say, "Good-bye, Mama. I love you."

Having spoken those final words, Jenny stepped back, looking at the still form of her mother in the coffin. The undertaker stepped up, quietly closed the coffin lid, then returned to the spot beside his assistant.

While the minister and Jenny's friends looked on, she placed the flowers on the coffin lid, stood there a moment, then turned to her friends and thanked them for being there.

Dr. Griffin gave her a brotherly embrace, as did Zack and John. Emma and Dorothy put their arms around her and held her for a few minutes, then each kissed her cheek and released her.

"We'll take you home, honey," said Dorothy.

"Jenny," said Zack, "you get yourself a good rest. Emma and I will manage. Don't come to work until you feel up to it."

Jenny gave him a weak smile. "Thank you. I'm sure I can be back on the job within two or three days." Glancing once more at the coffin, she turned and walked away with John and Dorothy.

When the Bowden buggy pulled into the Linden yard, John and Dorothy walked Jenny to the door and offered to come inside with her. She explained that she needed to be alone, but thanked them for their kindness to her. They made sure she understood that if she needed them, all she had to do was let them know. Both of them embraced her one more time and headed for their buggy.

Jenny moved inside, closed the door behind her, and walked slowly into the parlor. This was the only house she had ever known, and at that moment, it was quieter than she could ever remember. To her, it was like the silence of a tomb.

She walked to the rocking chair by the large front window and laid a hand on its high back. It seemed so empty. She rocked it slowly for a minute, then lowered her tired body into it and stared at the same view her mother had gazed upon day after day, year after long year, waiting for Captain William Linden to come home from the War.

Jenny's mind wandered back over her happy childhood as she grew up in this house with her parents. As with every family, they had good and bad times, but always they had each other and the love that bound them together. Now there was only herself.

She left the rocking chair, and with an aching heart, she moved slowly through the house, entering every room and recalling memories of the past. With each memory, her heart grew heavier.

When she had been all through the house, Jenny returned to the parlor and began to pace the floor. Wrath burned in her soul toward Dan Tyler. Her mind went back to the day her mother died. She was standing over her mother's body in the hospital room after the staff physician had gone. The nurse had an arm around her, still trying to console her, when Dr. Adam Griffin came in. He had just arrived at the hospital to visit some of his patients and had learned from a nurse that Myrna Linden had died.

While the nurse sat down with Jenny, Dr. Griffin examined Myrna's body, and agreed with the staff physician that Myrna had died of a stroke. Dr. Griffin then added, "With the emotional problems your mother was already suffering, Jenny, no doubt the shock and violent impact of your father's death was what brought on the stroke."

With those words echoing through her mind, the hatred she felt for Tyler twisted her face. The bloody murderer had now taken both of her parents from her. "I've got to find him and put the punishment on him he deserves!"

Pondering the situation, Jenny sat down in the rocker again and stared out the window. She knew that if she went to the Confederate capitol building in Richmond, Virginia, they would no doubt still have records of all the men who served in the Confederate army during the Civil War. Once she learned where this Dan Tyler lived, she would go there and find a way to shoot him some dark night without being seen by anyone. She would never rest until the man who took both her parents from her was dead.

With her mind made up to make the search for Dan Tyler until she found him, Jenny hurried out the door and headed toward downtown.

Zack and Emma were both behind the counter when Jenny came into the store. Emma had a customer, but Zack was busy filling a large glass jar on the counter with candy canes.

As Jenny moved around the end of the counter, Zack looked up. "Hey, little gal, I told you to get some rest. We can handle things here."

"That's right, dear," Emma said, turning toward her. "Now you go home and rest."

"I didn't come to go to work. I need to talk to Zack."

"Oh. All right. Let's go back to the office."

When they entered the office, Zack pointed to the chair in front of his desk. "Sit down, Jenny."

"Thank you, but it won't take that long. I just wanted to tell you that I need to take a week or so off."

"Why, of course. You've been through a lot."

"No, no. Not to rest. I have to make a trip in regard to my father's death. I can't tell you exactly how long I'll be gone, but I don't think it will be much more than a week. I'll be back as soon as I can."

"That's fine, Jenny. Take as long as you need. A little trip will be good for you after all you've been through. Your job will still be here waiting for you."

Jenny hugged him, speaking words of appreciation, then hurried out of the store, waving to Emma as she passed the counter.


When Jenny arrived home, she went to her father's den and took a .38 caliber revolver from a drawer in his desk. She swung the cylinder out to make sure it was loaded, then snapped it shut and slipped it into her purse.

At that moment, there was a knock at the front door. She laid the purse on the desk and went to the front door to find Laura Denton standing there. "Laura! How nice to see you. Please come in."

As they walked toward the parlor door, Laura said, "Honey, I just arrived back in town last night. You know that Shirley Atwood is living in Pittsburgh now?"

"I'd heard that."

They moved into the parlor.

"I've been visiting Shirley. I went to the general store to see you a few minutes ago, and the Hendersons told me about your father having been murdered and that your mother died three days ago. They said she was buried this morning."

Jenny's countenance was a grayish color. "Yes."

"I came to tell you how sorry I am for what has happened."

They embraced, then Jenny said, "Come over here and sit on the sofa."

Laura settled on the sofa and placed her large purse at her feet. Jenny sat down beside her. "It's sweet of you to come and see me, Laura."

Laura patted her hand. "I care about you, Jenny. Do you mind talking about your parents? I'd like to know more about what happened to both of them."

"I don't mind."

Jenny gave Laura as little information as possible, saying only that a Confederate guard at the Andersonville Prison Camp had murdered her father. She then explained in brief about her mother's stroke that was brought on at the news of her father's death.

Laura tried to comfort Jenny, and while speaking to her in a kind, tender manner, she reached into her purse and took out a small Bible.

Jenny stiffened at the sight of the Bible.

Laura reminded Jenny of the times she and Shirley had talked to her about the Lord during their school days, then brought up the day at the store when she and Shirley tried to help her to see that she needed the Lord Jesus Christ as her Saviour.

Jenny nodded. "I mean no offense, Laura, but I still can't see it."

Laura smiled and opened the Bible. "I want to show you something. She turned to 2 Corinthians chapter 4 and drew closer to Jenny so she could hold the pages in plain view. "Follow it while I read it to you."

Jenny was uncomfortable with what was happening, but did not show it.

"Verses 3 through 6," said Laura. "'But if our gospel be hid, it is hid to them that are lost: In whom the god of this world hath blinded the minds of them which believe not, lest the light of the glorious gospel of Christ, who is the image of God, should shine unto them. For we preach not ourselves, but Christ Jesus the Lord; and ourselves your servants for Jesus' sake. For God, who commanded the light to shine out of darkness, hath shined in our hearts, to give the light of the knowledge of the glory of God in the face of Jesus Christ.'"

Laura looked at Jenny, who had noticed that the four verses had been underlined with red pencil. "It says the god of this world has blinded the minds of those who are unbelievers, Jenny. Notice the small 'g' on the word 'god'. That's not the God of heaven. That's Satan, who is indeed the god of this world. Satan is the one who has blinded the human race so they can't see the truth. Jesus said in Mark 1:15, 'Repent ye, and believe the gospel.' Here, it says Satan has blinded the minds of unbelievers lest the light of the glorious gospel of Christ should shine unto them.

"You aren't going to repent and believe the gospel until its light shines into your darkness. And here in verse 6, it is stated of believers that God has shined His light into our blinded hearts. I was once like you, Jenny. I heard about salvation in Jesus, and all that goes with it, but I just couldn't see it. But when I found my life so miserable and was fearful of what lay beyond death, I allowed Him to shine His light into my Satan-blinded heart and mind. I saw the truth, and in repentance of my sin, I opened my heart to Jesus and received Him as my personal Saviour."

Jenny's face had a deadpan expression.

Laura smiled. "Notice here in verse 6, Jenny, that it refers to God, who commanded the light to shine out of darkness. See that?"

"Mm-hmm."

Laura held her place in 2 Corinthians and turned back to Genesis chapter 1. "Look here in verse 1. 'In the beginning God created the heaven and the earth. And the earth was without form, and void; and darkness was upon the face of the deep. And the Spirit of God moved upon the face of the waters.' Now watch verse 3. 'And God said, Let there be light: and there was light.'"

Jenny's expression had not changed.

Laura turned back to 2 Corinthians 4. "Now, look at verse 4 here again, Jenny. Read it to me."

Reluctantly, Jenny read verse 4 aloud.

"All right. You get the picture, don't you? Satan has blinded you so the light of the gospel should not shine unto you. He doesn't want you to be saved. He wants you to die without Christ and spend eternity in hell. Now look at verse 6 again and read it to me."

Jenny nodded and read the verse aloud.

Laura smiled at her. "Look there. 'For God, who commanded the light to shine out of darkness, hath shined in our hearts'...the hearts of those like myself, who have put our faith in Christ. When I gave God the chance, Jenny, He shined the light of the gospel into my spiritual darkness. What I couldn't see before that moment, I could see clearly then. And when I saw what the gospel was, I realized that Jesus had gone to the cross of Calvary, shed His precious blood for my sins, died for me, and came out of the grave three days later so He could save me if I would open my heart to Him.

"That's what the gospel is, Jenny, according to 1 Corinthians 15:3 and 4: 'How that Christ died for our sins according to the scriptures; And that he was buried, and that he rose again the third day according to the scriptures.' There is no one else in the gospel, because only Jesus can save us. We must put our faith totally in Him for our salvation, Jenny, based on the finished work of His blood-shedding death, His literal burial, and His literal resurrection from the dead.

"If you will let God shine His gospel light into your darkened heart and mind, He will do it. He will not force it on you. But if you will, you will see the light. When you do, you will repent and open your heart to Jesus."

Laura flipped back to Romans chapter 10. "Here, honey. Read verse 13 to me."

Noting that this verse was also underlined in red, Jenny read it aloud. "'For whosoever shall call upon the name of the Lord shall be saved.'"

"It's that simple, honey. Put that together with what we've already read. If you call on Jesus to save you in repentance of your sin, believing the gospel, He will save you. You will then have Jesus living in your heart. God will say, 'Let there be light,' and all your darkness will be gone. All your sins will be washed away in His precious blood, and you will go to heaven when you die, not to a horrible burning hell."

Jenny licked her lips but did not respond.

"I'll be glad to help you, honey."

Jenny shook her head. "I still can't see it, Laura. I'm really busy right now. I need to get back to what I was doing when you knocked on the door."

Laura surprised Jenny by closing the Bible and placing it in her hands.

"What are you doing?"

"I'm giving this Bible to you. I bought it for you when I was in Pittsburgh. Did you notice that I had the verses underlined that I showed you?"

"Yes."

"I did that so you could find them easily."

Jenny smiled. "Laura, that was sweet of you. You're very kind. Thank you."

"You're welcome. Will you promise me something?"

"What?"

"That you will read the underlined passages over and over again, on your own."

Jenny nodded. "I will."

"And may I come back and talk to you again about this?"

Jenny felt her stomach tighten. "I'm…ah…going to be gone for a little while, but maybe sometime later."

Laura would have liked a more positive answer, but she wouldn't push Jenny too hard. She wanted to deal with her again after the Word had some time to take root in her heart. She hugged Jenny, saying again how sorry she was for the loss of her parents. Jenny laid the Bible on a small table by the sofa, then walked her to the door. When she closed it, she went back to the parlor, sat down in the rocking chair, and put her mind on the search she would make for Dan Tyler.

A few minutes later, she left the house and walked to the railroad station to see when the next train was leaving that would carry her to Richmond.

When Jenny returned to the silent house, she took her satchel from the storage closet, and without much thought of what she was doing, began to pack a few items for her trip. Closing the fasteners, she placed the bag near the front door.

Her next stop was the kitchen, which once was the liveliest room in the house. She stoked up the stove, filled the kettle with water, and placed it where it would get hot the quickest.

*I'm not the least bit hungry,* she thought. *But for the task ahead of me, I must maintain my strength.*

After eating a light supper and washing her few dishes, Jenny stood at the cupboard, drying her hands. Her heart began to race in anticipation of her trip and eventual quest to find and destroy Dan Tyler.

She decided to give the house a good cleaning, since she would probably sleep very little, anyway. She tied on her apron and decided she would start in her parents' bedroom. Pouring hot water from the kettle into a bucket, she picked up a mop. Upon entering the room, she saw a gorgeous sunset through the window. She paused a moment and watched the sun throwing its slanted rays through the lace curtains, duplicating their pattern on the wooden floor.

Her eyes traversed the room. There was the bed, standing in stately fashion near the window, overlaid in a blue and white coverlet with a colorful quilt folded across the foot. The next to draw her attention was the washbowl and pitcher on the dresser, decorated with painted flowers and ivy. Next to them were her mother's comb and hairbrush. Pegs along the wall by the closet still held some of her mother's clothes. There was even her father's favorite jacket on a peg, left their purposely by her mother.

Tears filled Jenny's eyes. She moved to the items on the pegs and touched them. "I love you, Mama." She told her father she loved him too.

The moment became too much. A deep sob escaped her lips.

She whirled about and threw herself facedown on the bed, sobbing into the pillows in an attempt to rid her heart of the unending ache inside.

The next morning, Jenny went next door and told the Bowdens she was taking a little trip in regard to her father's death, and asked them to keep an eye on the house. As she had stated to the Hendersons, she told the Bowdens she wasn't sure exactly how long she would be gone, but she was estimating it would be a week or a bit longer.

At seven o'clock that evening, Jenny boarded the southbound train that would take her to Baltimore, through Washington, D.C., and on to Richmond.

While the train rolled southward in the night, Jenny was alone on the seat. She watched the lights in the windows of farmhouses for a while, then put her mind back on the purpose for her trip. She slipped her hand into the purse and gripped the .38 revolver. She gritted her teeth. *I'll find you, Dan Tyler, wherever you are. You will pay for what you did. You put my papa in his grave, and by so doing, you put my mama in her grave. I am going to put you in your grave!*

When the train stopped in Baltimore, Jenny watched passengers get off and go into the arms of loved ones. Tears spilled down her cheeks as she faced the realization that never again would she ever be in the arms of her father and mother.

Her mind went back to the night in April 1861 before her father left home to go into the Civil War the next morning...

Myrna Linden was helping her husband pack his bags in their bedroom, while fifteen-year-old Jenny was doing the dishes and cleaning up the kitchen.

When Jenny finished her work in the kitchen, she walked down the hall toward the bedroom and heard her parents talking about the War and how it was tearing families apart. When Jenny appeared at the door, her father was holding her weeping mother in his arms. William Linden set loving eyes on his daughter and opened an arm for her.

Jenny hurried to him and let him encircle her in the arm. Tears were in her own eyes. She put an arm around him. "Oh, Papa, please come back to us. Please don't get killed in that awful war!"

William squeezed his daughter tight. "Honey, I'll come home to you and your mama when the War is over."

Jenny sniffed and blinked at her tears. "Promise?"

William Linden wanted to encourage his daughter. "I promise, sweetheart." He then looked into her tear-dimmed eyes. "Now, if this war goes on for a few years, you're not going to get married while I'm gone, are you?"

Jenny sniffed and blinked at her tears again. She thought of Nate Conrad. Nate had left for Washington, D.C., two days earlier to be inducted into the Union army. He would also be gone until the War was over. She forced a smile. "No, Papa. When I get married, I want you at my wedding."

William leaned down and kissed her wet cheek. "I want you to have a church wedding, and I'm going to be there to walk you down the aisle."

"Promise?"

"I promise."

The train was pulling out of the Baltimore station when Jenny's thoughts came back to the present. She wiped at her tears and whispered, "And I know you meant that promise, Papa, but that murderous Dan Tyler took your life. He made it so you couldn't keep your promise."

Vengeance burned within her as she told herself she would figure out how to kill Tyler once she located him. Once again, her hand slipped inside the purse and gripped the revolver. *I'm not an expert with a gun, Dan Tyler, but you can bank on it. I'll come up with a way to be close enough when I pull the trigger. I won't miss.*

Soon the train was once again rolling through the countryside. While Jenny watched the twinkling stars in the sky and the winking lights in the farmhouses, her thoughts went to Nate Conrad, and how he had betrayed her.

She wondered if she would ever get married.

219

# 18

THE TRAIN PULLED INTO THE RICHMOND DEPOT at nine-thirty the next morning. With the satchel in one hand and the purse in the other, Jenny Linden walked out to the street and hired a buggy to take her to the capitol building.

The woman at the receptionist's desk directed her to the offices that had been occupied by officials of the Confederate army during the War. She found a small number of men there, doing paperwork in regard to the War. One of the men directed her to the Confederate military records office, which was on the second floor.

Topping the stairs, Jenny moved past three other government offices, then spotted the sign that read: *Military Records.*

The door was open. Jenny stepped in and approached the counter. A handsome young man rose from his desk, smiled, and moved up to the counter. "Good morning, ma'am. May I help you?"

Jenny noted that the nameplate on his desk identified him as Eldon Wheeler. She smiled in return. "I believe so, Mr. Wheeler. I'm from Pennsylvania. My father died in the Andersonville Prison Camp in Georgia during the latter part of the Civil War. Of course, I didn't know about his death until some time after the War was over, you understand."

"I understand."

"Several weeks after the War ended, the Union soldiers who had been in Confederate prison camps came home. I was told by a Union officer who had been with my father at Andersonville that he had died there shortly before the War ended. This officer told me that one of the camp guards, a Sergeant Dan Tyler, was the last man to see Papa alive. I desperately need to locate Dan Tyler and talk to him."

Wheeler nodded. "Certainly, ma'am." He now had a pencil in hand, and a pad of paper. "What is your name, ma'am?"

Jenny's heart lurched. She dare not leave a trail that could lead the authorities back to her when they found Dan Tyler dead. The first name that came to mind was her mother's maiden name. "My name is Jenny Blair, sir. B-L-A-I-R."

Eldon Wheeler scratched the name on the pad. "And the Confederate guard's name is Dan Tyler. He was a sergeant, you say?"

"Yes."

"Would you happen to know where Sergeant Tyler is from? What state, I mean."

"No, sir."

When Wheeler had written down this information, he said, "I'll put a clerk on it right away, ma'am. It could take some time, like maybe a couple of hours for the clerk to find Tyler's file."

"That will be fine. Is there somewhere I can wait?"

"Yes," said Wheeler, heading for the small gate at the end of the counter. "There's a small room a couple of doors down."

Wheeler led Jenny down the hall to the room, opened the door, and motioned for her to step in ahead of him. The only light was from the hall, but Jenny could see the overstuffed chair, a small table beside it, and three wooden chairs nearby. A ticking clock hung on the wall.

Wheeler quickly lit two lanterns. "There you are, Miss Blair. I assume it is *Miss* Blair. I noticed you're not wearing a wedding ring."

Jenny smiled thinly. "Yes, it is *Miss* Blair."

"As you can see, there are some magazines on the table here by the chair. Make yourself comfortable. I'll be back as soon as the clerk brings me Sergeant Tyler's file."

"Thank you, Mr. Wheeler. I very much appreciate your help."

Wheeler stopped at the door. "Would you like this open or closed?"

"Close it, please."

He nodded and closed the door. She could hear his rapid footsteps fading away.

Jenny looked at the spot where she last saw him and her mouth turned down. "You just see that they find the file, mister. I want Dan Tyler dead!"

She set her purse and satchel on top of the magazines, eyed the chair, then shook her head. She paced the floor for a few minutes, wringing her hands, then finally eased into the chair. Laying her head back, she closed her eyes and tried to think of just how she would shoot Dan Tyler and get away with it.

After a few minutes, she raised her head. "No, Jenny, there's no use trying to plan it, now. You'll have to figure it out once you find him and know the circumstances. But when I do find him, he'll wish he'd never laid eyes on Captain William Linden!"

Suddenly the small room seemed to be closing in on her. She jumped from the chair and opened the door. "There. That's better."

She returned to the chair, and sat down with a sigh. Time seemed to drag. Every time Jenny heard footsteps in the hall, she looked up expectantly only to be disappointed. The person always passed on by.

Periodically, she glanced at the clock. When two hours had passed, she hissed, "Come on, Wheeler. Come on."

Finally, after almost three hours, the footsteps she heard in the hall belonged to Eldon Wheeler. He came through the door, carrying a file folder, shaking his head. "Sorry, Miss Blair. Since we didn't know what state Dan Tyler is from, it took longer than I thought for the clerk to find his file."

"But you have it there, right?"

Wheeler pulled up one of the wooden chairs. "Sure do. I haven't looked at it, yet." He sat down and opened the file.

She waited patiently while his eyes ran over the first page. He flipped to the second page, read it over, then looked at Jenny. "Mr. Tyler is from Chattanooga, Tennessee, and he has a good record as a Confederate soldier. Served in the cavalry for most of the War, then was transferred to Andersonville to be a guard."

"Chattanooga," Jenny said, rubbing her temples. "That's in southeastern Tennessee, isn't it?"

"Yes, ma'am. Right on the Tennessee-Georgia border."

Jenny rose to her feet and picked up her purse and satchel. "Thank you, Mr. Wheeler. You've been a real help."

Wheeler set the wooden chair back where it had been. "You're welcome, Miss Blair. I'm glad we were able to find the file, even though it took so long."

Jenny set the satchel down and extended her right hand. "Please tell the clerk I appreciate his effort, too."

"Sure will," he said, gently shaking her hand. "And if we can be of any further help, please let us know."

Jenny nodded her head and hurried out the door. She hired another buggy outside, and her heart was racing while the buggy conveyed her to the railroad station.

She purchased a ticket on a train to Raleigh, North Carolina, where she would take another train to Chattanooga.


Two days later, Jenny's train arrived in Chattanooga at ten o'clock in the morning. Bone weary from the long days and nearly sleepless nights since leaving Harrisburg, she picked up her purse and satchel and followed the other passengers from the coach.

When she walked out of the terminal onto the street, it hit her that she was in the very city where Dan Tyler lived. She patted her purse, feeling the lump made by the revolver inside. The revenge she sought was almost in her grasp. This thought gave her a fresh boost of energy, and the weariness she had felt was gone.

She made her way to the line of buggies and approached the first. The youthful driver was giving his horse a drink from a bucket as she drew up. He smiled. "Yes, ma'am. I'll be finished in a second or two. Where can I take you?"

The horse was slurping the last of the water in the bottom of the bucket.

"I'm here to look up an old friend of the family. I don't know his address, but he lives here in Chattanooga. The conductor on my train said I needed to go to the Bradley County Courthouse—they would help me locate him."

"All right," said the young man, tossing the bucket on the floor of the buggy, next to the driver's seat. "County courthouse it is."

He helped Jenny into the backseat of the buggy, climbed up onto the driver's seat, and put the horse in motion. "Where you from, ma'am?"

"Pennsylvania."

He nodded as they passed a heavily loaded wagon, pulled by two horses. "Well, welcome to the Deep South."

Jenny wanted to slap the cap off his head and pull his hair out. She restrained herself. "Thank you."

As the buggy made its way toward downtown Chattanooga, Jenny looked around. It was a beautiful morning. She noted the plentiful pink and white dogwood trees along both sides of the street. Their pleasant scent rode the gentle breeze that brushed her face. She breathed in the delightful aroma, smiling and allowing herself to enjoy it.

The pleasure of the aroma lasted only a few minutes, then the reality of her quest to find Dan Tyler set in. Once again, her young face put on its mask of determination. She was there to kill the man who had murdered her father and subsequently caused her mother's death.

Soon, Jenny was out of the buggy and making her way inside the stately courthouse. She drew up to the reception desk. A middle-aged woman smiled at her. "May I help you, young lady?"

Jenny explained that she was trying to find an old family friend who lived somewhere in Chattanooga and needed help in locating him. The receptionist gave her directions to the proper office, and a few minutes later, she was standing before the desk of a matronly looking woman in her late fifties. "Can I help you, dear?"

"I sure hope so. I'm from up north, and I'm trying to locate a man named Dan Tyler. He was a sergeant in the Confederate army during the Civil War. I was told by the military records people in Richmond that he lives here in Chattanooga."

The woman smiled. "Well, you've come to the right person. I know Dan."

Jenny's pulse quickened. "You do?"

"Mm-hmm. Actually, I knew the whole family. They didn't live here in Chattanooga, however. They had a cattle ranch some twelve miles west of here."

Jenny's features pinched. *"Had* a cattle ranch? You mean they're not there anymore?"

"Correct. The ranch no longer belongs to the Tyler family. Dan's parents both died several years ago. He was an only child. While Dan was away in the War, he had renters living on the ranch to take care of the place and the stock. When he came home in April, after the War was over, he sold the place to a family named Freeman."

The weight of the woman's words was pressing like a steel rod against her spine. "Do…do you know where Dan is now?"

"Sorry, I sure don't. But the new owners probably know. I suggest you go to the ranch and ask the Freemans."

This gave Jenny a thread of hope. "Can you tell me how to find the ranch?"

"I'll do better than that. I'll draw you a map. It's really an easy place to find. You can't miss it."

Jenny left the courthouse with the map in her dress pocket and hired a buggy to take her to the ranch. She felt relief when she showed the driver the map, and he told her he knew the area well. He had been past the ranch many times.

In just over half an hour, the driver turned the buggy off the road onto a tree-lined drive, and within seconds, Jenny got her first glimpse of the house Dan Tyler once called home. It was a large two-story white frame house that stood in a grove of trees, surrounded by an array of brightly colored flower gardens. A closer look showed her that the house could use a fresh coat of paint, but the magnificent flowers led her eyes away from that fact.

As the buggy drew nearer to the house, Jenny saw a middle-aged couple sitting on the front porch. They were watching the buggy, and when it drew close, they both stood up and walked down the porch steps.

The driver pulled rein. "Hello, folks. I have a lady here who would like to talk to you."

The couple smiled at Jenny.

"I'm Ben Freeman," said the man. "This is my wife, Florence. We haven't met before, have we?"

Jenny smiled. "No sir. My name is Jenny Blair. I'm from Pennsylvania."

She gave her story about Dan Tyler being the last man to see her father alive at Andersonville Prison Camp, then explained what she was told at the courthouse in Chattanooga, and said she desperately needed to find Dan Tyler. She needed to ask him some questions about what her father might have talked about before he died.

Ben scratched his head. "Well, Miss Blair, when Dan sold us the ranch, he told us he was going out west to meet up with two of his army pals and start a new life."

"Do you know *where* out west?"

"No. Dan didn't tell us."

Jenny's heart sank. "Would there be anyone around here he might have told?"

"Don't have any idea. Guess all you can do is ask some of the neighboring ranchers and farmers. Dan might have told some of them exactly where he was going."

Jenny spent the rest of the day having the buggy driver take her to the surrounding ranchers and farmers. None of them had any idea where Dan Tyler might have gone.

She had the driver take her back to Chattanooga, telling him she needed to stay in a hotel for the night. She explained that she would need one that was not too expensive. He recommended the Ridgeside Hotel, which was clean, but quite reasonable. It was also relatively close to the railroad station.

At the hotel, Jenny was directed to a small, but sparkling clean, comfortable room. When she laid her purse and satchel on the bed, her first inclination was to lie down and drown in its softness. But practicality dictated that she have a substantial meal. She hadn't eaten since having a light breakfast in the dining car a couple of hours before the train arrived in Chattanooga.

She removed her hat, shook the road dust from it, and laid it on the bed. Then she moved to the dresser and looked at herself in the mirror.

Turning back to the bed, she opened the satchel and took out her comb and brush, as well as her night garments and a fresh dress for tomorrow. Returning to the dresser with comb and brush in hand, she released her hair from its pins, letting it fall to her shoulders. She poured water from the pitcher into the washbasin and dipped in a cloth. She passed it over her dusty face, then dried it with a towel. Feeling somewhat refreshed, she drew the brush through her thick blond hair several times, then secured it at the nape of her neck with the pins.

She patted an errant strand into place, put the hat back on, then shook the creases from the dress she had been wearing since she left home. Moving back to the bed, she picked up her purse and opened it. She touched the revolver as if it were some prized possession, then took out the dwindling wad of currency, counted it, and put it back. With purse in hand, she left the room.

In the hotel dining room, Jenny chose a table near one of the windows. A diminutive young lady wearing a crisp white apron approached the table with a menu in hand. Speaking in a southern drawl, she said, "Good evening, Miss. Our special is a roast beef dinner with all the trimmings. Or you can order off the menu."

At the mention of food, Jenny suddenly realized how hungry she was.

"The special sounds good to me. And a pot of tea, please."

"All right. I'll be right back with your tea."

As the waitress walked away, Jenny eased back in the chair and let her gaze roam around the room. The place was almost full, and suddenly she realized that at every occupied table, there were couples or families. She was the only person there who was alone.

Her thoughts ran to her parents. Both dead.

Then to Nate Conrad. She had lost him.

Jenny sighed. *I see nothing but loneliness in my future.*

The waitress returned, carrying a tray with steaming teapot, cup and saucer, cream and sugar. She poured the tea into the cup, saying the roast beef dinner would be there shortly.

Jenny pushed the sugar bowl and small cream pitcher aside, picked up the cup, and took a sip. Her mind went to Dan Tyler. She felt frustration caused by the fact that she had failed to find the dirty killer. Now what? She was just too tired to think about it at that moment.

Soon her dinner was served by the waitress. Jenny managed to devour most of it, and felt a bit more energy coursing through her body as she walked to the counter and paid the bill.

When she entered her room, she laid the purse on the dresser and took off her hat. With her mind on Dan Tyler again, and feeling the frustration of not finding him, she fidgeted and paced the floor. How was she going to stand it, knowing her father's killer was walking free and unpunished somewhere out west?

Jenny's pacing went on until deep into the night. Finally she sat down on the edge of the bed and resigned herself to the fact that the west was too big for her to be able to track Tyler down, even if she had the money to go out there.

She must accept it. She would never have the satisfaction of exacting justice on the man who murdered her father, and by so doing, took the life of her mother.

Feeling sick at heart, she prepared herself for bed, put out the lanterns, and slipped between the covers. Moments later, sleep claimed her.

Suddenly, Jenny was dreaming.

Time had slid back some ten years. She was on a picnic with her parents at the Harrisburg Park. Other families were there. Children were laughing, playing, and having a good time.

Nine-year-old Jenny was among them. She knew most of the boys and girls; they were her schoolmates.

While playing a game of tag with the other children, Jenny noticed a girl her age who she knew well, sitting alone at a picnic table, crying. Her name was Maggie Knowles. Maggie's mother had died of consumption a few months previously. At the moment, Maggie's father was playing horseshoes with some of the men on the other side of a stand of trees, and apparently thought Maggie was involved with the other children in their games.

Jenny's heart was suddenly heavy for Maggie. She dropped out of the tag game and hurried to the table where Maggie sat. Maggie looked up at her through a wall of tears while drawing a shuddering breath.

"Maggie, what's wrong?"

"All…all the other children here have their mothers with them, Jenny. But my mother is dead."

Jenny put her arms around her. "I'm so sorry that your mother died, Maggie. If I could, I would take all the hurt out of your heart."

Maggie hugged her tight. "Thank you, Jenny. You are a true friend."

Jenny continued talking to Maggie in a soft voice until the weeping stopped. Maggie thumbed the tears from her cheeks and told Jenny she felt better. She would be all right now.

Jenny headed back to the picnic table where her parents were sitting and talking to the parents of a boy and girl from her school. She set her eyes on her Mama and Papa and told herself how awful it would be if one of them were to die.

The sound of her own sobbing awakened Jenny. She sat up in the hotel room bed, trembling. "Oh, Mama! Oh, Papa! It *is* awful! It's terrible! I miss you so much, and I will never see you again!"

Early the next morning, while Jenny was brushing her hair at the mirror, she stopped and looked at herself in the reflection. "Since you're already in the South and you still have some money, why not go over to Andersonville and see if you can find Papa's grave? I think it would make you feel better if you could visit his grave."

She firmed her jaw and nodded. "Yes. I like that idea."

When she arrived at Chattanooga's depot, she approached a ticket agent.

"Good morning, young lady. May I help you?"

"Yes, sir. I need to go to Andersonville, Georgia. Can you route me there?"

"I can put you on a train that will take you to Atlanta, ma'am. You will change to another train there that will take you down to Macon. At Macon, you will have to hire a buggy at the depot that will take you down to Andersonville."

"All right. How soon can I get a train to Atlanta?"

"There's one that leaves in forty-five minutes." He checked a sheet of paper. "You'll arrive in Atlanta at nine-fifteen. The train I'll book you on in Atlanta will leave at nine forty-five. You'll arrive in Macon at eleven-thirty."

Jenny opened her purse and took out the wad of currency. "Let's do it."

229

At noon, Jenny walked out of the Macon railroad station and approached the driver of a buggy who was putting grease on an axle. He rose to his feet and smiled, wiping grease from his fingers with an old rag. "You needin' a ride, ma'am?"

"Yes, sir. I want to go to Andersonville."

"Well, it just so happens that this ol' buggy has been wantin' to get down to Andersonville again and so has my horse."

"I…I need to go to the prison camp there. My father was a prisoner in the camp during the last few months of the War. He died just before the War ended. I want to visit his grave. Do you know where the prison camp is?"

"Sure do. Been right by it many times."

It was just past two-thirty when the driver pulled the buggy up to the gate in front of the Andersonville Prison Camp. The gate stood open, and from what they could see, the place was deserted.

Jenny craned her neck, peering as well as she could inside the stockade. "Do you know where the graveyard is?"

Before the driver could answer, an elderly man appeared from under the guard tower and came through the gate. "Somethin' I c'n do for you folks? I'm Jess Walz, the attendant here."

"Mr. Walz," said Jenny, "my name is Jenny L—ah…Jenny Blair. My father was a Union soldier. He died as a prisoner in the camp shortly before the War ended. I would like to visit his grave."

"Well, ma'am, I need to explain somethin'."

"Yes?"

"First, let me say I'm sorry that your father died here."

"Thank you, sir."

"You see, ma'am, the prisoners weren't buried in individual graves, but in mass graves. There is no way to know which of the mass graves holds the body of your father."

Jenny bit her lower lip. "Oh." She took a deep breath. "Would it be all right if I just go there for a little while?"

"Of course."

"Where is the graveyard?"

He pointed north. "It's just over that ridge, ma'am."

As Jenny alighted from the buggy, the driver asked, "Would you like me to go with you, Miss?"

She set soft, teary eyes on him. "Thank you, but I'd like to go alone."

"Sure. I understand."

"I won't be very long."

"Take your time, Miss. I'll be right here."

Jenny slowly made her way over the ridge and down the gentle slope to where the mass graves scarred the land. She stood on level ground and ran her eyes over the countless lengthy mounds of dirt, now speckled with weeds and tiny patches of grass.

"Papa...I'm so sorry I won't be able to bring justice to the man who murdered you. I love you. I always will. Good-bye, Papa."

Jenny turned and with shoulders slumped, made her way toward the slope, her eyes scanning the massive stockade wall that surrounded the Andersonville prison camp.

*19*

THE NEW MEXICO SUNSET WAS A GLARING BLAZE without clouds. It was Thursday, June 1, and Dan Tyler stood on the small balcony outside his second story room in Santa Fe's Buena Vista Hotel, looking west toward the rugged Jemez Mountains. The mountains were taking a dark, uneven bite out of the sunset, and their long shadows were shading the desert in purple toward the spot where Dan stood.

"Lord," he said, his voice full of awe, "You sure know how to paint pictures that would bankrupt the greatest orator on earth for words to describe them. That is beautiful!"

Dan was feeling the exhaustion of the long train rides he had taken since leaving Chattanooga seven days ago. The two-day lay-over in Little Rock due to a train wreck that tore up a lengthy section of track served only to weary him more.

His stomach growled. "Okay, okay. I know it's time for supper." He turned and went back into the room. He stopped when he saw the golden light of the lowering sun painting the walls with gold bars that were slowly changing to red. "Lord, if this is any example of what kind of sunsets You paint farther west, I'm sold on this part of the country already."

He stepped out into the hall and headed for the staircase that would take him down to the first floor and the restaurant. He was about halfway down the hall when he heard angry voices inside a room a few steps ahead.

Suddenly the door came open and a young woman came out, weeping. A male voice snapped, "Marlene, you get back in here, or I'll beat you half to death!"

She paused and looked back inside. "If you touch me, I'll scream for the people down at the desk to call the law on you!"

Dan was moving toward her when a big, husky man came through the door, red-faced, with bulging eyes. "Get back in the room, Marlene! Right now!" As he spoke, he raised a hand, ready to strike her.

Dan rushed up. "Hold it, fella!"

Both the man and the woman turned to see who had spoken.

The man's beefy features grew darker. "You stay out of it, mister!"

Dan shook his head. "If you touch her, I'll have to take you down."

The look in the woman's eyes spoke a world of relief.

The man's face looked like a thundercloud. "This is none of your business! She's my wife, and if I want to beat her good, there's nothin' you can do about it. You ain't man enough to take me down. You get out of here before I pound you like a nail into the floor!"

Dan's piercing eyes locked on the man. "No man is going to beat on a woman, no matter who she is, as long as I'm around. Now you just cool off, mister."

The big man cursed through his red blur of anger and stomped toward Dan. The woman put a shaky hand to her mouth and took a step back.

Dan braced himself, fists balled.

The beefy man's eyes blazed as his right arm shot forward like a piston behind his fist. Dan saw it coming and dodged far enough that the fist whistled past his ear. He countered with a savage blow to the man's mouth.

The man staggered back. His massive head settled into his shoulders until his neck was no longer visible. There was a low, rumbling sound in his throat.

Dan knew better than to let him set himself. He smashed him in the mouth again. The man staggered back, shaking his head, and fell on his back with a loud *whump*. Drops of blood flew from his mangled mouth.

Briefly, Dan saw the woman. Her own fists were doubled and her lips were drawn tight. "I'm going down to the desk for help." She ran toward the stairs.

The big man was rolling onto his knees, fire in his eyes.

Dan stood before him, fixing him with a cold stare. "Better let it go, mister."

The man stood up and wiped the back of his hand over his bloody mouth. He looked at the crimson brightness on his hand and let out an animal-like roar. He charged like a mad bull.

Well-experienced in handling the enemy on the battlefield when both were out of ammunition, Dan was on the balls of his feet. He dodged the muscular frame as it came his way. The big man roared, came to a stop, and whirled around, fury in his eyes. Before he had a chance to make a move, Dan's fist caught him flush on the jaw with a loud cracking sound. The man's head bobbed like his neck was made of rubber. Dan stepped in, cocked his fist, and unleashed another powerful blow, then hit him with the other fist.

The man's knees buckled and he fell to the floor facedown in a heap. He was out cold.

Dan heard rapid thumping on the stairs. He turned to see Wally Ames, the clerk who had waited on him at the desk when he checked in.

Dan looked back down at the unconscious man, then met the clerk's wide eyes. "Mr. Tyler, Mrs. Watson told me what happened up here. I've got a messenger on his way on horseback to the sheriff's house. He just lives two blocks away. He'll be here soon."

"I was heading down to the restaurant for supper, but I guess I'd better wait till the sheriff gets here," Dan said. "I'm sure he'll want to talk to me."

Mrs. Watson topped the stairs, panting, and hurried to the spot where her husband lay on the floor. She set admiring eyes on Dan. "Sir, I appreciate what you did. Louis was really angry. He would've hurt me."

Suddenly there were more footsteps on the stairs. A husky man in his early forties with a badge on his vest appeared. He looked at Wally. "I was just down the street when your messenger spotted me and told me what was going on."

Wally nodded as the sheriff looked down at the big man on the floor, who was now beginning to stir.

"Sheriff," said Wally, "his name is Louis Watson. And this is his wife."

The sheriff touched his hat brim and nodded. "Mrs. Watson. I'm Sheriff Burt Benning." Then to Dan: "I understand this man was about to rough up his wife. I assume you're the one who intervened."

"Yes. My name is Dan Tyler."

"Well, Mr. Tyler, you did the right thing. Sometimes family squabbles are best left alone, but not when a man is about to beat up on his wife."

"I can't stand to see any woman manhandled. God made men physically strong so they could protect women, not beat up on them. Whenever I see a girl or a woman being manhandled—or even about to be manhandled—it gets to me, and I have to do something about it."

Benning grinned. "Like I said, Mr. Tyler, you did the right thing."

Louis Watson moaned and moved his head.

Mrs. Watson smiled at Dan. "Your wife is a very fortunate woman, Mr. Tyler. I know she appreciates your protective attitude toward her."

Dan grinned. "Well, I'm not married, ma'am, but when I do find the right woman, I'll take care of her."

"I don't doubt that. Bless you for it."

Louis Watson rolled over, moaning louder.

The sheriff turned to Dan. "If you had something to do, Mr. Tyler, you can go. I'll handle the situation."

"All right. I was on my way down to the hotel restaurant when all of this started. I'll just move on then."

As Dan headed for the stairs, Mrs. Watson called after him, "Thank you again, Mr. Tyler."

Dan smiled over his shoulder.

Just after sunrise the next morning, Dan was standing in front of the Wells Fargo office in Santa Fe, waiting for the stagecoach to come from the barn behind the office where the coach and team had spent the night. The Fargo agent had told him he would be the only passenger on the short trip down to Albuquerque this morning. At Albuquerque, Dan would board the stage that would carry him all the way to his destination, which was the town of Mogollon, Arizona.

His head came around when he heard the rattle of the stagecoach and it came round the corner from the alley. To Dan, the stage was a thing of beauty as it bobbed serenely down the street behind the prancing team with chains jangling and harness rings shining in the early morning sun.

When the stage rolled to a halt, the driver smiled down at Dan. "You must be Mr. Tyler."

"Sure am."

"Since you're our only passenger this morning, you can just take your bags inside with you."

Dan placed his two bags on the front seat, climbed in, and sat on the backseat. The stage rolled south out of Santa Fe.

Two hours later, Dan boarded the westbound Wells Fargo stage with a well-dressed man in his early fifties and two elderly women. As the stage pulled away from the Fargo office, the ladies introduced themselves as Sadie Collins and Ruth Barton. Sadie explained that they were only going as far as Gallup. She added that both she and Ruth were hard of hearing and wouldn't be very talkative on their short part of the trip.

The man nodded and smiled. "My name is Pastor Richard Kelmar, and I'll be getting off at Holbrook, Arizona. I pastor a church in Holbrook. I've been in Albuquerque on business."

"I'm going just a little further than you, sir," said Dan. "I'm going to Mogollon. My name is Dan Tyler."

The men shook hands. Kelmar asked, "Are you going to Mogollon on a visit?"

"No, sir. I'm going to make my home there. I was in the Civil War as a Confederate soldier. Two of my army pals have gone to Mogollon to live, and I'm going there to join them."

The preacher nodded. "Well, let me tell you, Mr. Tyler, Mogollon is in a beautiful area. I've been there many times. The town is some sixty miles east of the San Francisco Mountains, and is situated in the magnificent Valley of the Little Colorado River. You'll love it."

"That's what my friends told me in the first letter they sent. They really made it sound inviting." Dan paused briefly. "Pastor Kelmar, may I ask you something quite personal?"

"Of course."

"Do you believe the Bible is the perfect, inspired, infallible Word of God?"

A wide grin spread over the preacher's face. "I sure do. And I preach the Lord Jesus Christ as the one and only way of salvation."

Dan shook his hand a second time. "Well, praise the Lord. It's always a joy to meet a brother in Christ."

"Amen! Are your two army pals Christians?"

"They sure are. They go to church there in Mogollon. Their pastor's name is David Denison."

Kelmar smiled. "Well, that's great. I told you I've been to Mogollon many times. I've preached several revival meetings for Brother Denison. The two of us are good friends."

"Small world, isn't it? This is really great."

"What are your friends' names?"

"Clay Holden and Joel Stevens."

"What do they do there?"

"They own the C and J Livery Stable in Mogollon. They bought it right after moving there. Changed the name, of course."

"Sure. It used to be Bob's Livery Stable. So what are you going to do there?"

"Well, in their first letter, Clay and Joel told me there are many cattle ranches in the area. I should explain that I was born and raised on a cattle ranch in Tennessee, just west of Chattanooga. My pals say with my experience, I'll have no problem getting a job on one of the ranches. You see, for most of the War my pals and I were in the cavalry. We love horses. So by having the stable, Clay and Joel get to work with horses. They also have a blacksmith shop and a wagon repair shop."

"So is their business doing well?"

"Quite well, from what they said in their second letter. They would like to bring me in as a partner someday, but it will take some time to build up enough business to support a third man."

"Well, it sounds like the Lord has things all worked out for you. And let me say this, Mr. Tyler, you will like Pastor David Denison as a person and a preacher."

"This is what my pals told me in their second letter. They really love him."

Dan asked Pastor Kelmar questions about his background, where he was from, and about his family.

Soon, from the seat in the box above, the stage driver called out that they were coming into Gallup.

When the stage rolled to a stop in front of the Wells Fargo office, the two men hopped out and helped the elderly women from the coach. Friends stepped up and welcomed the ladies, then escorted them to a waiting buggy.

Kelmar noticed a man come from the office carrying a satchel. "Hey, Mike! Are you going home on this stage?"

"Sure am, Pastor," replied the middle-aged man. "I didn't realize you and I would be on the same stage."

They shook hands. "I didn't either. Let me introduce you to a brother in Christ."

Kelmar introduced Mike Guzman and Dan Tyler to each other, explaining to Dan that Mike was one of his church members and the owner of Holbrook's tailor shop. The two shook hands, then Dan and the preacher took time to go to the washroom and splash some of the dust off their faces.

Moments later, the stage pulled out with the three men in the coach.

Kelmar and Guzman sat together on the front seat, facing Tyler. The preacher filled Mike in on Dan's story, then he and Mike began discussing matters that had to do with their church.

Dan looked out the window of the rocking, swaying coach as it crossed the New Mexico–Arizona border. He ran his gaze over the magnificent scenery, taking in the beauty of the wide-open desert land. In Dan's estimation, the farther west they traveled, the more beautiful it was. When there was a break in the conversation, Dan said, "Gentlemen, I'm overwhelmed at the beauty of this land. It's marvelous!"

Kelmar smiled. "I know how you feel. Just look out there. We are now in the area known as the Painted Desert."

Dan chuckled. "It's well painted, I'll say that."

The preacher pointed out his window, which was south. "And take a look at that forest."

Dan leaned toward his window and ran his gaze to the breathtaking sight before him.

"That's the Petrified Forest, Mr. Tyler."

Dan kept his eyes on the forest for a long moment, then looked out the other window. He chuckled, shaking his head. "Yes, sir, evolution sure painted this desert beautiful and petrified that forest marvelously, didn't it?"

Kelmar and Guzman laughed, and for a few minutes, Charles Darwin's godless theory of evolution—beginning with the big explosion—was discussed.

The preacher said, "It's a lot easier to believe what the Bible says: 'In the beginning God created the heaven and the earth.'"

Dan grinned. "Right. And it was Almighty God who said, 'Let there be light.' Like the heaven and the earth, the light didn't evolve. God spoke it into being. And it wasn't some accidental explosion that divided the light from the darkness. Genesis 1:4 says, 'And God saw the light that it was good: and God divided the light from the darkness.'"

Pastor Kelmar nodded. "Amen. It was all *His* wonderful handiwork, not the effect of some fortuitous explosion."

"Yes, praise His name. Ephesians 2:10 says that we who are born again are *created* in Christ Jesus. It wasn't an explosion that made us God's children. It was the Lord. And the gospel light that shined into our spiritual darkness was no accident. The precious Holy Spirit directed that light into our darkened hearts and minds on purpose."

Kelmar smiled. "You're right, my brother. Are you sure God

doesn't want you to be a preacher? I think you'd make a good one."

"Well, sir, if God called me to preach, I would most certainly obey Him. But He also needs laymen to back their pastors and help build the churches."

Kelmar rubbed his chin. "Well I can't argue with that. The laymen you just described?"

"Uh-huh?"

"There's one sitting beside me right now. Mike has been such a blessing. He's a soul winner. He backs me all the way and is a tremendous asset in our church. So is his wife."

Dan set his eyes on Mike. "God bless both you and your wife. Keep it up."

Mike smiled. "We plan to."

"Tell you one thing, Mr. Tyler," said the preacher, "Pastor Denison will be glad to have you in his church."

"Well, I'll do my best to be a blessing. I want to help him all I can. My two pals have really pitched in to help, I know that."

"Great. Ah…"

"Yes, Pastor?"

"Do you and your pals have girls back home? I mean who will be coming to join you later? You know…to get married, settle down, and raise families?"

"No, we don't. We talked about it just before they left for Arizona, and we agreed that since we have put our lives in the Lord's hands, He will bring the young ladies He has chosen for us into our lives when it's His time."

"Well, that's the way to look at it," said Kelmar. "Marriage is a wonderful thing. A man sure needs to get the woman God has planned for him."

"I can say amen to that, Pastor," spoke up Mike. "My older brother back in Michigan married the wrong woman. He's a Christian, and I believe she is too. But he married her on the basis of physical beauty without earnestly seeking God's will in the matter. The marriage was miserable for both of them, and after only a few months, they divorced."

Kelmar shook his head sadly. "That's too bad, Mike." Then he said to Tyler, "Be sure to seek God's will in the matter of marriage, my friend, whenever you find a young woman you think might be the one."

"I'll do that."

Soon the stagecoach pulled into Holbrook.

When the three men stepped out of the coach, Dan shook the hands of Pastor Richard Kelmar and Mike Guzman. "It's been a real joy meeting you, my brothers. The Lord bless you."

"We'll see you again, Mr. Tyler," said Kelmar. "And please greet my friend Pastor Denison for me."

"I sure will. And I'll look forward to seeing both of you gentlemen again."

The driver and the shotgunner took two pieces of luggage out of the boot at the rear of the coach and handed them to Kelmar and Guzman.

As they walked away, Dan waved and smiled.

The driver said, "Okay, Mr. Tyler, we're ready to head for Mogollon. Thirty miles to go, and we'll have you there."

"Sounds good."

As Dan stepped into the coach and took his seat, the crew climbed up to the box. The whip popped over the heads of the team, and the stage pulled away from the Wells Fargo office. Soon they were out on the desert with dust flying from the horses' hooves and the wheels of the stage. The bright sunshine reflected off the huge mounds of sand. Here and there, blossoms of ocotillo shone a brilliant red. The surrounding area was bedecked with ironwood and mesquite and an occasional cactus. Desert marigold, with its showy, long-stemmed yellow wheel-shaped flowers, made golden patches along the side of the road.

It was quite warm inside the coach. And Dan was glad for the breeze that whipped through the windows. He caught sight of a desert hawk periodically, as well as shiny black ravens. Once he spotted a vulture on the limb of a dead tree, twisting its head on its red neck.

The stage had gone about ten miles from Holbrook when the road swung parallel with a shiny river that wended its way through the land.

The driver called down from the box, "Mr. Tyler! That's the

Little Colorado. Branches out of the big Colorado River up north in the Grand Canyon. We're now in the Valley of the Little Colorado River."

Dan stuck his head out the window and studied the Little Colorado as it wound through the valley. It seemed wide enough to him. He wondered how big the actual Colorado River was. The golden sunshine on its surface showed that the water had a red hue. It seemed silent as it glided along. It was magnificent to see. He was captivated by the beauty of the river and by the vast rugged land around him. He had heard how the lure of the desert could capture a person, and now he knew it was so.

He was captivated, not only by the sweeping golden-red river, but the marvelous formations of red rock and the long reaches of desert; the undulating bronze slopes waving up to the dark, tree-shadowed mountains.

The miles passed, and when the sun was lower in the sky, the driver called to his passenger, "Mogollon up ahead, Mr. Tyler!"

Dan stuck his head out the window so he could catch a glimpse of the town. He saw the uneven rooftops of the commercial buildings on Mogollon's Main Street, and the houses that covered broad areas on both sides. They were of many sizes and shapes. Most of them, he saw, were made of adobe.

Soon they were in town, moving along Main Street, and Dan grinned when he saw the stable with its sign on a pole:

*C and J Livery Stable*
*Blacksmith Shop*
*Wagon Repair Shop*

His heart quickened pace. His new life in Arizona was about to get its start.

When the stage pulled up in front of the Wells Fargo office, Dan grinned again when he saw the smiling face of Clay Holden.

"Hey, Clay!" Dan shouted through the window, then opened the door and jumped out.

The two friends embraced, each pounding the other on the back. When the pounding stopped and they each took a step back, Clay said, "Joel stayed at the stable to take care of customers, but he's anxious to see you. I assume you've got some luggage."

"Sure do. Couple of bags."

Even as Dan spoke, the shotgunner pulled the bags out of the boot and carried them to Dan. "Here you are, Mr. Tyler."

Dan thanked him, and before he could grasp the bags, Clay had them in hand. He pointed to a nearby wagon with his chin. "Your chariot, sir."

Dan laughed and walked beside his friend toward the wagon which had *C and J Livery Stable* emblazoned on its side. Clay set the bags in the wagon bed. "Okay, pal, let's go."

They climbed in the seat, Clay put the horses in motion, and the wagon headed down Main Street.

While they were moving along Main and Dan was taking in the sights, Clay said, "Got good news for you."

Still grinning, Dan looked at him. "I can always use good news."

"Joel and I learned of a ranch job that's open. It was advertised yesterday in the *Mogollon Dispatch,* and the ad is in today's edition, also."

"Well, tell me about it!"

# 20

THE WAGON ROLLED SLOWLY DOWN MAIN STREET. Brilliant shafts of light shone between the buildings on the west side of the street as the sun's upper rim dropped beneath the horizon. Earth and sky were bathed in sunset light.

Clay Holden waved at a friend on the street, then looked at Dan Tyler. "The *Box B Ranch* is seven miles west of Mogollon. I've seen it several times. It has five hundred acres of pasture and wooded land and some three hundred head of cattle. I've never met the owners, but from an article in the *Mogollon Dispatch* last week, I learned that the rancher, Jim Brady, died suddenly on Tuesday of heart failure at the age of eighty-four. He left behind his widow, Suzanne—who is eighty-one. The lengthy job ad says she is looking for a man to come and live in the small cabin on the ranch and run it for her."

Dan's eyebrows arched. "Mmm. That sounds ideal. I'd like to talk to her about it."

"Well, there's one little hitch you need to know about. Since it is a comparatively small ranch, Jim had no hired men. Mrs. Brady explained in the ad that because of a substantial amount of money she sends periodically to take care of her sister in Texas who is very ill, she can only afford to pay a hired man thirty dollars a month. Carl Axton, the owner of the *Dispatch,* was in our wagon repair shop yesterday and commented that Mrs. Brady was going to have a hard time finding a man to work for those wages."

Dan opened his mouth to speak, but before he could get it out, Clay said, "Joel and I talked about it after Carl left. We decided that if you took the job, we would supplement your income until the day comes when we can take you in as a partner in the business."

Dan grinned. "I appreciate your kindness, Clay, but if I am hired by Mrs. Brady, I'll be fine. When I sold the family ranch in Tennessee, there was a mortgage on it, but I still came out with a few hundred dollars. I can afford to work for thirty dollars a month for a year or so." He glanced at the sun. "It's probably too late to do it now, but if you will take me to the *Box B* first thing in the morning, I'll talk to Mrs. Brady."

"Be glad to, but would you rather see if you can get a better-paying job on one of the larger ranches?"

"I'd rather talk to Mrs. Brady first. The idea of running the ranch for her by myself and living in the cabin sounds really good."

"Well, Joel and I sort of thought the same thing, that's why we got excited about it. I know you've got to be tired, so we'll just go out to the ranch first thing in the morning. As you know, Joel and I are living in the same room in a boardinghouse. We only have two beds, but I'll sleep on the floor and you can have my bed tonight. If you're hired in the morning, you'll be in your own cabin tomorrow night."

Dan shook his head. "You're not sleeping on the floor so I can have your bed. We've passed two hotels. I'll stay in one of them tonight."

"But—"

"No arguments, ol' pal. I'll stay in one of the hotels."

Clay grinned. "Yes, sir, General Tyler, sir. Joel and I will be taking you to Pastor Denison's home for supper. It's already planned. The Denisons want to meet you—and believe me, she and her daughters cook up a delicious meal."

"Sounds good to me. From what you said in your letter about Pastor Denison, I'm eager to meet him. You only wrote about his preaching and what a great pastor he is. I assumed he had a wife, but I didn't know he had children."

"Well, you'll meet all four of them in a little while." Clay waited a few seconds, then said, "Joel and I have some good news we want to share with you, but we want to do it together."

They were drawing near the stable. "Good news, eh? I can't wait to hear it!"

Clay swung the wagon through the open gate of the stable and pulled rein. Dan saw Joel walk through the door of the office. He jumped out of the wagon and they wrapped their arms around each other, pounding each other on the back.

When the pounding ceased, Joel gripped Dan's upper arms. "Sure is good to see you, ol' pal!" Then he said to Clay, "You didn't tell him, did you?"

"No, sir!" said Clay. "As excited as I am about it, I managed to keep from telling him."

"Well, I'm glad of that! But before we tell him, is he interested in seeking the job at the *Box B Ranch?*"

"Most definitely," said Dan. "Clay's taking me out to see Mrs. Brady first thing in the morning."

"Good! And if you get the job, you're going to accept our offer to supplement your income until we can make you a partner in the business, right? Clay did tell you about that, didn't he?"

"He did, but I explained to him that I have some money left over from the sale of my ranch in Tennessee. I can make it comfortably on thirty dollars a month for a year or so. You guys are very kind to make such a generous offer, but I'll be fine."

Joel chuckled. "Well, we plan to have you as a partner within a year, so it'll all work out."

"Sounds great. Now I want to hear this good news."

Clay and Joel looked at each other and grinned.

"Okay," said Joel, "which one of us is going to tell him?"

"I'll humbly pass the honor to you," said Clay.

A wide smile spread over Joel's face. His eyes danced with joyful light. "Dan, Clay and I are both engaged to be married."

Dan's eyes widened. "You're kidding me!"

"No, it's the truth," said Clay.

"Tell me who these most fortunate women are!"

Clay grinned. "I told you Pastor and Mrs. Denison have two daughters."

"Yes, but I figured they were children."

Joel laughed. "They were children once."

Dan snorted and shook his head. "Okay, okay. You two are marrying the pastor's daughters?"

"Right," said Clay. "I'm going to marry beautiful Mary, and Joel is going to marry beautiful Martha."

"Mary and Martha, eh? Are they from Bethany, and do they have a brother named Lazarus?"

"Not exactly," said Joel, "but I'm sure these young women love Jesus as much as the Bethany ladies did. Upon meeting these sweet Christian ladies when we arrived here, Clay was attracted to Mary, and I was attracted to Martha. We joined the church, and in a short time, Clay and Mary fell in love as did Martha and I. It's all set. We are going to have a double wedding on Saturday afternoon, September 2."

Dan chuckled. "Well, praise the Lord! I guess you guys know that here in the West, there are two hundred men for every single woman. I read that in a newspaper when I was on the train crossing the Texas panhandle."

Clay nodded. "That same information has been printed in the *Mogollon Dispatch* several times. Joel and I know the Lord had Mary and Martha picked out for us, so there were no other suitors for us to compete with. God is good, Dan."

"He sure is! So which of the Denison sisters is the oldest?"

"Mary is."

"And how old is she?"

"Nineteen."

Dan looked at Joel. "How old is Martha?"

"Nineteen."

Dan's face went blank. "Huh?"

Clay and Joel smiled, then Joel said, "They're identical twins, Dan. Mary is fifteen minutes older than Martha."

"Identical twins! Isn't that something. Well, since they're identical, how do you tell them apart?"

"It's easy," said Clay. "Mary is just more beautiful than Martha."

"Oh no!" said Joel. "It's the other way around!"

The three friends had a good laugh.

"Well, pals," said Dan, "congratulations to both of you. I know these engagements came about after much prayer and seeking God's will."

Clay nodded. "You're right about that. And the toughest part of it was asking Pastor and Mrs. Denison if we could marry their daughters."

"Yeah," said Joel. "It sure was!"

Again, the trio had a good laugh together.

On a serious note, Clay said, "Dan, there are two Bible-believing churches in Mogollon. The pastor of the other church is Lance Kemper. If you want to check out the other church before you decide which one to join, we'll understand."

"I'll make that a matter of prayer. But I'll visit your church first."

Joel cuffed him playfully on the chin. "Wise move, ol' pal. Wise move."

"How about taking me and my luggage over to one of the hotels? I'll get checked in, then whenever it's time to go to the Denisons' for supper, you can come by and get me."

"Hotel?" said Joel. "Clay, didn't you tell him we'd make room for him?"

"I did, but he insisted on staying at one of the hotels tonight."

Joel shrugged. "Okay. Well, Dan, I recommend the Avery Hotel over the Sanford. Folks hereabouts say the Avery is better, and a little less expensive."

"Then the Avery it is."

"Better get going, then. It's almost time to close up shop here. And Mrs. Denison wants us at the parsonage at seven o'clock sharp. You guys go on, and I'll close up."

At 6:45, Clay and Joel were waiting in their wagon in front of the Avery Hotel when Dan came out. Clay was at the reins. Joel slid closer to him on the seat to give Dan room. When Dan settled on the seat, Clay put the team in motion, and they headed down Main Street to the south.

The melancholy desert twilight rapidly succeeded the last rays of the sun. Soon they pulled up into the parking lot of the church, which was a white frame building with a belfry that was topped by a white cross. The parsonage was also white frame and stood a few yards from the church building.

Dave and Clara Denison were the first to meet the three young men at the door. They welcomed them, invited them in, and when introductions were made by Clay Holden, they gave Dan an especially warm welcome. As Dan was telling the pastor about meeting Pastor Richard Kelmar on the stagecoach, Mary and Martha appeared.

Joel introduced Martha to Dan, and Clay introduced Mary. The twins were petite and had light brown hair and hazel eyes. When all were seated at the dining room table with a delicious-looking meal before them, the pastor asked Dan to lead in the prayer of thanks. All were touched when Dan not only thanked the Lord for the food, but thanked Him for bringing Mary and Clay, and Martha and Joel together.

All four Denisons asked questions about Dan's life in Tennessee as he grew up on the cattle ranch. Clay and Joel had already told them about Dan's parents having died several years before, and Pastor Denison said that Dan's parents were waiting in heaven to welcome him there someday. Dan wiped away a tear and said he was looking forward to that day.

The next morning at eight o'clock, Clay was waiting in front of the hotel when Dan came out, carrying his bags.

Clay chuckled. "Looks like you're pretty sure you'll be hired."

Dan placed the bags in the wagon bed and climbed up beside his friend. "I prayed about it last night and again this morning. I've got perfect peace in the matter. Mrs. Brady is about to hire her new ranch hand."

Clay snapped the reins. "Well, we'd better get out there!"

Soon they were out of town, headed west on a dusty road.

Dan's eyes busily searched the landscape as the road stretched out level for some three or four miles, then crossed arroyos and ridges among massive rock formations. As they moved along to the sound of pounding hooves and spinning wheels, Dan ran his gaze to the wooded areas on both sides of the road, deep in shadows cast by the sun from a cerulean sky. "I tell you, Clay, this land is plenty different than the South, but it has a singular beauty all its own."

"That it does, Dan. And it grows on you too."

"Tell me about it. I'm already under its spell!"

Soon they arrived at the gate of the Brady place. Clay swung the wagon between the heavy posts that bore a sign some ten feet high between them that identified it as the *Box B Ranch*. The wagon made a rumbling sound as it crossed over the iron rods that made up the cattle guard, and as they headed down the lane toward the house, corral, barn, and outbuildings, Dan noted the beef cattle in the fields on both sides of the lane.

Clay set his eyes on a spot at the corral's split rail fence. "That must be Mrs. Brady over there."

"I'd say so."

When the wagon swung up close to where the silver-haired woman was struggling to carry a bucket of grain that she had just filled from a large metal barrel nearby, she set the bucket down and looked at the wagon and its two occupants. A half dozen steers were at the feed trough inside the corral, waiting patiently for their meal.

A wide grin split Dan's face at his first close glimpse of Suzanne Brady. She stood no more than five feet in height. Her plump body was clad in a brown dress sprigged with yellow and white flowers, and she wore a voluminous white apron. A bright yellow sunbonnet shaded her wrinkled face and her wiry hair was protruding out all around it.

The two men jumped out of the wagon, and as they hurried toward her, Dan said, "May I help you with that, ma'am?"

She sighed and wiped the back of her blue-veined hand over her forehead. "I'd sure appreciate it, young man."

While the woman and Clay watched, Dan picked up the bucket and poured its contents in the feed trough. The steers began eating hungrily. He turned around and asked, "Do you want more grain in the trough?"

"No, thank you. That'll be enough for now."

When Dan returned with the empty bucket, Clay said, "Mrs. Brady, I'm half-owner of the C and J Livery Stable in town. I'm the C. My name is Clay Holden."

Drawing her head back, she looked up under the brim of her bonnet and both men saw two twinkling blue Irish eyes and a smile that would charm all the leprechauns in Ireland. Dan immediately lost his heart to the dear little lady.

"I've been told that the two new owners of the stable are born-again men."

"Well, you heard right, ma'am."

"I'm a born-again child of God too, Mr. Holden. I belong to Pastor Lance Kemper's church, as did my late husband."

"May I say that I'm sorry about his sudden death, Mrs. Brady? Even when we lose a loved one that we know went to heaven, it's still hard to let them go."

"Yes. But thank God for His grace."

"Yes. Mrs. Brady, this young man is Dan Tyler. He is also a Christian. My partner at the stable and I were in the Civil War together with Dan. He just arrived here yesterday. He is single and is interested in the job offer you have in the *Mogollon Dispatch.*"

Suzanne's eyes lit up. "Mr. Tyler, do you have experience with cattle and horses?"

"Yes, Mrs. Brady. I was born and raised on a cattle ranch in Tennessee, and I know the business. I was also in the Confederate cavalry for most of the War. I love horses, and I love cattle."

"Good. And the thirty dollars a month is all right?"

"Yes, ma'am."

Suzanne cocked her head and let her mouth curve into another charming smile. "Well, Mr. Tyler, you're hired!"

Dan grinned from ear to ear while Clay whispered a word of thanks to the Lord. "Well, now that you're my boss, ma'am, you can call me Dan."

"I'll do it if you'll call me Suzanne."

"If you say so, Mrs. Br—I mean, Suzanne."

"Well, let me take you over on the other side of the barn and show you the horses, then we'll go to the cabin."

Dan and Clay walked alongside Suzanne as she guided them to the corral where three saddle horses stood, ears pricked up, looking at them. There was one mare and two geldings. Dan commented on what fine-looking horses they were, saying his first pick would be the bay gelding with the white face and white stockings.

Suzanne chuckled. "Well, he's yours, but you'll have to ride the other two periodically to keep them in shape."

"Be glad to."

As Suzanne led them to the cabin, which stood under two cottonwood trees some thirty yards behind the ranch house, she explained that her husband had built it with plans to take on a hired man when he wasn't able to do the work around the place anymore. Jim was still carrying the workload up till the day the Lord took him home.

When Dan saw the one-room log cabin, he liked it at first sight. It was neat as a pin. The bed was made of peeled logs and covered with a deep feather tick. A washstand and dresser occupied a portion of one wall. There was an overstuffed chair at the large open window in the front of the cabin, with a small table beside it. The welcome morning breeze toyed with the blue cotton curtains. In one corner near another open window was a square table with two wooden chairs. The cabin had two other windows, and the curtains in each one were in constant motion from the breeze. A woodstove stood in the middle of the room. Although it was not needed now, Dan knew its warmth would feel good in the cold winter months.

"Well, Dan," said Suzanne, "what do you think?"

"I love it. I'll get my luggage from Clay's wagon and move in. You can fill me in on the work schedule around here and I'll start earning my pay."

Suzanne smiled. "Wonderful! Now, one thing must be understood..."

"Yes, ma'am?"

"I'll do your washin' and ironin'."

Dan chuckled. "Praise the Lord! I appreciate that."

"And you'll take your meals with me."

"Sounds good. I'm not much of a cook."

"There's a large galvanized tub on the back porch for takin' your baths. You can get your water from the well pump at the water tank over there at the corral."

Dan looked at Clay. "I'll get my luggage, ol' pal, and let you get back to town."

The following Sunday, Dan went to church with Clay and Joel and very much liked Pastor David Denison's preaching. The members welcomed him warmly and he felt at home. During the week, he prayed about visiting the other church, but felt led of the Lord to return to the same church. The next Sunday, when the invitation was given after the sermon, Dan joined the church.

As time passed, Suzanne Brady was very pleased with Dan's work and thanked him every day for being such a good worker and working for such low wages. She also complimented him on being such an excellent horseman.

In conversations at mealtime, Dan learned that Suzanne had never been able to have children, and other than her ailing sister, who was in a sanatorium in San Antonio, Texas, she was the only one left of her family on either side.

Dan spent much time with Clay and Mary and Joel and Martha. He was glad for his two friends, that they had found the young ladies, but inside, he was wishing he could find a nice Christian young lady too.

One evening when he was eating supper with Suzanne Brady, she asked him if he had left a young lady back in Tennessee.

He swallowed his mouthful of fried potatoes. "No, ma'am. I'll just have to wait till the Lord sends the right one into my life."

Suzanne looked at him. "Dan, don't you know there are two hundred men here in the west for every single woman?"

"Yes, I do. But the Lord provided Mary and Martha Denison for Clay and Joel. He can provide the right young lady for me."

"Well, maybe the Lord would have you try the mail order bride system, like so many other men are doin'. If you put a lot of prayer with it, the Lord just might send you the young lady as a mail order bride."

Dan took a sip of coffee and set the cup down. "I…I don't know about this mail order bride thing, Suzanne. I'm not too sure it will work for Christians."

"Well, it does. There are married couples in my church, and in yours, whom the Lord brought together through the mail order bride system."

"Really?"

"Yes. Really. And to my knowledge, every one of them is superbly happy in their marriage."

"Hmm. Well, I'll give it some thought and pray about it."


That night as Dan lay in his bed, he pondered his conversation with Suzanne, but still was a bit uneasy about the thought of seeking a wife through the mail.

He lay awake for some time, talking to the Lord about it. Just before sleep claimed him, he decided that since there were couples in both churches who had found each other through the mail order bride system, he would seek God's leadership in it before taking that step.

That night he dreamed about his wedding. He was standing at the foot of the platform in the church building, looking down the aisle, while the organ played the wedding march. He recognized the faces of his fellow church members in the pews and saw Suzanne Brady sitting on the aisle a few rows back, smiling at him. But when he set his eyes on the young lady coming down the aisle toward him in a white wedding gown, *she had no face!*

The next morning, Dan was haunted by the dream while driving the *Box B* wagon toward town to pick up a load of grain. He shook it from his thoughts as he pulled up in front of the C and J Livery Stable. He would pick up the grain after having a talk with his two best friends.

Clay and Joel were in the wagon repair section, putting a new rear axle on a wagon, when Dan walked in. They both greeted him warmly and Joel asked what brought him to town.

"Well, first I have to pick up a load of grain for the cattle and horses. Second, I need a little information."

Clay chuckled. "You'll have to get the grain from the feed and grain store, but we've got all kinds of information around this place. What do you want to know?"

Joel laughed at his partner's humor.

Dan made a mock scowl. "Funny, Clay."

The three of them laughed together, then Dan told his friends about his conversation with Suzanne concerning the mail order bride system at supper the night before. "She said there are couples in our church, as well as hers, who came together through the mail order bride system. Who was that? I'd like to talk to one of the couples."

Joel paused. "Well, there's Tim and Lisa Cole, Earl and Emmylou Washburn, Jack and Lorna Sparks, and Forrest and Cynthia Hyde."

"I'm not sure who they are. Isn't Jack Sparks the one with the eye patch? He's manager of the hardware store."

"Sure is."

Dan's eyes lit up. "Good! He and his wife have been especially friendly to me at church. I'll talk to them."

Joel told him where the Sparkses lived. "Dan, Clay and I have been praying about this very thing. We've seen the look in your eyes when you're with us and our gals. It's time you were finding your gal. Suzanne's suggestion is a good one, as you'll find out from Jack and Lorna."

"We'll keep praying too," said Clay. "Let us know if you decide to go for a mail order bride."

Dan said he would.


That night, Dan rode the bay gelding into town after supper and knocked on the door of the Sparks home.

A handsome man opened the door. "Well, Dan Tyler! Come in!" He turned and called toward the rear of the house: "Lorna! Someone's here to see us!"

As Dan stepped in, Jack laid a hand on his shoulder. "I haven't said anything to you at church about it, but I was a Union soldier in the War. We can still be friends, can't we?"

Dan looked at him seriously. "We're brothers in Christ, Jack. Even when you wore blue and I wore gray, we really weren't enemies."

"Amen to that."

"Why, Dan Tyler!" Lorna said as she drew up. "It's nice to see you. To what do we owe this pleasant surprise?"

Dan ran his eyes between them. "I need to talk to you. Am I

coming at an inconvenient time?"

"Not at all," said Jack. "Let's go sit down in the parlor."

When the Sparkses were seated so they could face Dan, Jack said, "So what can we do for you?"

"Well, I…ah…I understand you two were brought together by the Lord through the mail order bride system."

Jack took hold of Lorna's hand and kissed it. "We sure were! And we thank the Lord every day for it."

"I'm glad to hear this. Jack, would you mind telling me the story from your side?"

"It's quite simple," said Jack, adjusting his eye patch. "I was in the same boat you're in a couple of years ago. Some of the other 'mail order bride' couples urged me to seek a mail order bride. At first, the idea of getting a bride through the mail didn't set well with me, but as I prayed about it, God gave me peace in the matter. So I went to Carl Axton at the *Mogollon Dispatch* and had him wire my ad to several eastern newspapers."

Dan smiled. "Well, that's encouraging."

"Let me hasten to say, Dan, that in order to make sure I got a genuine Christian bride, I put right in the ad that I was only interested in a born-again bride. I asked that any interested young lady include a testimony of her salvation when she answered the ad."

Dan smiled at Lorna as he said to Jack, "Well, it sure worked for you, didn't it?"

"It sure did. It has worked out wonderfully."

"Yes," said Lorna. "Jack and I are so happy together. The Lord certainly chose us for each other, there's no question about that. He can do the same for you and that young lady somewhere back East that He has all picked out for you."

Fully encouraged by his talk with Jack and Lorna, Dan rode toward the ranch, eager to put his ad in the newspapers back East.

The next morning, with Suzanne's blessing, Dan rode back into town and entered the office of the *Mogollon Dispatch*. He sat down with Carl Axton and dictated the ad to be sent to two dozen newspapers back East.

On Tuesday, July 11, a Wells Fargo stagecoach pulled into Holbrook, Arizona.

On board the stage was Edgar Toomey, who stepped out of the coach to stretch his legs, along with the other two male passengers. A woman who had ridden with them since Albuquerque was met by family members and walked away with them.

The three men noticed the driver hurry down the street and turn into a blacksmith shop while the shotgunner was inside the Fargo office.

Some five minutes later, the driver approached the three men. "Gentlemen, I'm sorry, but there'll be about an hour's delay before we can head for Mogollon. One of the horses threw a shoe just before we came into town. The blacksmith is going to forge a new shoe and put it on the horse. My shotgunner and I will take the horse down there right now. If you decide to walk around town some, be sure to be back by eleven-thirty."

The three men nodded, and the driver hurried into the office.

One of the men said to the other, "Well, since you and I have seen all there is to see of Holbrook, let's just go inside and sit down."

"I'm for that," said the other man. He looked at Toomey. "You want to stay with us, or would you like to take a look at the town?"

Toomey glanced down the street. "Guess I'll just take a walk."

As Toomey started down the street, the driver and shotgunner came out of the office, meeting up with the two passengers. They told the driver that Toomey was going to take a walk.

"Mr. Toomey!" the driver called. "Don't forget! Be back by eleven-thirty!"

Edgar waved back and nodded.

Strolling along Main Street, he chuckled to himself. He was now just thirty miles from Mogollon, where he would find Dan Tyler and send him into eternity. Toomey was glad he remembered that Clay Holden was from Birmingham, Alabama. He thought about how he had gone to Birmingham and found Holden's family, feigning friendship with Clay. He told them he needed to find Clay's friend, Dan Tyler, and wondered if they knew where Tyler might be. He was happy to learn that Clay was in Mogollon, Arizona, with his army friends, Joel Stevens and Dan Tyler.

Feeling elation because he would soon be able to put a bullet through the heart of Dan Tyler, Toomey heard a shout across the street from inside the Holbrook Bank. Suddenly, three masked robbers burst through the door, guns and money in hand, heading for their horses, which were held by a fourth man in front of the bank.

At the same instant, three men came out the door of the bank, guns blazing. The robbers started shooting back. Bullets were flying.

Women and men on the boardwalk on that side of the street were running for cover.

Holbrook's town marshal burst out of a nearby store, his own gun spitting fire. While people all along the street were trying to get out of danger, Edgar Toomey headed for a water trough. But before he reached it, a stray bullet plowed into his chest, and he fell in the dust of the street.

When the gun battle was over, the marshal was standing over the dead bodies of the four robbers when his deputy came up. "Marshal, we've got two dead men who took stray bullets during the gun battle. One of them is Dale Brooks, but the other one is a stranger, over there by that water trough. He's not carrying any identification, so I have no idea who he is. None of the other spectators know him. No way to tell which horse at the hitch rails belongs to him. Too many of them."

"Well, since we can't identify him, take his body to the undertaker. The town will just have to foot the bill for his burial."


At 11:45, it was past time for the stagecoach to leave. The two male passengers boarded, talking about the bank robbery that had just taken place. The shotgunner was already up on the seat in the box. The driver turned to the Fargo agent. "I can't wait for Mr. Toomey to show up. I told him to be back here by eleven-thirty."

The agent grinned. "He probably got interested in the bank robbery and can't pull himself away from the excitement. When he comes back, I'll tell him he can go to Mogollon on tomorrow's stage."

"Okay. Do that. See you later."

The agent watched the stage roll down the street, then turned and went back into the office.

# 21

ON THE HOT, STICKY THURSDAY EVENING of August 3, 1865, Jenny Linden entered her yard with the day's edition of the *Harrisburg Journal* in hand. The day had been a busy one at Henderson's General Store, and she was feeling a bit weary. The sun was more than an hour from setting and it put off plenty of heat.

As she stepped up on the porch, her eyes went to the empty rocking chair in the parlor. She paused and a lump rose in her throat.

When she moved into the house, its cooped-up heat hit her. She quickly went from room to room, opening windows, hoping to allow what little breeze was in the air to circulate.

In the sun-filled kitchen, she paused and took stock of her cupboards. She sighed. "It's almost too hot to eat, and eating all by myself has no pleasure. But Jenny Linden, you've got to keep up your strength."

She pumped water into the basin, splashed it on her warm face, and dried it with a towel. "Guess I'll just have a ham and cheese sandwich and a glass of water. It's too hot to fire up the stove."

Jenny set about preparing her small supper. She put it on a tray, along with the day's newspaper, and headed toward the front of the house. When she reached the parlor door, she stepped in and laid the newspaper on the small table beside her favorite overstuffed chair. With tray in hand, she moved out onto the front porch, which was in the shade of the house. She placed the tray on the small round table in the corner of the porch and sat in one of the chairs that were pulled up to it.

While she was eating, the flowers in her mother's garden gave off a fragrant scent when stirred by a quickening breeze. She was thankful for the coolness of the breeze and for the pleasantness of the flowers. Coldness washed over her as she thought of her mother.

By the time Jenny had finished her supper and cleaned up the kitchen, the sun was going down and the breeze that circulated through the house made it more tolerable.

She went to the parlor, sat down in her chair, and picked up the newspaper. She read the front page, which had news about President Andrew Johnson's untiring effort to bring the entire nation back to unity, though many of the Southerners were making it clear they had not surrendered to the Union in their hearts.

On the second page, she read an interesting article about the orphan trains, sponsored by the Children's Aid Society in New York City, that were carrying children off the streets of the city to homes in the Midwest and the far west, all the way to California, Oregon, and Washington Territory.

When she turned her attention to page three, she found a large article about Harrisburg men who had fought in the Civil War and now carried wounds of one kind or another. Many had lost limbs, while others had lost their sight or their hearing. Jenny thought of her father, wishing he had merely sustained a wound in the War, instead of being murdered by the beastly guard at the Andersonville Prison Camp.

The name *Dan Tyler* came off her lips, causing her to almost taste the bitterness it brought. She hissed, "Tyler, I wish I knew where you were. I'd see that justice was done."

Jenny kept turning pages, reading those articles that interested her, until finally, she was at the classified section. She read ads about fall clothing that would be available in Harrisburg's department stores in late August.

Letting her eyes run quickly over these ads, she started to close the paper and lay it aside when her attention was drawn to the mail order bride section. Having read the ads in this section a few times, she chuckled. "What fools those young women are who go out west and marry some man they have never met!"

Suddenly her eyes froze on a mail order bride ad that had been placed in the *Journal* by a man in Arizona named Daniel Tyler. She frowned and focused on it closely. In the ad, this Daniel Tyler said he worked on a cattle ranch called the *Box B* near Mogollon, Arizona.

Jenny's heart quickened and her mouth went dry. *Daniel Tyler. Dan Tyler, for short.* Could this be him?

As she read the rest of the ad, she was surprised to see that this Daniel Tyler wanted to marry a born-again woman and asked for the testimony of her salvation in her reply to the ad.

Jenny shook her head. "No, this can't be Sergeant Dan Tyler, who murdered my father. Even though I'm quite uncomfortable around these born-again types, I know they would never murder anyone."

She folded the paper, tossed it in the wastebasket that sat by the small table and picked up a novel she had been reading.

Going to the spot about halfway through the book where she had left a bookmark, she opened it, laid aside the bookmark, and began to read. From time to time she shook her head, flipped back a page, and reread part of it. She closed the book, holding the place with her finger, and sighed.

With her father's killer having been brought freshly to mind, her thoughts kept going to the mass grave where the body of Captain William Linden had been buried with hundreds of his Union comrades.

Fresh hatred for Sergeant Dan Tyler was burning inside her.

Jenny opened the book and tried to read but simply could not concentrate. Shaking her head, she put the bookmark in place and closed the book. "It's no use," she said. "I can't get that dirty murderer out of my mind."

Even while preparing for bed, Jenny was wishing she could get that killer in her gun sights. It would be a pleasure to put a bullet in him and send him into eternity. She smiled to herself. *And if I could later stand over his grave, I would laugh and spit on it!*

She doused the lantern, slipped between the covers, and tried to go to sleep. But sleep eluded her. She thought again of the mail order bride ad placed in the *Harrisburg Journal* by ranch hand Daniel Tyler. Once more, she told herself this cowhand out West couldn't be the man who murdered her father. Born-again people didn't go around murdering people. They just wouldn't do that.

Suddenly Jenny sat up in bed, the silver light of the moon shining on her face. "That is, unless they are hypocrites, and really don't believe what they profess. I've seen some of that kind. Maybe that's what this cowboy Daniel Tyler is—a hypocrite. I have to find out!"

She threw back the covers, lit the lantern, and made her way into the parlor. There, she took the newspaper out of the wastebasket, sat down, and read the article again.

"Mmm. Mr. Daniel Tyler, you just might be the man I've been looking for. Mm-hmm. Looking for so I can put a bullet in your vile, wicked heart, that is!

"I'm going to do it! I'm going to send a reply. It'll come from Jenny Blair. I'll ask for more information about him, his past, where he was born and raised. If he answers back that he was a sergeant in the Confederate army and served at Andersonville Prison Camp, I'll do my dead-level best to convince him that Jenny Blair is the woman he should marry. Hah! If he falls for it, Jenny Blair will go to Mogollon, Arizona, and give him the justice he deserves. What better opportunity to put a bullet in his wicked heart if I'm his trusted wife?"

With this settled in her mind, Jenny Linden returned to her bed and slept well the rest of the night.

The next morning, while eating breakfast, she thought about her plan. In order to fool Daniel Tyler into thinking she was one of the born-again types, she must come across with the right words.

When Jenny had finished doing the dishes and cleaning up the kitchen, she hurried to her bedroom and went to the chest of drawers where she had put the Bible Laura Denton had given her. She took the Bible out of the drawer and wiped the dust off of it. Opening another drawer she took out a photograph of herself that was taken for her high school graduation, and carried the Bible and the photograph to the desk in her father's den.

She sat down and read every passage Laura had underlined, and went over in her mind several times exactly what Laura had said she would have to do to be saved—to be born again. She rushed to the parlor, picked up the newspaper, and hurried back to the den.

At the desk once again, she took out pen and paper, dipped the pen in the inkwell, and began her letter:

August 4, 1865
Dear Mr. Tyler,
My name is Jenny Blair, and I am nineteen years of age. I am five feet four inches tall and weigh a hundred and ten pounds. The enclosed photograph was taken for my high school graduation a little more than a year ago. You can see that I'm blond. My eyes are blue.

Yesterday, I read your ad in the Harrisburg newspaper, and because of so many disappointments in my later teen years in trying to find the right man to marry, I feel that possibly you are the man that God has chosen for me. I know He does things like this for His born-again children.

You sound like a very nice man, and though you are a few years older than me, I believe we just might be meant for each other. I am intrigued with your occupation. Since I was a little girl, I have had a deep admiration for horses and cattle, and I have long been interested in the West. My parents are both dead, and I work as a clerk in the general store not far from my house. I'm sure I could fit into ranch-style living.

You asked for my testimony. Just a couple of years ago, I started attending a church that preaches the Bible as the holy Word of God with a friend of mine from school. After hearing that I was a lost sinner on my way to hell, I talked to my friend, and she showed me many Bible verses on salvation—verses that the pastor preached from many times in the pulpit.

I saw the light that God gives through the gospel. I realized that Jesus had died for me on the cross, shed His precious blood for my sins, and rose from the grave three days later so He could save me if I would open my heart to Him. I repented of my sin and took Jesus into my heart as my Saviour.

I hope this makes it clear to you that I am born again. If you are interested, please write back as soon as possible. Tell me where you were born and raised. Have you always worked as a ranch hand? I will be waiting with great antici-pation for your reply, and I will be praying that God will lead us together if it is what He wants for our lives.

Sincerely yours,

Jenny Blair

Box 23

Harrisburg, Pennsylvania

Jenny read the letter over to make sure it was exactly what she wanted to say. "There you are, Daniel Tyler. If you tell me you were a sergeant in the Confederate army, and served as a guard at Andersonville Prison Camp, and you want me to come and be your mail order bride, you have only a short time to live."

She left the house a bit early to go to work, so she could stop by the post office and mail the letter. Somehow, the more she thought about it, the more she was convinced that she had the right man. Her heart jumped inside her. If Daniel Tyler of the *Box B Ranch* near Mogollon, Arizona, indeed was her father's killer, she would have the sweet taste of revenge.

She greeted one of the general store's faithful customers who was coming out of the post office, then moved inside and drew up to the counter. Postmaster Bill Marvel smiled at her. "Good morning, Jenny."

"Good morning, Mr. Marvel. I need to tell you that some mail may be coming to me as Jenny Blair. It's a long story, and I won't bore you with it. 'Blair' was my mother's maiden name, and I'm using it for a very special reason."

"Whatever you say, Jenny. I'll see that you get the mail when it comes."

She handed him the envelope addressed to Daniel Tyler with *Jenny Blair* in the upper left-hand corner, along with her post office box address. "And here's a letter to be mailed."

Marvel didn't look at it but simply dropped it in the box of out-going mail. "Anything else, Miss Jenny?"

"That's all for now, thank you." She turned and went out the door.

A feverish excitement made her tingle all over as she thought about the letter being on its way to Daniel Tyler. "Papa," she said in a whisper as she walked briskly down the street toward the general store, "if this Daniel Tyler is the man who took your life, I will avenge you. And I have a strong feeling it *is* him!"

Thinking of Tyler, Jenny wondered if her father's killer knew where in Pennsylvania he was from. Then she shrugged it off, telling herself that even if Tyler knew Captain William Linden was from Harrisburg, he could make no connection.

She entered the general store and smiled at Zack and Emma Henderson, who were both behind the counter getting ready for the day's business.

Emma elbowed her husband. "Zack, do you see what I see?"

Zack nodded. "Uh-huh. Our little Jenny is smiling. We haven't seen her smile like that for quite a while."

"No, but it sure looks good on her, doesn't it?"

"Sure does, Em. Sure does."

Jenny moved behind the counter and began taking out pads and pencils. "How are my two favorite bosses today?"

"We're fine, honey," said Emma. "What has you in such a good mood today?"

*Careful. Don't give them even so much as a hint.* "Oh, nothing I can really put my finger on," she lied. "I've just decided I've been down-in-the-mouth long enough. I woke up this morning and told myself it was time I was rising above the heartaches I've been carry-ing. My parents are gone. I have to face that fact and get on with my life."

Moments later, they opened the store and customers were filing through the door.

As the morning progressed, Jenny had a hard time keeping her mind on her work. She kept thinking of Dan Tyler and pictured him lying in a coffin with his arms folded across his chest—the chest that would have a bullet hole right through his heart. *Yes, you dirty killer, and after they have buried you, I'm going to spit on your grave!*

That afternoon, Jenny was busy tallying a bill for a customer at the counter when she saw Laura Denton come into the store.

Laura smiled and gave a tiny wave. "Hello, Jenny."

Jenny smiled back. "Hello, Laura. Nice to see you." She finished tallying the bill, took the customer's money, and gave him his change.

She had waited on three more customers when she saw Laura standing in her line, which was longer than Emma's line.

Several minutes later, Emma looked at Laura, who still had two people ahead of her. "Laura, I can take care of you here."

"Thank you, Mrs. Henderson, but I need to talk to Jenny. Let one of these people in this line step over there."

Emma called for the next person behind Jenny's present customer to come to her, which she did. By the time Laura stepped up to the counter, there were no others in either line. Emma said, "Jenny, I'll go back and help Zack with that paperwork in the office. Give a holler if you need me before I get back."

"Will do," said Jenny, then smiled again at Laura. "So how's everything with you, Laura?"

"Just fine, Jenny. And you? There's a sparkle in your eyes that I haven't see for a while."

"I'm doing better, thank you."

Jenny tallied the bill and put the small amount of goods in a paper sack.

When Laura had paid her and was ready to take her sack and leave, she said, "Jenny, have you been reading the passages in the Bible that I underlined?"

Thinking that she had just read them that morning to use them for her testimony to Daniel Tyler, she said, "Sure have."

"Do you understand them better?"

"Well, a little bit, but it still doesn't make sense to me. I mean no offense, Laura. It's just that…well, it seems too easy. I'd think a person would have to do more than simply put their faith in Jesus to make it to heaven. I'd think they'd have to do lots of good deeds and never do any bad deeds."

"Honey, I explained that to you. Salvation isn't something you can earn by doing good deeds or merit by not doing bad deeds. It's by grace, not works."

Jenny shrugged. "Guess I'll have to read those passages some more."

"Yes, Jenny. Please do. And I suggest you read more Scriptures too. You can read the whole gospel of John, and while you're reading, let God speak to your heart. One day soon the light will break through into your darkness, like it did mine."

Jenny nodded.

Laura picked up her sack, then reached her free hand across the counter and touched Jenny's arm. "I bought the Bible for you and am encouraging you to read it because I care about you, honey. I want to have you in heaven with me for all eternity. You understand that, don't you?"

Jenny made a smile. "Yes. Of course. Thank you, Laura."

When Laura had passed through the door, Jenny's mind went to the *Box B Ranch* in Arizona. "I've been thinking, cowboy," she said in a whisper, barely moving her lips, "if you're the Dan Tyler who took my parents from me, whether you want me as your mail order bride or not, vengeance will be mine. I'll get you no matter what!"

MAIL ORDER BRIDE SERIES
NO. 10
1865
USA
AL & JOANNA LACY

# 22

IT WAS A HOT DAY IN MID-AUGUST as Dan Tyler drove the *Box B* wagon through the gate, onto the Mogollon road, and headed for town to pick up some supplies.

It was late morning, but the temperature—according to the thermometer on Suzanne Brady's back porch—was already 101 degrees.

The dust lifted from the hooves of the horses as they trotted along the road with catclaw and mesquite lining it on both sides. A hot wind was blowing, and Dan heard its melancholy moan in the mesquite. Squinting his eyes as he held the reins, he ran his gaze over the sunbaked land all around him. He noted the dancing heat waves off to the north with the blue distance of the San Francisco Mountains seemingly in motion.

As he turned his attention back toward Mogollon, he shifted on the seat and looked at seemingly distant lakes quivering in the mirage of heat waves.

Dan smiled to himself. In spite of the heat, he was adjusting happily to the desert more every day. He was beginning to feel a part of the land and loved its vast openness. In daylight, the wide open spaces and the endless blue sky did something to him. And at night, the great black velvet canopy, with its silvery moon and the shimmering heavens, affected him in another marvelous way.

"Lord," he said, "thank You for bringing me to Arizona. Thank

You for my job and for the blessing Suzanne has been to my life. And again, Lord, as I've prayed many times a day since placing my ad in all of those newspapers back East, I'm asking You to show me the right young lady to be my mail order bride—like you did for Jack Sparks and those other fellows."

Dan thought about the six letters he had received from young women already in response to the ad. Each one appeared to be a fine Christian, but none of them seemed right. Upon placing the ad, he had claimed Colossians 3:15 to guide him to the right woman: "Let the peace of God rule in your hearts."

The Lord had not given him peace about any of them, so he had written and told them this in a kind way, saying he wanted God's will for their lives, as well as his own.

Dan's eyes drifted to the massive collection of giant cacti on both sides of the road. Clay and Joel had told him these lofty, fluted columns of green were called saguaro, the mighty sentinels of the desert. Another odd-shaped cactus sprinkled among the saguaro was the ocotillo. Each of its branches rose high and symmetrical, furnished with sharp blades that seemed to be at once both leaves and thorns.

Suddenly movement in the sky overhead drew Dan's attention. Looking up, he saw two bald eagles in flight. Since coming to Arizona, he had seen a lot of birds: the magnificent swift-winged hawks, the great blue condors, and the grisly red-necked vultures. All of them held a fascination for him, but not the degree of fascination he had for the majestic, broad-winged bald eagles. He had often marveled at the eagles as they sailed wondrously, with graceful movement of wings, sometimes shooting across the heavens like thunderbolts, and at other times, circling around and upward to suddenly vanish in the deep blue.

Lifting his hat to use as a shade for his eyes against the blazing Arizona sun, Dan wiped sweat from his brow and focused on the two eagles. He noted that they were male and female. Eyeing the larger and imposing male eagle, he said, "What a fortunate fellow you are! I almost wish I was an eagle, like you—having a mate and nesting on the lofty crags of those mountains up north. I hope you appreciate what you've got."

At that moment, a still, small voice somewhere deep in Dan's heart said, "Be patient, son. You will have your mate."

He experienced a singular exhilaration and became conscious of the quickened beating of his heart. "Thank You, Lord." He set his eyes on the town, which was only a mile away.

Dan went first to the general store and made grocery purchases Suzanne wanted him to pick up.

His next stop was the hardware store. He needed some new tools and supplies for the repair work he was doing on the barn, the outbuildings, and the corral gate. When he stepped into the store, Jack Sparks was stocking one of the shelves with nails of various sizes. He set his single eye on Dan and grinned. "Howdy, Arizona cowboy!"

Dan chuckled. "That sounds good to me. You doing all right?"

"Sure am. What can I sell you today?"

"I need a hammer, a crowbar, some wire, and some nails and screws."

"Well, you came to the right place. Let's see what we can find."

After they had carried the items Dan needed to the counter, Jack started tallying the bill.

"Lorna doing all right?" asked Dan.

Jack paused in his figuring. "Sure is." A grin spread over his face. "But then, being married to me, how could she do otherwise?"

"I'll say no more!"

Jack laughed, shook his head, and went back to his arithmetic. A moment later, he came up with the total, drew a line under it, and looked up. "That'll be twelve dollars and ninety-four cents."

Dan plunked down a twenty-dollar bill. "Can you squeeze twelve ninety-four out of that?"

"It'll be difficult, but a man with my expertise and intelligence can do it."

Dan shook his head. "Why do I come in here?"

Jack handed him the change. "Because you like dealing with an intelligent expert like me."

"No. Because it's the only hardware store in this town."

They both laughed together, and while Jack was bagging the items, he asked, "How's the mail order bride situation doing?"

"Well, when we talked about it last, I had received three letters."

"Uh-huh. And you had written those young ladies and told them you didn't have peace about asking them to come."

"Right. Since then, I've received three more."

"Oh. And…?"

"Same thing. One of them was a blue-eyed blonde but I just couldn't get peace from the Lord to invite her to come. And the same thing with the other two."

Jack slid the paper bags across the counter to Dan. "I commend you, my friend. I well remember the temptation to invite a particular young lady who seemed just right when I was seeking my mail order bride. When I started to write the letter, it was like I had a tornado churning up inside me. No peace. If I'd ignored it, I would have gotten the wrong woman. Sure glad I let the peace of God rule in my heart. Lorna was definitely God's choice for me. You've told Lorna and me about your fixation for blue-eyed blondes, but you don't want to make a drastic mistake and get the wrong gal, no matter what color of hair and eyes she has."

"That's for sure."

"I told you before, and I'll tell you again. Lorna and I are praying daily that the Lord will help you to know when you get the letter from the right young woman."

"I appreciate that more than I can tell you, Jack," Dan said, picking up the paper bags. "See you later."

"Keep us posted."

"Will do."

Dan's final stop was the post office. He pulled the wagon to a halt, tied the reins to a hitching post, and went inside.

Bill Marvel was waiting on a customer at the counter. He looked past the man and said, "Hello, Dan. Be with you in a minute."

Dan smiled and nodded.

Marvel's minute was almost exactly sixty seconds. When the man turned and walked away, Dan stepped up to the counter. "Just need the mail, Bill."

"Sure enough," said the postmaster as he hurried behind the wall and returned with two envelopes. "This is it for today."

Dan took the envelopes. "Thanks."

"You're welcome. How's Mrs. Brady doing?"

"Pretty good. She has her moments when she gets lonesome for her husband, but that's to be expected."

"Sure. Well, tell her hello for me."

"Will do."

As he walked toward the wagon, Dan looked at the envelope on top. It was addressed to Suzanne, and was from the Alamo Sanatorium in San Antonio, Texas. When he looked at the second letter, he saw that it was addressed to him from a Jenny Blair in Harrisburg, Pennsylvania.

He climbed up into the wagon and opened his own letter. A broad smile spread over his face when he pulled out the photograph with the letter, and saw how lovely Jenny Blair was.

As he began reading the letter, his heart quickened when he read that she had blond hair and blue eyes. He was thrilled the way Jenny expressed herself, and he was impressed with her testimony of salvation.

When he finished reading it, he looked back at the photograph. "Jenny Blair, you're blond and blue-eyed…my ideal girl! And I feel—well, I feel good about you!"

Dan folded the letter and replaced it in the envelope with the photograph. "Lord, I believe You are speaking to me about this one. I'll let Suzanne read it and see what she thinks. When she read the other six letters, she had the same feeling about them that I did."

Suddenly, Dan found himself covered from the harsh rays of the sun and looked up. A high wind was shoving dark, heavy clouds across the sky from the west. "Hmm. Looks like we're going to get some rain."

By the time the *Box B* wagon was turning off the road and passing through the gate of the ranch, there was no sunshine to be seen. Lightning spread jagged branches across the dark sky, shooting fiery roots toward the earth.

Dan noticed Suzanne looking at him from the kitchen window as he drove the wagon up to the back porch. She opened the door while he was hopping down, and stepped out on the back porch. "Looks like we're going to get rain, Dan. We don't get rain often here, but when we do, it's usually a gully-washer!"

"So I'm told," he said, gathering the grocery sacks from the wagon bed.

When his arms were loaded, he moved up the steps and carried them into the kitchen. The aroma of hot food cooking made his mouth water. "Mmm! Smells good. What are we having?"

"Irish stew."

"Suzanne, you're going to make an Irishman out of me if you're not careful."

She laughed.

As Dan set the sacks on the cupboard, he said, "There was a letter for you. I stuck it in the sack with the nails and screws. I'll bring it in when I come back."

Suzanne nodded and watched him dash out the door, closing it behind him. She went to the cupboard and began taking out the groceries.

Outside, the wind was growing stronger. Dan climbed back onto the wagon seat, put the horses in motion, and drove up in front of the tool shed, which was near the barn. He deposited the tools and supplies inside the shed, slipped both letters inside his shirt, and led the team to the barn. Leaving the wagon under its usual shelter beside the barn, he unhitched the team and led them inside the barn.

When he had removed the harness and hung it up, he took off the bridles and put the horses in the corral, where they joined the saddle horses.

As Dan was closing the barn door, the smell of rain was strong in his nostrils. A strong gust of wind plucked at his hat, but he was able to grab it before it was gone. He pulled it tighter on his head, and with long strides, headed toward the house. He was almost there when stark white bones of lightning cracked through the blackness of the sky directly overhead. As he hopped onto the back porch, a roar of thunder like a bellow of rage shook the air.

A sudden deluge came out of the clouds, splashing on earth and buildings like a waterfall. Dan stopped at the door, glanced at the heavy rain, then moved inside. He hung his hat on a peg by the door, then reached inside his shirt and pulled out the letters. He looked at Suzanne, who was at the stove, and said above the roar of the rain on the roof, "Looks like your gully-washer is here."

"I'm not surprised. Those clouds have looked plenty heavy since they first started to gather."

Dan handed Suzanne the white envelope. "Here's your letter."

She took it, noticing at once the letter still in his hand and the big grin on his face.

The woman looked at her letter and frowned.

"What's the matter?"

"Well, as you saw, it's from the sanatorium where my sister is. It's probably a bill for something extra they had to have done for her. What's that you have there?"

Dan looked at the envelope in his hand and the grin made its way from ear to ear.

Since he didn't reply, Suzanne said, "Well, if you don't look like the cat that swallowed the canary! What's in that letter that's got you so happy? Who's it from?"

He cleared his throat. "It's from a prospective bride, and it looks pretty good to me."

"Oh, really? Must be really a good one from the looks of you."

"It is. And it's far above the other six. Hey, I just thought of it! This is letter number seven, and seven is God's perfect number! This has to be the right girl!"

"Now, Danny boy, be careful. Tell me she's not blond and blue-eyed."

Dan cleared his throat again. "I can't tell you she's not, but I was already planning to have you read the letter and give me your opinion, just like I had you do with the others. I trust your judgment better than mine in this bride search. I'm too close to the forest to see the trees."

Fierce lightning fluttered through the windows, followed by a deafening clap of thunder that shook the house. Fat drops of rain were splashing against the windows, driven by the wind. Dan said, "I see you've already closed the windows in here. How about the rest of the house?"

"All done. I was pretty sure we were going to get this rain."

"Do you want to read this letter now or wait till after supper?"

"I can read it now. The stew won't be ready for another twenty minutes."

Dan took the photograph out of the envelope and handed it to Suzanne. "Take a look at this."

She stepped to the cupboard, picked up her half-moon spectacles, and looked at the photograph. "She's a pretty one, all right. And she's a blonde. And from what you said a moment ago, she has to have blue eyes."

"Yes. She says so in the letter." As he spoke, he took the letter from the envelope and extended it to her.

She smiled, handed him the photograph, and began reading the letter.

Dan looked at the picture, drinking in her beauty.

When Suzanne finished the letter, she looked up at Dan with a twinkle in her eye. "You'd better get a reply to Miss Jenny Blair quickly, Danny boy. She may have answered other mail order bride ads. Not only did she write a heart-touching letter, but she is exceptionally beautiful."

"That's my opinion too."

A slight frown pinched Suzanne's brows together. "She's almost too good to be true."

Dan chuckled. "Yes. I was thinking the same thing. But I imagine that's how Jim Brady felt when he first laid eyes on you."

Suzanne looked up at him and smiled. "Now, aren't you the diplomat?"

"Nothing diplomatic about it. I think you're still beautiful, and you are one of the most charming ladies I have ever met."

Suzanne shook her head and took off the spectacles. "That sweet compliment will get you a double portion of Irish stew!"

"Great! And when my stomach's full, I'll write the letter to Jenny and put sufficient travel money with it. I'll ride into town and mail it first thing in the morning."

"Smart boy!"

"Do you want to read the letter from the sanatorium before we eat?"

"Guess I'll do that. Why don't you go get washed up?"

Dan wheeled and went to the washroom just across the hall from the kitchen. The rain beat on the roof of the house and soaked the windows while he washed his hands and face.

When he was through, he returned to the kitchen to find Suzanne sitting on a chair by the table, letter in hand, weeping. Her spectacles lay on the tabletop. When she looked up at him, a veil of sadness covered her usually lively eyes. Dan's heart went out to her. He rushed to her, bent over, and put his arms around her.

"Suzanne, what is it?"

"My sister died on August 4. They buried her the next day."

"Oh, I'm so sorry," Dan said softly.

"They have included the bill for the funeral and burial plot."

Suzanne clung to him and wept for a long moment, then pulled a handkerchief from her dress pocket. Dan released her and stood back so she could wipe the tears from her eyes and face.

Sniffling, she said with a shaky voice, "Sarah—my sister—was my last relative on earth. I'm…I'm the only one in my whole family that is still living."

"I can relate to that. I know what it's like to have no living relatives, Suzanne. I, too, am a sole survivor. But you know what the Lord said in His Book. 'I will never leave thee, nor forsake thee.' All of those we hold dear may die before we do, but our heavenly Father will never die."

Suzanne sniffed and dabbed at her nose. "That's so true, Danny boy, and it's wonderful to know. I told you Sarah was saved at the same time I was when we were children."

"Yes."

"It's such a comfort to know that she is no longer sick and lonely, but she is safe and well in the arms of the Saviour. I can't wish her back in this world for a moment, but as old as I am, I know it won't be long till I'm in the arms of Jesus—and with my loved ones who are there with Him in heaven." A watery smile graced her lined face.

Dan nodded. "I'm sure Jim is waiting, ready to be the first of all your loved ones to meet you at the pearly gates."

She sniffed again. "Oh yes. What a glorious day that will be. Of course, I want to see Jesus first of all."

"I'm sure you will."

She looked him square in the eye. "I want to tell you something."

"Yes?"

"Since I won't be sending money periodically to the sanatorium for Sarah's care anymore, I'm going to give you a substantial raise in salary."

"Oh, Suzanne, that isn't necessary. And especially since you have to pay for the funeral and burial plot."

"I've had money set aside for that for quite some time, so that's already taken care of. I'm going to triple your salary."

Dan shook his head. "Now, Suzanne, you can't—"

"Oh yes, I can. The ranch makes me a good living, and without the expense of caring for Sarah, I can afford to pay you well."

Dan rubbed the back of his neck. "How about just doubling my salary?"

Suzanne set her jaw stubbornly. "No. You're doing a wonderful job, and I'm tripling your salary. Anyway, you're going to need it when you marry that girl the Lord is sending you."

Dan's face tinted. "You're a case, Mrs. Brady, a real case. I don't know how to thank you, but to say thank you. I appreciate having the job in the first place."


On Thursday, August 24, Jenny Linden picked up the mail at the post office during lunch break, and her heart leaped in her breast when she found a letter from Dan Tyler.

She rushed out of the post office and sat down on a bench in front of the building. With trembling fingers, she tore the envelope open, and with the letter were two hundred dollars in cash and a photograph of three smiling young men in Confederate uniforms.

Her eyes went quickly to the letter:

August 5, 1865
Miss Jenny Blair
Box 23
Harrisburg, Pennsylvania
Dear Miss Jenny,
I received your most welcome letter yesterday, and I wish I could deliver this one in person. Yours was the seventh letter of response to my ad, which I placed in several eastern newspapers. The other six were from fine Christian young ladies,

but after much prayer over each letter, I did not have God's peace about any of them. After reading your letter, a sweet peace came over me, and I knew you were the one the Lord had chosen for me.

I have enclosed a sufficient amount of money for the trip, which your railroad people will schedule for you. You will travel by rail to Santa Fe, New Mexico—and by stagecoach to Albuquerque, and on to Mogollon. Please advise me of your arrival time in Mogollon, so I can be there to meet you.

In your letter, you asked about my past. I was born and raised on a cattle ranch near Chattanooga, Tennessee. When the Civil War broke out, I joined the Confederate army and chose the cavalry. I served in the cavalry until some six months before the War ended. They needed guards at the Andersonville Prison Camp in Georgia, so I was sent there to be a guard. Two of my close friends in my cavalry unit were also sent there at the same time. Their names are Clay Holden and Joel Stevens. They are both Christians. They are with me in the photograph I have enclosed. I'm the good-looking one in the middle!

Clay and Joel are the reason I'm in Arizona. They came here ahead of me. They own and operate a combination stable, blacksmith shop, and wagon repair shop.

In my ad, I explained that I work on the *Box B Ranch* near Mogollon. I work for the elderly widow who owns the ranch and live in a log cabin behind the ranch house. Her name is Suzanne Brady, and you will love her. I have made arrangements with her so you can live in the ranch house until we get married. You and I will discuss a wedding date after we have gotten to know each other and have prayed about it.

We have a great church here. You will love Pastor David Denison, his family, and all the wonderful members of the church.

I will be eagerly waiting to hear of your arrival time. No doubt you are aware of the significance of the number seven in the Bible. God planned for you to write the seventh letter so I would know that you are the PERFECT one for me!

Until I meet the beautiful blue-eyed blonde in the photograph in person, I will try to contain myself.

Yours expectantly,

Dan

Jenny bit her lips. This is the man who murdered her father. She studied his face in the photograph, considered the letter, and told herself he seemed like such a nice man. Generous, too. He had included far more money than she would need for the trip to Mogollon. How could he be a murderer?

A coldness settled over her. "Mm-hmm. But then, hypocrites are like that."

She studied his face again. "I agree, Dan. You are quite good-looking." A frown creased her brow. "You'll be a good-looking corpse, won't you?"

The next day, Jenny went to the railroad station and made reservations on the trains and stagecoaches that would carry her to the man she would shoot, and bought her tickets with his money.

That evening, she wrote her acceptance letter, giving Dan the time she would arrive in Mogollon on the Wells Fargo stagecoach. It would be at four o'clock on Tuesday afternoon, September 5.

The next morning, a sense of deep satisfaction enveloped Jenny when she handed the letter to the postmaster. Yet, when she walked out of the post office, a mental picture of Dan's smiling face came to her mind. A strange, unexplainable feeling washed over her. She shook it off and hurried on down the street.

Though it was her day off, she would now go to the general store and give the Hendersons a false reason why she had to be gone for an indefinite period of time on a trip out west.

As she walked toward the store, she told herself once again that she would have to wait till she was in Mogollon to make her plans on how to shoot her father's murderer and get away with it. She might exact her justice before they married. On the other hand, though Dan worked the ranch for this widow woman, maybe he had some money in the bank. If that was the case, she would shoot him after they got married, make it look like someone else did it, and as his widow, she would collect whatever money was his.

Either way, Dan Tyler didn't know it but he had only a short time to live.

Jenny arrived at the store, and the Hendersons accepted the reason she gave for needing to take a trip out west. Zack assured her that her job would be waiting for her.

When she arrived home, she went next door to the Bowden home, gave the same reason for the trip west to John and Dorothy, and left her house in their care. They volunteered to take her to the railroad station the next morning.

Sleep was very elusive for Jenny that night. As she lay in her bed, she let her mind have free rein, and it transported her back to her childhood. She thought of the days when she was a happy, carefree little girl with parents who doted on their only child. One pleasant scene melted into another as the years passed by in her mind.

Finally, in her memory, she was watching her beloved father walk out the door to fight in a war from which he would never return, then found herself standing over her mother's open coffin, with tears streaming down her face.

Lying in her dark room, Jenny let her mind run to the good-looking hypocrite who had murdered her father. She could almost feel the grip of the revolver in her hand, and pretending it was aimed at Dan Tyler's heart, pulled her finger back as if she was squeezing the trigger.

"I know it won't bring Papa and Mama back," she breathed, "but that bloody killer has to pay for what he did!"

After only a few hours sleep, Jenny rose wearily from bed the next morning. A fevered excitement filled her as she prepared a hasty breakfast.

Downing the last drop of coffee, she quickly rinsed the few dishes and glanced around the kitchen to make sure that all was in order. She then moved from room to room, and once again, her mind was filled with memories. This house had been her home all of her life, and now she was the only member of her family left.

Frustrated with the tears that filmed her eyes, she quickly wiped them away.

Returning to her bedroom, Jenny let her gaze linger on her own things. Suddenly she became aware of the time. She tied her bonnet on with the ribbon under her chin, then picked up her purse from the dresser and opened it to check on the revolver. It was there, and seemed to say, "I'm here, Jenny, and I'm ready to be your weapon!"

On the dresser, next to her purse, was the small Bible Laura Denton had given her. Since she was supposed to be a believer, she knew she would have to carry a Bible to church in Mogollon. She placed it in the purse alongside the revolver that was to end Dan Tyler's life. She picked up the satchel she had packed the night before and went through the bedroom door without looking back.

Once again, Jenny went to the kitchen, made sure the fire was out in the stove, then headed up the hall toward the front door. She paused for a moment at the parlor door and set her gaze on her mother's rocking chair by the big window. Fresh tears threatened to spill. She swallowed hard, rushed to the rocking chair, set the satchel down, and ran her hand over the arms of the chair. Blinking at her tears, she said in a low voice, "Mama, I'm sure you wouldn't approve of what I'm about to do, but I know for me to have any sense of peace, I must see that the man responsible for your death and Papa's pays for it. I have to do it. I love you."

With those words, her resolve took control. She hurried into the hall and out the front door. She closed it, locked it, and headed for the porch steps. At the curb, John and Dorothy were waiting in their buggy to take her to the railroad station.

Just as she reached the steps, an ugly thought struck her, and she stopped. What if the authorities would catch her after she killed Dan Tyler, in spite of the care she took to kill him without being detected?

She bit her lower lip. *If they were to learn that I had done it and arrested me, I would never be able to come home again. I would spend the rest of my life in prison. Am I prepared for this?*

The unexpected thought gripped her for a moment; then again the horrendous thought of her father's murderer getting away with it and being free to live out his life overtook her mind.

Jenny drew a deep breath, squared her shoulders, and descended the porch steps. She smiled at the Bowdens as she hurried toward their buggy, satchel and purse in hand.

# 23

MAIL ORDER BRIDE SERIES
NO. 10
1865
USA
AL & JOANNA LACY

ON FRIDAY MORNING, SEPTEMBER 1, Clay Holden and Joel Stevens were busy in their blacksmith shop. Clay was putting shoes he had forged the day before on a draft horse from a nearby ranch, while Joel was working the bellows, preparing to forge four more for a customer's horse that was waiting in the stable.

Clay nailed the first shoe on the hoof of the horse's right foreleg. As he bent down to pick up another shoe, he saw movement at the wide double doors from the corner of his eye, and turned to see the form of Dan Tyler coming in with a wide grin on his face. Dan's eyes were sparkling. There was an envelope in his hand.

Clay straightened up. "Hey, Joel. We've got a happy man here."

Joel stopped working the bellows and turned to look at the man who was walking toward them. "Yeah, he sure does look happy. I'd say that letter in his hand is probably from that cute little blue-eyed blonde in Harrisburg, Pennsylvania."

Dan used a thumb to push his hat back a little on his head. "Well, Joel, ol' pal, you are dead on center." He lifted the envelope up so both could get a good look at it. "I just stopped at the post office, and here was this letter from Jenny in Harrisburg. She's coming to be my mail order bride! She'll arrive in Mogollon on the four o'clock stage on Tuesday, September 5!"

Both men laughed happily.

"That's great, ol' pal!" said Clay. "Congratulations!"

Joel popped his palms together. "Yeah! Congratulations!"

Clay rubbed his jaw thoughtfully. "Too bad she couldn't have come in time to attend the wedding tomorrow."

Joel nodded. "Yeah. Too bad. It would have been nice to have her here to see Dan perform as best man for this double wedding. It's going to help prepare him to be a groom. Jenny would probably like to see how he functions in a wedding atmosphere."

Dan chuckled. "Well, I'd like to have her here for your wedding, gentlemen, but even more important—she'll be here for ours!"

Clay and Joel laughed.

Dan snapped his fingers. "Hey, I just thought of something!"

"What's that?" asked Joel.

"Well, since I get to be best man for both of you guys, maybe we can work it so both of you can be best man at my wedding."

Clay moaned and shook his head. "No, Dan. Two guys can't be best *man*. It would have to be best *men,* but that would be impossible, because I'm better than Joel! I'd be the best *man*. He'd only be second best."

Joel gave him a mock scowl. "Oh, yeah? You've got that backwards, ol' pal!"

Dan laughed. "Okay, okay, sorry I even brought it up. When it's time for my wedding, we'll flip a coin to see which one of you will be best man."

"Hey, flipping a coin won't change anything!" said Joel. "Even if I lost in the coin toss, I'd still be the best man at your wedding."

Clay cuffed Joe playfully on the chin. "Hah! That's a matter of opinion. If all the people who know both of us got to express their opinions as to which one of us is the best man, they'd vote for yours truly!"

Grinning, Dan said, "Sorry, boys. I didn't mean to start a fight. I'll get out of here so you can make peace and get back to work."

Clay snorted. "You mean you're not going to let us read that letter in your hand?" said Clay.

"Not on your life! What that cute blue-eyed blonde said in here is just between her and me!"

Joel nodded. "Of course. Seriously, Dan, we're both very happy for you. We'll tell Martha and Mary about it this evening when we eat supper at the Denisons."

"Thanks, but you won't need to. I'll be going to the parsonage with this good news before I head back to the ranch for lunch."

"Well, they're going to be as happy for you as we are. Our father-in-law and mother-in-law to be will be happy for you too."


Jack and Lorna Sparks were behind the counter at the hardware store when they saw Dan come in with the same wide grin and sparkle in his eyes. There were no customers in the store at the moment.

Lorna elbowed her husband. "I think we're about to be told that a certain happy cowboy has received a letter from a certain girl in Pennsylvania."

"You've got that exactly right, Lorna," said Dan, drawing up to the counter and flashing the envelope. "Jenny's going to be here on the Wells Fargo stage at four o'clock next Tuesday."

"Wonderful!" exclaimed Jack. "I just know it's going to work out beautifully between you and Jenny."

Lorna nodded. "Has to. The Lord is bringing them together without a doubt."

"Yes. Praise His name!"

"Just like He did us, sweetheart," Jack said, putting an arm around her. "When God's in it, everything goes right. I'm really glad for you, Dan."

Lorna smiled. "Me too. And you be sure we get to meet her as soon as possible."

"I'll do that, you can bank on it. Well, I've got to let Pastor Denison, Clara, and their daughters know. Then I'm riding to the ranch so I can tell Suzanne she's about to have a lovely houseguest."

When Dan arrived at the parsonage, the pastor, Clara, Mary, and Martha rejoiced at the good news. Clara told him she would prepare a nice meal for next Tuesday evening. The newlyweds would be invited, as well as Suzanne Brady. Together they would give Jenny a royal welcome.

Dan was pleased at this gesture and thanked Clara for her kindness. Then, as happy as the proverbial lark, Dan mounted the bay gelding and rode for the ranch.


Suzanne Brady was in the kitchen preparing lunch while wondering what was keeping Dan. She had expected him back by about eleven o'clock. It was now ten minutes till noon.

She pushed the pans and the coffeepot partially off the hot part of the stove, wanting to keep them warm.

When she stepped away from the stove, she stopped, closed her eyes, and put a hand to her forehead. She opened the cupboard and took out an envelope of salicylic acid powders. She measured the dosage into a cup with a teaspoon, then went to the water bucket at the end of the cupboard, filled the cup with the dipper, and stirred it with the spoon.

She was just finishing the last of the mixture when she heard rapid hoofbeats pounding past the side of the house. She swallowed it quickly and used a little more water from the bucket to rinse out the cup.

Footsteps were heard on the back porch and Suzanne turned around when the door came open.

Dan stepped in, a crooked grin on his mouth. "Am I in trouble for being late for lunch?"

Suzanne gave him a loving look. "Not if you have a good reason."

Dan lifted up the envelope. "How about a letter from Jenny saying she's coming to be my mail order bride? I had to share the news with Clay and Joel, Jack and Lorna, and the pastor and his family. Is that a good reason?"

Suzanne's eyes widened. "Really? Is she really coming?"

"Sure is! She'll be here next Tuesday on the four o'clock stage."

"Oh, Danny boy! That's wonderful. Praise the Lord!"


The next morning, Dan Tyler awakened in his cabin to a beautiful sunrise. His first thoughts were of Jenny, then his mind went to the wedding that would take place at the church that afternoon at three o'clock. He wondered if his two pals had gotten any sleep at all.

He got out of bed, washed, shaved, and combed this hair, then put on Levi's, a shirt, and socks. He slipped into his high-heeled western boots, then sat down at his small table, read his Bible, and had his prayer time. When he was finished, he put on his wide-brimmed cowboy hat, left the cabin, and headed for the barn and corral to do his chores.

A half hour later, Dan was approaching the ranch house when he noticed that there was no smoke rising from the chimney above the kitchen. Something was wrong. Suzanne always had breakfast ready when he came in after doing his chores.

He hastened his pace, and hopped the steps of the back porch in one bound. When he opened the door, his heart skipped a beat. Suzanne was lying on the floor in front of the cupboard. Her eyes were closed and she wasn't moving.

He dashed to her, knelt down, and touched her face. It was warm and she was breathing. Taking hold of her chubby hands, he squeezed them. "Suzanne! Suzanne! Can you hear me?"

There was no response.

While he ran toward the barn and corral, Dan said, "Oh, dear Lord. Help me to get her to the doctor in time."

Moments later, he snapped the reins and hurried the team up to the rear of the house. Hopping down from the wagon seat, he dashed back into the house. He checked Suzanne again. She was still breathing, but had not come to.

He dashed to the spare bedroom, gathered up an armful of pillows, and hurried to the linen closet in the hall. With two blankets added to his pillow supply, he ran outside to the wagon and made Suzanne a soft place to lie in the wagon bed next to the tailgate.

He was still praying as he dashed back into the kitchen and gathered her limp form into his arms. He carried her quickly to the wagon and laid her on the pillows, then covered her with the blankets. After running back to close the back door, he climbed into the wagon seat, looked at Suzanne one more time, and put the horses to a gallop.

During the fast trip toward town, Dan looked over his shoulder repeatedly. Suzanne had not moved, and her eyes were still closed.

When the wagon came to a halt in front of Dr. Wesley Foreman's office in Mogollon, he hopped down from the seat, ran around to the tailgate, and flipped it down.

He reached in to gather Suzanne up in his arms, and as soon as he touched her, he knew she was dead. Her skin was cool, and she was not breathing.

Sick at heart, Dan picked up the lifeless body, and with people on the street looking on wide-eyed, he carried it inside. The nurse at the desk stood up and looked at the body. "Oh, dear. It's Suzanne Brady. Is she—"

"Yes, ma'am. She's dead. I'm her hired hand, ma'am. I found her unconscious on the kitchen floor when I went into the ranch house to have breakfast with her as usual. By the time I got her here in the wagon, she was dead."

The nurse dashed to the examining room at the rear of the office, and brought Dr. Foreman into the office. His face pinched when he saw the limp form in Dan's arms. He asked Dan to follow him, and when they reached an examining table in a secluded corner of the room, he asked Dan to lay the body on it.

When it was done, Foreman told Dan to wait out in the office. He would do a thorough examination and let him know what caused her death.

A half hour had passed when the doctor appeared and told Dan that Suzanne had died of heart failure.

Dan frowned. "Had she been having heart trouble, Doctor?"

"No, but like her husband, her heart just gave out. Since you're the hired hand, I'd suggest you go to her attorney and let him know. He will have to handle the legal papers for the sale of the ranch. Have you met him? His name is Derek Campbell."

"No, sir. I recall her mentioning her attorney a time or two, but I didn't know his name."

Foreman nodded. "His office is in the next block across the street."

"Yes, I recall seeing the sign many times. Since there are two other attorneys in town, I wasn't sure which one was hers. I'll go see him right now, then I'll go to her pastor's house and let him know. I'll let him make the funeral arrangements."

"Fine. I'll just keep her here till I hear from him."

When Dan sat down in attorney Derek Campbell's office, Campbell said, "I'm sorry to hear this news, Mr. Tyler. Suzanne was a fine woman."

"That she was, sir."

Campbell leaned over the desk. "Did Suzanne tell you about the will?"

"The will?"

Campbell eased back in his chair. "Then you don't know."

"Know what?"

"Well, on the day after she learned that her sister had died, Suzanne sent one of her neighbors to bring me to the ranch. You were with the cattle in the pastures at the time."

"Oh."

"Suzanne willed the ranch to you, Mr. Tyler."

Dan's features blanched. "She did?"

"Yes. She didn't want you to know about it until she found the right time to tell you. Apparently she hadn't found the right time, yet."

Stunned, Dan said, "I…I guess not. I had no idea she liked me that much."

The attorney smiled. "She spoke quite well of you, and since she had no living heirs, she wanted her faithful hired man to have the ranch. You will also get the money she had in the bank. I'll draw up the legal papers so we can put the ranch in your name."

"All right."

"While I'm at it, do you want to change the name of the ranch? You know, like the *Box T,* or the *Bar T,* or the *Circle T,* or something like that?"

Dan ran a palm over his eyes. "Well, let's keep the 'Box' in it. We'll go with the *Box T.*"

"Fine. Come and see me on Monday, and I'll have the papers ready."


From the attorney's office, Dan went to the parsonage of the other Bible-believing church in town and informed Pastor Lance Kemper of Suzanne's death. A shocked Kemper agreed that he would make the funeral arrangements.

Dan's heart was heavy as he drove the wagon into the ranch yard. Everything looked the same, but it wouldn't *be* the same without sweet Suzanne. He was going to miss her terribly.

While he dressed up in one of his Sunday suits in preparation for the wedding, he was still in shock over Suzanne's sudden death and the fact that she left everything to him.

As he stood before the mirror in his cabin and tied his bow tie, he said, "Lord, she was such a dear lady. I prayed that You would not let her die, but You always know best. I know this much: heaven is all the more special with Suzanne there."

It was almost two o'clock when Dan mounted his bay gelding and rode toward town. He was very much looking forward to being best man for his two closest friends and their brides. He would wait until after the wedding to tell Clay and Joel about Suzanne's death. Nothing should put a damper on their big day.

Suzanne Brady was buried on Monday morning. Dan's friends and their new wives sat with him at the well-attended funeral service in the church, and stood beside him at the graveside service, which had the same crowd. Pastor Lance Kemper brought two excellent messages.

After the graveside service, Dan went to attorney Derek Campbell's office, and the legal formalities were finished. When Dan rode away, heading for the ranch, he thanked the Lord for making it possible for him to own the ranch. It would give him the opportunity to provide a good living for Jenny and him.

When he arrived at the ranch, Dan moved all of Suzanne's personal belongings into the large storage shed near the toolshed and took his own few belongings from the cabin to the ranch house.

He smiled when he thought about how clean the house was, and how everything was in its proper place. That was Suzanne's custom. Even at eighty-four, she worked every day inside and outside the house. Her handiwork was evident wherever he looked.

When he had changed the bedding on the bed that was now his, he could still almost feel Suzanne's presence in the room. "I'll do you and Jim proud, Suzanne," he whispered. "This ranch will prosper and make a lovely home for Jenny and me and however many children the Lord gives us. Thank you, Suzanne, for your sweet generosity and all of your hard work. You rest, now, there in heaven. You certainly deserve it."

Just before sunrise on Tuesday morning, September 5, Jenny Linden's stagecoach stopped in Gallup, New Mexico, allowing two passengers to get off. While she was out of the coach, stretching her legs, she saw the stage driver, Will Hentzel, and his shotgunner, Harry Eubank, come out of the Wells Fargo office with two men who were handcuffed together. One of the two men was wearing a U.S. deputy marshal's badge and wore a Colt .45 in his holster, which was on his right hip. His left wrist bore the handcuff.

The four men stopped a few feet from the stage, and Jenny picked up by their conversation that the deputy was taking his prisoner to Holbrook, Arizona, to stand trial for murder.

Driver Will Hentzel stepped up to Jenny and said, "You can get back on the stage now, Miss. Once you're settled, the deputy and his prisoner will board."

While Jenny was climbing back into the coach, Hentzel and Eubank were making their way toward the front of the stagecoach.

Just as Jenny sat down on the seat, she heard a heavy grunt and a scuffling sound. She turned to see the deputy and his prisoner wrestling for control of the deputy's revolver, which the prisoner had evidently snatched from the deputy's holster. It was in the prisoner's hand, and the hammer was cocked. The driver and shotgunner were running toward the struggling men when the gun went off.

The bullet buzzed past Jenny's right ear, so close she felt the heat and breath of it. A tiny gasp escaped her lips. Her body stiffened and felt like it had turned to stone. She fell back against the back of the seat.

The deputy and his prisoner were still struggling, each for control of the gun. Shotgunner Harry Eubank cracked the outlaw savagely on the back of the head with the butt of his shotgun. The impact of the blow dropped him to the ground like a broken doll. The revolver fell from his hand and was instantly retrieved by the deputy, who was on one knee beside him. He holstered the gun, then used the key to unlock the handcuff on his own wrist.

By this time, the Fargo agent was on the scene, standing over the unconscious outlaw beside the deputy. The outlaw's head was cracked and people were gathering around, eyes wide.

The door of the stagecoach swung open. Will Hentzel stuck his head in and saw the hole in the opposite side of the coach next to the window. "Miss Blair, are you all right?"

Jenny's features were white. She licked her lips and stammered, "I…I…think so. Th-the bullet just missed m-my right ear."

"Hang on. I'll get you some water."

Hentzel dashed to the front of the stage, reached up, and took down his canteen from the seat. He hurried back to Jenny and uncapped the canteen. "I filled it with fresh water in Albuquerque."

With trembling fingers, Jenny grasped the canteen, put the spout to her lips, and took a long pull. Managing a tiny smile, she handed the canteen back to him. "Thank you, Mr. Hentzel."

"You're welcome, Miss. I'm sorry this happened. By the position of that bullet hole over there, I'd say you came within an inch or two of being killed. You sure you're all right?"

Jenny nodded in jerky movements. "Yes. Just a little shaken."

"I can understand that," Hentzel said, backing out of the coach. "We'll be ready to leave in a few minutes."

Jenny clasped her hands together and looked toward the scene. The outlaw was lying on the ground, his head bleeding. He was still unconscious. The deputy was asking two townsmen to help him carry his prisoner to the doctor's office down the street.

Together, driver and shotgunner stepped up to the side of the coach. The door was still open. Hentzel leaned in. "We're going to pull out, Miss Blair. You sure you're all right?"

"I'm fine, thank you."

Hentzel closed the door, turned, and climbed up onto the seat. Eubank joined him on the other side. A moment later, the stage was rolling out of Gallup, heading due west.

Sitting alone in the coach, a shaken Jenny Linden was trembling all over as she thought how close the bullet came to her head. Suddenly her mind went back to Laura Denton and how Laura had shown her in the Bible that if she died without Christ, she would go to hell. The Scripture passages Laura had underlined and shown her—and that Jenny had gone over while writing the letter to Dan Tyler—came to mind sharply. She tried to shake them out of her mind, but they remained there, ripping at her heart until the stage stopped in Holbrook.

At Holbrook, they picked up a passenger. She was middle-aged, and introduced herself as Alice Rodine, saying she was on her way to visit her nephew and his wife, who lived in Mogollon. Jenny Blair introduced herself. The stage pulled out. The Scripture passages were still stabbing Jenny's heart, but as she and Alice began talking, the passages faded from Jenny's thoughts.

The time seemed to pass quickly while the two women talked, and before Jenny realized it, the driver called from up top, saying Mogollon was in sight.

A tremor ran through Jenny's body. She was about to meet the man who murdered her father.

Alice began dabbing at the hair beneath the brim of her bonnet. Jenny did the same, and worked at rubbing what wrinkles she could from her dress. Her heart was pounding, but her resolve to exact justice on Dan Tyler came to the forefront of her mind.

Dan Tyler was standing in front of the Wells Fargo office in Mogollon. It was 4:25, and he was getting concerned as to why the stage was late when he saw a dust cloud on the road to the east. Seconds later the stagecoach was in plain sight ahead of the dust cloud.

Dan's heart lurched in his chest.

Moments later, the stage drew up and the Fargo agent moved past Dan, asking the driver what made them late. Will Hentzel told him they had a little incident in Gallup that delayed their departure, but everything was all right.

Dan stepped up close to the coach as the shotgunner opened the door and helped a middle-aged woman out. Just behind her was a blue-eyed blonde.

Dan's heart lurched again.

Harry Eubank helped the blonde down, and Dan moved up, smiling for all he was worth. Jenny let go of Eubank's hand and painted a smile on her face. "Dan?"

"Yes, Jenny. I...I'm so happy you're here. Could—could I give you a welcome hug?"

The thought of her father's murderer touching her was disgusting, but she knew it had to be. Holding the smile, she nodded. "Uh-huh."

While Dan was giving her a brotherly hug, Jenny felt revulsion, and her hatred for him seethed in her like cold acid, but she had to keep up her act. She hugged him in return. When they released each other, Jenny covered her true feelings. "I'm so glad to finally meet you."

Dan looked down into her blue eyes. "Same here. You're even more beautiful than your picture."

She gave him another smile just as Harry Eubank stepped up with her satchel in hand. "Here you are, Miss Blair."

Dan took the satchel and thanked the shotgunner. "The wagon's right over here."

As Jenny walked beside him, she felt the weight of the .38 caliber revolver in her purse. It sent a tingle slithering down her spine. Dan placed the satchel in the wagon bed and helped her up into the seat. To keep up her act, Jenny slipped close to him when he settled on the seat and took up the reins.

As the wagon headed out of town, Dan told Jenny about Suzanne Brady's sudden death three days ago, and how surprised he was to learn from Suzanne's attorney that she had willed the ranch to him, including what money she had in her bank account.

Jenny found herself strangely attracted to Dan, but struggled against it. This news settled the question as to whether she would kill him before or after the wedding. She would wait until they were married, then as his widow, the ranch would be hers. She would sell it and go back to Harrisburg a wealthy woman.

Dan then explained that since Suzanne wouldn't be at the ranch, it would not look good with just the two of them out there, and not married.

Jenny agreed.

"I want you to see the ranch, then I'll bring you back to town. My friend Clay Holden and his new wife, Mary, have offered to let you stay in their home until the wedding. The house has a nice spare bedroom."

"That's fine, Dan. It won't be very long, anyway. That is, if you agree. You see…I already know I'm in love with you. As far as I'm concerned, we can get married real soon."

Dan slipped his free arm around her and gave her a big smile. "Jenny, I'm already in love with you too. I know you are the one the Lord has chosen for me. I have perfect peace about it."

"Me too," she said, secretly meaning something totally different. Her plan was working already.

"To be proper, we should wait at least a month, then marry."

Jenny would rather get it over with sooner, but she told herself it would take a little while to figure out how to shoot him and make it appear that someone else did it. "A month is fine, darling."

As the wagon drew up to the gate, Dan pulled rein and explained that the sign that hung over the gate on the thick posts would soon be changed from *Box B Ranch* to *Box T Ranch*.

Jenny smiled up at him and squeezed his arm. "Sounds wonderful to me."

Dan put the wagon in motion again, and as they moved down the lane, Jenny ran her gaze over the wide fields dotted with cattle. "This is sure different than Pennsylvania, but I like it."

Dan smiled. "I knew you would."

They were drawing near the ranch house. It stood proudly in the bright September sunshine. To Jenny, every window sparkled, as if with a smile of welcome. *Oh my. Under other circumstances I would really love this place. Well, at least it will be mine for a little while…till he's dead, and I sell it.*

Dan helped Jenny from the wagon and held her for a moment.

She forced another smile and tilted her face toward him. Though it repulsed her, she let him plant a soft kiss on her lips.

Dan's heart pounded as he took her through every room in the house. From the kitchen door, he showed her the cabin out back where he used to live. Jenny found that she genuinely liked the ranch and the house, but lied once again as they stood on the front porch. "Oh, Dan, I'll be so happy here as your wife!"

Dan kissed her again, then helped her into the wagon seat.

That evening at the parsonage, Jenny found that she actually liked Pastor David Denison and Clara. And strangely enough, she liked Clay and Mary, and Joel and Martha. The dinner Clara and her daughters had prepared was exquisite. Later, when the Holdens showed her their guest room and welcomed her warmly, she thought that these born-again people did have some fine qualities.


On Sunday, Jenny carried her Bible to church and found that she also liked the members, who welcomed her so warmly.

Dan had told her she should join the church right away, so at the invitation, an inwardly nervous Jenny walked the aisle and told the pastor she wanted to become a member. He asked for her testimony of salvation while the congregation continued to sing the invitation song, and because what Laura had shown her in the Bible was fresh in her mind, she was able to fool the pastor.

On Monday, Dan and Jenny sat in Pastor David Denison's office, and Dan explained that they were already in love and were certain the Lord had chosen them for each other, but felt they should wait at least a month before getting married.

Denison smiled and nodded. "I believe that's wise, Dan." He looked at the small calendar on his desk. "How would Saturday, October 14, be? That's just a little more than a month."

Dan looked at Jenny, who was once again wishing it could be sooner.

"That sound all right to you, sweetheart?"

"Sounds perfect! October 14, it is!"

As the days passed, Jenny nursed her grudge against Dan Tyler for what he had done to her family, but as she became better acquainted with him, she struggled with the uncontrollable emotions that ran through her when she was with him. She could hardly believe that this kind and gentle man was capable of murder. But she knew he was, because Edgar Toomey was there at the prison camp and told her so.

On Sunday, October 8, Pastor David Denison reminded the people from the pulpit at offering and announcement time that the Tyler-Blair wedding would take place at the church on the following Saturday afternoon at three o'clock.

Sitting in the pew with Dan at her side, Jenny's heart pounded within her. He looked at her and smiled, and she smiled back. The Holdens and the Stevenses were in the same pew, and flashed their smiles at Dan and his prospective bride.

Jenny told herself that once they were married, she would finalize her plan as to how she would exact her justice on Dan and make it look like someone else had shot him. When he was buried, she would work with the attorney to sell the ranch and collect her money. And then, it was back to Harrisburg.

A ladies' trio sang a special song, then Pastor Denison stepped up to the pulpit and opened his Bible.

"My initial text this morning is Genesis 1:3. Please turn there with me in your Bibles."

When Jenny opened her Bible to that familiar page, her eyes fastened on the verse, which Laura Denton had underlined. The words "Let there be light" seemed to be written in letters of fire.

After reading the verse to the congregation, Pastor Denison commented on how God dispelled the darkness found in verse 2 with the light. He then took them to 2 Corinthians 4:3–6 and preached on how God brings the true gospel light into Satan-blinded, sin-darkened hearts through hearing and reading the Word.

As he preached, something was happening in Jenny's heart. Suddenly she saw the truth of the gospel, and of heaven and hell.

She saw her lost condition before God so clearly, it startled her. At that moment, as the preacher went on, to Jenny it was like God was speaking to her almost audibly, saying, "Yes, Jenny: Let there be light!"

Tears were misting Jenny's eyes as she moved her lips silently. "And there was light!"

She blinked her eyes in an attempt to keep the tears back. She was successful. She didn't want Dan to see her tears.

The preacher went on in his sermon and described hell from a graphic Bible passage. He then warned of clinging to the darkness when God had shined the light of the gospel into a lost sinner's heart. He closed the sermon and gave the invitation. Two teenage girls and one man walked the aisle to receive Christ.

Jenny stood there during the invitation, struggling with the light that was penetrating her darkness, but she managed to hold on till the invitation was finished and the service was over.

The sermon in the evening service was on Christian living, but the gospel was also included. Jenny had another battle when the invitation was given, but once again, managed to stay in the pew.

24

As Dan Tyler walked his bride-to-be to his wagon after the service, he could tell that something was bothering her. When they drew up to the side of the wagon, he said, "Sweetheart, is something wrong?"

A bit distracted by what the gospel light was doing in her heart, she looked up him. "Hmm?"

"I asked if something's wrong."

"Oh. No, darling. I…I was just thinking about the friends I left in Harrisburg, including Zack and Emma Henderson, who were so good to me on my job. Please don't misunderstand. I'm happy to be here, but I still miss them."

"Well, of course. I understand. I'm glad that's all it is."

Dan helped Jenny into the wagon at the same time Clay was helping Mary into their buggy close by.

Dan and Jenny followed the Holdens to their house. Dan was invited in, and after coffee and oatmeal cookies were served and devoured, Dan and Jenny walked out onto the front porch. They kissed good-night, and Jenny waited on the porch and waved to him by the light of the porch lamp.

When Jenny was in her room for the night, her stomach was churning. She picked up her Bible and once again read the verses Laura had underlined.

Tears were blurring her vision when she read Genesis 1:3 and 2 Corinthians 4:3–6 one more time. Laura and Pastor Denison were both right. Satan had her blinded, but God was now shining His light into her darkness. Suddenly, she burst into sobs and dropped on her knees beside the bed.

She trembled and her voice quivered as she bowed her head, closed her eyes, and sobbed, "Dear Lord Jesus, I clearly understand now why You went to the cross, shed Your precious blood, died, and raised Yourself from the grave. It was to give sinners like me salvation. I have no doubt that hell exists and is real eternal fire. I know I'm lost and walking the road that leads to hell. I…I can't stand it anymore!"

Jenny gulped at the tears in her throat. "Lord Jesus, here and now I repent of my wicked sin. Please come into my heart and save me. Forgive me and wash me clean in Your blood."

When Jenny rose to her feet, she picked up the Bible and held it close to her heart. God's Word said if she would repent and receive Jesus into her heart as her Saviour, she would be saved. Because she now believed every word in the Bible was true, she knew she was saved.

She had been born again. She was now a child of God and would go to heaven when she died.

She sat down on the edge of the bed, wiping tears. "Lord," she said in a soft voice, "thank You for saving me. I…I know that my plan for vengeance is over. Now that I'm Your child, there is no way I could kill Dan Tyler. In fact, I must now tell him that I can't marry him—that I'm going back home. The…the strange thing about this whole thing, Lord, is that in spite of what he did to my family, I…I have these strange feelings toward him. Please help me to do this thing right."

All day Monday, Jenny struggled with what she had to do. She still harbored the grudge toward Dan as before, but she told the Lord she would leave the punishing of the man who murdered her father to Him. She wouldn't bother to tell the hypocrite that she had gotten saved. She would simply tell him she needed travel fare to get back home, and then she would get out of his life. If it broke his heart, so what?

That evening, Dan and the Stevenses arrived at precisely six-thirty, for the Holdens had invited them on Sunday for supper.

Dan was asked to lead in prayer over the food, and Jenny felt anger inside toward him. *How could that hypocrite word such a beautiful prayer?*

During the meal, the subject of the Andersonville Prison Camp came up. While Clay and Joel were talking about different incidents that had taken place at the camp, Clay glanced at Jenny, then said to Joel, "Something just dawned on me. Wasn't Captain William Linden from Harrisburg?"

Jenny's ears perked up. She ran her gaze to Joel.

Joel nodded. "It seems he told me that. Yes, I'm sure he did. I hadn't thought about it."

Clay's eyes were on Jenny. Her heart froze as he said, "Jenny, did you know or know of Captain Linden?"

Jenny's mouth was suddenly dry. Her throat tightened. "I…I knew Captain Linden. I was told that he was murdered by one of the prison camp guards."

Dan's features pinched.

Clay shook his head. "Not so, Jenny. Let me ask you this. Do you happen to know Lieutenant Edgar Toomey, who is also from Harrisburg? He wouldn't be a lieutenant anymore, of course, but—"

"Yes, I know him. Why?"

"It was Toomey who murdered Captain Linden, Jenny."

While Jenny's face registered surprise, Joel said, "Dan was accused of killing Linden, can you believe that?"

Jenny felt the edge of a fog trying to seize her brain. "Why… why of course not."

Clay set steady eyes on Jenny. "It was Toomey who accused Dan of killing Linden. But when the guards put the timing of it together, it was quickly proven that Dan couldn't have done it because at the very time Linden was stabbed to death, Joel and I were with Dan in his tent, reading the Bible and praying together."

Clay's words cleared up the fog in Jenny's brain. She was stunned. "Why wasn't Toomey prosecuted for killing Captain Linden?"

Joel looked her in the eye. "Jenny, the camp commandant agreed with the rest of us that it was Toomey who killed Captain Linden. With the circumstances that prevailed that night, it had to be Toomey. We knew that for some reason, Toomey hated the man who had been the leader of his unit and killed him. But there was no way to prove it. News of the War's end came at that very moment, and Toomey got off scot-free."

Jenny looked like she had just taken a shot between the eyes. The food stuck in her throat. She felt as if all the air had been sucked out of her lungs. Her face turned ashen.

Dan saw the distress in her eyes. He immediately left his chair, dropped to his knees beside her, and took hold of her hand. "Jenny, what is it? What's wrong?"

Her widened blue eyes focused on his face, but she was unable to force a word past the lump in her throat. Her breathing suddenly became rapid. She swallowed uncontrollably over and over.

The Holdens and the Stevenses looked at each other in puzzlement.

Dan laid a palm on her cheek. "Jenny, do you want me to take you to the doctor?"

Jenny shook her head, and with a herculean effort, took a breath of very welcome air. Struggling to clear her throat, she coughed, then drew more air into her lungs. Her lips moved silently for a few seconds, then with squeaky voice, she said, "Dan…can I…talk to you alone?"

"Well, sure. Let's go out on the front porch." He helped her from the chair and put a strong arm around her. "Folks, we'll be back in a little while. Please excuse us."

"Of course," said Clay. "If you need anything…"

"We'll be fine, thanks."

When they stepped out onto the front porch, the porch lamp was giving off a circle of yellow light. Dan still had his arm around her. "Do you want to sit down over here?"

"Let's…let's just move over here and lean on the railing."

They stepped to the railing, and Jenny braced her hip against it. "Sweetheart, what is it?"

Trembling all over, Jenny spoke in halting words as she opened her heart and bared her soul. She confessed who she really was, and told him how she had been led by Edgar Toomey to believe that this guard named Dan Tyler had murdered her father. She explained how she searched for Dan with the intent of killing him, and how she finally found him through the mail order bride ad, and that she had come there to marry him, then kill him in a way that would make it look like someone else had done it.

Still breathing shakily, Jenny studied Dan's face, fearful of the revulsion she was sure would be there.

Stunned beyond words, Dan stared at her, speechless. A thousand thoughts were vying for a place in his confused mind.

"There's something else, Dan," she said. "I've been a hypocrite. When I wrote that letter and put in what was supposed to be my salvation testimony, I lied. I have a friend in Harrisburg who is a sweet and dedicated Christian. Her name is Laura Denton. She witnessed to me over and over, even gave me that Bible you see me carrying to church. She had underlined many salvation verses and tried her best to get me to open my heart to Jesus. But I refused. This was why I could put that false testimony in the letter. I knew exactly what to say. At that point, I would do anything to get to you so I could put a bullet in your heart."

Dan shook his head. "Jenny, I—"

"Please let me finish."

Dan stared at her as she went on to tell him how the Lord had dealt with her yesterday in the church services. She explained what was really wrong with her, which he had asked about, was the conviction that was eating her up, then went on to tell him how she had fallen on her knees beside her bed last night. She had repented of her sin and received the Lord Jesus into her heart as her Saviour.

Dan was stunned. Jenny's eyes were riveted on his face. She was sensitive to the change that was dawning on his countenance. A broad smile suddenly curved his lips, and his eyes came alive with happiness.

He opened his arms, and with a tentative step, Jenny moved into them. Dan held her tight, and his own breath was a bit ragged. "Jenny, sweetheart, I'm so thrilled with the way the Lord has worked in your heart. I'm glad that you're saved. I still love you as I've already told you over and over again. But…what now?"

She eased back in his arms and looked up at him through a mist of tears. "Dan, all along—ever since I came here and met you—I have had these strange emotions toward you, in spite of the fact that I thought you had murdered Papa. I couldn't understand these emotions. But now I know what they are. I have fallen head over heels in love with you!"

Dan drew her to him. They kissed, then he looked into her eyes and said, "Jenny, I have been that way about you ever since I received your first letter. I knew then that I had fallen in love with you, even as I know right now that I am still in love with you. God knew the whole thing before it ever happened, and He planned that you and I would fall in love in spite of all these circumstances. I still want you as my mail order bride."

Tears were streaming down Jenny's face. "Oh, Dan! Oh, darling, I love you so very much!"

They sealed it with a kiss, then went inside to tell the Holdens and the Stevenses the whole story.

At one point, Mary Holden asked Jenny what she would do about Edgar Toomey.

Jenny drew a deep breath. "Well, Mary, since there is no way to prove that he murdered Papa, I will just leave him in God's hands. Just this morning, while I was reading passages in the book of Romans that Laura had underlined, I came across Romans 12:19, which she had not underlined. It's where God says, 'Vengeance is mine; I will repay.' So, like I said, I'll just leave Edgar Toomey in God's hands."

"That's the way to do it, honey," said Martha Stevens. "Let the Lord take care of punishing Edgar Toomey."

Everyone at the table agreed.

The next evening, Jenny and Dan went to the parsonage and told the pastor and his wife the whole story. The Denisons rejoiced in God's marvelous working, and it was set that Jenny would be baptized the next night in the Wednesday evening service.

Jenny and Dan left the parsonage and took a drive under the stars in his wagon. Jenny brought up Laura Denton, saying she had written to her that day and told her of how she had received Jesus as her Saviour. Again, she mentioned Laura having underlined passages in the Bible she gave her, and told Dan that Pastor Denison had used some of those very verses in his sermon last Sunday morning. "Remember, darling? Genesis 1:3: 'And God said, Let there be light: and there was light.' And 2 Corinthians 4:6: 'For God, who commanded the light to shine out of darkness, hath shined in our hearts, to give the light of the knowledge of the glory of God in the face of Jesus Christ.' What a powerful connection there is between these two verses!"

"Amen to that, Jenny, darlin'! And praise the Lord for shining His gospel light into your heart."


The Arizona sun was gleaming brightly out of a glorious blue sky on Saturday afternoon, October 14. But it couldn't begin to outshine the glow on the faces of Dan Tyler and Jenny Linden when the pump organ was playing the wedding march and Jenny headed down the aisle toward the man she loved.

Jenny was dressed in a simple white organdy gown and carried a small nosegay made up of late summer desert flowers. She was a vision of loveliness to the smiling man who waited for her at the altar.

The congregation watched with pleasure as Jenny came to a graceful halt and looked up at her groom. Her face beamed and she smiled at him as he offered his arm.

Sliding her hand into the crook of his arm, she looked up at him and whispered, "'And God said, Let there be light: and there was light!'"

A wide grin spread over Dan's shining face as they mounted the steps to the platform, where Pastor David Denison waited to hear their vows.

Multnomah Publishers®

The publisher and author would love to hear your comments about this book. *Please contact us at:*
www.allacy.com

# Mail Order Bride Series

Desperate men who settled the West resorted to unconventional measures in their quest for companionship, advertising for and marrying women they'd never even met! Read about a unique and adventurous period in the history of romance.

# An Exciting New Series by Bestselling Fiction Authors

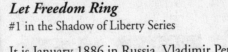

### Let Freedom Ring
#1 in the Shadow of Liberty Series

It is January 1886 in Russia. Vladimir Petrovna, a Christian husband and father of three, faces bankruptcy, persecution for his beliefs, and despair. The solutions lie across a perilous sea.

ISBN 1-57673-756-X

### The Secret Place
#2 in the Shadow of Liberty Series

Popular authors Al and JoAnna Lacy offer a compelling question: As two young people cope with love's longings on opposite shores, can they find the serenity of God's covering in *The Secret Place?*

ISBN 1-57673-800-0

### A Prince Among Them
#3 in the Shadow of Liberty Series

A bitter enemy of Queen Victoria kidnaps her favorite great-grandson. Emigrants Jeremy and Cecelia Barlow book passage on the same ship to America, facing a complex dilemma that only all-knowing God can set right.

ISBN 1-57673-880-9

### Undying Love
#4 in the Shadow of Liberty Series

19-year-old Stephan Varda flees his own guilt and his father's rage in Hungary, finding undying love from his heavenly Father—and a beautiful girl—across the ocean in America.

ISBN 1-57673-930-9

# Angel of Mercy Series

Post-Civil War nurse Breanna Baylor uses her professional skill to bring healing to the body, and her faith in the Redeemer to bring comfort to thirsty souls, valiantly serving God on the dangerous frontier.

# Hannah of Fort Bridger Series

Hannah Cooper's husband dies on the dusty Oregon Trail, leaving her in charge of five children and a general store in Fort Bridger. Dependence on God fortifies her against grueling challenges and bitter tragedies.

A FREE "BEHIND THE SCENES" LOOK AT YOUR FAVORITE FICTION AUTHORS!

www.letstalkfiction.com

*Let's Talk Fiction* is a free, four-color mini-magazine created to give readers a "behind the scenes" look at Multnomah Publishers' favorite fiction authors. *Let's Talk Fiction* allows our authors to share a bit about themselves, giving readers an inside peek into their latest releases. Published in the fall, spring, and summer seasons, *Let's Talk Fiction* is filled with interactive contests, author contact information, and fun! To receive your free copy, get on-line at www.letstalkfiction.com. We'd love to hear from you!